The Cloud Chamber

CLARE GEORGE

The Cloud Chamber

SCEPTRE

Copyright © 2003 by Clare George

First published in Great Britain in 2003 by Hodder and Stoughton
A division of Hodder Headline

A Sceptre Book

2 4 6 8 10 9 7 5 3 1

A CIP catalogue record for this title is available from the British Library

ISBN 0 340 82421 2

Typeset by Palimpsest Book Production Limited,
Polmont, Stirlingshire
Printed and bound in Great Britain by
Mackays of Chatham plc, Chatham, Kent

Hodder and Stoughton
A division of Hodder Headline
338 Euston Road
London NW1 3BH

For my family, with love and thanks

I am the daughter of Earth and Water,
And the nursling of the Sky;
I pass through the pores, of the ocean and shores;
I change, but I cannot die –
For after the rain, when with never a stain
The pavilion of Heaven is bare,
And the winds and sunbeams, with their convex gleams,
Build up the blue dome of Air –
I silently laugh at my own cenotaph,
And out of the caverns of rain,
Like a child from the womb, like a ghost from the tomb
I arise and unbuild it again.

Percy Bysshe Shelley, 'The Cloud'

1

George Henderson's coat was too large. It was a ridiculous garment, dragging along the ground with the stitching coming undone. His instinct was to grab it, gather its folds at his ankles, and carry the tails like a Victorian lady walking downstairs. This, however, was not an appropriate gait for a civil servant. So instead it swished behind him across the crystal-polished pavements, a reluctant retinue to his frost-bitten parade.

He would not have been wearing the coat – it had belonged to his dead brother-in-law – but his own had proved too draughty for this line of work.

'Take Leonard's coat,' Phoebe had begged him each night, when he came in from his first days of pacing the streets, his fingers blue with the cold, the blood constricted almost to his armpits. He had dodged the suggestion for days, unable to confront the neediness in her eyes, but also unwilling to feel the prick of dead man's flesh between the wool and his own skin. But in the end the cold had proved too much. 'Yes, all right then,' he'd said at the fourth day's entreaty, as if it were no great capitulation. And then as soon as he'd said it, Phoebe's fragile eyes snapped shut, and she left him to find the coat himself, while she busied herself with ironing next week's shirts.

It was, at least, better to be warm. The ice struck cold from the paving stones and through the too-thin soles of his shoes. He trudged the usual route from High Street Kensington tube station to Stafford Terrace in the last darkness of the night, thinking, as always, bloody Nunn May, bloody Nunn May. For four months and nineteen days George Henderson's working life had been dictated by the movements of this man, who, to all appearances, was merely a harmless academic, with little in his life other than his work in the Physics Department of King's College, London.

'The British Museum,' his boss, Mr Aitken, had told him. 'We are expecting him to make a rendezvous with his Russian contact outside the British Museum some time in October or November. The meeting place is on Great Russell Street, at the junction with Southampton Row. His code name is Alek. He will be carrying a copy of *The Times*; his associate will make himself known using the phrase, "What is the shortest way to the Strand?"'

It had all sounded rather unlikely to Henderson. How could Aitken know such things? In the war, when his place had been at the very bottom of the Intelligence pile, his job had mainly consisted of poring over translations of German newspapers, piecing together strands of knowledge on whatever topic the authorities thought fit to investigate. Now that it was all over, and most of his more senior colleagues had drifted back into their old occupations, he wondered whether there was a job to do at all. Perhaps Dr Nunn May really did have some sort of connection with the Russians. But, he thought, *but* – and the coat sat uncomfortably at his neck and arms as it always did when such things crossed his mind – the Russians were, had been, were, allies. Phoebe's brother Leonard had drowned in the waters of the Arctic defending the supply convoys to the Soviet Union, while George himself had sat stifling in a basement in Whitehall, half-hoping that a German bomb would score a direct hit and give him the opportunity to find it in himself to be a hero and a man.

'Asthma' was the answer he had learnt to give almost before the question was asked. 'What—' men and women had asked him, and he'd answered 'Asthma,' until they had looked at him queerly and rephrased their questions. 'No, I mean what is your address?' Or, 'What are you thinking of doing for lunch?' Sometimes he supposed that these really were the questions they'd meant to ask. At other times he was sure that they had been simply dodging their own embarrassment by foisting it upon him. We were a poor crowd, he thought, remembering his wartime colleagues at the Bureau: a gaggle of wheezers, limpers and astigmatics. And now here he was, the damp seeping through the thick serge of the coat, tightening his lungs until he thought he would not be able to walk when the time came.

'They shouldn't send you out in weather like this,' said Phoebe sometimes. 'Not with your asthma.'

'Phoebe,' he said, 'we *mustn't complain.*'

'The war's over now.'

'I cannot use asthma as an excuse all my life,' George told her. 'I am not a shirker.'

And at that the conversation was always done with, because they both knew that he was.

A light flicked on in Nunn May's rooms. Henderson squinted up at it and looked at his watch. Seven fifteen. It would be half an hour now, for a shower and whatever else it was that Nunn May did in the mornings. At the end of that time there would be the blessed relief of movement, the pain of blood coming back into fingers and toes, breath whistling through the constricted cavities of his chest— And as he observed the shadow against the curtains of the room above, he counted his blessings. They were not very many, but though it seemed his fate to be a mere bug clinging to the surface of Nunn May's life, he knew in these moments that in this case the parasite was better off than its host. When Nunn May came out, he would be alone, and none but Henderson would follow him. There was no Phoebe in that flat to warm

3

the bed from which he emerged, no companion with whom to share his morning cup of tea or to fasten his coat before he left. In four months and nineteen days Henderson had never witnessed a single moment of companionship between Nunn May and a fellow human being. His communications were as functional as the pressing of a doorbell or the ticking of a clock. I am his only company, Henderson thought, and he does not even know that I am here.

Before the war, this had been a very grand street. Now all the railings were gone, taken up to make armaments. The road and pavements were pocked with holes. The holes were not bomb craters, but had been created by the simple action of six years of weather without repair. At one end of the terrace, there was a gaping void where the road's single bomb had fallen on one home, leaving the interior walls of its neighbours exposed and crumbling. The houses on either side of it were occupied by a raggle-taggle crew of squatters. Henderson knew this because the people who shuffled in and out at odd hours were not of the type who would ever have lived here before. A bus conductor, slipping out in his uniform for the night shift, his face drawn and pale with malnutrition. A mother pulling a clutch of bedraggled children behind her when she crept out to the shops. In some of the other houses, the old families continued with their business wearing their fine clothes and fancy airs in just the same way they always had. But few of them had servants any more. They had gone away to fight, or make bombs, and had not come back.

The light in Nunn May's rooms moved from one to the other and then back again. Behind the screen of moth-eaten fabric the coat and hat were donned, the imagined keys taken from the hook on the wall, the final checks performed, and then the lights extinguished once more. Slowly, Henderson trudged across the road and took up his position behind the bare cherry tree. The front door swung open and Nunn May appeared. He walked up the drive to the place where the gate had once been, and turned away from Henderson towards the tube. He did not look back. He never did.

If all the world and love were young . . .

Walter Dunnachie stared out of the train window, the contents of the world slipping past him in a slow, deliberate blur. Grey rooftops. The unconsidered flight of grubby pigeons. Men and women waiting on platforms amongst rotting leaves in brown tweed coats that swept the ground, a creaking transit along tracks lined with boarded-up windows and streets that plunged below the rails, the smoking chimneys protecting their citizens from view, up to the high ground where the trees stood cold in their nakedness.

Why had that poem popped into his head? He knew well enough where it had come from. Years ago. A girl on the deck of a ship on the other side of the world.

'Walter,' she had said, grinning wildly, pressing the book into his hands. They'd started using each other's Christian names only the day before, and were drunk on their newborn intimacy.

'Grace,' he'd responded shyly, not looking at the poem at all. His eyes were caught up in the sun that shone through her unrestrainable hair.

'*Look* at it, Walter.'

He'd looked down, and saw those words. He'd wondered whether to read them out loud, but could not.

'He has the same first name as you.'

Sir Walter Ralegh, 1552–1618.

'And he was an explorer, too—'

He'd laughed, and so had she, and the sun had sparkled on the endless sea, and all the world and love were young.

Walter felt old. There was a day's work ahead of him, and of late he'd begun to wonder what it was for. He'd never thought he'd end up here, tethered to a single spot on the surface of the earth by wife and children and the interminable routine of lectures and examinations. I am thirty-seven, he thought, I am not old. But as he looked around the carriage at his fellow passengers and their sleep-stricken faces, not one of them showed a sign of the youth that had once roared around his veins.

Henderson waited outside the tube station while Nunn May bought his newspaper. It was *The Times*. It always was. It signified nothing at all.

Their daily route had not varied once in four months. Down into the tunnel, and onto the anti-clockwise platform of the Circle Line. Each morning the train wound around the edge of Central London, returning its occupants to the light at various appointed locations. Nunn May's destination was Temple. He was a Reader in Physics at King's College London, on the Strand. Henderson had spent many mornings puzzling over this particular geographical fact. The Russians, so Aitken thought, had arranged to meet him in Bloomsbury, which was perhaps a twenty minute walk from the Strand. And the man appointed to meet Nunn May would announce himself by asking directions to the very place where Nunn May worked. So perhaps this would give him the opportunity to accompany his contact back towards King's, and they would conduct their business en route. Henderson knew that it was not really his job to consider such details – Aitken had made that pretty clear – but this hypothetical appointment was the only focus of his days, and it had come to hold a disproportionate fascination. There were two ways in which the rendezvous might happen. Nunn May might pop out from King's during the working day, or he might make a detour to Bloomsbury on the way to or from work. If he chose to go on the way, then the clockwise platform would be the logical choice.

Each morning, Henderson waited for his quarry to head clockwise. And each day, Nunn May went the other way.

Nunn May passed the ticket inspector, and Henderson followed, barely bothering to keep an eye on him. He examined the walls. A year ago, they would have been dominated by public information posters giving advice about everything from doodlebugs to powdered eggs. Now they were gay with blandishments to attend the latest theatrical production or try a new sort of soap. The world seemed determined to behave as if none of it had ever happened. Henderson found it strange. It did not seem possible that it would ever be forgotten, or that he would ever be forgiven. He turned the corner—

—and saw the empty tunnel stretch before him.

He stopped dead.

The sight of Nunn May's nondescript back had incorporated itself so firmly into his vision that he felt blind without it. He swung round, and loped back along the tunnel, trying not to break into a run.

There he was. A lone figure, shuffling along with *The Times* pressed between briefcase and arm.

In the direction of the clockwise platform.

'Tickets, please.'

Walter looked up at the ticket inspector and did not see him. Then he pulled himself out of his reverie and smiled politely. It was always the same man, always the same words. He produced the ticket.

'Thank you, sir.'

'Do you think we'll be delayed long?'

'Not long, no, sir. Waiting for the signal.'

The train was at a halt just outside Willesden Junction. The rails stretched to either side, dozens of them. He'd never seen so many tracks before he came to London. When he was a boy, in Australia, the railway line from Newcastle to Sydney had passed close to his house. But there had been only two sets of tracks. His Uncle Joe had been a train driver, spending his days travelling out along one track, then back along the other. Sometimes Walter used to hear the engine whistle about half a mile after passing Adamstown station, and he would know that Joe was passing the point nearest to the house.

'He's a fine lad, young Walter,' he'd heard Uncle Joe saying to his father once, 'but a bit funny.'

The reason why Walter was funny was that all the other boys had dreamed of being a train driver, like Joe. Walter's little brother, Jim, had idolised Uncle Joe and followed him around making engine noises. And Walter never did. Trains were fine, but he'd wanted more. He had wanted a hundred things, to be an inventor, an astronomer, an explorer. His dad worked as a clerk for a ship chandler down at Newcastle docks and sometimes he had to go down to the docks to settle up the accounts just before a ship sailed to some distant port in Europe or South America. Occasionally, when Walter was a young boy, his dad had taken him along. Newcastle was a very busy harbour, but its capacity was limited by a rocky outcrop which formed a bar across its entrance, and if it was full, the craft had to wait outside for there to be room for them to come in. Walter had watched in wonder when the willowy masts and billowing sails of fifty or more sailing ships gathered in the back harbour, unable to take their cargo on board because of the steamships blocking the way in, until his father had dragged him away. Sometimes Walter had got the chance to ask the ships' captains about the places they came from, and once a Norwegian had offered to take him back to Norway with him. The small boy and the captain were well advanced in making their arrangements when his dad had pointed out that it would be teatime soon, and that Mum would be expecting him. As he was led from the port, he kept glancing over his shoulder, watching his ship sail off to those strange-sounding places, and he'd tried to imagine what it might be like one day to go too.

There was a hiss from the wheels beneath the carriage. The seat jolted and moved forward, and the engine heaved its cargo of commuters towards Euston.

The best way to get to the British Museum would be to change at Notting Hill Gate and take the Central Line to Tottenham Court Road. Henderson shifted nervously in his seat as the train slowed, and watched Nunn May's dull image in the glass, waiting for him to pack up his paper and get ready to move.

But instead he was unfolding it on his knees.

The train stopped. Several people got off. The muscles in Henderson's legs were tense with the readiness to go. Nunn May carried on reading the paper. The doors closed and the train went on.

Bayswater. Nunn May stayed put. Paddington. Edgware Road. Henderson's legs were beginning to ache with their tautness. Baker Street, and still on.

We are on the Circle Line, thought Henderson. If we stayed on long enough we'd go right round and end up back in Kensington. And then we could still keep going.

Great Portland Street. Nunn May glanced up at the platform and began to fold his paper. The train pulled out of the station and trundled into the tunnel. Nunn May snapped his briefcase open—

—and put the newspaper inside.

Henderson stared in confusion. No copy of *The Times*. A ruse? He was getting out of his seat. The train pulled to a halt. Nunn May felt his way down the carriage, holding his briefcase and umbrella in one hand and keeping hold of the safety rail with the other. The doors opened. Henderson jumped to his feet.

Euston Square.

Henderson consulted his mind's eye's map of London. It was, he realised, a perfectly sensible route. From Euston Square one could cross the Euston Road and walk straight down Gower Street to the British Museum.

He let two men get off after Nunn May and then followed him out, his heart pounding painfully. The paper would come back out of the briefcase soon enough. It's now, he thought. It is finally going to happen.

And then he would be free.

Walter walked slowly down the platform towards the Euston concourse. The cold bit hard at his face and neck. It had never stopped surprising him, this cold, not in fifteen years. The viciousness of it assaulted him afresh every winter morning.

'You must have a coat,' his mother had said to him all that time ago, when he was just twenty-two and had delivered to her the miraculous, unbelievable news that he had won a Travelling Scholarship. He'd not known where he was going – the award did not specify, it just endowed him with the money to study for a Ph.D. abroad. But as his professor at Sydney had made enquiries at Oxford and Cambridge, it seemed likely that he was going somewhere that was colder than New South Wales. He'd thought her rather comical as he'd stood with her in that Sydney department store, fussing over clothing when his head was full of the whole world. But he was glad of it once his journey was over.

He had wondered, that first winter in Cambridge, whether his short lifetime in the sun had made it actually dangerous to attempt to withstand such a climate. His father's family, four Australian generations back, had been Scottish, and so he reasoned that his small Celtic body ought to be able to cope. But the cold took root in his bones and radiated loneliness from inside. He'd felt sick with it, for months and months, until spring came and England softened into familiarity.

Now, as he walked out of the station onto the Euston Road, England was so familiar that Australia felt like a half-remembered dream. But this winter, the loneliness was setting into his bones once more.

'Get me Aitken,' Henderson barked at the operator. 'Get him NOW!'

He had never spoken so rudely on the telephone. The tone of his own voice made him cringe. But it was necessary. In all his imaginings, he had never quite been able to work out how he was going to achieve this part of the job. His instructions were that if it became clear that Nunn May was about to keep his appointment, Henderson must contact his superior. Aitken would arrange for the police to come to the museum, and Nunn May and his contact would be arrested in the very act of passing information. At that point, Henderson's role would be to look out for confused-looking policemen and point them in the direction of their man. But the thing which had always been a mystery to him was how he was going to make the phone call without losing Nunn May.

He was lucky. After surfacing from the tube, Nunn May had stopped in a coffee shop. Outside the shop was a phone booth, where Henderson stood now. He could see Nunn May through the glass of the box, sipping from his cup, reading the paper once more. Perhaps there was still time to kill before the rendezvous. But still – who knew how much time, or how little— The telephone operators at the Bureau were notoriously inefficient. He might easily spend these precious moments tangled in the loop of wires that linked the rooms of the maze.

'Is that you, Henderson?'

'Mr Aitken!'

'Do you have news?'

He was suddenly tongue-tied. Someone stopped on the pavement, blocking his view of the shop. When they moved on, Nunn May was glancing at his watch. 'Aitken!'

'Henderson?'

'He's – it's going! It's happening! He's in the coffee house.'

'Coffee house?'

'I'm on Gower Street. No, Euston Road. We just have to go down Gower Street. And then it's the – British Museum!'

'Do you still have sight of him?'

'Yes!'

'Keep with him. We'll have our men there straightaway.'

'Yes! I—'

But the line was dead. Henderson slammed the receiver back onto the hook. Nunn May was talking to the waitress and settling his bill. Henderson stayed in the phone box and waited for the man to emerge. He looked to be struggling rather to get his newspaper folded up.

For a moment, George felt a pang of affection, and then pity.

And then Nunn May came back out onto the street, and Henderson was on his tail once more, and the anger he'd felt through all the four months of this job merged with exhilaration that he was going to make a success of something at last.

Walter's office was on the top floor of the University College Physics Department, overlooking Gordon Street. It was the same office he'd had before the university had been evacuated, and the same job, and ever since he'd come back just over a year ago, before the Christmas of 1944, he'd felt the horrible sensation of time going backwards.

The office was piled up on every shelf and table with journals. In the old days he'd been punctiliously neat –

he'd felt that if he had a clear room, it would help him to have a clear mind. During the war, of course, there had been very little in the way of journals. But now the scientific community seemed to be getting back into gear, and publishing, publishing, for all it was worth. He was beginning to think that if he did not catch up on his reading soon, the university would have to subject him to taxidermy and stick him in a glass case in the entrance hall alongside Jeremy Bentham, on display as a relic from the past.

There was no time for reading this morning, anyhow. This afternoon he was due to give a lecture in Modern Physics to a hall crowded with demobbed soldiers, who far outnumbered the undergraduates fresh out of school. The ex-servicemen were hard enough to teach at the best of times, constantly questioning things from the most unacademic standpoint. And Modern Physics was a nightmare. When he and the rest of the Science Faculty had been evacuated to Bangor, in North Wales, he'd taught the same course for five years on the trot. There had been no new developments to incorporate. Hardly anyone was around to do any new work, and the research which was being undertaken was all under military embargo. Now, much of what had happened had suddenly, explosively, become public knowledge. And all the students wanted to know about was fission.

He'd fobbed them off all of last term. 'The fission lecture will be in February,' he'd told them sternly, shuffling his lecture schedule in his head. The war might have been over but its last calendar year had seemed to stretch on for ever, and back then February 1946 had sounded to him a very long way off, part of a new era in which he would be able to confront anything. Even fission.

But like tomorrow, February always comes. There had been no miraculous dawning of a new era, no sudden rebirth of his soul. Nevertheless, he had promised them a lecture, and now he could put it off no longer.

Last year's notes were on the table in front of him. They outlined the basics, as they had stood, freshly discovered, at the end of 1938 and the beginning of 1939. If he narrowed his eyes he could still catch sight of the romance of it, could still glimpse the things inside the things inside. When he was a boy at Newcastle High, the science teacher had described the way all the things they saw were made up of molecules. She'd told them all to turn out their pockets, and from the collection of assorted marbles and conkers that resulted, selected the best. Then she'd taken a box and filled it with the missiles, and shook it around to show them how the particles jostled in a body of liquid, such as the sea which beat against the rocks below Walter's house. He'd experienced a thousand moments of discovery. Soon the class had been told about the way heat worked to agitate the water molecules, until the bonds which tied them were shaken apart and they floated in freedom into the atmosphere to form a gas. The heat caused them to rise, and as they ascended, they moved into cooler air, where they settled once again in tiny droplets and formed the ever-changing structures of the clouds.

Every day Walter had known more than he had the last, and he saw the quest for knowledge stretching out before him for ever. When he was doing his homework, he'd sat on the verandah at the back of the house and gazed out across the bush through the gaps in the hills to the sea. He had sucked his pencil and watched the clouds drift in from the ocean and out again, forming themselves into turrets and battlements – real, true life castles in the air. The plumes of smoke from the steelworks and the collieries of Newcastle had streamed upwards in dark grey puffs, then softened as they joined the constellations of vapour. The clouds had taken on the shape of Walter's dreams, and he saw them follow the ships into the ocean. He had wondered where they were taking his water molecules, and what they might do when they got there. Would the stream that rose from his cup of tea one day fall as rain on a boy in Jakarta, or Calcutta, or Moscow, or Spain?

Walter stared at his notes and held his forehead. The blood in his fingers beat hard against his skull. Fission had once been a lecture he'd particularly enjoyed. He'd drawn the images on the blackboard – the uranium atom, cumbersome and weighty, almost, but not quite, overloaded by the forces holding it together. Then the neutron, fired into its bulk. The neutron was a big sub-particle, as large as a proton, and its mass was a threat. But it also had stealth, its neutral charge allowing it to pass straight through the barrier of the electrical field that protected the uranium atom's core. It shot past the circling electrons and was not deterred by the strong positive charge of the nucleus. If its trajectory was right, it would make a direct hit—

—and would not bounce back. It vanished.

Walter used to leave his tale hanging at this point. *Where is it? What has happened to the neutron?* were the questions in the air, even though the students ought already to have known.

'The neutron has been *captured*.'

Captured, but not subjugated. It was a Trojan horse. For a moment nothing happened. Then the uranium atom began to distort. The new addition was too much for the tension of its surface to contain. It tottered, squeezed, elongated, until it formed the shape of a dumbbell, with two growing bumps at either end, the forces within them propelling them apart, until the neck which held them together was stretched, pulled, tugged – and finally gave way. The two positively charged fission fragments spun apart in repulsion, in a storm of unprecedented thermal energy. Amongst the wreckage of the now non-existent uranium atom, two or more free neutrons had escaped and were spinning off too, heading for more uranium nuclei. They did not generally make contact. But they might, and then the whole thing could start all over again.

'Have you ever seen it?' a student had once asked with wide eyes.

'You can't *see* it,' he had objected. Which, for him, had been part of its grandeur. He and his students had looked back at the simple drawings on the board. 'It's nothing like that,' he had said. 'You must use your brain. You must use your imagination.' He'd spoken of the simplicity of physics, of its mystery, of how utterly different it is from what you could see, and how profound nature was.

But the world was different now. On 6 August 1945 an act had been committed by physics and by nature, and both were changed for ever. And now, when fission was mentioned in lectures, Walter no longer had the usual struggle to hold his students' attention. It was there already. Their eyes blazed with desire for knowledge, and it was not science they burned for.

It was death.

'Mr Aitken!'

'Henderson?' The archness in Aitken's voice had become parodic.

'He's not going to the British Museum.'

'Well, where is he going, then?'

'He's gone into a building. It's a university building.'

'*Which* university building?'

'Just off Gower Street. University College, I think. Hold on a second—' Henderson shoved more coins into the slot, and leant out of the booth. 'Excuse me!' he yelled at a passer-by. The young man stopped. 'Is this University College?'

'Yes,' said the dumbfounded student.

'It's University College,' confirmed Henderson breathlessly, back in the booth. And then subsided. 'I think – I think it's a false alarm, sir. It must be university business.'

'Henderson,' said Aitken, in a tone too underwhelmed for impatience, 'the association between the different colleges of London University is very loose.'

'I know.' He knew. He'd done his background reading. But still—

'Get off the phone. Find out where the HELL he's gone.'

'Do you think—'

'GET OFF THE PHONE.'

Henderson leapt out of the booth and scuttled back in the direction whence he'd come.

Walter had read his old notes three times. He had been through the official document released by the US government on the matter, and had cross-referenced it against those scientific papers he'd managed to root out. And still he could find nothing he could bear to add to the lecture he'd written in 1939.

The phone rang. It was the porter downstairs.

'There's a gentleman to see you, Dr Dunnachie,' the porter said.

Walter's heart sank. The last thing he needed now was a student with an essay crisis. 'Well, who is it?'

The porter said a name. It skimmed off Walter's brain. Then his whole body clenched in outrage.

'*Who?*'

Henderson loitered around the corner while Nunn May knocked on the door. There was a pause, and then it opened.

For a moment, silence. Then,

'Alan!'

It was the first time Henderson had heard Nunn May's Christian name uttered to his face.

There was a pause. 'I suppose you'd better come in.'

'Thank you,' said Nunn May quietly.

And then the door closed behind him, and Henderson was left scrutinising the nameplate on the wall.

'Dr Walter Dunnachie. Lecturer in Physics.'

Another one. Henderson sighed. He'd never been very good at science at school.

2

Henderson and Aitken sat in the coffee shop on Euston Road. Aitken was sprawled around his chair. He was an aristocrat of the fat sort, built to make his accommodation look inadequate on all occasions.

'Well,' said Aitken, 'he's on our files. Dunnachie, I mean.'

'Oh.' The silence gaped. Henderson knew by now that it was not his business to understand the nature of his investigation. Early on, he had occupied the wandering hours with speculation. Nothing had seemed plausible. The man appeared to have no military or official connections. Even now, his only contact had been with another teacher. Henderson could not imagine university lecturers being involved in anything sinister. But after a dozen fruitless sessions with Aitken, he knew that it was pointless to care.

Aitken expected conversations to be facilitated by his interlocutor. It was therefore necessary to ask questions. The problem was that those questions could not be too direct. It was a matter of trying to work out which pieces of information Aitken was prepared to part with. The best technique Henderson had found so far was to ask half a question and let Aitken turn it into whatever enquiry he wanted to answer.

'You mean,' he hazarded, 'that he is also—'

'In contact with the Russians?' Aitken snorted. 'Don't be so obvious, my boy. There's more than one way to skin a cat.'

Skin a cat? With great difficulty, George restrained himself from letting out a deep sigh. He found his boss more obscure than any of the Latin teachers who had made his schooldays such a misery. He took a little rest, gazing at the tablecloth. Then,

'So why—'

'Is he on our files? He's a conchie.'

'A conchie.' George's muscles relaxed instantly. If there was one creature further down the food chain than an asthmatic shirker, it was a conchie.

'And also' – and here George watched the very slow uncurling of Aitken's upper lip, in an elaborate gesture of distaste – 'an Australian.'

George had never met either a conchie or an Australian.

'Came here years ago, as a young man. Stayed, made a life for himself here. Got mixed up in the' – Aitken puffed – 'Peace Movement. Lots of speechifying. Sat out the war in *Wales*.'

Were they both pacifists? It did not explain why Aitken might be interested in them. After all, there was no war now, and it was difficult to understand what damage a conchie could do in peacetime. All the same— 'So do you think—' It was looking ever more likely. The assignation had been made. The business with the British Library had been a diversionary tactic.

'That he's the contact? Unlikely.'

George's heart sank.

'Has to be considered as a possibility. But it was never likely to be someone he knew.'

'They know each other?'

'Looks probable. They were contemporaries at Cambridge. Dunnachie's a bit older, but still. Both physicists. Both political. Both dissident. There's more here than meets the eye. But it's not enough to justify an arrest.'

'Oh.' No release, then.

Aitken watched him. 'Not enough to justify *Dunnachie's* arrest, I mean. We've got more than enough on Nunn May. Time to stop this wretched cat and mouse. The British

Museum isn't going to happen. We'll tie up a few more bits and pieces, then pull him in.'

George could not stop the smile from breaking out all over his face.

'Thought you'd be pleased,' said Aitken impassively. 'I can tell you're ready for a change of scene.'

Oh God. He could go home to Phoebe now. He could tell her it was over. He would take her to the little restaurant on the corner, where they used to go when they were first married. And then tomorrow he could go back to the office and get back to trawling through those blessed, warm, dry papers.

'You can switch your attentions to Dunnachie now. Much easier job, less delicate. You can make yourself known to him. Find out what he does, where he goes, who he knows. What he talks about. Particularly that.'

No— 'You mean you want me to trail Dunnachie?'

'You can start tonight. Follow him home.'

Walter turned his key in the front door. His head was still burning with remonstrations, both real and imagined. *How dare you*— Had he said that? He probably had, at some stage or other in the conversation. The accusations and demands had flown back and forth and he could no longer distinguish between them. They had probably both said it. But not enough. Alan, how dare you, how dare you, how dare you—

Grace was coming towards him in the hallway, ready with a kiss. He looked at her and saw no more than the forces of mass and motion propelled in his direction. The only way to avoid collision would be to step aside. But human imperatives are subtly different from physical ones. He remained still and his impassivity was enough to deflect her. She stopped. Her shoulders lifted and then dropped, and her mouth pursed in annoyance. How strange it is, he thought through his anger, that our sensory mechanisms are so finely attuned to these tiny

21

movements, which would be impossible to distinguish using the most sophisticated measuring equipment, and which have no physical impact, yet can set in motion a whole train of consequences.

She stared at him. Once, such a rejection would have provoked a lively stream of protest, a vigorous debate, and finally, a reconciliation. But the laws of their relationship had changed and both knew that things were not guaranteed to turn out that way any more. She took a step back.

'I'm sorry I'm late,' said Walter, trying to force them both into a semblance of normality. 'Are the children in bed?'

Grace responded in kind. 'Only just. Dinner'll be half an hour. You can read them their story while I'm making it.'

But she continued to glare at him. She was not going to let him get away with it.

'How was the lecture?' she demanded.

'Lecture?'

'The fission lecture. Come on, Walter, you've been dreading it for months. How did it go? Or were you obliged to postpone it again?'

He registered the injury those few words inflicted upon his state of mind. It was not as great as she intended. The lecture had taken place; Walter had discharged his duty by delivering it from his old notes, merely omitting his old inspirational asides. He had sensed the frustration of his audience but had defused each query with a retreat into the literalness of the equations. It had not been very difficult given the way he was feeling after Alan's visit. If Alan had done him one favour, it was that.

'I gave the lecture,' he said with dull defiance.

'Did it go badly?'

'No,' said Walter, 'it went perfectly well.'

'Then why are you in such a filthy mood?'

She had previously accused him of having been in a filthy

mood for six months. For a moment he considered concealing
from her the events of the day and sparing himself the ordeal
of the inevitable interrogation. But it was true that the mood
was exceptional on this occasion, and Grace could not be
deterred as easily as his students.

'I had a visitor.'

'What sort of visitor?'

'Alan Nunn May.'

All of a sudden, she relaxed. He saw the relief flood across
her face, followed by sympathy. 'Oh, Walter,' she said, 'how
horribly difficult for you.'

No one else would have understood how difficult. Yet, he
thought as she hugged him, it is an illusion. She only thinks
she understands. In reality it is much, much worse than that.

'What on earth possessed him to think he could turn up
uninvited?' Then she stopped. '*Was* he uninvited?'

'Yes!'

'How is he? What did he have to say for himself? Did he
mention—'

How could he possibly describe their conversation, even if
he wanted to? It remained in his mind as a mess of emotion.
He could hear the sharp, dissonant music of their raised voices
above the words they had actually said. Exhaustion surged
through him. He was still wearing his coat and did not have
the energy to take it off. He made a dash to the sitting room
and threw himself onto the sofa. Grace sat down next to him
and took his hand, gazing at him in expectation.

'He's back from Canada,' said Walter eventually.

'Obviously. How long has he been back?'

'A few months, I think. He's taken up a place at King's
College.'

'A few months? Why on earth didn't he get in touch
before?'

'For the same reason it was difficult to see him.'

She huffed in frustration. 'How was his time in Montreal?'

Walter seized upon the only triviality he could remember. 'Well,' he said. 'He would keep going on about the Canadian Mounties.'

'The what?'

'The Canadian Mounties.'

'You mean those policemen in red uniforms and big hats who sit on horses?'

'Presumably, yes. I got the impression that these ones didn't actually have horses.'

'What on earth does Alan have to do with the Canadian Mounties?'

'Apparently they made life rather difficult at the laboratory. They were in charge of security out there.'

'But how completely silly.'

'That's what Alan thought.'

'I mean silly that that was what he talked about.'

'Oh. Well, yes. I suppose so.'

'Didn't he say anything about the work out there?'

Walter's hand flicked out of hers. It was an involuntary movement, as if he'd been scalded. She grabbed it back. 'Walter, my love,' she said, but the gentleness was flecked with steel, 'you are going to have to talk about it one day.'

Was he? His whole ambition in life was never to have to talk about it and never to have to think about it. Yet life would not let him rest on the matter. 'He talked about the secrecy. I suppose that was his way of talking about it.'

'Didn't you ask him?'

'Well. You know. We had a conversation.'

'And he didn't like the secrecy.'

'Hated it.'

'But he didn't talk about the rest of it. To you.' She dropped his hand and stood up. 'Oh, you *men*. It's no wonder, you know, that the world's in the state it is. Go on, go and read your story. They'll be asleep soon.'

'Grace—'

'I know you don't want to talk about it.'

'I'll try,' he lied. 'One day.'

'One day.'

He took his opportunity to escape, and retreated to the children's world of Wendy and Peter Pan.

Watford.

Henderson stared at the house from the other side of the road. It was a red-brick semi, probably built not long before the war. The front garden was better tended than most, with small trees and weedless flowerbeds. The lights glowed from behind cheerful orange curtains.

Henderson had rarely ever been so far north.

And newborn hatred bubbled through every cell of his body. Watford. He stared up at the smoke-smeared sky. What worse place on earth could there be? Polluted by the filth of the city, yet miles away from its living heart. At least Kensington had been the shortest possible hop from his home in Clapham.

A car backfired against the dark silence and a flock of black birds flew wildly into the night from their rookery, cawing in protest. Henderson spun on his heel, coughing along with them. He whipped his dead-man's coat around him and stormed back out of the cul-de-sac towards the station.

Walter stared at the ceiling.

She'd been awake still when he'd joined her. She always was. It was an axiom of their life that she could not sleep until he did. She said it was because his waking movements disturbed her, but he knew that she thought of it differently. She thought that she was guarding his sleep.

It was true that she rarely slept before he did. But it was not true that she could not sleep while he was awake. When these particular nightmares had begun, he had woken her with his shouting and thrashing a few times, and had scared her as much as he'd scared himself. She'd then interrogated him on what he'd been dreaming about, on and on, until he was half-crazed with exhaustion. However many times she asked, he could not tell her. The eyeballs melting from their sockets like pink ice cream on a hot day, the cracking bones, the igniting flesh – this was not the stuff of fantasy. It was documentary fact. He would rather have returned into his dream's visceral cocoon than recite those realities in the cold light of the bedside lamp. Now, the dreams still woke him, but they did not rouse her. His fear of her cross-examination had worked itself into as deep a nook of his brain as the horrors themselves. He woke in petrified silence, and she slumbered on.

As the sounds and the stink began to be muffled by the clicks of the house and the smell of Grace's skin, he listened to her even breaths. In sleep she was fragile. He wanted to touch her, but knew that to do so would be to banish her peace and what shreds there were of his own, and he understood the comfort she drew from his own sleeping form.

Tonight's carnage had erupted from a tangle of Tinkerbell and sea, Nunn May and Cambridge spires. The details were forgotten now. He was left with as congealed a mess of waking thoughts, which would not be put to sleep.

On the wall opposite the bed was a print of Trinity College. Now that the blackout was gone, he could see its outline, where once all had been darkness. He did not need to see it. It was years since he'd been back to Cambridge, and those painted stones had replaced the shape of the real ones in his memory, as if he'd lived in a place made of water-colour paint.

'Mr Dunnachie!'

It was the memory of an urgent voice, the sound of running feet and panting, his own head turning to see the dishevelled undergraduate hurtling to a halt.

'Hello?'

'You don't know me. My name is Alan Nunn May.'

And as he lay as still as he could in his bed, his head full of Alan, he remembered the way he'd stared at the young man who'd just broken into his life, and how he'd then seen a look on that face which stopped his resentment. It was the untainted glow of respect.

'How can I help?' he'd said more kindly.

'I'm terribly sorry to disturb you. I'm studying physics, you see, and thinking of staying on for a doctorate.' Nunn May's words had tumbled over one another in his attempt to get out all the necessary information at once. 'Dr Chadwick said – he said you might be prepared to show me your experiment.'

'Oh!'

Dr Chadwick had been Walter's supervisor, the Assistant Director of the Cavendish Laboratory. He was a quiet and clever man. Walter had been so in awe of him that he'd found it difficult ever to ask for his help. News of such a commendation, even made to an untidy undergraduate, was precious indeed.

'If Dr Chadwick has recommended me to you,' Walter had said proudly, 'then I shall be happy to give you a tour.'

And so, on the lick and the spit of a promise from Chadwick, they had become acquaintances.

Chadwick. Walter stared at the shadowy painting and another picture presented itself to his memory. It was a grainy newspaper photograph, out of date but very recognisably Chadwick, and beside it lay an article outlining the British contribution to the development of the atomic bomb.

3

When all the world and love were young, in Cambridge 1931, a youth stepped through old gates and saw, a new world at the atom's core.

Walter trembled at its brink, his bones brittle with the feeling that nothing would ever be the same again. He was a slip of a thing, shivering on a warm October day in his new coat, gown and college scarf. The door was the entrance to the Cavendish Laboratory, and the inscription above it read 'Magna opera exquisita in omnes voluntates eius'. The works of the Lord are great; they are studied by all who delight in them. A mighty injunction.

Until now he'd always been sure that he was a great scientist already. The conviction had been there so long it was impossible to remember forming it. He'd not even known what science was until he went to Newcastle High. But somehow it had already been there when, to his and everyone else's surprise, he'd emerged from Cook's Hill Primary with a scholarship place at the town's only academic secondary school. And when he got there, science was waiting for him, as if he'd had it by him always and he'd just never noticed. After that it had just been a matter of stretching the limits. Newcastle, Sydney – how far could he go? How far *was* there to go?

The six-week boat journey from his home had ended only two days before. He'd arrived in Cambridge in a mood of great excitement, cloaking his luggage at the station and catching a bus to Trinity College, where he found that his lodgings were all ready for him. When he had finished unpacking, he looked around the little attic room, and saw all the same objects which had populated his cabin on the ship. He'd felt the sensation of having spun in the air for an unaccountable length of time and of landing on soft earth with the lightest touch.

Now Walter Dunnachie looked up at the gates of the Cavendish and felt small.

The Cavendish Laboratory was founded by a scientific-inclining duke of the same name in the eighteen-seventies, his weighty blood having prevented him from pursuing his calling in any serious way other than the provision of capital. A man named James Clerk Maxwell was its first professor, and Maxwell secured its reputation straightaway, by making a series of discoveries which heralded the most profound change in the concept of physical reality since the time of Newton. Whether he meant to or not, he took a step forward into a mysterious and wavering world, for he found out about electro-magnetism, and this was the first sign that the world does not operate simply by the force of objects moving around and hitting one another. Thomson's electron followed, and Rutherford's atomic nucleus, and all around Walter, huddled over their experiments, were men intent on probing deeper into the strange unworldly universe of the intensely real.

The place looked like a Victorian rectory from the outside, overloaded with ornamentation and obscured by ivy. But it was a rectory adapted to the eccentric scientific leanings of its inhabitants. Some of the windows had a wide flat ledge on the outside so that the sun's rays could be reflected into the room by a heliostat; the interior was partly panelled in varnished pitched pine.

Amongst all this old-fashioned paraphernalia, a modern scientific community throbbed and hummed in activities that looked like the purest manifestation of chaos that Walter had ever seen. He passed through its rooms, guided by a researcher named Jack Constable, and stared about him in disbelief. A jungle of wires was suspended from ceilings, pipes and light fittings. Ladders lay propped against shelves, often with someone halfway up, tinkering precariously with a black box, or a dial, or a piece of tubing. The tables were crammed with equipment; pulleys attached to levers; cogs and pistons; bottles and batteries and corkscrews of piping, all jostling with one another for space. It was impossible to tell how anyone could possibly get at the machines in the middle of the tables, so knotted and obscured were they by the apparatus inching in from the edge.

But there they were, the researchers, all crowded round their experiments, ducking under the wires and stretching over the retort stands with a practised dexterity.

Walter's head darted from side to side as he tried to imagine himself ever being able to take his place amongst them. He caught sight of a sign hanging from the ceiling. It was an oblong electrical box, etched with glass lettering which was clearly designed to light up. SHUT UP DAMN YOU, it demanded imperiously. Constable followed his line of sight and grinned mischievously. 'That's mine,' he said. 'Had to do it. Equipment highly sensitive to sound, you know. If anyone makes too much noise, it tells them what to do. It's the only way to keep things under control.'

Walter smiled nervously and carried on walking. Suddenly, from somewhere at his feet, he heard a yelp.

He started and looked around him.

'Oh, Dunnachie,' said Constable in sorrow. 'You've trodden on Dr Cockcroft's hand.'

Beside them was the most extraordinary contraption. Two giant metal balls hung motionless in mid air, one above the other, the upper suspended by a slim pole connected to the ceiling, and the lower supported by a large black plinth. It was attached by a system of rigid pipes to a huge piston arrangement, which stretched from a kind of hat fixed to the roof, down to the top of an insulated wooden crate on the floor.

Inside the crate was a man, sucking his fingers. The crate was so small his knees were pressed hard against his chest and his head against the top of the box. The interior of his cubbyhole was lined with wires and dials.

A volley of apologies and refutations passed between them, while Dr Cockcroft remained in the refuge of the crate and Walter squatted to talk to him. 'I'm most terribly sorry.' 'No, it's quite all right.' 'Are you hurt?' 'Not at all, it was my fault really.'

'What is that machine?' Walter asked in mystification after they had left the scientist to his finger-sucking and his dial-twiddling. 'I've never seen anything like it in my life.'

'It's Cockcroft's particle accelerator,' said Constable in a confidential whisper. 'He's trying to get protons to travel at higher and higher speeds, to see what damage they can cause. Rutherford hates it, or at least he pretends he does. He says it takes up too much electricity, and anyway he has an absolute horror of complicated equipment.'

Walter looked around and it struck him that this horror did not seem to be reflected in his surroundings. Constable saw his expression, and said, 'Oh, none of this is really complex, you know. We try to keep things as simple as possible. It's just – well, there isn't really enough space. There are too many people here. Rutherford just keeps on accepting more research students – it seems he can't say no to anyone with real promise – and then it's up to Dr Chadwick to find them all work to do, and places to carry it out.'

'Oh,' said Walter. This was not welcome news. He was due to meet Chadwick later that day for that very purpose.

'It's better than it used to be, of course,' continued Constable. 'In the old days, there was so little equipment to go round between all the students that they used to carry out raids on each other's apparatus, and defend themselves with bits of rubber tubing.'

Walter was just trying to envisage this apparition when another appeared before him.

He knew Rutherford, the Director of the Cavendish, as soon as he saw him, for he had seen his photograph, and he was not a man to sink into the background. The New Zealander was standing in the middle of the large room at the heart of the laboratory, with his hands on his hips. His burly frame was squeezed into a dark three-piece suit. His jowls burst out above a wing collar, and in his mouth was a pipe, which spat sparks and ash into the air as his voice boomed out from under his walrus moustache. The professor appeared to be having a perfectly ordinary conversation with a young man about an experiment; but it was being conducted at full volume, and was interspersed with guffaws of laughter and wild gesticulations.

Constable looked rather daunted at the prospect of interrupting the conversation in order to introduce Walter, but fortunately Rutherford spotted them hovering meekly in the corner, and broke off the discussion to draw them into his orbit.

'Constable, I see you have a visitor with you. Would this be our new research student from Sydney?'

He stuck out his hand, and Walter did not have time to think about what was going on before his own was vigorously shaken.

'Dunnachie, sir,' he said weakly.

'Good to meet you, Dunnachie, good to meet you.' He snorted jovially, and Walter was enveloped in a cloud of choking tobacco smoke. 'How was the long journey from the other side, eh? Been a while since I did it, more's the pity.'

'It was—' It seemed terribly important that he found the right words. 'Most illuminating.'

'Illuminating? Jolly good. One can never have too much illumination, except, of course, when one is trying to eliminate it— Now, we need to get you fixed up with some sort of work, don't we?'

Walter agreed that indeed they did.

'Chadwick's the man. Have you met Chadwick yet?'

Constable and Walter both tumbled out some words to the effect that he had not.

'I expect he's hidden away in his office, working away, as usual. Well, I hope you have a very productive time here, Dunnachie. If ever you have a problem, just drop in and have a chat, I'm always happy to have a chat.'

'Thank you, sir,' said Walter, and retreated as Rutherford turned back to the experiment he had been contemplating before their arrival. As Constable guided Walter across the room, Rutherford suddenly turned again.

'And Dunnachie,' he shouted.

'Yes?'

'Dinner next Saturday evening. Newnham Cottage. Wife bakes a most acceptable apple pie. Eight p.m., anyone can tell you where it is.'

Walter nodded, and the Professor turned away again.

'Don't worry,' said Constable, recovering his knowledge-able and confident air now that Rutherford's attention was no longer focused in his direction. 'Everyone gets an invite every now and again. There'll be lots of other people there. He likes to have lots of people.'

Walter could not speak. He had met Lord Rutherford and had been invited round to his house for dinner.

*　　*　　*

Like most boys, in his days at Newcastle High, Walter was inspired by the achievements of his heroes.

Publicly, his idol was the New South Wales leg spinner, Arthur Mailey. But in the private world of his imaginings, the journeys taken within the minds of scientists were at least as exciting as the physical battles on the cricket field.

In the 1920s, there were two physicists whose fame had carried beyond academic circles. One was Einstein, whose bemused brown eyes and shock of hair were catapulted into the public imagination in 1919, when the Royal Society photographed the solar eclipse and verified his hitherto-ridiculed general theory of relativity. Walter was eleven at the time and asked his teacher to explain it to him. The teacher laughed and told him that much cleverer men than himself had failed to understand it.

Walter was stunned. He had never heard a teacher making an admission of inadequacy in the face of knowledge. And that was the moment at which he realised how far science stretched towards magic. He learnt the formula $e = mc^2$, and managed to glimpse a little of what relativity was about, but from that day onwards, for Walter, Einstein possessed a spectral type of greatness which he revered but feared touching, lest it shatter and lose its mystery.

The other physicist was Rutherford. And he was quite different. For despite being 'the colossus of modern physics', the photographs of the sturdy New Zealander showed him to be a very recognisable sort of human, who looked for all the world a particularly robust and energetic farmer. Walter conceived a desire to know more about his life, and when he was fourteen, looked him up in Arthur Mee's *Children's Encyclopaedia*.

He discovered that Rutherford had grown up in a community very like his own and, like Walter, had managed to pass a scholarship examination in order to get into the local

High School. My goodness, Walter had thought, tingling with excitement. And as he progressed through his own education, he kept coming back to that encyclopaedia entry, for his life began to take on a shape a little like that of his hero.

The young Ernest Rutherford came top in his school in the final year, and gained a scholarship to the local university. So did Walter. Rutherford took Maths and Physics, and gained first class degrees in both. So did Walter. Then Rutherford applied for a travelling scholarship, in order to study at the Cavendish Laboratory in Cambridge, and though he did not get the award at first, the successful candidate dropped out, leaving Rutherford to take his place. And, of course, exactly the same thing happened to Walter.

But in 1931 Walter knew that there was a world of difference between the scientific world he was about to enter and that which had lain before his Antipodean predecessor. In 1896, the atom did not even exist.

Men had always had an urge to subdivide their surroundings into the smallest possible components. The atom, along with the four elements, the four humours and goodness knows what other superstition and fantasy, was just one of them. The argument had raged from the age of Democritus right up to the cold winter's day in the Cavendish when Professor Thomson set up an experiment with the help of the young New Zealander, and succeeded in identifying and photographing a minute particle with a negative electrical charge. The pair then liberated electrons from every element they could lay their hands on, and whatever the material, it was always the same. They had come across a fundamental particle. The existence of the electron implied that it was part of an atom, and for the first time men knew that a rock was built from the same materials as a human heart.

It was, for Walter, the most incredible moment in the

history of science. But it was just the beginning of Rutherford's story.

The scientific knowledge which was so readily available to
Walter had been utterly unknown then. Many of the words
and equations had needed to be cobbled together piecemeal by
Rutherford himself. He peered at the strange radiations which
had been discovered emanating from matter, and classified
them as he went along: 'one that is very readily absorbed,
which will be termed for convenience the alpha radiation,
and the other of a more penetrative character, which will
be termed the beta radiation'. The simplicity of Rutherford's
mind was infectious. When another physicist discovered a
third type, he followed Rutherford's scheme and named it
gamma radiation.

Walter knew that 'the alpha radiation' consisted of particles
identical to the nuclei of helium atoms. Beta particles were
electrons, and gamma rays were a form of high-energy x-ray.
But Rutherford could not know any of this at the time. The
alpha radiation could not be recognised as helium nuclei
because the atom he had watched Thomson discover had
no nucleus.

It was more than a decade before Thomson's own pupil
put him right on the matter. By then the young Rutherford
was already a professor of physics at Manchester University. Whilst on the ship to England, Walter had read an
article about the breakthrough, written by a scientist who
had been present at the lecture at which the discovery of
the atomic nucleus was announced. He had written, 'Quite
what possessed Rutherford to announce these results at the
Manchester Literary and Philosophical Society is unclear. The
audience consisted of members of the general public who were
interested in literary and philosophical ideas. The first agenda
item was a statement by a fruit importer that he had found
a rare snake in a consignment of bananas. He produced the

snake. The next item was the communication by a professor of anatomy in the University. He produced a model of a skull and claimed that the cheek part went back to early man. My friend and I decided that the talk was extremely interesting, but in our opinion it was a mixture of Plaster of Paris and imagination. And then came Rutherford.'

Who stood in front of a crowded hall of Manchester businessmen on 7 March 1911, and founded the science of nuclear physics.

The article was written by a Dr James Chadwick, who had been reminiscing about his time as a Manchester undergraduate. Everywhere around Walter, books and newspapers were turning into people.

When he walked into Dr Chadwick's office, he felt the descent of an English chill. The Assistant Director of the Cavendish was sitting working at his table, melting a block of blood-red sealing wax. A pile of spent matches lay in neat rows on the table, next to his tobacco pouch and pipe. He looked up without greeting, as if Walter had been in the room all morning. 'Need to get the thing airtight,' he said, gesturing at the tubing on his desk.

Walter watched in confusion as he held the match to the wax. It softened and wilted at the edges. When it was almost liquid, Chadwick pulled a piece off and applied it to the joins in the glass.

'Dr Chadwick,' said Walter nervously. The words echoed against the room's austere walls, and Walter blushed at his own pronunciation of them. 'I'm Walter Dunnachie. I was told – to come to speak to you. About my Ph.D. project.'

The physicist did not react. Walter wondered whether he should leave the room again, or continue the conversation regardless. Then Chadwick's focus sharpened, and Walter felt his own face form as image on his retina, and

he acknowledged the presence of the interloper by looking away.

'Mr Dunnachie,' he said, fixing his eyes firmly on the
Wilson Cloud Chamber on his table.

He was a tall thin man, his legs sprawling out awkwardly
beyond his chair, and his arms all bony wrists and elbows.
Yet his appearance was of a greater neatness than any other
scientist in the building. His dark hair was lacquered tidily
to his head; his collar, cuffs and waistcoat all folded away in
their appropriate places.

'Dr Chadwick,' said Walter again, and took a step towards
him, holding out his hand.

Chadwick looked at the hand for a moment, as if wondering what it was doing there. Then he appeared to find the
answer. He stood up, and they shook hands.

'Good to meet you,' he said.

And that appeared to be the end of the conversation. Walter
was on the verge of leaving the office when it occurred to him
that really he could not. Dr Chadwick was responsible for
allocating him to a supervisor and a project. The weight of
twelve thousand miles spurred him on.

'Dr Chadwick,' he said desperately, 'will you be advising
me on the topic for my Ph.D. work at some stage?'

He blinked. 'Why, of course,' he said. 'What are your
particular interests?'

Walter hesitated. The paper he'd published during his
M.Sc. in Sydney had been on the behaviour of electrons
in a number of hydrogen-based molecules. But the subject
of electrons seemed to him to be child's play in comparison
with what was going on here. He would have been happy
with anything, really, as long as it was in keeping with the
work the laboratory was doing. Whatever he said, he was
sure it would sound naïve.

'Alpha particles,' he hazarded.

'Alpha particles? Anything in particular to do with alpha particles?'

Oh golly. 'Scattering?' suggested Walter.

'Hmm,' said Chadwick, and for a moment in his eyes Walter saw the spinning of tiny helium nuclei through a chemical void into the magnetic field of an atomic nucleus.

'Well,' said Chadwick, pulling himself together, 'we'll see if we can't find you something to be looking at with alpha particles.' He picked up a lump of wax and contemplated it. 'I have a little project I've been working on for a year or so now,' he said finally, 'and it happens to involve alpha particles. I think it's a field of research which we could quite easily extend into a couple of other areas which you could be getting on with.'

Oh, thank goodness. His stab in the dark had hit home.

'How's your carpentry?' demanded Chadwick.

Walter started. 'Erm—'

'You're going to have to become a carpenter, you know, before you can become an experimental physicist. I think we shall delay the start of your job. You can spend the next month or so in the Attic. There are a few things you can be occupying yourself with up there.'

'The Attic?' It sounded like a prison sentence.

'The Attic. How's your German?'

'Erm—'

'Don't be nervous, there's a good chap. We all end up fluent Germanists here. And you won't be needing to speak it, just read it. Easy as anything. Utterly logical language, all makes sense, not like English. Or French. You need to get down to some serious reading. I'll just jot down a few books for you.'

Walter stood in front of him while he hummed and ha'd over paper and pen. He scribbled down the titles of about twenty books and papers. When he handed the list over, Walter saw that more than half were in German.

'Thank you,' he said. Then he realised that he still needed to know who would be in charge of him. 'Who will be supervising me?' asked Walter.

'I will,' said Chadwick.

Walter's heart fell. Three years of meetings like this! Three years of having to fish out the answers from a sea of reticence! Really, he would need all the help he could get, and he could not see how he was going to get it.

'Thank you,' he said dully. Then he realised that he would need to know a little more about his job if he was to direct his reading properly. 'What exactly will I be doing with the alpha particles?'

'Why, disintegrating nuclei, of course.'

Walter stared at him, his breath having rushed sharply inwards. 'You mean—' His heart was pumping. 'You mean splitting the atom?'

Dr Chadwick's face hardened. He lowered his nose and looked over the rims of his glasses. 'Splitting the atom? That's newspaper-speak, Dunnachie. According to the press everything is splitting the atom. You can call it what you like but I will continue to refer to it as artificial disintegration of the nucleus. And I would advise you to do the same when you come to write up your thesis, or you will find yourself qualified for nothing but a career in journalism.'

Walter found himself exiled to a room at the top of the building, almost alone, and soon discovered that the Attic's other name amongst the Cavendish scientists was 'the Nursery'. Its purpose was to keep fresh new inmates out of harm's way while they learnt the tricks of the trade, and he smarted with the indignity of it. At Sydney he had been an academic star, spoken to as an equal by doctoral students and sometimes even by the professors.

But he soon found himself too humbled to complain.

Chadwick gave him a simple experiment to perform, with the novel factor that he was to build his own equipment. He was given a home-made, hand-operated pump and a poorly constructed system of tubing, and his mission consisted mainly of chasing the leaks in the glassware and working out how to replace various bits and pieces with things that would produce better results.

It did not go very well. He felt like a magician's apprentice, set upon by machinery which conspired against him in evil animation. It took him days to assemble a wooden frame which could have been built by a competent carpenter in the course of a morning. He attached screens and wires, and then moved on to the construction of the glass tubes in which his materials would, in theory, perform their tricks. At this point his work ground to an abrupt and painful halt, and then started determinedly to proceed in a backward direction.

At the end of such days of destruction he collapsed in his room. The daylight was quickly shortening to a few precious hours; the sun never had the energy to warm the earth; and each day shocked him by being colder than the last. The fire in his room became an obsession. He spent hours feeding and tending it, and it rewarded him with a bright but hopeless glow which on the coldest days stretched barely beyond his feet. His desk existed in a climatic zone completely untouched by its warmth, and he sat shivering there hour after hour, poring over his German dictionary, scribbling his diary and writing letters home.

He wrote to his parents, trying to describe his activities so that they sounded at least vaguely like achievements, and into each letter he inserted a postcard to his brother Jim. Jim was fifteen and, in Walter's opinion, at a very impressionable age. The boy had not seen fit to give Walter a proper farewell at Sydney Harbour while all the friends and relations were milling around him; Jim had looked away in sulky dismissal, and Walter thought he had seen accusation in his eyes. He felt bad enough about leaving his parents for such a long time, but he felt worse about abandoning Jim. So he scoured the streets of Cambridge in search of informative picture postcards, and wrote carefully composed missives which he hoped would inspire his brother to work hard at school and learn all he could about the world.

He had still received no replies to any of his letters. They had too far to travel.

The dining room in Newnham Cottage was long and narrow and filled from one end to the other with men discussing science. Lord Rutherford sat at one end of the table, a huge moustachioed bear, jumping boisterously upon any poor strand of conversation that caught his attention, and worrying it to death as if it were a rat or a badger. Scattered amongst the severely jovial professionals were the new research students, of whom Walter was one. Two distinguished foreign visitors flanked Rutherford. To Walter's left, and at the opposite end of the table to her husband, was Lady Rutherford. She was being very kind, coaxing him and those of the others who were less confident into conversation. Walter was glad of it. The only person he knew was Dr Chadwick, who was deep in debate with Rutherford and the visitors. He could hardly hear what Lady Rutherford said, the noise of laughter and shouting from the other end of the table was so loud. 'Alpha particles – resonances – cross-section – damn spectroscope—'

'Pardon?' said Walter.

But she did not answer him. Between her remark and his faltering response, her attention had been distracted by the antics of her husband.

Walter had heard what Rutherford had said himself; his voice had drowned out his wife's words from the other end of the room. He was in the middle of some debate about electrical currents and a particle accelerator. He broke off mid-sentence.

'More pudding, please!' he barked in his New Zealand accent to the maid.

Then he continued the discussion exactly where he'd left it.

Lady Rutherford's eyes were on the dish on the cabinet at the side of the table. Walter followed her gaze and saw that there was only a small amount of blackberry and apple pie left. The maid was advancing on it.

She screwed up her face in annoyance. 'Ern, you will wait!' she commanded, cutting across the noise, and the room fell silent.

Rutherford looked down at his plate in guilt.

'Professor Bohr, would you care for some more pudding?' she said to the distinguished visitor at Rutherford's side.

Niels Bohr's big, amiable, bloodhound face creased in smiling embarrassment, and he declined.

'Dr Chadwick, more pudding?'

'No, thank you.'

It went all round the room. 'Dr Fowler? Mr Cairns? Mr Nicoll?' Each man declined bashfully. Finally she came to Walter.

'Mr Dunnachie, surely I can tempt you with some pie?'

He blushed. 'No, thank you very much, Lady Rutherford.'

She huffed. 'Ern, pass your plate,' she said. Her husband submitted it, and she divided the small piece of pudding into two halves and sent the remaining portion back to the kitchen.

There were quite a few men struggling to hold back laughter, seeing their mighty leader chastened in this way. As for Walter, he was overwhelmed with awe. Lord Rutherford was quite possibly the greatest scientist in the world. To Walter, the name had always been an abstract noun, a thing with meaning and not substance, a phrase like 'the King' or 'the electron' or 'the Royal Navy'. One knew what it signified, but never expected it to materialise in entirety or actuality. And there he was, in the very same room, occasionally addressing Walter by name, wolfing down his pie and exchanging light-hearted insults with Bohr, who was in Cambridge visiting his old mentor. He was as real as the stain which Walter had made on the tablecloth and was trying to cover up with his plate.

At that moment it dawned on him that all of this was happening. He watched Chadwick's face, bright with conversation. Each one of the scientists' faces was animated with the joy of discussing their work. Suddenly all his travails seemed trivial, and he realised that however bad a physicist he was now, in this place, there was no doubt that he would learn.

'Don't you agree, Mr Dunnachie?' Rutherford suddenly fired at him.

'Why yes,' said Walter. 'That's absolutely right.'

'You see!' cried Rutherford, shaking his fist at Bohr. 'Even the younger generation agrees with me.'

The other men laughed with him. Walter quivered. He had made it at last. He had come to the centre of things and was talking with the man who had given the world its present picture of the atom.

4

Henderson pushed at the door of the church hall and found it open. He walked in nervously, feeling out of place. It was a Methodist chapel, and he was a Church of England man when he made it to church at all.

He looked around. A woman stood on a stepladder at the far end, fiddling with a board on the wall. She turned awkwardly. He walked towards her. She glared down at him through dark-rimmed spectacles.

'Hello,' she said. 'Can I help you?'

Henderson opened his mouth, and coughed, as he generally found himself doing when he walked from the cold into the warm or, indeed, the other way round. He recovered himself and wondered what to say. He'd come here because it had said on Dunnachie's file that he was 'an active member of the Methodist church', and looking at the map, this had seemed the most likely church for him to be an active member of.

'I'm thinking of joining the church,' he said.

The woman raised her eyebrows, let go of the attachment, and came down the stepladder.

'Are you a Methodist?' she asked.

He stared at her. Her voice—

'No,' he said. 'I'm Church of England. But I—' Oh God. This was an altogether foolish move. He was sure that religious conversions could not possibly be part of the job. But still. Her voice— 'I've heard a lot about Methodism, and I wanted to find out more.'

'Well,' she said, 'we're an open church. The minister would be delighted to welcome you to the congregation.'

He was right. It was faint amongst the almost-perfect gentility of her enunciation, but the vowels in the words 'welcome' and 'congregation' had made it unmistakable. She was Australian.

'Oh good,' said Henderson in excitement, and stuck out his hand. 'I'm Mr Henderson.'

'I'm Mrs Dunnachie,' she said, shaking it. 'We've got an evening service tomorrow, if you'd like to come along.' Her face flushed a little. 'My husband will be preaching. He's rather good.'

'Is your husband the vicar?' said Henderson in confusion.

'*Minister*. No, no. He's a local preacher.'

She was a good-looking woman. Better than he'd have expected of Dunnachie, though somewhat imposing behind those glasses.

'Excellent!' gushed Henderson. 'I'll be sure to come along.'

She looked at him shrewdly. 'Mr Henderson,' she said, 'how tall are you?'

His eyes widened. 'Five foot nine,' he responded before he knew what he was saying.

'Then you have a good four inches on me. I wonder if I could prevail upon you to have a go at sorting out this blasted hymn board.'

He stared at her. She looked at the stepladder.

'Sorting out what?'

'The hymn numbers, of course.'

'Oh.'

She held out four wooden panels painted with white numbers. Henderson took them and found himself climbing the stepladder. He examined the fittings on the board.

'Fourteen first,' said Mrs Dunnachie. 'Then one-two-one. Twenty-three. Then seventy-six. You see, you can actually reach it and see how it works. I had to do it all above my head. I don't know what possessed the people who built this place to put it so high up the wall. Really the minister should have got a man to do it. But men are hard to come by at this time of day. What's your profession, Mr Henderson?'

He froze for a moment, and then got busy with the screwdriver. 'I'm a civil servant.'

'Have you taken a day off? Just to investigate our church?'

Oh God. If he was going to spend his days hanging around Watford, trying to make the acquaintance of Dunnachie's associates, he was going to have to think of a better cover than that. He thought quickly. 'I work night shifts,' he said.

'*Night* shifts?'

'Yes.'

She was silent.

Henderson fiddled self-consciously with the panels. The numbers eventually slid into place and he descended to the floor.

'Thank you,' said Mrs Dunnachie. Her nose and eyes wrinkled with mischief. 'Now,' she said, 'would it be terribly rude of me to ask you to do the one on the other side too?'

Yes, thought Henderson, and then was submerged in confusion. He had told her that he wanted to become a member of this church, and such a desire should naturally enough entail a willingness to contribute. The fact that he had no such aspiration was – well, irrelevant, at least for as long as she believed his lies.

'Not at all,' he said, with as much enthusiasm as he could muster, and she gave him more numbers.

Mrs Dunnachie wandered off, and Henderson found himself alone halfway up the wall of an alien domain. He had not thought this through properly.

Mrs Dunnachie returned suddenly to the room. 'Do you have a wife, Mr Henderson?'

He could not make Phoebe a spy's wife. But nor could he deny her existence.

'Yes,' he said.

'Will she be coming to our service?'

'I—' There was no way he could bring her. He could not embroil her in something of which she had no understanding. Phoebe knew well enough not to ask him the details of what he got up to during the day. She'd learnt reticence in the war, when it had been normal enough not to know. Sometimes now she objected, mildly, to the fact that for them it was still going on, and for so little money. But they'd met a year after fighting broke out. George was not sure he could have talked to her about his work now even if he were a postman.

'She is Church of England,' he said. 'I don't think she'd like it.'

'Does she know you're here?'

Perhaps I could get another job, thought Henderson desperately. But the thought was too outlandish to be held for long. 'No,' he said.

Mrs Dunnachie's short silence was kindly but severe. 'Come down, Mr Henderson,' she said. 'Leave that for a while. I have some tea going in the kitchen.'

Henderson could no more have disobeyed her than smash all the windows of the church. He descended.

The kitchen was sparse and clean. In the corner was a huge metal urn which dispensed hot water into the pot which Mrs Dunnachie held beneath it. Henderson sat at the chair indicated to him.

'People say I still behave like a teacher,' she said. 'It annoys them. But it's hard to avoid it, when it is so much easier just to get things done.'

'You were a teacher? Before your marriage?'

'In Australia.'

'Did you meet your husband in—' He stopped himself. He

was not supposed to know where he came from. 'Is your husband Australian too?'

'Yes. We met on the boat to Europe.' The awkward look of pride he'd seen the last time she'd mentioned Dunnachie crossed her face again. 'He was on his way to take up a scholarship at Cambridge University, and I was going to Paris to study for a postgraduate diploma at the Sorbonne.' Her delineation of their qualifications was most precise. 'So it was natural that we should become friends.' She poured the tea. 'I was a Church of England girl then, you know. Right up until we got engaged.' She passed Henderson his cup and looked at him expectantly.

'Really?'

'Your wife may be more tolerant of your—' Her brows creased for a moment, as she searched for the right word. 'Beliefs. Than you expect.'

'Perhaps.' Henderson's stomach tightened.

'Why Methodism, Mr Henderson? It is not such a very far step away from the Anglican church. John Wesley himself always wanted his followers to be welcomed back into the Church of England. I think that if you are looking for something very different from what you have known before you may be disappointed.'

He looked at her clear, earnest eyes and was inspired to a lie which felt like truth. 'I don't know very much about it,' he admitted. 'But what I have heard made me think that it is perhaps more – pure. Than the Church of England is now. Closer – to what Christ intended.' He listened to his own words and was amazed.

She scrutinised him. 'The Hindoos would not agree with you,' she said.

'The Hindoos?'

'My husband is – was – very interested in the Hindoos. And the Mohammedans. We used to have many friends—'

She stopped and wriggled, as if trying to tear her mind away from something. 'Our friends used to say that it was the spirit of the seeker which is the most important thing. Not the route you choose to take.'

'I was not considering Hindooism—'

Mrs Dunnachie grinned. 'No, Mr Henderson, I was not suggesting you should. It is natural enough for any of us to look for the way that suits us best. And I can vouch for the fact that this way has suited me very well. But that has been to do with Walter as much as anything. You must promise me one thing.'

He knew what she was going to ask before she said it. As he steeled himself to give his consent, he saw the broken promise join his small pile of lies.

'Tell your wife.'

Walter was searching for an anglepoise lamp in the lab. His own had died on him and it was impossible to carry on writing in the evening darkness. The place was dim and eerie in the lee of the day, the evidence of earlier chaos scattered around in the pencils on the floor, the books left open, the equations still scrawled on the board. He found a lamp in a corner. It had been commandeered by some undergraduate, who also seemed to have stockpiled the most enormous hoard of stationery. Walter climbed under the table and discovered that its flex was wound three times round the table leg. For a moment he felt a warm rush of memory, for days he had never even known, when the Cavendish students had set upon one another with pieces of rubber tubing in defence of their precious equipment. Except that they had been fighting over spectroscopes, not coloured pencils.

He returned to his office with his spoils and adjusted the lamp so as to cast the light most effectively over his desk.

The anger he'd felt all day after his encounter with Alan

had subsided, and he wished he had it still. Anger was a simple emotion, a straightforward rebellion against fate. He was left now with a deep, corrosive anxiety, as if his soul were eating itself from within. It was a mood he slipped into much of the time these days, whenever he was left alone and there were no outside stimuli to distract him. He found himself worrying about the silliest things in the most desperate way, such as a lost vacuum flask. Or a broken lamp. And then when the apparent source of his discontent was fixed, he was left with the reality. That it was not lamps or pieces of equipment, or even long lost friends, which were the real cause of his worry. It was himself.

The task he'd set himself for today was to finally get to grips with rewriting the Modern Physics paper. As soon as he'd got back to his office he'd known that he'd let the students down badly with his fission lecture. They'd deserved to hear the truth, and though he had not lied, he had not given it to them. In Wales he'd longed for a full hall of students, eager to discover the secrets of physics. He'd ached to resurrect his stagnant career and inspire a new generation of scientists, just as he'd been inspired by Rutherford and Chadwick. But all year he'd been unable to do it. The course he was delivering was the same one he'd taught in 1939. It was time, he realised, to pull his socks up and do something about it. So he'd set pen and paper on his desk, and had written the words 'Modern Physics' at the top of the sheet.

His normal procedure when writing a course of lectures was exactly the same as that which he'd first developed for planning his work as an undergraduate. He usually jotted down a few ideas, joined them together, and gradually the blobs and the lines knitted into a spider's web, expanding across the page and onto the next one. The pace of his thought tended to quicken as he wrote, the ideas coming thicker and faster, until the web was so tight that it threatened to solidify and defeat its own purpose. At that point, the planning had to stop, and it was time to set the sheets of paper aside and start to arrange the thoughts into a recognisable structure.

Now the light was gone, and it was evening. There was not a single blob or line. The page was blank.

Throughout his career, he'd listened to many a pupil bemoan the inability to put pen to paper. He'd given the complaint short shrift, having never suffered such an affliction himself. 'It's simple,' he'd told them. 'Just get on with it.' And much of the time they'd gone away and done exactly that. But staring at the white rectangle on the table, he understood the hostility of the untrodden path and the almost physical impossibility of treading it. Who was there to tell *him* to get on with it now, as he always told his own students? His professor at UCL, Poltine, had once been a brilliant scientist, but was now a self-obsessed neurotic with more concern for his endless rivalries with his peers than the quality of the teaching in his department. Over the years, Walter had circumnavigated his whims more adroitly than most, but the man was far from being a mentor.

He stared up through the window at the sky. Rutherford, he thought, painfully. Rutherford, come to me now.

The old Crocodile had died in 1937, almost a decade ago now. He'd not lived to see any of the science which Walter was trying to transcribe. He hadn't seen the world slide into war, hadn't watched his old friends battling against one another on opposite sides, hadn't witnessed the perversions of science and the human spirit which had taken place during the last nine years. His spirit was long gone, alien to all that surrounded Walter now.

But at least it was still pure.

For a moment Walter sensed a blast of the physical presence of the man, felt the force of his step beneath his feet, the clouds of smoke in his nostrils, the boom of the mighty laugh in his eardrums.

Then it was gone, and Walter was left with the stale, mundane air of his room, and the memories, and the absolute absence of the reality they'd once inhabited.

Surely, he thought, even memories have something to teach me. They cannot be useless, because then they would not have been worth living. And they were worth living.

And then he heard Rutherford's voice. It was a snippet of memory, a fragment of conversation, disembodied from time or location. The words might never have been said at all. But they were said in Rutherford's voice, spoken with Rutherford's absolute confidence, and Walter knew that they were true.

Teacher, teach thyself.

The small church was filling fast. Henderson was sitting at the back with Mrs Dunnachie's children. She was, it transpired, expected to help the minister with welcoming people to the chapel. Her husband had not yet arrived.

'Are you a scientist?' demanded the Dunnachie boy of Henderson.

'No, I'm not.'

'Daddy's a scientist.'

'I know.'

'Where's Daddy?' demanded the girl.

'I don't know. He'll be here soon.'

This new role as childminder was utterly unexpected. His only prior experience of children was of Leonard's little girl, long vanished with her mother back to Yorkshire. It occurred to him that Aitken would probably expect him to interrogate Dunnachie's offspring. But he had no idea what to ask.

Mrs Dunnachie was greeting the visitors austerely, except when she knew them particularly well, in which case there was generally some explosion of giggles. From his seat at the back, Henderson could hear her words.

'Caught up at work,' she'd said to begin with when they asked after her husband. 'He'll be along soon. He's taking the sermon, you know.'

Now the situation was becoming urgent. There was no longer any mention of the sermon.

The congregation began to settle itself. Mrs Dunnachie rushed over to Henderson. Her face was scarlet. 'Mr Henderson,' she said, 'you don't mind taking care of the children like this, do you?'

'It's absolutely fine,' said Henderson, but she had dashed off again already and was deep in fervent conversation with the minister.

'Daddy's been naughty,' the girl told Henderson confidentially.

It occurred to Henderson that it might be polite to find out what they were called. 'What's your name?' he asked the self-contained little blonde scrap.

'I'm *Bridget*,' said the girl scornfully, as if he should definitely have known. 'Don't you know Patrick's name either?'

'I do now,' said Henderson, and then felt pleased with himself for having made a joke which might be understood by a child. 'Do you want to know my name?'

'We know it already,' said Patrick without even bothering to turn to look at him.

Henderson felt suitably snubbed, and then cross. He might have known that the progeny of a physicist and a graduate of the Sorbonne would be too clever by half. His neck began to itch under his collar. And then he looked up. Mrs Dunnachie was storming back down the aisle. Her children looked up at her in dread, their insouciance gone.

'Move *up*,' said Mrs Dunnachie sharply to Bridget. Bridget

shuffled hastily, Patrick giving way quickly for her. She stared straight ahead. The children fiddled with their collection money.

Henderson shot a glance at her rigid back and wondered what had gone wrong. Why wasn't Dunnachie here? What was he up to? He felt a stab of doubt. This had seemed a perfect opportunity to meet Dunnachie in social circumstances, and to find out what made him tick, as Aitken might have said. But perhaps it would have been better to stick with his old methods of trailing, trailing, trailing. Then he would have known what Dunnachie's wife still did not know now.

A man in a lounge suit stepped up to the pulpit.

'It's Mr Gregory,' Patrick whispered to Bridget.

'*Why* is it Mr Gregory? Where's *Daddy*?'

'Shhh,' commanded Patrick, and dug his sister in the ribs. Their mother ignored them.

And Henderson found himself following her occasional, hopeless glances towards the back door of the church.

The point, Walter realised, was that he could not teach something which he did not understand himself.

The equations were not the problem. Equations, experiments, scientific logic – all of those came very easily to him. The instinctive command of the language of science that he'd discovered as a schoolboy had never deserted him. Few colleagues could better him when it came to science, whether theoretical or experimental.

And once he'd understood the rest of it, too. How human endeavour tended towards trial and error, trial and error, until out of all the errors a new truth broke forth, sundering all previous truths and leading to more trial and error, trial and error, ever onwards. It was like a jigsaw puzzle, except that with each newly inserted piece the whole twisted a little, jolting a few of the other pieces out of place. It would never be finished. It would just become bigger, and broader, and deeper, and more magnificent, and would inspire more men to keep toiling away with more misfitting pieces of jigsaw, until they too found one that fitted and made more work for all the rest.

All of that is still true, thought Walter. So what is it that I don't understand?

It was what went on outside the world of the jigsaw. He had always made sure to emphasise to his brightest students that they should not get science confused with nature. The two were not the same. Nature was outside, huge and all-consuming, whereas science was simply the faulty though ever-improving apparatus which mankind had built with which to understand it.

Yet in a way, they had always been linked. Man's knowledge of the laws of physics had given him greater and greater power to manipulate nature. When Walter was a young man, it had been thought that the equations and their impact on the world were better dealt with entirely separately. The best science was conducted with no other aim than to understand nature better. Technology could only be pursued with the very different aim of serving the interests of whoever was paying for it. But now an equation had been found which was capable of destroying the whole world. And suddenly the simple chain of cause and effect, of scientists toiling in the pursuit of knowledge alone, was exploded, and none of it made sense to Walter any more.

I must make sense of it, he thought. If I can't, then nothing is of any consequence.

He looked at the heading he'd written at the top of his page.

Modern Physics.

Walter wrote a sentence, and then crossed it out.

What was it that he was trying to describe? Where did its limits lie?

He summoned Rutherford's spirit once more. An image appeared in his head of the man himself. He appeared not as the scientific potentate Walter had known, but as a student as young and foreign as Walter had been on the day when he'd first met him. Once, Rutherford had blundered into the Cavendish with all his brilliance trapped inside him. He must have felt as stupid and scared as Walter had. But he would also have known that he was entering the scene of a story which had been proceeding for thousands of years. On that day, a new chapter had begun.

Suddenly Walter no longer cared about the Modern Physics lecture course he was supposed to be writing. It was the story that mattered, a story which had driven him almost all his life and which had only recently begun to unravel around him. His desire now was to go back to the time when nothing had been known about the atom, to start again with the basics, and piece together for himself how it had all happened, and where it had gone wrong.

And now the pen was speeding along, as fast as it ever had.

1. THE ELECTRON

In the year 1897 the electron was discovered, and the centuries-old debate as to the fundamental structure of all matter was resolved.

The electron itself, if not its nature, was known of since the mid-nineteenth century. In those days it was called a cathode ray, and it was used to perform popular tricks. The scientific lecturers of the day took a glass tube, pumped out most of the gas, and ran an electrical current from one end to the other, making the interior glow in marvellous patterns and the spectators gasp in admiration.

When subjected to serious experimentation, the cathode ray remained mysterious. Some physicists thought it was similar to a light wave and others speculated that it was some sort of material particle. The evidence suggested both hypotheses and neither. The rays could be pushed about by the field of a magnet like a particle, yet they moved in a way different to any yet discovered, and passed through thin metal foil like a ray. They possessed a negative electrical charge, yet the ratio of their charge to their mass was over one thousand times greater than that of the smallest charged molecule. If they were particles, they were infinitesimally small and very strangely behaved.

It was Joseph John Thomson who saw the truth. He expelled enough gas from the cathode tube to allow the rays to move freely, and proved by their movements that they were indeed particles. He reconfirmed the experiments which had shown the ratio of their mass to their charge, and proved that they were indeed far smaller than any previously known particle. And then he speculated. He proposed that although an electron is almost nothing, it is everything. It is not light, and it is not just an independent form of matter. It is a constituent of all matter. He called it a corpuscle. At the annual Cavendish dinner that year, the staff and students sang a song in Thomson's honour. They sang, 'The corpuscle won the day, And in freedom went away, And became a cathode ray.'

At that moment, the science of Atomic Physics was born.

Beginnings, thought Walter, are so much lovelier than endings. He remembered his own beginnings as an experimental physicist, the water-dappled light dripping in through the big windows onto his and Alan's sleeves, which must be wrong, because his memory of that first year in Cambridge was that he had found it dark. And now he worked it out, he knew that particular exploit had taken place in as deep a winter as it was now. But still there it was, in his picture book of the past, that light, making the glass sparkle and their skin glow.

Nunn May was not supposed to have been helping Walter with his experiments. He was meant to have been working for his finals. But there had been a good excuse. Just before the Christmas holidays, Walter had received news from Chadwick that he had inherited great riches. A man named Hugh Webster had left to take up a post at Bristol University, and all of his equipment was waiting up at the Observatory to be claimed. Nunn May, on hearing this from Walter, had immediately volunteered to help him bring it all down to the Cavendish. It had been back-breaking work, and once it was done, Walter had felt that it would have been churlish to keep him out just when it would all bear fruit. He'd had a frustrating time of late, having been pulled off his own work to help Chadwick with a project which had subsequently been abandoned. He'd needed all the help he could get.

The pride of Webster's collection was the Wilson Cloud Chamber. It was a fairly ancient contraption, passed down from generation to generation of research students, while its inventor still lived and breathed in the Cavendish.

Walter and Nunn May had cleaned and polished it until it shone. 'Have you ever heard the story of how CTR invented the cloud chamber?' Walter had said.

C T R were Professor Wilson's initials, and also constituted his name – behind his back for the students and junior staff, and to his face for his contemporaries. Nunn May's eyes had widened and he'd shaken his head.

'Well,' Walter had said, and prepared to embark upon the story. The tale had been passed on to him only a couple of months before and he had been as goggle-eyed as Nunn May was then. It had been wonderful to find himself cast in the role of Old Man of the Cavendish so quickly. 'When CTR was a young man he was a keen climber.'

The Jacksonian Professor was a deeply shy man, and such a notoriously terrible lecturer that neither Walter nor Nunn May had ever attended any of his lectures. But he was a familiar enough figure around the lab, famed for his Cloud Chamber.

'Whenever he went home to Scotland, he used to go up into the highlands on his own. And—' Walter had hesitated before allowing his romantic appreciation of the scene to take wing, but at the sight of Nunn May's eyes, decided to go on. '—up there on his own, there was nothing between him and the weather systems.'

'He's a meteorologist mainly, isn't he?' Nunn May had said excitedly. 'That's how he discovered it. That's what I heard, anyway.'

Walter felt that his gun had been jumped. 'Amongst other things,' he'd said sniffily, though that was exactly what CTR was. 'Anyway, he used to stand up there and watch the clouds come in from the sea. When they hit the coast of Scotland they rose to get over the mountains, just as he'd been taught. He saw it all happening. The air rising, expanding, cooling, and he saw that all it took to form a great big cloud was a speck of dust. Like—' He'd stopped in embarrassment, but this *was* how he'd imagined it. He had not been to Scotland yet, but he'd wanted to go. It was the land of his fathers. 'Like a grain of smoke from a crofter's fire, or the tiniest piece of feather or skin. And it was then that he realised that some of the things which formed clouds were invisible. A cloud was actually visible evidence of something too small to be seen.' He was getting excited. 'Something too small to be seen, like—'

'A subatomic particle!' Nunn May had burst out.

'They weren't called that then. It was before the proton. Even Rutherford still thought that everything might be made of electrons. But Becquerel hadn't long discovered radiation, and Rutherford was finding new types of it all over the place, and when Rutherford found CTR working away—'

'He'd come back from Scotland?'

'He was back. Rutherford found CTR grinding a piston into a cylinder and wanted to know what he was up to, and when CTR told him that he was trying to get supersaturated air into a bottle—'

'—so that he could trace charged particles—'

'—obviously he was very pleased.'

'So they built the cloud chamber! I didn't know Rutherford was involved with that too.'

Walter had smiled. Even then he was discovering new things which Rutherford had influenced. There seemed hardly a scribble of physics in the past forty years which did not bear his signature. 'Sort of. Except that Rutherford was just on his way back to New Zealand to visit his family. And—' He'd wondered whether Nunn May understood the enormity of such a journey, and had decided to give him the benefit of the doubt. 'And when he came back, there was no cloud chamber.'

Nunn May's silence had been fraught with anticipation.

'Instead, there was CTR, still grinding exactly the same piston into the same cylinder. He'd probably still be going now if it hadn't worked in the end.'

By the time of that sunny morning in the Cavendish, every fortunate physicist in the world had one. Walter's possession of the Observatory cloud chamber had felt like his scientific coming of age. He'd adjusted its position on the table. If, like CTR, he persevered, and he and his chamber worked well together, the cylinder would soon be filled with clear vapour, just on the verge of mist, and each of his alpha particles would carve a foggy track through its heart.

In his office at UCL, Walter now stared at the old contraption. It had pride of place still. It had broken down beyond repair shortly before he left Cambridge, and in a fit of sentimentality, he'd parted with a few pounds to purchase it from the laboratory as a memento of his incredible years there. It was very quiet up here. He'd done so much work alone throughout his scientific career that it ought to be no hardship. But he longed for the particular noises and stillnesses of the Cavendish. Rutherford's voice booming through the laboratory, Chadwick pottering away ominously in his office, Alan adjusting the polonium source at the table, taking issue with him over Peace—

The pen slipped from his hand and pierced the floor with its nib. He stared at its small upright shape, standing to attention, and realised what he had just remembered. For a moment he sat there, frozen.

His body came back to life. 'DAMN!' he shouted at the top of his voice, and then there was nothing to do but run.

The Methodists seemed to be a sociable bunch. Most of them had stayed behind after the service. Mrs Dunnachie's children were occupied in games with their friends in a special corner of the hall, and their mother was free to be the life and soul of the party. Henderson tagged around after her.

'This is Mr Henderson,' she said repeatedly, to each of the people they met in turn. 'He's interested in joining the Methodist church.'

He noticed that no one sprang forward to relieve her of him, not even the minister. He looked at her, detecting a drawn look of distress beneath the brightness, and thought that she might actually be glad to have him there. Gradually the crowds thinned out.

'Mr Henderson,' she said at a moment when there was no one else standing with them, 'you don't have to stay to the absolute end. There is no rule that says that new members of the congregation must wait here until a particular hour.'

He realised that when the population of the room had reached a particular density he would indeed have to go. But having committed so much of his evening, he wanted to have a glimpse of the elusive Dunnachie to show for it. 'I'm fine,' he said. 'I'm enjoying myself. I'm learning.'

'Hmph,' said Mrs Dunnachie. 'I can't imagine what you're learning now, amongst all this *small talk*.'

Henderson was taken aback to hear her spit the words with such vitriol, having just proved herself to be a mistress of it.

'Anyway,' she said, 'how does this fit in with your night shift?'

He'd had time to prepare for that one. 'It's an early morning shift. Starts at midnight. I sleep in the early part of the day.'

'All in the service of the government. Ah well, I suppose it knows what it's doing.'

This, he supposed, was the sort of comment he was supposed to be looking out for. He had no idea how to follow it up. 'I was sorry not to hear your husband speak,' he said.

Her eyes flashed. 'Not half as sorry as I am,' she countered brutally, and then collected herself. 'I'm sorry, Mr Henderson,' she said, with only the smallest concession to good grace. 'This is not like him. He has never – *never* – missed a service before. Not if he was preaching. It's so unfair on whoever has to stand in.'

Henderson's natural reticence made him want to make his excuses and run from the church. He forced himself to stay. 'You must be very worried.'

'Indeed. I'd ring the hospitals, but – well, one doesn't want to start along that track, does one? Anyway, of course it isn't that. Probably got caught up in some stupid committee. He has so many committees these days. They should promote him and be done with it.'

For a moment he could hear Phoebe's voice. But one sight of that intimidating chin banished it.

'What does your husband preach about?' he asked.

She frowned. 'He hasn't given a sermon since – since the end of the war. This was going to be the first. But he always used to talk about Peace. He was a conscientious objector during the war.' She flashed a glance at him.

I know, Henderson almost said, and suppressed it. 'Oh,' he said, as it was all he could think of to say, and suddenly realised how all those people had felt when he'd told them he was asthmatic.

'I suppose I ought to ask what you did during the war,' she said. 'It's generally expected.'

'I was unfit,' said Henderson, and had never felt so easy saying it before. 'Asthma.'

'Aha. Neither one thing nor the other. A safe bet.'

'It's not usually a safe bet.'

'It is here.'

They looked at one another.

'Well, Mr Henderson,' she said suddenly, 'it's all very well chatting with you here, but there are cups to be washed up. And a husband to wait for.' She let her façade drop again. 'You see, he will come here. He'll be hoping the service is still going.'

'But it finished more than half an hour ago.'

'Good point! Amazing the resources of optimism in the male animal, isn't it? And – goodness! As if on cue, the husband arrives.'

There was a great clattering at the door. Dunnachie was dragging himself through, hat and briefcase and umbrella, all at once. His wife stood ramrod straight, waiting benignly. She looked briefly at Henderson.

'You may go,' she said.

5

Tonight Walter had faked sleep. Grace was collapsed beside him, worn out by her tears. 'I'll look like a frog in the morning,' she had complained as he held her close, the sobs subsiding, so he'd hopped out of bed and got a wet flannel to dab her eyes. She'd let him kiss her better. As he'd felt her slip towards sleep, the fire had reasserted itself, and she'd murmured, 'How can I help you when you won't say what it is?'

'Grace, we both know what it is.'

'No, you're wrong. I don't know. Things have been far worse than this, before. And you were always so strong. But you didn't turn up tonight. You've never done that. Was it Peace, Walter? Do you really hate it so much, now?'

'I don't hate it,' he'd said. But his words were a screen.

'What is it, then? Is it Alan coming back?'

Exhausted, he'd not known how to respond.

'It can't just be him,' she'd said, 'because you were unhappy before he turned up again. But he's made it worse. Hasn't he?'

The explanation was too trite to approximate to truth. 'I suppose so,' he'd said, capitulating.

'Well, I'll give him a piece of my mind if I see him.'

Now that she was asleep, he thought about what she'd said about things having been worse, and him having been strong. He had not been. It had always been her. Grace was the strongest person in the world. Sometimes he thought he'd done a terrible thing by taking all that strength and burying it here, when she could have had the world at her feet.

'But I don't want the world,' she'd said when she was young and they were talking about their marriage. 'I want *you*. That'll be the whole world. You'll see.'

And he'd known it was true, that he really was what she wanted. It was still true now. He was her quest, as surely as the atom had been Rutherford's. She would never give up on him. But back then, even when he'd been most afraid of not being worthy of her, he'd at least been able to trust that somehow he'd manage it. Now he knew that he could not.

When Walter had first met Grace on that ship to England, he had not been able to understand what she saw in him. He'd seen a willowy thing with a bright, pretty face and an air of animation which could keep a whole table entertained. While he'd been bothering the crew to show him the ship's engine, she'd been dancing with half the men on board. But there it was. She'd asked him what book he was reading, and from then on they'd been inseparable.

'Men,' she confided to him later, 'are very splendid creatures, but most of them can get rather dull after a while.'

There were not many of them about, dull or otherwise. The boat was crammed with young women. It was a strange, enclosed place, a sealed bottle floating on an infinite ocean, and the community attempted to ape normality by doing things that one might assume it was not possible to do. For Walter, raised on an Australian diet of constant physical activity, normality meant sport. So he played deck tennis, and deck quoits, and even deck cricket, against a procession of female opponents, young and old, a series of Miss Watsons and Miss Rileys and Mrs Godfreys. Occasionally another form of exercise was proposed, in the form of a promenade around the ship's perimeter. But only Grace Padgett could keep up with him.

'Why are there so many women?' he asked Grace in bewilderment, over the course of one of their hectic per-ambulations.

'They've all been dispatched to Europe by their fathers or fiancés,' Grace pronounced archly. 'Their families are relying upon them to acquire a cultural veneer and thereby secure the social advancement of the whole clan.'

'Really?' Walter said, shocked, thinking it a rather vicious sentiment, but unable to deny its possible truth. 'But what about you? Is that what your family has done?'

'Oh, I don't have that sort of family. Our glories all lie in the past.'

Her father, she confessed with alarming frankness, was a drinker, and she herself a first-generation immigrant, having been propelled to Australia whilst still a toddler as a result of his great capacity for losing things. 'His job. His house. My mother's parents' house. My mother's connections. His country. He is still in some ways a wonderful man. But my mother is no longer a wonderful woman. I dragged myself up. Ever since I was old enough to understand her constant complaints, I've been trying to regain what she lost.'

'Oh,' said Walter helplessly. It was such a melodramatic story that he felt sure that she would cry, at which point he would have no idea what to do at all. But she looked perfectly cheerful.

'If you must know,' she said, 'I earned the money for this excursion myself. I've been listening to stories about Europe all my life and I'm bored of them. I'm going for my own benefit. I've been teaching French for three years and yet I've never had a conversation with a native speaker. I want to know what it is like to really *live* in a different language. I don't want to sit in the kitchen at home listening to what my mother says about places I've never seen. I want to know about the world for myself. Do you understand?'

He did. 'So do I,' he said, very relieved to have found something in common. 'That's why I'm going to Cambridge. I want to know about the world too.'

They discovered it together. As the ship crossed the South China sea, the heat increased. One morning, they met on deck just after breakfast, and sighted their first foreign soil. The mountains of Ceylon rose in steep rugged walls from the sea, fringed by white sand. Colombo harbour raced towards them until they could make out the boats clustered in the port in front of a mesh of trees and white buildings. The ship pulled past the breakwater, and the hundreds of masts in the harbour jerked out of stillness and started to surge forwards. Suddenly, their ship was surrounded by a swarm of small boats. Their crews scrambled up the sides of the ship, and before they knew it, the deck was infested with men wanting to take up Walter's suit or sort out his laundry. When they boarded the ship at the end of the day, they watched the natives loading Adelaide wheat onto the lighters moored to the ship. Some of them lit fires on the lighters and cooked rice and coconut, chattering loudly and eating in turn, with their fingers, from a single plate.

The ship moored at Bombay, a grand imperial port tumbling into the crowded streets of Kalbadevi, decorated with strings of lamps in preparation for Diwali. At the island of Perim the vast canvas of water was suddenly bounded by land, for the ship had entered the seas sheltered by the mass of Eurasia, and the days of endless blue were replaced by the red and yellow of rock and sand. Walter and Grace stood and watched the barren mountains of Arabia close on their starboard side and the distant coast of Africa to port, until the land was obscured by dust storms which seemed to blow out of the sea itself. At sundown a large searchlight was attached to the nose of the boat to light its way through the hair-breadth straits of the Suez Canal.

They'd stayed up on deck that night, camping on their chairs under coats and blankets, with the ship's nurse as chaperone, and talked about all manner of things. While Sister Chapman snored, Walter and Grace talked of camels and sand dunes, bazaars and oases, and Grace showed off the few words of Arabic she had learnt. She explained to him how the languages of the world were related to one another, and Walter had told her that different religions had much in common too. He showed her a book he'd managed to borrow from one of the Indians who'd boarded the ship at Bombay. It was quite new, and this was the first edition to be translated into English, but Grace had already heard of it, for it was making quite a stir around the world. It was called *The Story of My Experiments with Truth*, and it was by Mohandas K. Gandhi.

He tried to explain what the book was like. It was the story of a young boy growing up in a remote Indian village, part of a culture of which Walter knew nothing. And yet it could have been any childhood, any boy. Walter recognised the schoolfriends, the teachers, the scrapes, and was at the same time entranced by the differences. Though it had seemed overpowering at the time, by comparison they'd caught only the smallest whiff of that scent of otherness in Bombay. Between the covers of the early part of that book, it was the whole world. And then Gandhi had left his village and travelled across the sea to study in England, by the same route they were taking now, and had seen it all with eyes untainted by the West.

'But it isn't just that,' Walter told Grace. 'It's the absolute *candour* with which he tells it. That's what the title is about. He's trying to tell the truth. When he tells us about the things he stole when he was a child—'

'Stole?' interrupted Grace. 'The Mahatma can't possibly have stolen. Even as a child.'

'Well, quite. But he did. And he manages to explain exactly how naughty it was, and why he'd done it, and it's all just as it really was, not as he would like people to see him.'

'But how do you know that it's exactly as it was?' objected Grace.

'Well, he says it isn't. But I think it is.' And he grinned.

From there they got onto Gandhi's principle of non-violence, and how it might be emulated. Neither of them really knew, particularly not Grace, who hadn't read the book, but she had opinions enough to be getting on with.

'The thing that puzzles me most is that he kept getting involved in wars,' said Walter. 'Whenever the Indians were violent in the cause of Home Rule he virtually disowned them, and yet he had already assisted the British against the Boers, and actually went around recruiting Indian soldiers for the Great War. I just don't understand it.'

'Just because you agree with some of the things he says doesn't mean you have to go along with all of it,' Grace pointed out.

He looked at her in surprise. 'No,' he said. 'I suppose I have to do some thinking for myself.'

'It sounds to me as though you already have.'

Did it? He was rather suspicious of her good opinion of him, feeling sure that she would find him out in the end and despise him. 'I don't know. I think my ideas are rather fuzzy.'

'Are you a pacifist?'

He twitched. It was not a question he'd ever been asked, and he had certainly never posed it to himself. Would she hate him if he was or, alternatively, scorn him if he wasn't? He knew that he must take the risk either way and, as Gandhi had urged, tell the truth. The problem was that he wasn't entirely sure what the truth was.

'Yes,' he said quickly.

'Why?' demanded Grace.

She never was one to give him an easy ride.

Peace begins with war. Without it no such concept could exist. For Walter it had begun in school-yard scuffles, games of British Bulldogs pursued across scorched earth in the blazing heat of the first winter of the Great War. The toilet block, formerly known as 'the Traps', was newly rechristened 'Wipers'; the tree at the end of the yard 'Arras'; and the ditch in front of the headmistress's house 'Nerve Chapel'.

Walter enjoyed these contests immensely, thriving as always on anything that involved lots of running around and getting excited. On one occasion he managed to knock a particularly obstreperous boy to the ground. He sat on James Gough's stomach, pinning his arms to the floor, shouting with triumph at his conquest of an older and larger opponent. 'Submit!' he shouted. 'Submit!'

Gough's legs flailed behind him, his knees occasionally making contact with Walter's back. 'I won't submit to you. Your dad's a coward and a shirker.'

'He is NOT.'

'He is so. My dad says so.'

Gough Senior was the butcher at New Lambton. The Dunnachies and the Goughs had always been on perfectly good terms, but it suddenly occurred to Walter that his mother had recently taken to travelling into Newcastle to buy meat. Was this due to Mr Gough's dastardly accusations of Dad's cowardice?

The game stopped. All around them, the boys were jostling in excitement. 'Scrap on!' somebody yelled, and from every corner of the yard, children were pushing through to get a better view.

Gough saw he had an audience and his pink face screwed

up in wickedness. 'Dunnachie's dad's a coward!' he crowed. 'Dunnachie's dad's a coward!'

Everyone was listening to him. Walter's first instinct was to cry. He crumpled in confusion and his hands loosened their grip on Gough's arms. Gough wriggled his shoulders and his head rose towards Walter's, his mouth opening to shout once more.

The response was perfectly obvious. Walter's right hand let go of Gough. It rose behind him, as if preparing to throw a cricket ball, tightened at its furthest limit, and then smashed that imaginary ball right through Gough's gaping mouth towards the hard earth below.

There was a gasp from the crowd and then silence. Walter began to panic. His victim lay still. He started to scramble to his feet. Gough's eyes rolled and closed, and his head tipped to one side. On the ground laid bare there was a sharp boulder, and a dark red pool of blood spread outwards from Gough's hair, seeping slowly into the sand.

'He's dead!' shrieked a small girl. 'Dunnachie's killed him!'

To the considerable disappointment of the audience, Gough turned out to be alive. Still, there was the drama of a visit from the doctor, and much scurrying of pupils past the door of the headmistress's office, whence muffled voices could be heard if you stayed there long enough without being caught.

The headmistress had left Walter in class, clearly having decided that this would be a greater punishment than isolation. His schoolmates kept him informed of progress during the course of the delicate operation: 'His head's been cracked open', 'A bit of his brain's fallen out', 'They've sent for the minister', 'I heard them calling the police', 'They've sent for his father', and, worst of all, 'They've sent for *your* father.'

The moment he was dreading arrived. The headmistress opened the door of the classroom and the teacher stopped talking. Miss Cartwright walked to the front and stood beneath the tablet displaying the Ten Commandments.

'Walter Dunnachie, please come with me to my office.'

The condemned boy followed her out.

Mr Dunnachie had come from the port. Walter knew that this meant that even Dad's boss would know about it by now. The headmistress left them alone and for a while his dad sat staring out of the big window that overlooked the yard and said nothing.

'Walter,' he said in the end, 'why did you hit that boy?'

Walter made a noise into his collar.

'What did you say, Walter? I can't hear you.'

'I don't know,' mumbled Walter.

His dad frowned quizzically and undid his left cufflink. He laid it out on the headmistress's desk and ran his finger up and down it. It was horrible to see Dad in Miss Cartwright's domain. After a full examination of the cufflink, Dad put it back into his shirt. He turned to look back at Walter.

'It was because he called you a coward,' Walter blurted. 'He said his dad said so.'

And the look on his father's face at that moment gave Walter a greater pain than any he had previously experienced. He did not at all understand what it meant, only that nothing was as Walter expected, and nothing was right.

'Walter,' said his dad, 'you do know that it's wrong to hit people, don't you?'

'I couldn't help it! He called you a coward!'

'You do know that sometimes if you hit someone they can be hurt very badly, don't you?' His father's voice was shaking. 'You do know that sometimes they die?'

Walter froze. 'Is Gough dead?'

'James has been concussed.' His voice had steadied and was as quiet and soft as ever. 'He will be well again in a few days if all goes well. But that's because he was lucky. If his head had hit that stone a bit differently then it might have hurt his brain. Your brain is needed to keep every part of you alive and if your brain gets hurt then sometimes the rest of you can't work any more. His lungs might have stopped breathing and his heart might have stopped beating and then his brain would have stopped thinking and there would have been nothing of him left in his body and his body would have had to have been put in the ground at the churchyard.' Dad paused. His eyes creased in concern, and then he went on. 'His body would have rotted away to nothing, and there would be no James any more. He wouldn't have been able to play with his friends, or go home from school to his mum and dad, and his mum and dad would have been sad for ever, because there would always have been a gap where James was supposed to be.'

'I didn't mean it!' shrieked Walter.

'Of course you didn't mean it, Walter. But you shouldn't have done it. It's not a brave thing to hit someone, even if they do things you don't like. It's much braver to let it pass, whatever they do, and forgive them, and offer them peace.' His eyes examined Walter's face intently. 'Just because of the war—'

Walter did not in the least understand what the war had to do with it. The war was all newspapers, and sometimes widows and wounded soldiers and funerals, and all the mothers knitting red socks to stop the troops from getting Trench Foot. Once Walter had been into the centre of Newcastle with his friends to watch the recruits parading on the beach, and just a week ago, so he had heard, there had been a brawl in the streets about something called conscription, which was connected in some way with the war. It was a distant source of excitement and it was nothing whatsoever to do with Gough. 'The war?' he said in bewilderment.

'The soldiers who are going to the war are very brave,

because they may be killed themselves. But war itself isn't a brave or wonderful thing, Walter. Whatever people tell you, you must never think that it is a good thing to hurt people.'

'I don't!' pleaded Walter.

'You mustn't listen to them, Walter,' said his dad, his voice shaking again. 'You must never think that it is a brave thing to kill.'

Grace was leaning on the guard rail and staring out across the inky sea. The moon smiled beneficently upon the waves, a small chunk of its left cheek shaved off. A cloud drifted slowly across the sky just above the horizon, revealing the Southern Cross in the space it had just vacated. By morning, Walter and Grace would have left those stars behind.

'Your father is a pacifist,' she said.

Walter was shivering, even though he was not in the least cold. It seemed very strange to be saying these things to a woman he barely knew. But his old self had been left beyond many horizons now, and she seemed as knowable as he was to himself now. 'I'm sorry,' he said. 'I hope you don't mind me telling you all of this.'

'Keep telling! I want to hear the end of the story.'

'There isn't one, really. James Gough recovered. He went to a different school when we left. But Grace – I don't think it's quite right to say that Dad is a pacifist. You see—'

'Of course he is. The things he said to you.'

'No – you see, there were big factions in Newcastle. About whether there should be conscription or not. Dad believed there shouldn't be, and said so. He said that the decision to fight ought to be left up to each man's conscience. That's why Mr Gough wouldn't serve Mum for a bit, because he was on the other side. But of course, most people wouldn't stand for being told what to do by the government, never mind whether it was right to kill or not, and so there never was conscription. And I think that if there had been, Dad would have gone away to fight. He said that it was his duty to abide by the laws of his country. I never quite understood it. It was like Gandhi, you know— I couldn't quite link it all together. Because what he said to me about Gough was so – so important, you know—'

'I think he was quite cruel to you,' said Grace. 'No one talks to six-year-olds about death like that.'

He was on his feet. 'Dad wasn't cruel!'

Grace took a step back in alarm. Then she recovered herself, and chuckled. 'Now, Walter, for a moment there I thought I was about to go the same way as James Gough.'

Walter stumbled away from her. 'Oh, Grace, I'm sorry—'

She was laughing still. 'Don't worry, I'm teasing you. I just think it's rather funny—'

'What's funny?'

'Well, for a pacifist you do display some rather violent tendencies.'

He stared at her. 'Don't you see?' he said suddenly, seeing it himself for the first time. 'That's why. That's why I'm a pacifist. Because I know what I'm capable of doing. And what I'm capable of is wrong. It *is* braver not to fight.'

Then he heard himself, and was sure he had made it all up.

'Well,' said Grace, 'if that's so I think it's the best reason for pacifism I've ever heard.'

He felt like a fraud. 'Really?'

'Really.'

They sank back into their chairs, and something which really did feel like peace entered Walter. He pulled his blankets around him and gazed at the moonlight shining in the curls of Grace's hair until he drifted off to sleep. At four in the morning they were awakened by a bright light in their eyes as they anchored at Port Said, in Egypt. The town had opened its shops in honour of the arrival of the mail boat. They hurried down to their cabins to change their clothes, so as not to look as if they had slept on deck, and scampered ashore to take advantage of the novelty of purchasing Turkish Delight, Egyptian table-runners and beads, with English money, at six o'clock in the morning.

Walter lay in the bed in Watford and listened to Grace's breaths. It was worth remembering that, for all the trouble it had caused them both, Peace had been there from the start, and she'd been in on it at the start. Perhaps if it had not been for Peace he would have got rather dull after a while, like all the rest.

He'd met her expecting to lose her. Those six weeks had been the longest and shortest he had spent on earth, speeding through space and time, frozen in a miniature universe beneath a sun and a moon that took different paths to those anyone outside the ship could see. The bright impatience in her eyes had seemed as impossible and transient as the smudges of sand in the darkening sky, and as sure to vanish into the haze of the past. Each moment he'd spent with her after that night out on the deck had burned deeper into him the excitement of the present. They'd written their diaries together, comparing notes and adding the details that were missing from their own, desperate to take some record of each other into the unassailable future.

At the end of the journey he'd lost his landing card when everyone else was exchanging addresses. He'd caught sight of her again, as her English relatives carried her away, and she'd laughed and waved, and when the world turned once more it took her across another sea and left him alone in London. The city he'd expected to shine with the glow of his dreams was dank with absence. And after that, though he fell in love with Cambridge, he felt as if there was something missing.

Time was bearing him away from her, and away from a part of the man he wanted to be. When he'd first dared to write to her, care of the Sorbonne, weeks after his last sighting of her, he'd been unable to believe that the world in which he lived now contained her too. 'You probably will not remember me,' he even wrote in one version, and then realised what an insult that might be. The end result was a tangle of humility and presumption. He had no news to report of the people they'd so briefly known together, and so there was too much about the laboratory, of which she knew nothing, and too little about her, because he had no idea what she was up to. Walter resolved not to send it, then stuffed it into the letterbox late one night, trying to blind himself to the idea of her actually reading it. Even after she'd replied, not long before the end of his first term, the arch script which bore her intoxicating signature would not connect itself with the constantly moving creature who had laughed at him and touched his arm and ordered him to call her Grace. He did not have the courage to write to her again.

It had always been impossible. That night on the boat, she'd looked straight into him with mocking, affectionate eyes and had seen things in him he hadn't even known were there to discover. He'd remembered a shameful scrap in the school yard, and she'd seen a man poised on the edge of violence, vibrant with action, potent with the capability to do good or bad. But until then he'd never known such potential was even possible. His greatest moments of vivacity before that moment had been within either the thunder of the sporting field or the lightning of his equations, and in both cases he had acted safely within the rules. A world in which the rules were there to be made by himself had not existed until she'd created it.

She'd been angry tonight about her humiliation in front of the congregation, and about poor Mr Gregory, who'd had to stand in for him at such short notice. But behind it all there was a hint of a greater betrayal. He'd let down the boy in the school yard and the girl on the boat. The man she'd been so sure she'd fallen in love with would never have missed an opportunity to stand in a pulpit and talk about Peace. That man, always mysterious to him, was slipping beyond reach, and there was no denying that he had indeed become rather dull in recent months.

Even in the cold, the weight of the blankets felt heavy. It's too much, he thought. I can't pretend any more. I just can't.

6

'We've managed to dig up the record of Dunnachie's hearing,' said Aitken.

The dossier was on the desk between them. George eyed it, envying the man whose job it had been to stay in a warm office and just leaf through the court records until he found it.

'It's turned up something of interest, as it happens. Take a look.'

George opened it and read. It consisted of a few brief notes. 'Citizen of the British Empire. Born Newcastle, New South Wales, Australia. Migrated to England in 1931. Active supporter of a number of pacifist organisations from c.1932. Published letters in support of the Peace Army early 1932. Joined Peace Pledge Union 1934. Speaker at meetings and conferences on the topic of peace, 1934–39. Called up February 1940. Applied for registration as conscientious objector. Summoned to this court May 1940. Registration granted, subject to diligent performance of community service at Bangor Hospital.'

George could not work out which part was supposed to be of particular interest, and had to ask Aitken.

'The Peace Army, of course,' said Aitken with vertiginous scorn. 'What were you doing down there all those years in the files?'

George burned with embarrassment.

'The Peace Army,' said Aitken wearily, 'was a crackpot scheme dreamed up by a bunch of religious do-gooders in 1932 in response to the Mukden Incident.'

'The Mukden Incident?'

'The Sino–Japanese War. First one. For God's sake, Henderson, you must have been well out of short trousers by then. Don't you read the papers?'

He had not, as it happened, been much given to newspaper-reading as a thirteen-year-old.

'These characters – vicars, meddling spinsters and such like – took it into their heads to gather an unarmed force to sail to China and put a stop to it.'

'Put a stop to it?' George was confronted by the image of a bunch of genteel middle-aged men and women wagging their fingers in the direction of a band of Samurai warriors.

'Well, exactly. They planned to form a human barrier, on the understanding that the innate human decency of the combatants would prevent them from assailing such a force. We know now, of course, all about innate human decency when it comes to the oriental races. Even then, any person with the least shred of sanity could see that the plan was the ravings of a particularly pernicious type of madman.'

There was the smallest emanation of heat from Aitken's last sentence.

'Gained some publicity. Led to a question in the House. They even assembled a raggle-taggle of women and cripples at Harwich.' He inhaled through narrowed nostrils. 'It was quite clear to those of us who had to concern ourselves with that sort of nonsense that any individual who was prepared to get embroiled in such wanton stupidity was a *dangerous element*.'

He left the phrase hanging in the air. George was not quite sure what to do with it.

'Find out what his involvement was,' said Aitken. 'Find out what it was all about. And be quick about it. Nunn May could be brought in for interrogation any day, and then your job will be very much more difficult.'

George had no idea what it was all about, but he did his best to find out. He tried the telephone directory, but there was nothing there. He found the Peace Pledge Union, which had an address and a telephone number, and was even so bold as to give them a call.

'I'm not sure whether we've got anything on that,' said the kind lady at the other end of the phone. 'It was never really an organisation as such. Most of the activists joined us in the end. Could you hold the line a moment?' There was the sound of conferring, and then she came back. 'Yes, yes. There's a book about it, apparently, but our copy's gone missing—'

Henderson frowned, his archivist's sensitivities aroused.

'You might be best off trying the British Library. It's a book by a chap called Henry Brinton. But you're welcome to come down and have a look through our archives if you're interested.'

Henderson did not think that a visit to the Peace Pledge Union would be a wise idea at this stage. It would be difficult to concoct a cover story associated with the Peace Army when he had so little idea of what it was. So the British Library it was.

On paper, he'd been a Reader of the British Library since his file-reading days. Everyone in the department was. But he had never darkened its doors. On occasions he'd made strenuous efforts to avoid it. He knew its reputation as a hotbed of knowledge, which bred in the most threatening way possible. Men and women had sat in that place and read, and had sat in there and written, adding their own tomes to those already snaking their way along the labyrinths which lay beneath. Like any good librarian, Henderson had an instinctive antipathy to publication. It messed things up. And in that place, the written word was particularly incendiary.

Marx, he knew, had written *Das Kapital* there. Lenin and Trotsky had followed him in. Darwin had sat there and pulled apart God's intentions for man. Sylvia Pankhurst had learnt all she knew of insurrection in the Reading Room, and had put it into practice in words and deeds. H. G. Wells had made his own dark predictions for humanity. And, thought Henderson, the thing all those books had in common was that they *had all come true*. Word had a nasty habit of becoming flesh in that place.

The gentleman behind the desk of the Public Reading Room looked at Henderson expectantly.

'Can I help you, sir?'

Henderson stood in shock. The blue and gold, the vast fretted dome, the thunder-trundling of the carriages, the mass of mumbling, bumbling readers—It was, he saw straightaway, a super-library, the epitome of libraries, the place where all librarians would be sent after they died, if they were very, very bad.

'I'd like a book,' he spat.

The assistant gave the very slightest glance towards the towers of volumes which lined the spiralling walls. 'Do you have an author?'

'Yes. Brinton.'

'If you'd like to take a look at the catalogue. Take a note of the press-mark, fill in a slip, and return it to me. Do you have a seat?'

'No.'

'Be sure to have your correct seat number before you hand in your slip. There have been instances of people waiting for their books all day in quite the wrong place.'

The catalogue was better ordered than that in the Bureau. Henderson flicked through the pages of the appropriate volume and found the entry pasted to the page. 'Henry Brinton,' it read. '*The Peace Army*.'

He copied the press-mark and returned his slip to the assistant.

'How long will it be?' he asked.

'About an hour, sir.'

Henderson went out to buy a newspaper. The weather was a little milder than it had been. He stood on the steps of the museum for a moment, reading the poster for an Egyptology exhibition.

'Excuse me,' said a voice.

Henderson looked round. He saw a man who was very much colder than he was. He knew that look. It was the look of having been standing around for a very long time.

'What is the shortest way to the Strand?'

Henderson's mouth dropped open. He clenched his copy of *The Times* in his hand. The beseeching look in the man's eyes flickered for a moment and then flared into panic. Henderson's arm shot out towards him. But the man was beyond his reach already, pelting down the steps, across the mighty courtyard, and out into the wilds of Great Russell Street.

'What,' said Aitken, 'were you doing in the British Museum?'

It was the worst thing that had ever happened to George. The disgrace was incalculable.

'I was looking for a book. About the Peace Army. I was passing the time while I waited for it.'

The folds of Aitken's face were motionless. His yellow eyeballs regarded George for perhaps thirty seconds. The sweat began to slide between George's collar and his neck.

'He ran, you say?' said Aitken finally.

'I would have gone after him. But – he already had a start on me—' Why hadn't he given chase? Mainly, he thought, because it would have looked so ridiculous. One man running down Great Russell Street could have been in pursuit of a bus. A second, on his tail, would have caused every bowler-hatted gentleman to lift his eyes from the pavement and stare.

'Ah well,' said Aitken, 'it's interesting to know that he's still there. *Was* still there, I should say.'

'Still there?'

'Poor blighter's been there for months. We had a man go there with *The Times* in December. Got asked for directions to the Strand in no time at all.'

'Since *December*.' George remembered January's coldest snaps, the earth sucking warmth through the soles of his shoes, the air razor-sharp to the touch. At least in his own job there had been some moving around.

'Unlike you, our man obliged the gentleman with directions to the Strand.'

'Oh.'

'I think you should know,' said Aitken, 'that I'm going to have to make some calls about this. Your name will be mentioned.'

George felt the same sting behind his eyes that had always followed his headmaster's application of the cane.

'Of course,' he said, keeping the wobble from his voice, as he always had then.

'In the meantime, isn't there a book waiting for you at the British Library?'

'You want me to go back?'

'Precious little damage you can cause there now.'

Walter was supposed to be marking essays and preparing for one of Professor Poltine's interminable and pointless committee meetings. But the words inside him were a fever.

He pushed the official papers aside, took the notes he'd started writing the day before out of the drawer, and picked up his pen.

2. RADIOACTIVITY

In 1896, the year before the discovery of the electron, a French physicist came across a phenomenon which would be of equal importance to modern physics.

It had, of course, long been known that cathode rays caused the glass tubing through which they passed to fluoresce. Recently, the same release of light energy had been observed coming from the glass up to a foot away. Even covering the apparatus with black paper did not prevent the rays from getting through and making nearby screens glow. And when one scientist held a hand between the covered tube and the screen, a darkened pattern appeared.

It was not an ordinary shadow. It was the bones of his own hand.

Henri Becquerel, a Parisian professor of physics, read about these effects and speculated. If the impact of cathode rays caused glass to emit these 'x-rays', perhaps they could be liberated from other fluorescing materials too, such as uranium. So he sealed a photographic plate in black paper, sprinkled a layer of uranium salt onto the paper and exposed it to the sun for several hours. When he developed the plate, he saw the silhouette of the substance in black on the negative, just like the skeleton on the screen. In a state of great excitement, he scribbled down his conclusions. The light of the sun had activated the uranium in just the same way that cathode rays had activated glass, and the resulting x-rays had passed through the black paper to the photographic screen.

It was important to repeat and thereby confirm his results. Unfortunately, by the time he had set up his equipment a second time, Paris had clouded over. So he put the photographic plate away in a dark cupboard and waited for another *day of sunshine. The weather remained overcast. After several gloomy days, he lost patience and developed the plate anyway.*

The image on the screen was more intense than ever.

This time, whatever had passed from the uranium to the photographic plate had not been stimulated by electricity, or light, or anything else which might be swimming around in the ether. Becquerel had stumbled across a power which was emitted from matter itself.

When they were young things had been simple. They'd wanted things, and they'd tried to get them. Walter remembered a day, in snow, when Alan had reached out and got what he wanted, and Walter had stood back in astonishment at the quietness of his cheek and the ease with which it had been accepted.

'Dunnachie,' Chadwick had said when Nunn May was helping him to lift the cloud chamber onto the table.

Walter had sprung alert so fast he'd almost dropped the cloud chamber.

'I'm reading a paper at the Royal Society next term. I thought it might be a good opportunity for you to experience one of these occasions.'

Walter's whole being had been a question mark.

'It occurred to me that you might benefit from accompanying me.'

Nunn May had been pulling the other end of the cloud chamber onto the table as quickly and strenuously as possible. Walter had given his own side a good shove and let it go.

'Why, thank you so much, sir! I'd most certainly like to—'

'Would that be your paper on the artificial disintegration of fluorine and aluminium by alpha particles, Dr Chadwick?' Nunn May had piped up.

Walter had stared at the young prig, aghast.

A lone eyebrow had risen. 'It would indeed, Nunn May.'

'I'm sorry to interrupt. But that's a field which I've been following with particular interest.'

Walter had heard himself gasp.

'Is it indeed?' Chadwick's steely gaze had given Nunn May a good examination. 'Well, I suppose if your interest is so particular, we might be able to accommodate a second spectator.'

'That's very kind of you, sir,' Nunn May had said. 'What date is it?'

The date was hardly a consideration.

'The eleventh of February,' Chadwick had said. 'Well, that's settled then. I'll book you both in. Look after that cloud chamber, Dunnachie, by the way. Be sure to put it to better use than Webster did.'

Walter sat at his desk in University College and held his hand out in front of him. It was not the same hand which had polished that old cloud chamber with Alan. The skin had worn away and been replaced, the muscles had thickened and been renewed. For a moment he saw his own brittle skeleton through the skin. I wish, he thought. I wish.

He did not even know what to wish for, except that the past should live again, and not lead to the present.

3. ALCHEMY

In the year 1900, Ernest Rutherford was twenty-eight years old. He was now Professor of Physics at McGill University in Montreal. Within a year of this precocious appointment, he reported the discovery of a gas emanating from thorium.

The scientific world was very impressed. Rutherford was not. It was all very well having identified a radioactive gas, but he had no idea what the gas actually was. He was a physicist, not a chemist. So he dropped in at McGill's chemistry laboratory, and found there a young Oxford graduate called Frederick Soddy.

'Soddy,' he said to the twenty-three-year-old research student, 'I've got this thorium emanation.'

Soddy was very excited and suggested, to Rutherford's delight, that the chemical character of the substance ought to be examined. They took a good look, and it proved to have no chemical character whatsoever.

Rutherford looked at Soddy and waited for his verdict. He already knew what it ought to be, but deferred to the judgement of the chemist. Soddy was as overcome as his methodical training would allow. He spat it out. 'It conveyed,' he said, 'the tremendous and inevitable conclusion that the element thorium was slowly and spontaneously transmuting itself into argon gas!'

One element had changed into another. Alchemy, the Philosopher's Stone, the elixir of life— They pushed such pre-scientific daydreams from their minds and got on with investigating the process they had observed.

Radioactive decay. Half-life. Isotopes. The new phenomena rushed from their test tubes, and 'for more than two years,' as Soddy later recalled, 'life, scientific life, became hectic to a degree rare in the lifetime of an individual, rare perhaps in the lifetime of an institution'.

And now Rutherford wanted to know what was going on within the radiations themselves. He proved that the beta radiation was a high-energy form of the electrons discovered by Thomson; and suspected that the alpha radiation consisted of helium atoms. These particles were emerging from the atoms within the decaying elements. He started to glimpse a new possibility – that this process of decay must release energy as well as matter. With Soddy, he made and published the first calculations of this energy release – greater than any other chemical change known – and privately began to speculate about its potential.

Rutherford used to joke about it. He suggested playfully

that 'could a proper detonator be found, it was just conceiv-
able that a wave of atomic disintegration might be started
through matter, which would indeed make this old world
vanish in smoke'. Remembering the chaotic conditions of the
Cavendish, he quipped to a Cambridge associate that 'some
fool in a laboratory might blow up the universe unawares'.

Soddy took the possibilities presented by this new energy
a little more seriously. 'If it could be tapped and controlled
what an agent it would be in shaping the world's destiny! The
man who put his hand on the lever by which a parsimonious
nature regulates so jealously the output of this store of energy
would possess a weapon by which he could destroy the earth
if he chose.' However, he dismissed the danger, reasoning that
in the long history of the world, if such a change were possible
it would already have taken place.

A few years later, the writer H. G. Wells read a book by
Soddy and took the matter more seriously still. In 1914 he
wrote the novel The World Set Free, *in which the spectre of*
atomic warfare was brought to life for the very first time.

The book was waiting at Henderson's desk. He might have
left it there all day and they would just have tidied it away
at the end as if nothing had happened.

He opened it and was instantly disappointed. It was
immediately clear what sort of book it was. He'd hoped for
something clear and concise, explaining the origins, history
and activities of the Peace Army. Instead it was a rambling
ideological tract.

He did not think he could possibly sit and read such a book.
His heart was ragged, his mind distraught. This was not a *job*.
All he'd ever wanted was a job, like anyone else. His mother
had been pleased with him when, at the age of fifteen, he got
himself the apprenticeship at the Bureau library. The idea had
been that he should stay on at the grammar school, but he'd

flunked his exams, and so when a sympathetic teacher had pulled those strings, a job working with books had, in her eyes, been the next best thing. He'd worked hard, and had done all right. Then the war came, and he'd put himself forward to fight. If only he'd gone, he might have come back to his old job like anyone else. Or died in battle like anyone else. By staying behind he had entered a strange underworld, and it did not now look as though there was any way out.

The people who did this sort of thing in books were valiant and brave. Their adversaries were masters of disguise who committed perfect crimes, and the heroes had to use every resource of cunning and strength to outwit them. They did not mooch around in libraries and church halls, chasing harmless academics. They did not come a cropper by stumbling into people on the other side who were doing just as bad a job as they.

I am no *good* at this, thought George tearfully. If he was no good at it he should not be doing it. But somehow he had sensed that in the underworld this did not follow. He'd seen it in Aitken's eyes. With each mistake he made, his next task would become harder and uglier. And no one else would ever be able to employ him, because he'd never be able to tell them what he'd done.

He knew that Phoebe could see that things were going badly. It did not matter that he did not tell her what he did. He carried the stink of failure home with him every day. She was tainted by it, and showed it, in the increasing drabness of her clothes and her dispirited eyes. He remembered the way that Mrs Dunnachie had looked at her husband as he'd struggled through the church door, and wished he could find a way to make Phoebe look at him like that. They ought to have had a perfectly good marriage. As far as he could see, they were both amiable people. But somewhere along the way, something had gone astray, and he knew that there was no real chance of getting it back. These days the mist only ever filled Phoebe's eyes when she spoke of Leonard.

But Dunnachie had stayed at home too. What triumph in his life kept that bold, proud look in his wife's eyes? George looked down at the book. The way Aitken had described it, the Peace Army had sounded like the most ridiculous thing in the world. But Aitken's tastes were narrow and unforgiving. Perhaps there was more to it than that.

He flicked the pages over until he came to a passage that held him.

'Apologists for war dearly love talking about human nature and saying that while human nature is human nature we shall always have war,' he read.

George was certainly of this opinion himself.

'Fighting, they say, is a natural instinct. Such a plea could hardly be successful in a murder trial, and, even if it was true, which it probably was not, about the kind of fighting that used to take place when professional soldiers went about dressed in a kind of boiler suit of armour plating, it certainly cannot be applied to modern warfare. War is an anachronism.'

It was an intriguing thought. George tried to make his brain consider the relations between nations as being similar to those which existed between individuals in a well-ordered country. He knew from his history lessons that things had not always been as they were now. Once even London had been a forest roamed by vagabonds. Perhaps the world was still waiting to catch up with the civilised nations.

'Peace treaties can never prove an enduring basis for the world order,' said Mr Brinton's book. 'That can only be achieved when we expect of the nations the same minimum standard of honesty as is demanded from individuals. The civil law of every nation does not recognise a pledge which is extracted by force; neither, in the long run, can a treaty dictated from the business end of a rifle be satisfactory. Some day the treaties have got to be revised and, whatever solution is arrived at, be the result of a mutual agreement independent of force either direct or indirect.'

George flicked back to the title page of the book, just to be sure: 1932. The author was, he realised, talking about the Treaty of Versailles. He was writing as if he had the authority to accuse the treaty-makers of having broken a basic tenet of civil law. There must be something wrong, thought George, with treating international relations in such a way. But he could not just now put his finger on what it was.

'Germany was forced to disarm and was left the bare minimum of forces necessary to maintain internal order. But, when this item was inserted in the Treaty, a specific pledge was given on behalf of all the Allies that there was no intention of keeping Germany at the mercy of the rest of the world, but that this was the first step in an all-round reduction and limitation of armaments "as one of the most fruitful preventatives of war". It cannot exactly be said that this pledge has been broken, but it certainly can be said that it has not so far been honoured. Either that pledge must be kept, however, or we must allow Germany once again to arm. For honourable people there is no third course. To confess our impotence to implement our promise would be such a confession of weakness that the result would inevitably be fatal to the tentative steps which have been taken toward a new world order.'

George wished he knew more about the events that had taken place during his teenage years. It had never occurred to him that history might be unfolding until the war, when history had become a commonplace of life. And by that time, he supposed, it had been too late to understand it. He had a feeling that this man's words had in some way predicted the future. When he was first working at the Bureau, which would have been 1934 or 1935, there had been something about a disarmament conference, and Hitler causing a scene, and things starting to get dangerous. He wished he knew what had happened.

'Mr Duff-Cooper has pointed out that we might as well try to revise the Ten Commandments: something like this: "Thou shalt not commit murder . . . but if thou dost, thou shalt only use weapons approved by the County Council". Even in the last war the inconsistency was apparent.'

George stared at the words and was suddenly aware of where he was. He ventured a sideways glance at the man sitting next to him. The sound of the scholar's scribbling was audible. His nose was very close to the book, and a cobwebby ginger beard scratched the page. He was wearing a kind of jerkin beneath a very dusty sports jacket, and his trouser legs were too short, displaying disarranged cycle clips. My God, thought George. The man was mad or dangerous or both. He might have expected no less. He looked back at his own book. Had Aitken known what he was doing by sending him back to this place? Every dangerous word he had read so far made sense.

'There is a phrase "a nation under arms", and it is not a metaphor but a literal description. Even in the last war the aeroplane had brought practically everybody within the danger zone and, if in those days the threat was more psychological in its effect than disastrous in its consequences, this will certainly not be true of the next war, should there be one. There is a story that a great inventor was asked recently by one of his friends if it were true that the whole population of London could be obliterated in the space of twelve hours. His answer, "No, it could be done in six!", may not be precisely accurate, but at least it gives some idea of what we may anticipate if we do not attain sanity in time.'

We were *not* destroyed, thought George, with the pride

of a true Cockney. Brinton had underestimated his own countrymen – London was too strong even for Hitler. But then he remembered the newspaper headlines, not from the beginning of the war but from the end. Tokyo was indeed destroyed in six hours. Then Hiroshima was obliterated in five minutes.

And now George sat and read properly, because he needed to prove Brinton wrong. The book posed various hypothetical situations, seeking a solution to international conflict which would avoid the predicted Armageddon.

'If a war is going on somewhere else and it is somebody else's country which is being attacked, to sit quietly by and watch the apparently triumphant progress of evil, without lifting a finger to stay it, would be an intolerable position to anyone with a strong sense of justice. The courageous thing to do, and the thing which we should most of us like to think we should do if faced with such a situation, is to try to separate them without injuring either and without using weapons oneself.'

To this end Brinton proposed the formation of a 'Peace Army', and the Peace Army of the author's imaginings took much the same form as the organisation Aitken had described: an utterly unarmed force with the mission of intervening between potentially warring nations. But in this theoretical context, without Aitken's raving spinsters and vicious Japanese warriors, it did not seem so strange.

'Let us imagine for example that France and Germany were to go once more to war (this will do very well for an example, as it is one of the most unlikely things to happen). Such a situation could not arise in a day and there would be ample time for preparations. Before hostilities actually broke out, we should have to announce that we were sending the "Peace Army" as a precautionary measure. It is possible that its landing would be opposed by force. If this were the case, there would undoubtedly be an awful slaughter. But that would probably be the end of the war. The knowledge of having killed thousands of men who had made no effort to defend themselves and who were only seeking to preserve their destroyers from war and destruction would be such a ghastly weight on the conscience of any nation that it seems incredible to believe that all the innate feelings of decency of the people would not rise in revolt and lead to such a reaction against war that it would vanish for ever.'

Innate feelings of decency. George saw Aitken's cynical eyes, and felt a surge of warmth for poor, deluded, trusting Brinton.

'If the landing were not opposed, the situation would be more complex and the result a little more difficult to foresee. We then have to imagine the "Peace Army" spread out in a line on the frontier between the two disputants. The strong probability is that, before endeavouring to start the war, the enemies would mutually agree, in the first place, to settle the question of what was to be done about it. The result would be protracted negotiations which would probably be fatal to the ambitions of the war parties in both countries. Attention would be drawn away from the feelings of righteous hate which had been worked up and, once such sentiments are allowed to die down, a war would be impossible. There is a third possibility, namely, that the war would start with the "Peace Army" in between the combatants. The situation would then become Gilbertian and it is impossible to say what would happen.'

George leapt from his seat and almost broke into a run. He rushed up to the enquiries desk. 'Do you have a dictionary?' he blurted.

The man scribbled a press-mark on a piece of paper and handed it to George, pointing towards an area of the book stacks. George grabbed a dictionary from its shelf and looked under G.

'Gilbertian,' it read. '(Of situation etc.) ludicrous or para-doxical, as in Gilbert and Sullivan opera.'

Gilbert and Sullivan? George found the corners of his mouth curling upwards in terrible appreciation of the blackest possible joke. Operetta was hardly what came to mind. Instead, an astonished line of sweet idealists, their limbs and intestines mashed to pieces beneath the Nazi tanks and planes.

So that was what the people at Harwich had meant to do in China.

Perhaps it was a terrible, unlawful thing to kill other human beings. Perhaps the only hope was to trust your enemy, because otherwise there was no chance that he would trust you.

But, thought George, such trust is fatal. There really had been no hope of a bloodless peace, not in China, and not in France. And then he saw what he hadn't been able to place before, the thing which was wrong with the way that Brinton treated the affairs of the world, the thing that made George a wiser man than him.

It was the Second World War.

7

11 February 1932

The clouds had loosed snow all night, and then parted and departed. It was the beginning of a clear day, bright with blue ice above the spires. Walter was hurrying from Trinity along King's Parade, but something in the cold dazzle of his surroundings stopped him, and he paused to look up in awe.

He had woken before first light, his breath forming crystal patterns in the air. As he'd fumbled for his spectacles on the little table beside his bed and squinted up through the clouds of water vapour towards the window, he'd known at once from the eerie glow that it had snowed again in the night. He had seen snow for the first time little over a month ago. Now he knew it on waking. Like the yellow stone of King's College, and like the earth falling into darkness at four in the afternoon, snow was becoming a fact of life. It was quite normal to dress in temperatures below freezing, with only a hint of warmth from the ashes of last night's fire. Quite normal to strap on layer after layer, and finish with his gown and the blue, red and gold scarf. And quite normal to shut the door behind him and crunch across Whewell's Court and out into the street, huddling against the cold in the twilight of morning.

Walter squinted up against the light. The stones above him had been placed there more than six hundred years before. It had taken hundreds of men to draw them from the earth, to transport them across the subsiding fens, and to lever and pulley them into place. The enormity of the task was unimaginable. And beneath the snow-capped spikes and buttresses of King's College Chapel, the architectural innovators of ages past had arranged an even greater achievement. They had taken the sand shaved from the chisels of the stonemasons and had made a clear, light-giving substance. Then they had fashioned this icy, fissurable matter into a sheet uncrushed by the tons of rock above it, providing protection and illumination for the worshippers within. Even after all these centuries, during which so much progress and discovery had intervened, it was still a thing to wonder at.

Walter let the glory of it zing through him for a moment. And then he pushed his bicycle onwards, eager to get going. In recent weeks, the weight of his homesickness had begun to lift. In the hectic and tolerant atmosphere of the Cavendish, he had finally come to a sort of truce with his equipment, and had managed to produce some results. Chadwick had even seen fit to toss him a compliment or two. 'You've got an instinctive feel for which course of action to take,' he'd said one afternoon. 'That's very important in a scientist.'

All the blood in Walter's body had shot to his face and he'd scuffled his feet, trying to kick a couple of fragments of broken glass under the table. 'Thank you, sir,' he'd said when he'd recovered his breath.

'You'll need more than instinct, my boy,' Chadwick had responded with tart amusement. 'It's not just genius which is ninety-nine per cent perspiration, you know.'

Walter had continued to blush, perspiring enough for any genius.

And now he was on his way to a meeting of the Royal Society with Chadwick, which he took as even better evidence of the esteem in which his supervisor held him. After all, he had only been in England for five months, and already here he was accompanying Chadwick on an important trip to London. He wondered whether he might glimpse more famous scientists at the meeting to add to his growing collection.

It wasn't just science that was exciting, either. Things were coming together in all kinds of marvellous ways. There were friends now, lots of them, an eclectically international crew from a dozen different cultures, all united by their scientific preoccupations and frustrations. And he was even getting to know a few people outside the laboratory. Shortly after arriving in Cambridge, Walter had made contact with the Methodist church, in an attempt to find something approximating to the community he'd left back at home. Like everything else, the church in Cambridge was an entirely different animal to the one in Newcastle, but he was enjoying his involvement immensely. The gaggle of relatives and family friends of Cook's Hill was replaced by an intense band of academics. The Methodist Group meetings were an opportunity to sit around with new friends all evening and inflict upon them his opinions about the state of the world.

The topic he chose most often was the one with which he'd wooed the girl on the ship. He had tried so hard to cling to his memory of what she looked like. But in the few snaps in which she appeared, she was always standing in a rather furious posture, swaddled with layers of clothing and forbidding him to try to make her look nice, and her hair was always blowing across her face, obscuring all but a trace of her outraged eyebrows and her wilful pout. He had to admit that the photographs showed a little of the truth, but that was not how he wanted to remember her at all. Her face, he knew, had been quite delicate, with a little girlish snub nose, and her figure had been slender and graceful. When he'd looked at her he'd always had to concentrate quite hard to avoid glancing at her ankles. Towards the end of the crossing, as they neared Europe, there had been a fancy dress ball, and while Walter had got kitted out as a cowboy in apparel which was variously too big and too small, she had arrived as the Black Swan of Western Australia, and the sight had been so distracting that it was only close up that he realised that the feathers were made of paper. When she danced that night, with him stumbling about after her, and her laughing at him, she was without doubt the most captivating woman on the floor. Everyone agreed on it. But though he could recall his thoughts about her appearance, he could not actually frame it in his mind. Perhaps she'd meant him to forget how pretty she was. She'd always seemed a little embarrassed about it. 'Our little Anna Pavlova,' one aged and gallant brigadier had dubbed her as they collapsed back at their table. The sparks from her eyes had brooked any divide in status or breeding. 'Hmph,' she had puffed. 'I suppose in Europe it is considered a good idea to dance like a pudding.'

The brigadier had feigned delight at her joke, but Walter had been very glad not to have ventured such a remark himself.

So he chose now to remember her the way he thought she might have preferred, in terms not of what she had looked like, but of what she had said. Whenever he could find a way to the subject, he steered his conversations round to Peace. The Methodists were remarkably responsive. They did not steal his gaze as she had done, so that he could not take it away, nor did they hint at vast resources of strength within him. But at least they were prepared to listen, and sometimes they agreed.

'Mr Dunnachie,' the Reverend Barnes had said one evening, taking him aside at the end of the meeting. 'Are you serious about Peace?'

Serious? Walter had summoned up every ounce of the seriousness he'd seen behind Grace's laughing eyes, and felt so full of it he thought his feet would burn a hole through the floor. '*Yes.*'

'When I say serious,' the Reverend had said, his rather loose mouth trying to purse itself for a difficult task, 'I mean is it something you would be prepared to make sacrifices for?'

For a moment he had glimpsed her, saw the upward tilt of her eyebrows as she demanded an answer. Then she was gone. 'Oh yes,' he'd said.

As he cycled to the station, the echo of Grace and the accompanying feeling of his own invincibility were with him still. Reverend Barnes had given him an address to go to in London. There would be plenty of time to go there after the meeting. He would achieve both things in one day. The road rushed by, eaten up by the uncontrollable pace of his bicycle. There was only one fly in the ointment, and that was—

—Nunn May. The undergraduate was standing at the near end of the station platform, stamping his feet and clapping his hands in an attempt to keep warm. All the colour of his face had concentrated into small pink peaks on his thin cheeks. His nose and chin were in the air.

'Good morning!' burbled Nunn May, and began to rush towards him.

'Hello,' said Walter frostily.

An awkward silence clapped tight over them.

'Jolly interesting talk at the Phoolosophical Society last night,' said Nunn May, in an attempt to make conversation.

Yes, well. If the truth were known, this was the main reason for Walter's annoyance with his uninvited companion. He had been embarrassed by Nunn May's unexpected appearance at the meeting the previous evening, and the mood had slipped over into the morning.

The 'Phool' was a spoof of the plethora of clubs and societies which so characterised the Cambridge scientific community. There was the Physical Society, a meeting of the more senior academics, and for lowlier mortals, the Junior Physical Society. There was the '$\nabla^2 V$ Club', the Kapitza Club, and, spanning the senior staff of the whole of Cambridge science, the Philosophical Society. It was this last august committee from which the Phoolosophical Society's name had been plundered. The Phool was a Cavendish affair, and it was restricted mainly to research students, because they did not care to have their supervisors hear them being facetious about their work. It was their one opportunity to indulge in the exquisite occupation of Poking Fun at Science.

As a rule, undergraduates were not invited to the Phoolo-sophical Society. But Nunn May was becoming such a part of the furniture that no one had looked particularly surprised when he sidled into the room. Walter had been in the middle of a particularly diverting argument with Jack Constable and Rafi Chaudhri, about whether Einstein or Bohr had made the greater contribution to quantum theory. Walter had been on the side of Bohr, as had Constable, chiefly because they had both met him, but Chaudhri was making rather short work of their arguments. 'Einstein may not be prepared to accept the implications of his own deductions,' the Indian had been declaring, 'but without Einstein, Bohr's theories would not exist. Simply would not exist.'

It was difficult to resist the will of Chaudhri. He was the man who had decided in India that he must study under Rutherford, had taken a passage to England, and had camped on Chadwick's lawn until they let him in.

'Yes, but—' Walter had contended. Then he'd seen Nunn May making his usual beeline towards him, was forced to move aside to give him space, and the argument had been lost.

'Interesting?' said Walter now, unable to help himself from delivering the put-down which he'd longed to give at the time. 'It's not supposed to be interesting. It's just a joke.'

'Oh, yes, yes,' bustled Nunn May, resolutely cheerful, and then, under Walter's sceptical gaze, his crest fell. 'Well, yes,' he said, in the tone of an admission. 'I'm not sure I got the joke, exactly. I mean, it did seem terribly amusing, somehow. But I couldn't quite work out how.'

Of course you couldn't, thought Walter, because you are not a research student and you weren't supposed to be there.

It had been a particularly elaborate and effective skit. On most occasions, the speakers were reduced to rather predictable conjectures about the feeding habits of Schrödinger's Cat. This time a Canadian named Ted Nicolls had stood in a warm college room, in front of a cloud chamber specially imported for the occasion, and had given a demonstration.

'I am here to announce,' Nicolls had proclaimed, 'a discovery of no small importance. In fact what I have to tell you will transform the way we understand the nucleus of the atom. Nay, it will transfigure, indeed transmute, the way we see the world. With the help of my dear lady wife, and the use of my Wilson Cloud Chamber, purchased for a very reasonable price at the pet shop on Trumpington Road, I have uncovered the existence of' – and here he'd paused for effect – 'a particle hitherto unknown to man.'

The audience had given appropriate oohs and ahs.

'Watch carefully,' Nicolls had said, and the sniggers began, for this was the catchphrase of a particular Cavendish demonstrator.

He'd produced a phial of what looked suspiciously like a radioactive source, necessary in any experiment which involved examining a stream of particles. There were gasps. It was not normal to see such dangerous materials in a college room.

Nicolls had taken a sniff. 'Hmm,' he'd said, 'that distinctive smell of cod liver oil, so essential in the chemical identification of radium.'

He'd wafted it in the direction of his audience, and sure enough the smell evoked memories of childhood wriggling and refusals to take one's medicine.

Nicolls had fitted it into the firing tube. 'Lights, Mr Miller!' he'd commanded of his accomplice.

The curtains were fastened to the walls to extinguish all chinks of light. They had been plunged into total darkness, two dozen men or more sitting in a normal-sized college room in front of an invisible demonstrator. Walter had heard his colleagues snuffling and fidgeting around him.

'You will now witness something which has only previously been seen by my own eyes,' Nicolls had declared. 'Fix your eyes very firmly on the cloud chamber. Very firmly, may I add.'

For about five minutes he'd rustled, accompanying these sound effects with huffs and puffs and the occasional 'Oh, dash! I'll have to start again now!' The attention of the blind spectators had begun to stretch thin, and falter. They'd wriggled. Someone had said, 'Get on with it, Nicolls!'

'Be patient in the cause of great science!'

Finally, just as Walter had been on the verge of sleep, there was a blinding flash. Every man in the room had bumped from his chair. Miller had flicked the lights back on and they'd looked around themselves, bleary and shocked by the sudden light. At the front, Nicolls had been holding a camera, which was directed at the cloud chamber.

'Lights, Mr Miller!'

They'd gone off again and then the audience had heard an almighty splashing. 'All right then, Mr Miller,' Nicolls had said. 'We are ready for the moment of truth.'

The room had been once again illuminated, and in front of the desk Nicolls had stood holding a photographic plate proudly in front of his chest.

There had been a breathless silence.

'Do you notice anything unusual about this photograph?' he'd demanded.

There certainly had been something very unusual about it.

'There's nothing on it!' someone had shouted.

'That,' Nicolls had said, 'is where you're wrong. Can't you see it?'

They'd peered. Nicolls had passed the plate to a man on the front row. The man had examined it closely, shaken his head and passed it on. When it had got round to Walter he was buzzing with anticipation. He'd held it close to his eyes, then far away. Even the most botched experiment will result in a photograph with something on it – just a streak of fluff or a crack in the lens. This one had been doctored. It was completely and utterly black.

'What you have just examined, gentlemen,' Nicolls had said when it was returned to him, 'is the world's first photograph of the Fewtron.'

The Fewtron? Brows had creased in an attempt to get the hang of the joke.

'The Fewtron is a very special particle, with a quite unique set of characteristics. I have taken the liberty of naming it the Fewtron because its properties are very Few. In fact it has no characteristics at all.'

And finally they'd got it, and the small room had boomed with laughter. Nicolls had shouted across the racket.

'No electrical charge. No tracks. No readings. In the course of three years of experimentation into this weighty matter, the Fewtron has yet to manifest itself visible by any of the established methods. In fact the indubitable conclusion must be that, if you perform an expansion in a Wilson Cloud Chamber and there are no tracks whatsoever, then this is absolute and positive proof that a Fewtron has passed through.'

Walter found himself smiling just remembering it. He

glanced at Nunn May, and, seeing his dismay, realised he'd made his point.

'The reason why you don't get it is that you haven't had to do it,' he explained, more gently. 'The joke was about all those hours we spend achieving absolutely nothing. It was to give us an excuse.'

'An excuse?'

'I asked Nicolls afterwards how he thought of it,' said Walter. 'Apparently it was something which he and Hugh Webster dreamed up last summer when they were working up in the Observatory.'

'Hugh Webster? The one we got your equipment from?'

'That's the one. Webster was doing some work for Chadwick. Chadwick told him to bombard beryllium with alpha parti-cles, pass the resulting gamma radiation through the cloud chamber, and look for very thin tracks. Then he went off on holiday and left Webster to it. Webster spent all summer taking photographs of that cloud chamber. He knew from the way Chadwick had spoken how important it was to find very thin tracks. Well, he and Nicolls looked at photograph after photograph and there was nothing. Sometimes they thought they'd got something, but it always turned out to be a bit of fluff caught in the lens. And as it got nearer to the time Chadwick was due to get back, Webster got pretty frustrated. So to calm him down, Nicolls invented the Fewtron.'

'Golly,' said Nunn May.

'You see,' said Walter, 'it was perfect. We spend so many hours, blowing up our glassware, spraying films all over the lab.' Actually this was Walter's own trademark, and could not honestly be attributed to the establishment as a whole, but Nunn May need not know that. 'Then finally, you get the apparatus sorted out, and then you spend another week or so trying to get the source prepared. But every time it's ready, Cockcroft's particle accelerator sparks over, and the whole thing's jigged out, and by the time all that's mended, the polonium's decayed, and you have to start all over again. Then one day it all goes fine, and it's all steady, and the particles should be streaming into the chamber, so you take your photographs. But when they're developed, there's nothing there. You spend hours staring at the plates and somehow you think there must be something. But you know really it's just a scratch on the lens. Well, Nicoll's demonstrated that it wasn't in vain. We did catch something after all. We caught a Fewtron.'

Nunn May's eyes were wide with horror at the travails he might be letting himself in for if he did his Ph.D. 'Don't worry,' said Walter magnanimously, deciding to behave in accordance with the elevated status which the undergraduate clearly believed he possessed. 'You'll get used to it. I was in despair at first. But it's getting better now.' He stamped his feet. 'No sign of Dr Chadwick?'

'None.'

'I wonder if his flu's come back.' Chadwick had taken a rare day off at the end of the previous week. He'd been looking distinctly odd ever since.

'What will we do if it has?'

'We can't go,' said Walter. 'For goodness' sake, Nunn May, it's the Royal Society. They wouldn't even let us in without him.'

'But I've already bought my train ticket. They have a library, don't they? We could have a look around there.'

Walter looked at him in incomprehension. 'There are plenty of libraries here. Don't you have finals to be studying for?'

'It's under control. Dunnachie—'

'Mmm?'

'I hope you don't mind me coming along with you. It's most awfully kind of you. In the lab too. I'm very grateful.

I just want to do as well as I can. Get started on the real stuff as quickly as possible. There's so much to learn.'

Walter looked at Nunn May's eager eyes. He recognised his own hunger and realised that the acknowledgement of his kindness was all he'd ever needed. 'Of course I don't mind,' he said quickly, bluffing away his annoyance. 'It's a pleasure—'

He stopped. The train was in sight, pulling slowly around the bend in the track, the steam vivid white against the blue air, its puffs like baby pockets of snow proceeding in the wrong direction. The moment was upon them. The noise of the engine was at first muffled by distance and the snow, then amplified, the tracks humming with the weight applied to them. Walter began to panic.

'Look!' cried Nunn May, and there was Dr Chadwick, dropping down the steps two at a time.

At the bottom of the steps, Chadwick turned to look at the moving train, and walked slowly and calmly to the students.

'Dunnachie,' he nodded. 'Nunn May.' His voice was almost drowned by the sound of the engine. 'All set for an interesting day?'

They nodded with enthusiasm.

With a whine and a screech, the train pulled to a halt, and Chadwick assumed his role as leader and guide, opening the nearest door before the porter could get to it.

The carriage smelt of brown paper and figs. Walter bounced himself up and down on the seat, making himself comfortable.

'You will excuse me,' said Dr Chadwick. It was a comment, not a question. He pulled crumpled papers from his case. 'I need to familiarise myself with this afternoon's paper.'

'Of course!' said Walter and Nunn May. Walter pulled the postcard he'd brought with him out of a pocket, and a pen.

He stared out of the window and attempted to pull together all the thoughts which had raced in his head on the way to the station. The perfect, insulated landscape gathered pace at his side, and the dazzling monotony of the snow confounded his vision, robbing it of any sense of distance.

'Dear Grace,' drifted his own voice in his head. 'The world is white. We always tried to imagine how it would look, didn't we? And of course we failed entirely. There we were, painting bush plants with a white brush, whereas here the fields are hugged by feathers, and though the sun is low, the light is brighter than anything we have ever seen. So much of this new life is like that. I always expected science here to be the same as at home, except more so, but as soon as Rutherford or Chadwick speak I can see that back then I had no idea how much there was to know. Has it snowed in Paris yet? My darling—'

Walter came to his senses, clutching the postcard, rigid with embarrassment and shame. What right did he have?

He pulled himself together and forced himself to address the task in hand. The pen was clumsy between his fingers. There was no way he could get it to express the smallest fraction of what he felt about snow or science or anything else.

'Dear Jim,' he scrawled slowly. 'It snowed last night. The picture on this card is a portrait of Niels Bohr, who is a very eminent Danish physicist and a former pupil of Lord Rutherford's, who came to visit us last week. He explained to us some very important discoveries he has recently made regarding quantum mechanics, which are too complex to explain here, though I hope to be able to sum up a part of them in a future letter. It is possible that I will meet men of equal distinction at the meeting today. I am very excited about it.'

Walter had a nasty feeling that Jim would think the cricket scores far more worthy of his interest. He tried to bury the thought. It made him feel too lonely.

He looked at Nunn May and felt a surge of affection for the young man who he knew was as excited as he was. Nunn May felt his glance and looked up from the paper on his lap.

'What's the news?' asked Walter.

'Very little,' said Nunn May. 'Woman in Trumpington's lost her cat.' Then his eyes lit up. 'It is not specified whether it was alive or dead.'

Walter grinned. It was the inevitable reference to Schrödinger's metaphysical feline, but at least it showed that he was catching on. He let out a very small miaow.

Chadwick stared at him in bemusement.

'Sorry,' said Walter, covered in embarrassment. 'It was just something amusing.'

'Amusing?' Chadwick sounded as though he had never heard the concept before.

'It's the sort of joke they tell at the Phoolosophical Society,' said Nunn May authoritatively.

Walter flashed him a look of warning. He did not know whether the staff were even supposed to know of the existence of the Phool, let alone what it did.

'Phoolosophical?'

'Like the Physical Society,' said Nunn May. 'Except foolish. Chaps read out papers about science, except it's a joke.'

'A joke?' It was clear from Chadwick's expression that the idea of science being a joke was utterly alien to him.

'Like the Fewtron,' explained Nunn May.

'The *Fewtron*?'

He was blundering now, knowing he was digging himself a hole, but unable to stop himself from continuing.

'It's – it's a particle with very Few properties. It's what you know has passed through your cloud chamber if you don't see anything on your photographs—'

He stopped. Chadwick had taken a very sharp breath and turned abruptly to face the window once more.

Nunn May turned scarlet. Walter gave him a stern look, blushing intensely himself. He looked back down at his postcard. It was a good thing he didn't have to explain to Jim what scientific fools he and his companion had just made of themselves.

4. THE NUCLEUS

When Thomson discovered the electron, he postulated that it was part of the atom. The next question he asked himself was how these electron-filled atoms were constructed. His answer was endearingly English. They were, he said, structured rather like a plum pudding. The negatively charged electrons were jumbled together like dried fruits, surrounded by a puddingy mixture, which gave the atom its mass and was probably in itself positively charged, to neutralise the negative charge of the electrons. The analogy was compelling and it lasted for more than a decade. Then it was destroyed, accidentally, by his own protégé.

Soon after his pioneering work with Soddy in Montreal, Rutherford was persuaded to return to England and take up a professorship at Manchester University. Whilst he was there, he built up a team which included some of the most talented physicists in the world. One day he was watching some experiments performed by Hans Geiger, who was bombarding metallic foils with alpha particles, and they noticed that when the particles hit the foil, some of them travelled through much larger angles than could possibly occur if the atom had a uniform structure. In fact, they returned to a point not far from where they had started out.

'It was quite the most incredible event that has ever happened to me in my life,' was Rutherford's reported verdict. 'It was almost as incredible as if you fired a fifteen-inch

shell at a piece of tissue paper and it came back and hit
you.'

It is difficult to see now what Rutherford found so aston-
ishing. In order to understand, it is necessary to cast away
one's assumption that what is known now was obvious then.
The words 'atomic' and 'nucleus' are so closely linked in our
minds that it is almost impossible to prise them apart. But if
you do, it is possible to glimpse how counter-intuitive the idea
was. An element was consistent in texture, in appearance,
and in the way it behaved. If it was made up of individual
particles, then surely those particles must themselves have a
uniform structure.

But the energy in the travelling alpha particles was far too
great to be deflected so far by the atoms in the static metallic
foils if they had a uniform structure. Only a considerable
electrical charge might be capable of doing that, and in
Thomson's plum pudding, the positive and negative forces
were too diffusely spread to turn a speeding alpha particle
through more than ninety degrees.

The problem which must then have presented itself to
Rutherford was: if the existing theory of atomic structure
was wrong, and it was not a plum pudding after all, then what
on earth could replace it? Zigzags? Wavy lines? Corkscrews?
It could have been anything.

He took more than a year to work it out. It was always
necessary to Rutherford to be able to visualise his theories.
So, in response to a flash of inspiration, he built an enormous model. His alpha particle was a heavy electro-magnet
suspended on thirty feet of wire, and his atom was another
electro-magnet fixed to a table. He arranged the magnets so
that their equivalent and repelling electrical poles were the
ones which encountered one another first, and allowed the
giant alpha particle to swing horizontally towards the atom.
The pendulum swung towards its target, and instead of hitting

it, began to curve through the air before looping back again. Just like Geiger's alpha particles, it had been deflected by more than ninety degrees.

The only way that an atom could cause such behaviour in an oncoming alpha particle was if all its positive charge were focused in one small space. The analogy Rutherford had imagined was the curved trajectory of a comet as it came close to the sun. The comet was the alpha particle, and the sun – an atomic nucleus.

In the illustrious debating hall of the Royal Society, Walter and Nunn May sat to the side of Chadwick and huddled together, barely daring even to breathe. Every now and again something burst out of Nunn May and his finger shot up to point towards some elevated personage, and Walter had to restrain himself from grabbing his colleague's hand and shoving it back down firmly at his side. One by one the members who were due to give papers stood up and addressed the audience. It was a bit like a series of lectures, except that the audience consisted not of students but professors, and each of the speakers was more famous and brilliant than the last. Walter wished he could have brought his camera. Then maybe even Jim would understand.

Chadwick's speech seemed to the two young students to be the most accomplished of them all, partly out of partisanship and partly because they'd been more familiar with the topic beforehand. But when they left the hall and were served tea with all the dignitaries, it became clear that Chadwick had lost any interest in his recalcitrant guests. 'You will excuse me,' he said brusquely, and went off to gossip about cross-sections with his friends. Walter and Nunn May considered themselves dismissed, and wandered out onto the street.

'You see,' said Walter, as they meandered onto the Mall and into St James's Park, 'science is not a joke.'

'But you said before that it was.'

How to explain this particular subtlety? 'It is only a joke once you have understood how serious it is.'

'I always thought it was serious,' said Nunn May miserably, somehow implying that the whole thing had been Walter's fault for leading him astray.

Walter felt sorry for him. Nunn May was not used to Chadwick's moods and probably thought that this might be his Ph.D. place gone. Of course, he might be right.

'I think it's – sort of – like there's stages,' said Walter.

'Stages?'

'The more you give to it, the more serious it gets. And the more serious it gets, the funnier it gets. In the Cavendish, we're at it all day, and it matters immensely, so it can't help but be funny. Do you see?'

'I think so,' said Nunn May doubtfully.

'And of course someone like Chadwick—' He paused to find an example. 'It's like when I went to Lord Rutherford's house for dinner.'

'*Did* you?'

Walter's chest puffed. He struggled for his humility. 'And so will you, if you do your Ph.D. The thing I found strangest about it was how much they were laughing. They talked about nothing but science, and yet they were laughing louder than I've ever heard in my life. I couldn't understand it at the time.'

He paused.

'But I do now.'

The snow was irresistible. Suddenly he took off from the path and charged into it, dancing his footprints into its freshness. He spun round, grinning. Nunn May was following hesitantly.

'Oh, Alan,' he said, and saw Nunn May's chin rise with the compliment of the familiar name, 'I do love the snow!'

He turned again and ran towards the bandstand. With a great leap he was upon it. He sat down. Alan clomped through the snow to join him. They sat down and gazed at the snowy park.

'What do you understand now?' Alan demanded.

'People like Chadwick and Rutherford, when they get together at a dinner like that, love science so much that they find almost all of it funny. Because the rest of the time it is so important. But if they see us laughing about it, it offends them, because we haven't given half as much. Do you know what happened to Chadwick when he was a young man?'

'No.'

'He was studying under Rutherford in Manchester. He'd just finished his undergraduate degree, and he needed to get a scholarship to keep studying. Rutherford found him one, but the condition was that he had to study abroad.'

'Like you.'

'A bit like me. Except that Rutherford sent him to study in Berlin under Geiger. And it was 1913.'

'Oh God.'

'He was interned for the entire period of the war. The internment camp was a racetrack and they lived in the stables. They had to sleep five to a stall. *And he carried on with his experiments.*'

'But how?'

'He made an electroscope from firewood, lined it with tin foil and used beer glasses and teacups instead of laboratory beakers.'

'But what did he use for a radioactive source?'

'Toothpaste.'

'Toothpaste?'

'There were rumours that this particular brand of tooth-paste had radioactive properties, because of the very dazzling smile of the woman on the posters. The guards got hold of some of it for him. The chemical composition had him confused for a bit, because he wasn't used to dealing with such quantities of baking soda. But eventually he pinned it down. It was thorium. Traces of thorium.'

'How do you *know* all this?'

'Oh well. You just sort of absorb it. You know.' The dust of the Cavendish was thick with its stories. Walter knew he hadn't heard the half of them yet. 'Anyway, after the war Chadwick was sick and malnourished and could barely work, but Rutherford was moving from Manchester back to Cambridge, and he gave Chadwick a job. Things were a bit of a mess after the war, and Chadwick was so grateful to Rutherford that he did anything he could to help out. Of course the problem with Rutherford was always that he couldn't bear to buy anything.' Their professor's miserliness was on an epic scale. 'And whilst Rutherford himself might be capable of performing miracles with the simplest equipment, Chadwick knew from his time in Germany that the rest of them couldn't be expected to do the same. So he started saying that they needed a particular piece of apparatus and ordering it. He had to do it very carefully, of course, or Rutherford would get upset about the money.'

'They say he's turned down more funds for the laboratory than he's ever spent,' said Alan. 'Is that true, do you know?'

'Far more. But you can imagine that Chadwick was able to use what money there was so quietly and so sensibly that Rutherford barely noticed, and of course things did get much better. In the end Rutherford relied on him absolutely. And that was how Chadwick became Assistant Director.'

'He's a very good scientist, isn't he?'

'Yes.' Walter knew now that it was not normal for a new research student to be taken under the wing of such a senior member of staff. It had come about through luck, but now it was done, it was done for ever. In his wildest moments of daydreaming, the fact took on almost religious significance. Chadwick was not only Walter's mentor, he was one of Rutherford's most favoured protégés. Rutherford in turn had been the disciple of J.J. Thomson, the discoverer of the electron and now the Master of Walter's own college, Trinity, an old man with half-moon glasses and an alarming shock of white hair, who could still be found occupying his spare time conducting experiments in the basement of the Cavendish. And Thomson was taught by James Clerk Maxwell himself. The lineage went back almost to the scientific equivalent of the Garden of Eden.

5. THE PROTON

Like the electron, the proton is a stable subatomic particle. The two differ in that while an electron has a negative charge, the charge of the proton is positive. The charges of the two particles are equal, and cancel one another out, so that where an equal number of protons and electrons are found, the net charge is neutral.

The proton's mass is nearly two thousand times greater than that of the electron. And while the electron circles the atomic nucleus in a wide orbit, the proton sits at its heart. In the case of the lightest isotope of hydrogen, the nucleus actually consists of a single proton. Its positive charge is balanced by a single orbiting electron. Heavier elements have more protons at their core, and more electrons circling them. This means that the nuclei of all atoms have a positive charge, but that the electrons surrounding them are negative. That is the way things are.

Thomson's first two hypotheses about the electron – that it was a charged particle, and that it was a constituent of the atom – were true, and had been confirmed by the experience of the advancing years. The third, that it was the only constituent of the atom, was false. This became clear slowly, as more measurements were taken of the atomic nucleus and its charge. Once again it was Rutherford who made the discovery. He divided positive from negative and identified the electron's bigger, bolder brother.

He did so by breaking up the atom itself.

'Why, good afternoon!' said Mr Brinton as he opened the door to his house on the road climbing up from Kentish Town towards Hampstead Heath. He was a very little man, probably not yet forty, but with the mannerisms and demeanour of an energetic pensioner. 'You must be Mr Dunnachie! At least – I presume that *one* of you is Mr Dunnachie.'

Walter stepped in front of Alan and stuck out his hand. 'It's me!' he asserted. Alan had insisted on barging in on things once again.

'Most wonderful to meet. Reverend Barnes tells me that you are a young man of the most sterling qualities. And this is—?'

Walter took a reluctant step back. 'Alan Nunn May,' he grumbled.

'Good afternoon,' said Alan politely.

'Most pleasant to meet you, Mr Nunn May. Now, I must show a little courtesy and invite you both in.' Mr Brinton led them down some steps into a small, dark room stuffed to the brim with books and cushions. 'I believe that you have been engaged in some terribly erudite scientific activities this afternoon. Am I right?'

'Yes!' How nice of Barnes to have told him that.

'Most impressive. I'm afraid I have no head for that sort of thing. But we most certainly need the contribution of people who do. Would you like some tea?'

Walter and Alan squeezed themselves between the cushions and nodded enthusiastically. They'd been well furnished with tea at the Royal Society, but all the debating they'd done since had been thirsty work. As Mr Brinton pottered about with kettle and teapot, Walter took a look around him. The books lining the walls ranged from Euripides to Bertrand Russell. He smelt the warm, musty aroma of knowledge and suddenly felt very much at home.

'I'm most grateful to you for agreeing to see me at such short notice,' he called out to the kitchen.

'And me,' piped up Alan. Walter glared at him.

'It is the *greatest* pleasure,' said Brinton, beaming, bearing a tray of tea paraphernalia. 'This movement is in need of bright young things like yourselves.'

'Reverend Barnes said that you were involved in something called the Peace Army,' said Walter.

'I would not call myself a leading light. That honour must go to Maude Royden, who is really the *presiding genius* of the whole affair. And of course Dick Sheppard has lent it his considerable intellectual force. They are doing all the thinking and the organising. My role at present is a rather quieter one. I am writing a book about it.'

'A book?'

'Miss Royden and Dr Sheppard have made a number of inspiring speeches. But we have come to realise that the case for the Peace Army is too complex to be dealt with in the small space of time in which it is possible to hold an audience's attention. My intention is to write something which will enable people to see all the facts placed together, and then go away and reflect upon them in private. Of course I am rather under the pressure of time. The matter is so terribly urgent, as I have no doubt you're aware.'

'Mr Brinton,' intervened Alan.

'Yes?'

'I'm afraid I don't know very much about the peace move-ment. I've come along because I was with Walter at the meeting this afternoon, and he said that he was coming to see you, and I thought it sounded interesting. Can you tell me what the Peace Army is? It sounds like a rather contradictory idea.'

Mr Brinton looked pleased to be asked. 'The irony is deliberate,' he said. 'The name is supposed to make you think. After all, in this age we all agree that Peace is the thing for which it is every civilised nation's utmost duty to strive. And yet we are still ploughing considerable resources into maintaining armies. The point we are making is that if one is to have a band of men whose aim is to protect the nation's interests, then its guiding preoccupation ought to be Peace.'

The simplicity was beautiful. 'That is a very *good* point,' proclaimed Walter.

'But Mr Brinton,' said Alan, 'if our army is a Peace Army, how will we defend ourselves in a time of war? War requires killing in self-defence. And if I have understood the peace movement correctly, it is based on the principle that it is wrong to kill. The pacifists in the Great War refused to fight at all.'

What *cheek*, thought Walter in outrage, and waited for Brinton to crush him with another piece of sublime logic. But Brinton was smiling indulgently. 'There will be no need for us to defend ourselves from military attack,' he said, 'when war has been outlawed across the world. And that is what the Peace Army aims to achieve.'

'Oh, but surely,' objected Alan, and there was even a little scorn in his voice, despite the difference in age and wisdom between Brinton and himself, 'war can never be outlawed. Fighting is a fundamental element of human nature.'

Stop it, thought Walter, but Brinton continued to smile, as if he had heard it all before. 'I would hope that you would not claim it as an unconquerable element of your *own* nature,' he said. 'I would hope that you would consider yourself capable of restraining yourself from the impulse to strike the first blow.'

Exactly, thought Walter. Such restraint was difficult, but he had proved to himself that it was possible. He had not inflicted physical harm on a single human being since the day with James Gough in the school yard.

'Yes, but there is always someone else who is willing to strike the first blow,' said Alan, undaunted. 'And when they do, I must have the right to defend myself.'

Walter looked at Alan in discomfort. He seemed to have an answer for everything, as if he did not *want* there to be peace.

'Those people are criminals, Mr Nunn May,' said Brinton gravely. 'In the civil arena they are arrested and detained. The force of public opinion allows us to restrain them, not by retaliating using their own means, but by using the letter of the law. The same can be achieved in relations between nations, once we see sense.'

Yes, thought Walter triumphantly, wanting to stand up and dance around. He wished he had something to contribute to the debate.

Alan remained calm. 'But Mr Brinton,' he said, 'surely you see that the rule of law depends on having a strong police force which outnumbers the criminal population by some considerable margin. Even with this advantage, they have the power to use force if need be. I can't see how an equivalent can be found when it is a whole *nation* playing the part of the aggressor. That, after all, is supposed to be the role of the League of Nations, and with no police force, they have proven themselves to be powerless in enforcing their decisions. Yet any international police force would surely not be a *Peace* Army, but an army of the regular sort.' He ended triumphantly, and looked back at Brinton in expectation, with wide eyes.

Walter saw Brinton falter, and his heart sank. If this man could be outwitted by a precocious undergraduate, what chance did the Peace Army stand against the military machines of the world? 'Mr Nunn May,' said Brinton, 'you argue very well. In fact I would venture to say that you have been well trained. Is that not so?'

Alan had the grace to blush a little. 'We had a debating society at school,' he admitted.

'I am sure you were one of its most distinguished speakers. It is a great talent to have. I do not possess it myself. This is why my weapon is my pen. When I have finished my little book, I would be most gratified if you would do me the honour of reading it. Because I hope that when you understand all the facts, you will join us. There *is* a way to oppose force without using it oneself. And if we are to communicate this to the world, we need speakers like you.'

Alan looked confused. Suddenly Walter realised what had happened. He had stayed silent and now Brinton was favouring Alan above him, even though he'd argued against everything he'd said. Walter could not see why such an easy facility for debate, regardless of the truth, should be prized so highly. The truth was so clear. Surely all that was needed was to explain it properly? And Mr Brinton *had* explained it properly. Yet Alan's impertinent, juvenile logic had never failed. He had, Walter acknowledged to himself, won the argument. But the argument was not the *point*. Rhetoric was a screen for the truth, something to hide it behind.

He could not keep quiet any longer. 'I think you're entirely wrong,' he said to Alan.

Brinton and Alan both turned to stare at him in surprise.

'I know I've been keeping rather quiet,' said Walter. 'But you see we didn't have a debating society at my school and I don't have any fancy ways for winning arguments. But – but – don't you see – you talk about police forces, and armies, and what they do now as if the fact of them doing it now makes it all right. And it isn't all right. It's never all right to hurt another human being. Alan, however much I might want to hit you' – and he suddenly realised how uncomfortably close to the truth his example was, so he rushed through it – 'it would never be right to do so. I must always restrain myself. And if it's not all right for me, then it isn't all right for the country I live in. I can't have one rule for myself and another for the people who protect me.'

'But I am not a foreign army,' said Alan with smug contentment. 'I don't have a machine-gun pointed at your head. I don't have a sword poised over your neck. You are comparing things which are not alike.'

Hot with rage, Walter had a sudden image of a sword severing Alan's head from his body. 'They are entirely alike,' he shouted. 'They're all about people. It doesn't matter who is inflicting the damage, it is always people who get hurt.'

The cushions absorbed Walter's raucousness. He stopped, and saw in his companions' eyes an expression rather similar to that which he'd seen on the faces of those children in the school yard all that time ago. They were shocked.

'I'm sorry,' he mumbled. 'I didn't mean—'

Mr Brinton collected himself. 'Don't be sorry,' he said. 'Your passion is quite inspiring to me. It is a while since – well, anyway, thank you.'

Walter blushed with gratitude. 'Mr Brinton,' he said, 'I want to join the Peace Army.'

'I would be delighted if you could. But you don't know what it will involve.'

'I don't care. I want to defend Peace.'

'Mr Dunnachie, it would require the most extreme sacrifices. You are a young man. You have your life before you. I don't know—'

'What sacrifices? What is it?'

Brinton told him. Alan's eyes grew wider and wider in disbelief. But he restrained himself from comment, watching Walter for his reaction.

'Oh,' said Walter. 'Oh.'

'We will leave from Harwich in April at the latest.'

'I suppose it will be the spring vac—'

'Walter,' said Alan, 'it takes *weeks* to get to China. Term would have started before you even arrived. Chadwick would never stand for it.'

Barnes had asked him if he was prepared to make sacrifices and now it was clear what had been meant. Walter realised that his idea of sacrifice had been entirely romantic and insubstantial, involving, primarily, the defence and seduction of Grace Padgett. But Grace did not need to be defended and was not around to be seduced, and all he had left were his dreams of science and peace. It had never occurred to him that the two might be at odds. After his lifelong quest to come to the centre of the world, and such a long journey to get here, it seemed horribly futile to travel all the way back again. He didn't mind one bit the idea of risking his life. But he couldn't leave his equipment.

'I can't do it,' he confessed. 'I'm in the middle of my Ph.D. They don't have many places at the Cavendish. I would never be allowed back in.'

'I understand,' said Brinton gently. 'You have a great deal to lose. It is easy for me to forget that not everyone has the leisure with which I am blessed.'

'But I'll do anything else! Anything else! I'll make speeches! I'll write letters! Anything, Mr Brinton, just tell me and I'll do it! I've never done any public speaking. Except once. And that was just receiving a science prize— But I want to learn. I want it more than anything in the world.'

He ran out of breath.

'Thank you,' said Mr Brinton. 'I assure you I won't forget your promise. We need people like you.'

Walter wondered whether they really did. He did not feel very proud of himself. The opportunity to do something real and courageous in the cause of Peace had presented itself, and he had turned it down. And though he felt a certain amount of satisfaction in having silenced Alan, he knew that he had done so by losing his temper. A harsh word might be one hundred times better than a blow, but, even on that basis, his technique for winning arguments could not really be said to be any more admirable than Alan's.

'Are you ever homesick?' asked Alan on the way back to the station.

Walter had been lost in a lonely reverie about Grace. His attempt to join the peace movement had brought her closer than she'd been since he'd written her that foolish letter, and his failure to do so was whisking her away again. He stared at Alan, taken aback by his prescience, and supposed he ought to reply.

'Well, yes,' he confessed, 'sometimes.'

'Do you think you'll ever go back?'

'Of course!' A battalion of geese stormed across his grave, guns blazing. 'Why wouldn't I go back?'

'I always wanted to get out of Birmingham. I never thought I'd want to go back. There were times as a boy when I wished the whole place really was twelve thousand miles away.'

Walter relaxed a little, glad to have the attention turned away from himself. 'Why?' he asked.

'Oh, there's nothing wrong with my parents. But they're not – well, intellectual, you know.'

'Neither are mine. But they're *wonderful*.'

'Mine are too, I suppose, in their way. I'm only just realising that now. Really I should never have wanted to go away at all. Oh, Walter – We should never be ashamed. Should we?'

Walter could not in the least work out what he was driving at. 'Ashamed?'

'What you were saying before about not having a debating society at school, and all that sort of thing. I suppose if you live all the way out there it's even more difficult than living in Birmingham.'

'What do you mean? It wasn't all the way out there. It was where I was.' He knew that Alan was being tactless, but Walter could not make enough sense of what he was saying to rise above it as he wanted.

Alan saw his face, and blustered. 'Sorry,' he said. 'I'm most dreadfully sorry. I didn't mean – to do that. It was wrong. You know I don't believe – in all that – at all.'

'All *what*?'

'Oh, colonials, you know. Class, or whatever you want to call it in your particular case. It's all nonsense. Men are born equal. Truly, Walter, they are.'

Class, or whatever you want to call it in your particular case. Walter felt cold. He had never let himself realise that he was a particular case. Alan had made him sound like an Indian. There were Indians in the lab. Walter liked them, and knew that they suffered the most appalling problems with discrimination, particularly from landladies, and he felt very sorry for them. He'd never allowed himself to see how he looked from outside, as an outsider, and that people might feel sorry for him too. 'I never thought I wasn't equal,' said Walter in a small, tight voice.

'Of course you didn't. But – you know, some people do. Without realising it. They're fools to themselves and to everyone else. We have to destroy all that, you know, Walter, you and me.'

Suddenly the words were beginning to sound familiar.

There was enough of this sort of thing bandied around by the hotheads of Trinity for him to recognise it when he heard it. Walter shrugged off the insinuations of inferiority in relief and gave his new friend a stern look. 'Alan,' he said, 'you aren't a communist, are you?'

'Would you despise me if I were?'

'*Are* you?'

'I haven't decided yet. I might join or I might not. It's difficult.'

Walter prickled, and found himself steering away from Alan's path. He'd always made sure he kept clear of the communists, and until now he'd done his best to avoid Alan too. The two combined in one person was anathema indeed. But now it seemed somehow too late to go back.

'I don't agree with your pacifism,' said Alan, trying again, 'but I respect it. I'm glad to meet someone who feels strongly about something at last.'

The compliment, however welcome, made him burn with the same sense of fraudulence he'd felt when he was with Grace. 'There are lots of people around who feel strongly about communism,' Walter retorted.

'It's all a pose. Can't you see that? They're all aristocrats playing. I've never really felt I belonged with them. And yet the people at home – who had real reasons for wanting equality – never read Marx, or knew much about revolution, except that it was probably something that might stop them from having their tea on time. It's all so confusing.'

Walter felt an overwhelming impulse to ask Alan what his father did for a living, and knew he must not. No one in Cambridge had ever forced him to answer that question. He had always been glad of not having been asked. The accent was burden enough, without having to explain that he came from a mining family. His father's elevation to the post of chandler's clerk, his own scholarship at Newcastle

High and the self-consciousness of Sydney might have beaten the extremes of his native dialect out of him, but however straitened his vocabulary, the accent came shining through. For a second he wondered what this new life was doing to him. He'd wanted the whole world, but he had never in a million years dreamed that it might stop him from being able to go home.

'Sometimes I just want to stand up and change everything,' said Alan wistfully. 'And then I remember the lecture I need to go to.'

Walter grabbed at the flicker of recognition. 'Like me not being able to go to China because of my Ph.D.'

'Exactly like. It's difficult, isn't it? Balancing the science with this sort of thing. I mean science is the most wonderful thing I've ever known. But sometimes it seems a bit remote. A bit irrelevant.'

'Yes,' said Walter. And looking sideways at Alan for a moment, he realised that this was the first time since he'd left the ship that anyone had asked him to be who he really was.

'I did think some of what Mr Brinton said was interesting, you know,' said Alan. 'That's why I was asking so many questions. The Peace Army itself may be a bit off-centre, but I can understand the rest. I don't much like the idea of violence either.'

'Perhaps we're both working for the same cause after all,' said Walter. 'Just in different ways.'

'Perhaps we are. Except that neither of us is doing much working for it yet. We're both too busy with science.'

They strode on into the gathering darkness as the snow fell around them. The flakes were piling deep on the road, falling in great fluffy slopperbumps – a word Walter could only have heard in England, and which he had stored up with the rest of his accumulating knowledge. He held out his hand and an inch-wide constellation of snow crystals alighted softly on his glove. It frayed at the edges, settling, puncturing its structure on the sharp edges of the wool. He closed his hand over it and it was gone.

'It's lovely, isn't it?' he breathed.

Alan and Walter stopped on the pavement and looked up. The moon cast the shadows of trees in crisp spiky shapes onto the snow. What colour was it, in the darkness? Not white exactly, not grey, for there was no mixing of the blackness of the sky with its whiteness. Silver suited its mood but was not correct. It shone, but was not metallic. It seemed to give its own light, like the radium that Otto Hahn handed to the Kaiser just after the war when they had wondered at its shining.

'It's beautiful,' said Alan.

They glanced at each other and saw equal fervour in one another's eyes.

8

Alan Nunn May pulled on his gloves and took the key from the hook on the wall. He turned out the lights, performed his final checks, and left his flat for the day.

He looked up at the dry scorch of the pale clouded sky and felt his retinas bleach. Light and air themselves were enough to hurt his skinless soul. I have no substance, he thought, no shell, and now even my shadow has gone.

His shadow had vanished for more than a week now, and to begin with he'd thought it might be flu. Alan had always worried about that cough. *You ought to get that seen to*, he'd thought. But now it was pretty certain. The man was gone. It felt like the silence he'd read about in the British newspapers when he was in Canada, when a doodlebug's engine cut out. Now it was only a matter of time.

Without his shadow, Alan felt naked and afraid. He had started having nightmares, arms reaching from walls, faces behind curtains, standard-issue stuff. Then, when his silent screams had woken him, he'd lain and entertained ludicrous fantasies about the possibility of being killed. In that dead time, it seemed possible. So many illusions about the honour and integrity of his own country had been destroyed that a discreet murder did not seem so very much greater a step. They would do anything, he thought at night, to keep this quiet. And sometimes, when he'd finished persuading himself that his dressing gown did not conceal a masked assassin, he considered taking its cord, making a loop, and sparing them the trouble.

During the day he knew that he was not worth a bullet or a blade. Some private deal had doubtless been made between British and American diplomats, and his destiny was part of the currency of exchange. But as the sun rose over the chimney stacks and lit the frosted grass of Holland Park, he knew that death was not the only fate worth fearing.

'Walter,' said Grace, 'I've worked out what it is about Alan turning up that has upset you so much.'

Walter breathed in. He was not in the mood for a great Grace theorisation.

'It was all very well him being in Canada. He might have been doing something you didn't like, but he was over there. But now he's back – and *particularly* back at London University – you have to accommodate it. He's part of our lives again.'

'He's always been part of our lives.'

'You know what I mean. Anyway, we might as well accept it. Get on with it. I thought we could invite him to dinner.'

'*No.*'

'What do you mean, no? We always would have done in the past. Now he's made contact, it would be rude to pretend that he's not around. Surely you see that?'

Walter stared at her in anger and realised what she was doing. To stop her, he would have to explain his reasons. He was trapped.

'I've thought of someone else to invite as well,' said Grace.

'Who?'

'He's a young chap who's been hanging around the church. Thinking of becoming a Methodist. He expressed an interest in meeting you, as a matter of fact. Because of Peace.'

'Alan won't want to talk about Peace.'

'The pair of you always end up talking about it anyway. The Hendersons won't make any difference to that.'

'Why, thank you,' said Henderson, startled by his serendipity. He was not used to strokes of luck.

'But there's one condition. You must bring your wife.'

Oh golly. How was he going to explain it to Phoebe? He looked at Mrs Dunnachie nervously. There wasn't really any choice.

'All right,' he said.

'Jolly good! There'll be another guest, hopefully. An old friend of Walter's who's just come back from Canada. They'll probably talk science a bit. You don't mind that, do you?'

'No! Not at all!' His heart was racing.

An evening with Dunnachie and Nunn May. He would hear what they talked about, see how they treated one another, perhaps even find out why Nunn May had visited Dunnachie in the first place. The decision to join the church was miraculously justified. There was a chance he might fulfil Aitken's nebulous mission after all.

'Is that Dr Alan Nunn May?' trilled the woman at the other end of the line.

He knew the voice. But he did not know to whom it belonged. For a moment Alan could say nothing, fearful of the consequences of making contact with it.

'Yes,' he said in the end, weakly.

'Alan! Alan, dear, it's Grace. Grace Dunnachie.'

Grace. Of course. He should have expected it. Then he was filled with confusion, and fear, and something infinitely more bumpy and uncomfortable. It was an emotion from which he thought he'd freed himself.

Hope.

'How are you?'

The question should have been innocuous but it was not. Her words transcended their formality, and demanded a truthful answer.

'I'm—' There was no answer, truthful or otherwise. The entity referred to as Alan Nunn May was no longer a thing to which either well-being or its opposite could apply. He stumbled out a reply. 'I'm very well, thank you.'

'It's wonderful to hear that you're back.' She got straight to the point. 'We want to see you properly. Come round for dinner on Friday.'

We want to see you properly? Walter wanted to see him? After what had happened last time? 'Grace—'

'Alan, I have no idea what has gone on between the pair of you but I don't mind telling you that I think it's nonsense. Please come.'

Then it was all her, not him. The hope shuddered out of him once more.

From the start he'd always told himself that whatever else he might betray, he would never betray his friends. To that end, he'd made an effort to see no one since his return to England except in the most limited professional capacity, lest he stain them with his indelible curse.

Except – he'd never stood a chance of keeping his vow, not with Walter. There had been times in Canada when memories had been all he'd had to hold himself together. Bright light, clear words and, always, Walter's infuriating doggedness. When he'd read his old friend's name on a committee list, a wild pensiveness had taken hold of him. He'd tried not to go, but in the end had not been able to help himself.

It had been a mistake.

'I'm really rather busy,' said Alan.

'Alan, I am married to a scientist. I know what you mean by busy. You mean that you would rather bury yourself in equations than converse with human beings. But you are terribly good company when you choose to be. Be a dear and come and see us.'

He wanted to see her. Their relationship had never been easy. In their youth it had been spiked by rivalry, each of them battling for Walter's soul. Walter had kept her a secret, mooning over her for years, and once Alan had finally heard about her he'd imagined a standard female, an amalgamation of all the fiancées and wives he'd ever come across. But in the flesh she had stormed into their cloistered lives like a battleship in swan's clothing, accepting nothing, disturbing everything, dressing up Walter's opinions in outrageous garb and claiming them as his own. And Walter had seemed to grow taller in her presence, more confident and articulate, a calm and reasonable foil to her storminess. She deferred to him always. Alan had watched them together, and had felt the same alarm and disbelief as when sodium was plunged into dilute hydrochloric acid and fizzed and spat and ended up with something as clear and natural as salty water. The loneliness of being outside that reaction was something he'd conquered over time. He'd learnt how to be a catalyst, if no more. It was strange, after having resented her for so long, that now he missed them both.

Was it one more chance?

He took a deep breath. 'Yes,' he said. 'That would be lovely.'

Walter sat up in his office, forcing himself to write, barely leaving himself a pause between paragraphs. The impending meeting with Alan was hovering at the edge of his thoughts and it was the only way of keeping it out.

The story was no comfort to him. It was an alternative pain, the action of a migraine sufferer pounding his head against a wall.

6. DISINTEGRATION

In 1917 Rutherford was still in Manchester. But his talented young collaborators were gone. One was in Berlin. Another was in an internment camp in Germany. Four were in the trenches. A fifth was dead.

He was alone. He had very little equipment. He carried on.

It was long since known that the radioactive element radium emitted alpha particles, and Rutherford had been studying the effects of these emissions on various substances for a number of years. In 1917 and 1918 he tried excluding all other gases from a vacuum tube and fired his alpha particles into pure air. The result was an increase in the volume of hydrogen in the tube. Rutherford had a hunch that the hydrogen was being emitted from the nitrogen in the air, and so he replaced the air with pure nitrogen. On being bombarded with the alpha radiation, the amount of hydrogen increased even more.

The hydrogen was in fact created as hydrogen nuclei, or, as Rutherford now named them, protons. The impact of the alpha particles had knocked a proton out of the nucleus of a nitrogen atom, leaving an isotope of oxygen. Alchemy had taken place once more. Only this time it was not the discovery of a naturally occurring phenomenon. It was the first artificial disintegration of the atom. Rutherford had broken through its barriers and had knocked a chink out of its core.

Alan glanced at his watch. The students were fidgeting. It was time to bring the lecture to a close. But he did not want it to end. The journey to Watford seemed immeasurably frightening.

'All right,' he said to the class. 'That's it. Have a good evening.'

They filed out. He fiddled with his lecture notes, arranging them into perfect order before putting them back into his briefcase. Then he wiped the equations from the board and went over to the door to fetch his hat and coat. He fumbled rather putting them on, getting his arms tangled up in his sleeves. When he was properly robed, he turned round, and found the door blocked by a very fat man.

Alan jumped backwards.

'Dr Nunn May, I presume,' said the very fat man.

Alan's eyes shut.

'If you wouldn't mind sparing me a few moments to have a quick word.'

The man turned without further formality, and left the lecture theatre.

Alan followed him out.

'Mrs Henderson!' said Mrs Dunnachie gaily. 'How lovely to meet you at last. I've heard so much about you.'

Phoebe took off her hat and handed it to her hostess. She was wearing make-up and her nicest frock, and smiling. George stared at his wife in pride.

'It's so kind of you to invite us to dinner,' said Phoebe. 'We don't get out much these days. George is always so busy working.'

'So I hear,' said Mrs Dunnachie. 'To tell you the truth I have the same trouble with Walter. But at least Walter doesn't work nights. Except when things are really hectic.'

They laughed together.

Breaking it to Phoebe had been remarkably easy.

'We've been invited to dinner,' he'd told her. 'Through work.'

'Really?' Her eyes had lit up straightaway. 'Who is it?'

'They're a very nice couple. He's an academic. She used to be a teacher. They've got two children. They're Australian.'

'Australian? That's rather outlandish.' But she'd looked pleased, and he knew why. Australian meant 'not posh'. There would be no social strata to scale, at least none they knew about.

'Yes. Now, Phoebe. It's rather complicated. I'm going to have to explain a few things to you.'

She had looked at him expectantly.

'You know that the work I do is rather confidential.'

'Of course I do.'

'And – well – though I met them through work, they don't know that I was working at the time.'

Her face had given nothing away.

'I actually met them through the Methodist church.'

She had not been able to hide her surprise then. 'The Methodist church?'

'Yes. And I had to explain why I was at church during the day, so I said that I worked night shifts.'

'For the civil service?'

'Yes.'

'That's a rather strange thing to say.'

'Yes. Well, anyway, it's what I said. They know you're Church of England. But they think we live in Watford. In a street called Jubilee Road.'

'I've never been to Watford. I'll have to have a look at a map. Did you say we'd lived there long?'

It was very odd. She'd picked up straightaway that she was being briefed, and had asked all the necessary questions, without asking to know anything she wouldn't need. Now that she was in the Dunnachies' dining room, acting the part, it occurred to him that she would be an awful lot better at this job than he was.

'It's so nice to meet people in Watford,' she was saying,

while Dunnachie provided them with glasses and fruit juice. 'We had so many friends where we used to live in Clapham. It takes a while to get used to somewhere new.'

'Have you made any friends through the church?'

'Well. They're a bit tight-knit, you know.'

'Your husband has told you about going to the Methodist church now, then?'

'It took me a while to get it out of him. I was jolly glad when I found out, I can tell you. I was wondering why he was acting so strangely.'

'You see!' Mrs Dunnachie's whole face flared with triumph. 'Didn't I tell you, Mr Henderson?'

'You did indeed,' said George. 'I followed your advice.'

'Men never understand how much we'll accept, as long as they just tell us about it.'

The two women smiled at one another. Oh goodness, thought George, they are allies already.

'Do you need me to do anything in the kitchen?' said Dunnachie.

'That's fine, darling. It's all under control.'

George glanced furtively at Dunnachie. It was the first time he'd had the chance to have a proper look at the man on whom he was spying. He had been afraid that Dunnachie might behave like his old science teacher, but Mr Furness had been a choleric and irascible man, who had gloried in making his pupils feel foolish. This man was nothing like that. He was not tall, but he was slim and athletic in build, and there was a gentleness in his eyes that made George think he would never shout at anyone for being stupid. Still, George was afraid. He could sense the presence of a Mind, which surely stretched far beyond the confines of that head, and further into the reasons for George's presence than he knew about himself.

'Do take a seat,' said Mrs Dunnachie, and showed George to his chair, while her husband pulled the one opposite back for Phoebe. 'We are waiting for one more guest, as you can see. His name is Alan Nunn May. But he's a scientist, like Walter, so doubtless he's got caught up with his work.'

George wondered what would happen when Nunn May saw him. He had always appeared to be unaware of George's presence, but now he was not so sure that it was any more than an appearance. Would he start, and stare? In a way it might be better if Nunn May did recognise him. Because George needed to watch Walter Dunnachie's reaction. If there was any sign of him understanding Nunn May's concern, George would know that he was in on it.

Whatever *it* was.

'Anyway,' said Mrs Dunnachie, 'I hope he gets a move on.'

'Do you mind terribly,' said Alan, 'if I make a phone call? I'm expected for dinner.'

'Feel free,' said Aitken, and gestured at the phone on his large, leather-clad desk. 'Dial 9 for the operator.'

Alan picked up the receiver and then stopped with his finger over the dial. He stared at the phone. No. He'd have to say the number to the operator.

'It doesn't matter,' he said, and replaced the receiver.

'Are you sure?'

'Yes.'

'Women can be very difficult if you stand them up for dinner.'

'It's not a woman. Well— That's fine.'

'If you're absolutely sure.'

'Presumably I will be able to go along later?'

'Oh, doubtless, if we make good progress.'

Alan's heart sank. In that case they were likely to be here all night.

*   *   *

'Well,' said Mrs Dunnachie. 'The time has come, the walrus said, to leave the blighter to it and tuck in.'

But she did not move. George and Phoebe waited in expectation.

'Walter,' said Mrs Dunnachie sharply.

Dunnachie jumped. 'Pardon?'

'I was just saying that we are going to have to stop waiting for Alan and serve up. Don't you agree?'

'Oh yes. Most definitely.'

She turned away from him in annoyance. 'If you'll just bear with me a moment,' she said to George and Phoebe, 'I'll sort out the first course. There's one thing in our favour. The soup can't have spoiled.'

Without her, the dining room fell into silence. George examined the tablecloth. Peace. Somehow he ought to lead the conversation on to Peace. He did not have a clue how to do it.

'It's a shame about your friend,' said Phoebe brightly to Dunnachie.

He did not appear to hear her. The pause stretched into embarrassment.

'Terribly nice tablecloth,' commented George.

'So, Dr Nunn May. I've had enough of this shilly-shallying. I know you want to get on too, so let's cut straight to the point.'

Alan sat as still as he could.

'I believe that you are perfectly aware that I know what you have done,' said Aitken. 'I can detail your actions if you insist. But it would seem – superfluous – to cause us both discomfort in the retelling, when we are both quite cognisant of what your actions were, and when you know full well the extent of my knowledge.'

Alan looked into the man's cold eyes. He really does believe it, he thought. He thinks I have been told what is known about me.

'Mr Aitken, I can assure you most categorically that what I know about what you know is limited to what you have told me this evening.'

Aitken's mouth opened in preparation for speech, then shut again. Oh God, thought Alan. He had as good as admitted that there was something for Aitken to know. And Aitken had chosen not to pounce on it.

'Whom are you protecting?' snapped Aitken. 'Is it the French?'

Alan's face crumpled. 'The French—' He could not afford to leave sentences unfinished. 'The French were just French, Mr Aitken.'

'The British, then. The Canadians. Who is it?'

'When I was in Montreal I was working very hard. I talked about work with my associates and had time for very little else. Since I returned I have had no contact with anyone connected with the project.'

'Why not?'

'Pardon?'

'You worked closely with those men for several years. Why cut off all contact? *Whom are you protecting?*'

I am protecting everyone I know, he thought. I am protecting everyone who has ever known me. He thought of Grace and her spoiled dinner, and of the outrage in Walter's eyes. He was not sure he wanted to go back out into the world after this. The safest thing now would be to give himself up. He teetered on the verge of confession, and then, seeing the impassive malevolence of his adversary, could not do it.

'I am protecting no one,' he said. 'I am just getting on with my life.'

Aitken stared at him. Alan had to look away.

'All right, Nunn May.' There was a new sharpness in his voice. 'Shall we start again, at the beginning?'

Who are these people? thought Walter. They were not Grace's type at all. Too slow, too uncultured, too ordinary. The man in particular seemed rather dense. His wife had more to say for herself, but most of it was pretty banal. But then Grace did have a habit of picking up lame dogs now and then. He wondered what she believed to be the particular affliction of these specimens. They seemed reasonably well-adjusted in their mediocrity.

He looked at Grace. She was looking very pretty tonight, her eyes very bright and her hair sticking out rather wildly as it always did when she was animated. The old swell of pride rushed through him. He had always loved watching her captivate others. Tonight she had limited her vocabulary and her topics of conversation to a level which could be understood by her guests, and yet was managing to be as entertaining as ever. But it was not quite right. It was not like the old days, when the guests had been his colleagues from the university, and the talk had been of science and literature, politics and art.

Then he realised that he had not invited a single colleague to dinner since their return to London.

'You see I have not seen any of my brothers or sisters since I left Australia,' she was saying. 'And that was more than ten years ago now.'

Her voice was still jolly but her eyes had creased a little with sadness. And Walter saw what it was. She was lonely. He felt a stab of terrible remorse and wanted to take her in his arms.

'My brother was in the Navy,' said Mrs Henderson abruptly. 'He was killed in the Arctic.'

Walter's fork clanked hard against his plate. He clutched its bone handle.

'Oh, I am sorry,' said Grace in a rush. 'Here I am boring everyone with my silly troubles, and forgetting as always what everyone else has had to deal with. Mrs Henderson, you must accept my apologies.'

'It's all right,' said Mrs Henderson dully. 'I'm not supposed to talk about it any more anyway, am I?'

'Oh, Mrs Henderson! Phoebe! You can talk about it as much as you like!'

No, thought Walter, she must not. He began to feel sick.

Mrs Henderson started speaking very quickly. 'They said at the time that the supplies to Russia were crucial to keep them in the war, that we would go under if they did not continue. But no one mentions the Arctic any more. I've only seen anything about once, when it was said that it was a terrible disaster. They never said that at the time. Was it, do you think?'

Grace looked rather confused. 'The Arctic? I'm afraid I was more preoccupied with the Pacific. You see, that's where most of the Australian forces were fighting. I can't really remember much about the Arctic.'

Mrs Henderson frowned, her eyes growing red with the beginnings of tears, and addressed Walter instead. 'Dr Dunnachie,' she said. 'Surely you must remember. Was it a terrible disaster, do you know?'

Walter said nothing.

'Phoebe,' said Henderson, looking very embarrassed, 'Dr Dunnachie was a conscientious objector.'

'Oh,' said Mrs Henderson, as if she did not see the relevance of this at all.

'We're both pacifists,' intervened Grace quickly. 'But that doesn't mean that we don't see how great a sacrifice was made by those who gave their lives. It doesn't mean that we're—' She stumbled and stopped.

'It's all so difficult, isn't it?' Phoebe burst out. 'There isn't a day when I don't think of Leonard. But it's – unmentionable, somehow. We are supposed to be all right now. We won.'

Once Walter would calmly have explained the ways in which they were all right and those in which they were not. Meanwhile, Grace would have bobbed up and down like a harridan, getting steamed up. Now the positions were reversed. She was in control of herself, speaking kindly to their guest, while his own head was a ferment of emotion. He did not know when or how it had changed. All he knew was that he could suppress his opinions no longer. '*We* did not win,' he said sharply.

Phoebe looked frightened and confused. 'The Australians?'

'The pacifists. We were fighting for Peace. We were fighting to stop the killing. Your brother was killed. We lost.'

'But there is peace now,' said Henderson with the sort of slow-witted simplicity that was always guaranteed to enrage Walter.

'The rate of killing has subsided. But the war machines grind on.'

'Walter—' Grace was looking nervously at Mrs Henderson. 'Walter, we should probably change the subject.'

You wanted me to talk about Peace, thought Walter in fury. And now surely she could see why he didn't. The things he had to say were not very nice.

'No, I want to know!' said Mrs Henderson. 'You're talking about us and the Russians, aren't you?'

'The Russians. The Americans. The British. The French. Nothing has ended. The hatred continues and we are expected to support it just as we were expected to support it during the war.'

'But this is what I cannot understand. Leonard died helping the Russians to fight.'

'And the British once fought with the Germans against the

French. This country has fought most peoples who have come near it at one point or another. On occasions it has seen fit to travel thousands of miles to export warfare to other continents.'

There was silence. All three of his companions seemed to have been frozen at the top of an inward breath. Walter felt a grim satisfaction.

Henderson shoved a forkful of food into his mouth and then spoke. Walter could see the lumps of potato between tongue and teeth. 'I was just saying earlier,' he said to Grace, 'what a very nice tablecloth this is.'

Walter snorted with laughter. Then he felt a sharp stab of pain to his ankle. Grace was glaring at him with a fury that might have evaporated a lesser man.

'You know,' said Walter, leaning down to rub his bruised ankle, but feeling a most inappropriate levity, 'I think it might be time for pudding.'

He stood in the kitchen, trying to block out the sound of their chatter, and felt as though he were about to explode, though whether with rage or laughter he did not know.

Alan would have laughed too, he thought. Where was Alan now?

'You may as well go,' said Aitken.

A kind of euphoria swept over Alan. He felt victorious, as though he had won life from the brink of death.

It was close to midnight. If he was quick he could still catch the tube. He hurried through the emptying streets, the water spraying from his umbrella and shoes. He reached the river and looked up for a moment at the waves of fairy lights marking its banks.

And then he remembered. Grace's dinner.

It was too late to go traipsing up to Watford now. But he ought at least to ring.

He stared at the river and a wave of anger rose in him so violently that he almost retched.

'Damn you all!' he hissed at the empty air.

It was the interminable guilt he could not bear. He carried it with him always, and now, just when he had found a moment of release, the new, stupid guilt of having missed a dinner party intruded and brought it all back.

His umbrella fell to his side. The rain began to seep into his eyebrows. Alan steadied himself against the railings and tried to counter his emotions with reason. He could not blame Grace for inviting him to dinner. Nor was it his fault that he had not turned up. The appointment had been of the most unexpected and unavoidable kind.

Whose fault was it, then? As he contemplated the multitude of forces that had led him to this place, the feeling of liberation he'd experienced on leaving Aitken's office slipped away with the river's flow. One way and another, every incident in his life had conspired to bring him into this trap.

This was not freedom. He thought back to Aitken's expression when he had released him, and knew that the authorities had not conceded defeat. They would be back for him in their own time, when it suited their purposes best.

He considered ringing Walter. It would be expected that he at least make some excuse. But the thought of any such explanation was surreal.

Damn you, *Walter*, thought Alan. Because it might have been in his power to save him. And when Alan had needed him most, Walter had turned him away. Now it was too late.

He turned his back to the river. The yellow of a taxi light shone through the drizzle. He raised his arm.

9

7. THE THIRD ELEMENTARY PARTICLE

In 1918 James Chadwick was released from an internment camp in Germany and returned to his home in Manchester

7. THE THIRD ELEMENTARY PARTICLE

In 1932

7. THE THIRD ELEMENTARY PARTICLE

In 1919 Rutherford was appointed Cavendish Professor at Cambridge University and asked his old pupil, James Chadwick, to join him

7. THE MOST HIDDEN RAY

In February 1932

7. THE MOST HIDDEN RAY

On 25 February 1932

Walter was in his eyrie above Gordon Street. The sky was close to the windows, the bleary clouds hanging wet at their panes. A ball of crumpled paper toppled from his overflowing waste-paper basket. He kicked it against the wall. It bounced back and hit him.

He had thought that seeing Alan again was the last thing

he wanted. But now Alan had rejected the chance to spend an evening with him, and had also failed to make any acknowledgement of the rejection. It was as if he did not exist. Or as if Walter did not exist. He did not know which.

Something old and fresh touched his nostrils, and the longing for the way things used to be pulsed a hard ache from the bones in his nose through to the back of his throat and the sides of his forehead. He blinked, and then quickly raised his left hand to catch the drop of salt water on the top of his forefinger.

On 25 February 1932 Walter had arranged to meet Alan for lunch. He emerged from the laboratory at midday and fought his way through the clutch of men standing with their notebooks right in front of the door.

'Excuse me,' he said tautly as their necks craned round him to see inside. They ignored him. He pulled the door shut behind him, almost trapping their noses, and pushed his way past.

Alan was waiting on the street. 'Who are those people?'

'Journalists,' said Walter breathlessly.

'But why?'

'There's been a bit of a development. I'll tell you about it when we get to the café.'

They went to a restaurant called Little Italy, which was Alan's choice. It had no connection with Italy except for a watercolour of Venice over the stairs.

'The Croque Monsieur is terribly good,' recommended Alan.

It was the cheapest thing on the menu, so Walter ordered it.

'What's going on?' demanded Alan.

Walter did not know where to start. People had been rushing about all morning and his blood was still racing with the adrenalin. 'Dr Chadwick has made a great discovery,' he said.

'When?'

'Just over the last three weeks. He finished yesterday and is busy writing a letter to *Nature*. The journalists have been trying to interrupt him all morning. He's in a frightful mood.'

'But what's the discovery?'

Walter paused. This was the moment. The old assumptions were as dust and everything was new and unfamiliar. He had been looking forward to the pleasure of imparting the surprise all morning. 'A new particle,' he said.

The expression on Alan's face rewarded him. Walter grinned inanely.

'What do you mean?'

'I mean just what I said,' said Walter. 'He's found a new particle. It's as big as the proton and it's found in the nucleus of every element except hydrogen. Every other atomic nucleus has as many of them in it as protons. Some have more.'

'Every element? But—'

'I know,' said Walter. 'We're going to have to rewrite everything. Relearn everything.' But he was still beaming. However daunting a task it was, they would be the first to do it in the whole world. It had happened in the room next to him, and the news was only just beginning to break. Perhaps even the great scientists across the seas – Einstein, Bohr, Heisenberg, Schrödinger – did not know it yet. Walter had been messing around trying to liberate the new particles for himself all morning. He had failed owing to faulty equipment, but at least he had tried.

'But when did he do it? This *morning*?'

'Of course not. That's one of the most marvellous things. It's taken him twelve years.'

'Twelve years? But I don't understand. Why didn't we know? Did – did you know?'

Walter felt his mood cloud over a little. 'No,' he had to admit.

'And why don't we know anyway? If it's so big, and it's in everything? The state of science is so advanced these days.'

'Well, you see, it's a very special kind of particle.' Walter stopped. The waitress had arrived with the Croques Monsieur and they had to move their elbows to make way for the plates. They let her put them down on the table and then ignored their food.

'Special in what way?'

Walter did not want to relinquish his authority on the matter, but he was struggling rather to get his head round the new concept. He screwed up his face with the effort, and then a phrase popped into his head.

'It's a particle of very few properties. In fact it has almost no characteristics at all.'

'*Pardon?*'

Walter began to smile.

'Walter, you're pulling my leg. It's – it's not April Fool's Day. Is it? It's February. You mustn't play jokes. It's serious. At least, it is to me.'

'I'm not pulling your leg.'

'You can't be telling me that Chadwick's discovered the *Fewtron*.'

'As good as. No electrical charge. No tracks. No readings.' His voice was rising dramatically in emulation of Ted Nicolls. He lowered it again. 'Chadwick's calling it the neutron.'

Alan's mouth gaped open. Walter opened his own and stuffed a mouthful of Croque Monsieur into it in triumph.

7. A PARTICLE WITH ZERO CHARGE

In 1920 Rutherford gave the Bakerian Lecture at the Royal Society for an unprecedented second time. Tradition dictated that the lecture was used to sum up the achievements of the past year. Rutherford followed the usual format, and explained the present understanding of the 'nuclear consti-tution', reflecting on the contribution made by his successful transmutation of the nitrogen atom. Into the midst of this retrospective, however, he inserted a nugget of speculation.

He suggested 'the possible existence of an atom of mass one which has zero nucleus charge'. The words 'atom' and 'particle' were at that time fairly synonymous. He meant that there might be such a thing as a particle with the same mass as a proton, yet which disguised its existence through its neutrality.

'Such an atom would have very novel properties. Its exter-nal field would be practically zero, except very close to the nucleus, and in consequence it should be able to move freely through matter. Its presence would probably be difficult to detect by the spectroscope, and it may be impossible to contain it in a sealed vessel.'

Amongst his audience was his young colleague, James Chadwick, whom he had brought to the lecture with him. He listened to the greatest ever flight of fancy taken by a man whom he'd heard say many times that to indulge in theory without backing it up with experiment was to 'draw a blank cheque on eternity'. Like most in the audience, Chadwick was sceptical.

But Rutherford's reasons for imagining such a thing went beyond any single observation. That winter, Rutherford invited Chadwick to help him with the work which would extend the nitrogen transmutations to heavier elements. In his early work at Manchester University, Chadwick had made himself a reputation with Rutherford for being quite handy as a chemist, and so it was partly on this basis that Rutherford enlisted his support. 'But also, I think,' said Chadwick later, 'he wanted company to support the tedium of counting in the dark – and to lend an ear to his robust rendering of "Onward Christian Soldiers".'

The technician, Mr Crowe, prepared the apparatus, evacuated it, put the various sources in place and made whatever arrangements had been agreed for that particular session.

'Now, Crowe,' said Rutherford, 'put in a fifty centimetre screen.'

'Yessir.'

'Why don't you do what I tell you – put in a fifty centimetre screen.'

'I have, sir.'

'Put in twenty more.'

'Yessir.'

'Why the devil don't you put in what I tell you, I said twenty more.'

'I did, sir.'

'There's some damned contamination. Put in two fifties.'

'Yessir.'

'Ah, it's all right, that's stopped 'em! Crowe, my boy, you're always wrong until I've proved you right! Now we'll find their exact range!'

Then Crowe darkened the room and left the two scientists to record the results. They had to spot the particles by watching for scintillations on a screen. The scintillation method was indispensable to much of Rutherford's research into radioactivity. 'In a dark room,' he wrote, 'the surface of the screen is seen as a dark background dotted with brilliant points of light which come and go with great rapidity. This beautiful experiment brings vividly before the observer the idea that the radium is shooting out a stream of projectiles each of which causes a flash of light on striking the screen.'

But before these effects could be properly observed, it was necessary for the experimenters to let their eyes adjust. Rutherford and Chadwick went and sat in a big box which

Crowe had prepared to shelter the equipment from any stray light which had found its way into the darkened room. 'And we sat in this dark room, dark box,' remembered Chadwick later, 'for perhaps half an hour or so and, naturally, talked.' Amongst other things, they talked about the Bakerian Lecture, which had niggled in Chadwick's brain, because he was sure that his mentor's conclusions could not be right. 'And it was then that I realised that these observations which I suspected were quite wrong, and which proved to be wrong later on, had nothing whatever to do with his suggestion of the neutron, not really. He just hung the suggestion to it. Because it had been in his mind for some considerable time.'

The problem was that Rutherford's intense visualisation of atomic structure still felt, to the man himself, incomplete. And the puzzle lay in something of which he had himself made physical sense – the periodic table.

The periodic table had been worked out by chemists in the nineteenth century, who had attempted to find a way to classify the elements in relation to one another. They had done this principally by measuring the relative weights of the particles within elements as they combined to make compounds, calculated originally on a scale which used a single particle of the lightest element, hydrogen, as its basic unit. The weight of hydrogen was one, followed by helium at around four, then lithium and after that beryllium, all the way up to uranium, whose weight was around 236 times greater than that of hydrogen. The chemists also classified the elements by means of their valency, which was the number of single bonds each of them could make in a chemical reaction. The result, refined over time, was a table of elements, grouped into 'periods'.

Rutherford's discovery of the atomic nucleus in 1910 had led to the determination of the electrical charge at the nucleus of a range of different atoms. It rapidly became clear that if *you measured this positive charge as a multiple of that of the negative electron, this ratio was roughly half the atomic weight in almost all elements. The closeness of the correlation meant that suddenly the periodic table began to look as if it had a firmer foundation than the librarian-like habits of the Victorian chemists – it was all tied up with atomic physics.*

But since those days the understanding of these relationships had grown and grown, and the more Rutherford understood, the more it looked as if there was something missing. By 1920 he had discovered the proton, a particle with a positive charge equal to the negative charge of the electron. In Rutherford's 'solar system' model of the atom, each of the electrons orbiting the nucleus was now matched by a proton at its core.

And the atomic weight of the proton was roughly one.

In the lightest isotope of hydrogen, at the very top of the periodic table, there was no mystery. Rutherford now knew that the atom consisted of a lone proton circled by a single electron, and the proton's positive charge was balanced by the electron's negative charge. The electron's weight was negligible, and so, naturally enough, the atomic weight of hydrogen was almost identical to that of the proton.

The conundrum began with helium, next along. In helium there were two protons, balanced by two electrons. Yet the atomic weight of helium was not twice that of hydrogen but roughly four times as large. And every other element was closer to helium in this regard than to hydrogen. After all, the original observation of the correlation between the periodic table and subatomic structure had shown that the number of electrons was usually around half the atomic weight. Now it was becoming clear that the protons at the nucleus, each with an atomic weight of around one, could account for only half the weight of the whole atom in all elements except hydrogen.

Where was the extra weight coming from?

*So Rutherford pondered aloud in the room with Chadwick.
'He had asked himself, and kept on asking himself, how the
atoms were built up – how on earth were you going to build
up a big nucleus with a large positive charge?'*

*And the answer, which had taken root in the young
Chadwick's mind even before his director spoke the words,
was a neutral particle. A particle of mass one, with zero
charge and zero external field, whose neutrality would enable
it to move freely through matter, without being attracted or
repelled by the charged particles it passed. Its presence would
be difficult to detect by the spectroscope, and it might be
impossible to contain it in a sealed vessel.*

*In other words, a particle of very Few properties. So Few,
indeed, that it appeared not to exist.*

It took Alan some time to recover his composure. Walter
gloated and ate, his appetite miraculously rekindled. 'You'd
better eat that before it gets cold,' he said, polishing off his
own last crumbs.

Alan took a perfunctory bite. 'Twelve years,' he said.

'It was because of a speculation that Rutherford made
years ago. But it was just a speculation, and he made it at
the Bakerian Lecture, and, well, nobody reads old Bakerian
Lectures. Do they?'

'No,' said Alan.

'No one remembered it. Even Rutherford got bored of it when
it didn't work out straightaway. It was only Chadwick who
bothered with it. And he's been bothering with it ever since.'

8. THE SEARCH

*By the end of 1931, James Chadwick was no longer a
favoured novice. He was Rutherford's Assistant Director of*

Research. Behind him lay a distinguished history of publications, each furthering the understanding of the atomic nucleus by small but important steps. Meanwhile, he had supervised a dozen or more research students, many of whom themselves produced valuable work.

And yet this façade of achievement hid a deep professional frustration. His conversations with Rutherford back in 1920 had convinced him that the neutron must exist, and 'the only question was how the devil could one get evidence for it. It was shortly after that I began to make experiments on the side when I could. Occasionally Rutherford's interest would revive, but only occasionally.'

The idea had taken root as an obsession long after the great man himself had tired of the idea. Chadwick pursued two lines of investigation. One was to try to synthesise the neutron from a proton and an electron, which he believed to be its constituent parts, and the other was to try to knock it out of the nucleus. Sometimes he set his research students off on perfectly valid projects which yielded interesting results in their own right, while secretly hoping to find some neutrons along the way. At other times, he set up his own experiments, almost at random, in the hope of catching the neutron unawares. He later admitted that some of these were 'quite wildly absurd'. In 1924, he wrote to Rutherford that: 'I think we shall have to make a real search for the neutron. I believe I have a scheme which may just work.' But it obviously did not, because no more was heard. Yet still he kept going. They may have been 'really damn silly experiments', but then 'if we'd got a positive result, they wouldn't have been silly'. He never lost faith that 'there was always just the possibility of something turning up, and one shouldn't neglect doing, say, a few hours' work or even a few days' work to make quite sure'.

The fruitlessness of the wild goose chase made it necessary

to pursue it almost in secret, above and beyond all his Cavendish work and the more mainstream research with which he was involved. The failures did nothing to lessen his own determination. If anything they made it greater.

And nothing had come of his quest. The invisible neutron stayed firmly locked up in his own imagination. None of his experiments gave any indications of its existence. He was no nearer now than he ever had been. Yet still he went on.

'When did it start going right?' demanded Alan.

'I think it was just a few weeks ago. In fact – do you remember the day Chadwick was off sick with the flu, just before we went to the Royal Society?'

'Yes—'

'I think that was the day it started.'

'But we were with him most of the day when we went to the Royal Society, and he didn't tell us anything.'

'He didn't tell anyone anything. Well, he might have told a couple of people, but not much, and only right at the end. Everyone was very surprised when he announced it at the Kapitza Club last night.'

The waitress was at the table again, taking Walter's plate and looking acquisitively at Alan's. 'Have you finished that, sir?'

'Yes! No!'

'Would you like anything else?'

'We'll have coffee!' said Alan with an extravagant wave of the arm.

'Alan,' said Walter when she had gone, 'how much is coffee?' He was afraid that his allocated funds for the day would run out.

'I don't know. It's a special occasion. Walter – the Fewtron! We talked to Chadwick about the Fewtron that day on the train.'

'I know,' said Walter. He had been trying to forget that particular fact all day. 'He must have been very angry.'

'Don't you see? He *must* have already told Ted Nicolls.'

'He hadn't.'

'He must have done. I don't believe it was a prophecy.'

'No, he didn't. I asked Nicolls. He knew no more than we did. But it wasn't a prophecy either. Well, not really.'

'How on earth did he know then?'

'You know I told you about the experiments Hugh Webster did up in the Observatory last summer, when Nicolls was up there too?'

'Yes.'

'Well, Webster didn't know it, and Nicolls didn't know it, but Chadwick was looking for the neutron.'

9. A MYSTERIOUS RADIATION

In the summer of 1931, Chadwick set a research student named Hugh Webster to work up in the Observatory. He gave Webster a supply of beryllium, and told him to get to work.

Chadwick had been interested in beryllium for many years. He had harboured fantasies that it might be possible to split it into two helium nuclei and a neutron, and had bombarded it with everything he could think of – 'with alpha particles, with beta particles and with gamma rays' – to no effect. But in 1931 he had read some results which suggested that he might have been on the right track after all. The results proved that if you bombarded beryllium with alpha particles, a rather strange thing happened. In response to its bombardment, the beryllium provided an emission of its own. The scientists who performed the experiment assumed that the radiation consisted of gamma rays, a high energy form of light, rather than any of the other emissions of charged particles with which they were familiar, because it left no tracks in the cloud chamber. But it was nearly ten times as strong as any equivalent gamma radiation that had yet been seen.

A mysterious radiation! Chadwick had been chasing the path of any such results for a decade. But so many avenues had turned out to be dead ends that he knew by now not to get his hopes up. He gave Webster the task of replicating the Germans' beryllium work. Webster made good progress, replicating their findings and making an observation of his own. He noticed that the radiation that continued in the same direction as the bombarding alpha particles was more penetrating than that which was emitted backwards towards the alpha source.

And now Chadwick was beside himself. Any emission of gamma ray energy ought to be the same in all directions. Only particles were likely to have more energy forwards than backwards. It was at this point that Chadwick allowed himself to think for the first time, 'Here's the neutron.'

Yet there was still the matter of proving it. Chadwick had booked a family holiday and had no choice but to leave the laboratory. He left Webster with a cloud chamber and a camera. 'Pass the secondary radiation through your cloud chamber,' he said, 'and look for very thin tracks.'

The tracks would be very thin because only a particle with an electrical charge can create a cloud in a chamber. And Chadwick was looking for something that was only very weakly ionised. Even he could not conceive of it having no charge at all.

Like so many students before him, Webster had no idea of his supervisor's hidden agenda. He spent the summer taking photograph after photograph, and each was blank. As each result proved negative, he discarded the plates. When Chadwick returned, all the photographs had been destroyed, and he became probably as angry as anyone had ever seen

him. He tried to be reasonable, knowing that Webster would
have kept anything that looked like heralding success, but
he wanted to see the pictures for himself. Perhaps there was
something they had missed – a flicker, a smudge, a fading
cloud – and he would never know. Webster had accepted a
post at the University of Bristol. The atmosphere between
him and Chadwick remained frosty until he departed at the
end of the summer.

'And then we went up there, and we took Webster's equipment
back down to the Cavendish,' said Walter. 'The first artificially liberated neutrons passed through my cloud chamber.'
    'Good heavens.'
    'But Chadwick couldn't prove it. They'd left no tracks.'
    'And so did he carry on?'
    'I don't think he did. He thought it was just another
failed experiment, like all the others. That is, he thought
that until—'
    'Until what?'
    'Until the article in *Comptes Rendus* came out.'

Walter had been there when the article arrived. He was
sure of it now. The thing on his mind at the time had
been his attempt to patch up the cracks in his tubing with
plasticine. The invention of plasticine had revolutionised the
laboratory – as a replacement for sealing wax it was a great
step forward, because it did not need to be melted, was easily
broken up and manipulated, and was not subject to the same
vagaries on the application of heat. Walter had pummelled
the putty in his hands for a minute or so, softening it with
the warmth of his blood, and was trying to hold the tube
in place with one hand while he applied the plasticine with
the other.
    A post-doc student named Feather pushed past him into

Chadwick's office, knocking Walter and his tubing to one side.

'Oy!' protested Walter, hot with the unsuppressable rage of the physically disrupted.

But Feather had not heard him. He was brandishing the journal, waving it above his head like a wild thing. Walter looked into the office. Chadwick was sitting at his desk, but the chair was back from his little table. He was leaning forward, his face tilted upwards to stare at Feather, just shaking his head over and over again.

'I know,' he was saying, 'I know, I know.'

'They say it's *gamma radiation*,' said Feather. 'It's the Curies. They're supposed to know what they're doing.'

'I know,' said Chadwick. It seemed to be all he was capable of saying.

'What do you think they're up to? Do you think they've bodged it? Why would they publish such stuff, for goodness' sake?'

Chadwick's eyes were suddenly steel. 'They haven't bodged it,' he said.

'Well—' Feather paused, nonplussed. 'Well, then what?'

Chadwick's gaze, previously fixed on Feather, lowered and rested on Walter, who was still staring at them. The door slammed shut between them.

Walter frowned, collected himself, and went back to work.

Ten minutes later, the door opened and Feather emerged. He was ramrod straight but unsteady on his feet. He looked as if he could not see anything in the laboratory. He made his uncertain way across the room, leaving the door open, and tottered towards the lavatories.

Chadwick stayed in the room.

Well, reasoned Walter, if it was anything important, he'd be off to tell Rutherford about it at eleven. It was the way Rutherford kept up with what was happening in the laboratory. His life was so caught up in the industry of being Rutherford that he relied heavily on Chadwick to keep him in touch with the decisions being made in his name.

Eleven o'clock arrived. Sure enough, Chadwick rose very slowly from his desk and made the journey across his office to the door. He was far more collected than Feather had been. His own copy of the journal was folded neatly in his hand.

Walter watched his back through the doorway to Rutherford's office. He was explaining something quietly and calmly, and at great length, holding the journal for Rutherford to see.

Chadwick finished his speech.

There was a crash. Rutherford had shot up out of his chair, sending it flying into the wall and onto the floor.

'I don't believe it!' he shouted in a boom which shook the whole room.

'SHUT UP DAMN YOU' commanded Constable's sign imperiously in illuminated letters, and half a dozen scientists scrambled onto chairs and tables in an attempt to switch it off.

10. THE NEUTRON

In February 1932 Irene Curie and Frederic Joliot published the results of a repetition of Webster's experiments.

Irene Curie was the daughter of Marie Curie. She had married a French chemist, Frederic Joliot. For some time they pursued their work separately, but recently they had started to perform experiments together. The combination of their different talents, and the riches of material at their disposal at the Curie Institute in Paris, were making them into one of the most formidable partnerships in science.

The Curie-Joliots had read Webster's results and, convinced that it was a very special type of gamma radiation which came from the beryllium, decided to find out whether the radiation would knock protons out of matter in the same way that alpha particles did.

It did.

The title of the paper was: 'The emission of protons of high velocity from hydrogenous materials irradiated with penetrating gamma rays'. But gamma rays are just a high energy form of light. They are virtually weightless. By comparison, a proton is a solid, weighty beast. It has a mass of one. One: the smallest of the natural numbers. But still a whole, an entirety, a universe unto itself. To imagine a gamma ray hitting a proton and setting it flying is to see the earth spun out of its orbit by the weight of Newton's apple.

No wonder Rutherford's chair went crashing to the ground. It was the fifteen-inch shell and the tissue paper all over again.

Why were the Curie-Joliots so sure that it was gamma radiation which was coming from the beryllium and dislodging the protons?

Because, of course, it left no tracks in the cloud chamber.

When CTR Wilson stood on a hill and dreamed of clouds in bottles, he invented a way to make the invisible visible. He devised a way to track charged particles. If the radiation left no tracks, then what was there left for it to be other than a very excitable form of light?

Scientists all round the world that morning read what Feather read, and some of them spotted the anomaly that offended him so much. But no one but Chadwick and Rutherford knew what it meant.

Chadwick saw beyond the irregularity. He was sure of it almost immediately. After all these years, after all his abortive attempts, the Curies had got there first.

They had liberated the neutron.

And they didn't even know it.

*　　*　　*

'My God,' said Alan. 'Why on earth didn't anyone think of it before?'

It was a fair question. Men and women had been peering into the atom for thirty-five years, and the pace of progress had been hectic. Walter and Alan knew that light was a particle, and that matter was a wave. They knew that time was curved, and that it changed its dimensions if one travelled through space. It was understood that it would never be possible to measure an object's position and its velocity at the same time, and that all the universe was disrupted by the act of just looking at it. The most wonderful theories, some of them incomprehensible to all but a few people in the world, had been postulated and then proved. Somehow, in all that time, one of the largest constituents of matter had rested quietly at the core of the atom, undiscovered and almost entirely unsuspected.

'I repeated Joliot and Curie's experiment,' Chadwick was saying to the umpteenth journalist as Walter slipped back into the laboratory, 'and took very careful notes of all the energy levels. Then I tried it again, only not with hydrogen this time. I worked my way up the periodic table, and the radiation from the beryllium knocked particles out of every atom it hit. The sums all made sense. It couldn't possibly be a gamma ray doing this. It had to be – something else.'

Walter tried to block out the voices, gave up on liberating neutrons, and went back to the experiment he was supposed to be doing. After the euphoria of lunch, he was feeling rather anticlimactic and excluded. Chadwick had not said a word to him all day. Of course, he could not be expected to, but Walter was desperate to feel a part of things. After all, when Rutherford had performed the first artificial disintegration of the atom, he had taken Chadwick to the Royal Society and

had told him all about his most brilliant new idea. Walter
might have gone to the Royal Society with Chadwick, but
he had been told absolutely nothing. He frowned, trying
to get his glassware lined up, and gave one of the metal
supports a tug.

'Oh, damn!' he shouted, as the vacuum tube slipped and
exploded, and his gold films flew in a shower around him.

The journalists were filing out of Chadwick's office. They
stepped over Walter as he crouched on the floor, picking the
films out from the cracks in the floorboards.

'You all right there?' enquired Chadwick coolly from above
him when his guests were safely out of the laboratory.

Walter felt very stupid. 'Sorry, sir,' he said.

'Not at all, not at all. Feel absolutely free.'

The irony was gentle enough. Walter stood up and saw a
lovely expression of exhausted, euphoric calm in his supervisor's eyes.

'Dr Chadwick,' he said tentatively, 'may I offer my con-
gratulations?'

'You most certainly may. Thank you.'

Walter blushed. 'Did it really take only three weeks?' he
blurted out, wanting to extend the conversation.

'Three weeks, twelve years, take your pick.'

'It must be the most marvellous feeling.'

'Oh, it is. I'm glad it's all over, to tell you the truth. It's been
a long twelve years.' He blinked with tiredness. 'Dunnachie,
would you mind doing me a favour?'

'Oh, yes! I mean, no, I wouldn't mind.'

'I'd get Rutherford or one of the other staff to read this
but they get a bit overexcited. It's the last paragraph of my
submission to *Nature*. I just want you to tell me honestly, as
– well, not as a layman, exactly, but as an outsider – whether
you think I'm being too harsh on the Curies.'

'Oh!' Layman? Outsider? Yet the honour of being the first

person to read it was so great that he had to brush the slights aside. Walter dropped all the bits of foil he'd retrieved onto the table. His hand shook as he took the sheet of paper from Chadwick's hand.

He read, 'It is to be expected that many of the effects of a neutron in passing through matter should resemble those of a quantum of high energy' – in other words, a gamma ray – 'and it is not easy to reach the final decision between the two hypotheses. Up to the present, all the evidence is in favour of the neutron, while the quantum hypothesis can only be upheld if the conservation of energy and momentum be relinquished at some point.'

It was certainly fairly damning. Without the conservation of energy and momentum, the whole of science would fall apart. Walter looked up at Chadwick.

'Well?' said Chadwick. 'What do you think? Do you think they'll be offended?'

'But it's true,' said Walter.

Chadwick relaxed and grinned, and for a moment Walter thought he was going to be slapped on the back. 'There is that, Dunnachie,' he said. 'That's just what I thought.'

'Dr Chadwick,' said Walter, 'did you know all along that you'd find it in the end?'

Chadwick sat down. 'No,' he said. 'No, mostly it seemed pretty certain that I wouldn't. And – well, you should ignore all the fuss. In a way I didn't find it at all.'

'You did!'

Chadwick still seemed euphoric, but behind the flush on his cheeks and the animation of his expression, his eyes were grim. 'I failed to think clearly enough about the neutron. I never thought hard enough about which properties would most clearly provide evidence of its existence. The decisive clue was provided by others.'

Walter knew that Chadwick was a modest man but he

thought that this time he was going too far. He seemed to be torturing himself for his failures even in his hour of triumph.

Chadwick leant back in his chair and sighed deeply.

'The problem is that I was always looking for what I expected. And one should never do that as a scientist. You will never find the truth until you start looking beyond what you want to find.'

Three days later Walter sat at the desk in his room and snipped all the cuttings from the newspapers to send to Jim. He thought it an excellent way to give him an education in science, now that it seemed certain he would finish school after his Leaving Certificate.

27 February 1932
Cambridge Daily News
A NEW RAY
Cambridge Scientist's Discovery
SPLITTING THE ATOM

A discovery, described by Lord Rutherford, Director of the Cavendish Laboratory, as 'of the greatest interest and importance – possibly the greatest since the artificial disintegration of the atom' – has recently been made by a Cambridge scientist, Dr J. Chadwick, Fellow of Gonville and Caius College.

Described as the most hidden ray, whose particles are said to be the fastest and most penetrating known, indifferent to the strongest electrical and magnetic forces, the radiation, a *Cambridge Daily News* representative was informed this morning, has been known for some time. 'It has been found recently,' said Dr Chadwick, 'within the last three weeks, that it has very peculiar properties which can be explained if we suppose the radiation is a particle which has no charge.'

As well as the local paper, Walter included the letter

which had been published in *Nature*, and pieces from the *Manchester Guardian*, the *Daily Express*, and *The Times*. The cuttings gave a marvellous sense of the historic nature of the occasion, but from a scientific point of view they were less than adequate. 'Now, Jim,' wrote Walter in the accompanying letter, unable to abandon his pedagogic mission even in the flush of triumph, 'apart from *Nature*, which is probably rather difficult to read, you must not take too much notice of the exact words these cuttings use. They have all got the wrong end of the stick in one way or another. The *Express* seems to have made a particularly poor job of it. "British Scientist Gropes Near the Origin of Life", indeed! I haven't a clue what they think they mean. I think they are just trying to be sensational. Really, it's very marvellous, but the neutron has done nothing to deserve all this. The important thing is the *discovery* and the fact that we know more about the atom.' He scratched his head, trying to think of a way to describe the thing that Chadwick had found. Already his own failed attempts to pin it down had made it feel like a sort of acquaintance, with whose frustrating yet endearing habits he was familiar. Its personality, as he had conceived it in his mind, was not unlike that of Chadwick himself.

'The neutron itself is a very harmless sort of individual, in fact most elusive. It all goes to show the devastating power of the press, far more devastating than all the poor neutrons liberated from beryllium.'

11. MOONSHINE

In September 1933, Rutherford addressed the British Association for the Advancement of Science, at which he recited a history of 'the discoveries of the last quarter of a century in atomic transmutation'.

Rutherford had presided over an extraordinary couple of

years at the Cavendish. The room was crowded and the audience buzzing with anticipation. He was quizzed in an intense but ignorant fashion by journalists, who wanted a sensational story. At one point, he lost his temper, and uttered the immortal words: 'Anyone who expects a source of power from the transformation of the atom is talking moonshine.'

Rutherford's utterances had a habit of taking root in the minds of other men. A few days later a Hungarian-Jewish émigré physicist named Leo Szilard read the account of the speech in The Times. *'Pronouncements of experts to the effect that something cannot be done have always irritated me,' Szilard wrote much later. 'This sort of set me pondering as I was walking in the streets of London, and I remember that I stopped for a red light at the intersection of Southampton Row and Russell Square. I was pondering whether Lord Rutherford might not prove to be wrong. It occurred to me that neutrons, in contrast to alpha particles, do not ionise the substance through which they pass. Consequently, neutrons need not stop until they hit a nucleus with which they may react. As the light changed to green and I crossed the street, it suddenly occurred to me that if we could find an element which is split by neutrons and which would emit two neutrons when it absorbs one neutron, such an element, if assembled in sufficiently large mass, could sustain a nuclear chain reaction. In certain circumstances it might be possible to liberate energy on an industrial scale, and to construct atomic bombs.'*

Walter laid down his pen. He did not think he could go any further.

10

'Excuse me, sir.'

The student who had put up his hand was younger than they mostly were these days. A normal school leaver, not a war veteran.

'Yes?'

'I had heard. From one of the other lecturers. That you were there when they split the atom.'

Walter stared at him. He wondered from whom the titbit could have come. It would have been an innocent enough remark, he supposed, and one which would capture the imagination of an undergraduate. Perhaps it was a good opportunity to digress from his standard lecture to clear up a few misunderstandings over terminology.

'In a manner of speaking. In which year was the atom first split?'

'1932.'

'And who performed the experiment?'

'John Cockcroft and Ernest Walton.'

'The reason I ask is because there are actually a number of events you might have been referring to. Several of them happened in 1932. Others happened in other years. What exactly do you mean by splitting the atom?'

But the undergraduate, exhausted by his contribution, looked tongue-tied and confused. A burly man from the navy put up his hand.

'Ridley?'

'Fission!'

Walter sighed. Here they went again. 'Ah. That's where it gets complicated. Fission did not take place in 1932, nor was it discovered by Cockcroft and Walton. In which year was fission first artificially performed, Ridley? We talked about this last week.'

Ridley subsided. The original undergraduate put up his hand.

'Smithson?'

'1938, sir. Hahn and Strassman.'

'That's correct. I believe that most of you attended my fission lecture. Can anyone remind us what it is?'

'Sir.'

'Smithson.'

'It's when a uranium atom captures a neutron and splits, and it lets off some more neutrons, and they get captured by more uranium atoms, then there's a chain reaction.'

'*No*,' Walter barked in anger, then stopped himself. It was not fair to be harsh when the boy was only exhibiting his enthusiasm. He could not help what had been done to his imagination by the intellectual climate. But it was very annoying all the same. Walter had not so much as mentioned chain reaction in his lecture. 'No, Smithson. Fission does not necessarily result in a chain reaction. You need to separate the two in your mind. But up to that point, yes, you are correct. Now, given that you have successfully placed the splitting of the atom and fission six years apart, can you tell me what differentiates them?'

Smithson was blushing. 'Fission is uranium, sir. Splitting is lithium.'

'Those were the elements in which the two phenomena first artificially occurred. But it is possible to split many atoms other than lithium. And fission has been observed in an element other than uranium. Can anyone tell me what it is?'

'Plutonium!'

'Ridley, please put up your hand first. Correct. *So*, are we any nearer to the distinction between the two? Smithson?'

'Fission is a special kind of splitting?'

'Ah. Thank you. The primary thing which is special about fission is that it is caused by neutron capture, which leads to a number of effects which are not present in other types of splitting. I am going to assume that you have all absorbed what we said about fission last week, and move on to the more general concept. What, precisely, is splitting?'

'An atom breaking up into more than one part?'

'That's probably the best way of putting it. But in fact atoms were first artificially broken into more than one part in 1919 by Ernest Rutherford when he knocked a proton out of the nitrogen atom. The press called that splitting the atom, but the correct scientific term is disintegration.'

Smithson looked nonplussed.

'I'll put you out of your misery. The point I'm trying to make is that *splitting the atom* is not a scientific term. It does not have a definition.'

The young men gawped gormlessly. Is it me, thought Walter, or are students getting denser as the years go on?

'Which invites the question of why I was prepared to concur with Smithson in placing the date of its first occurrence in 1932, and in attributing its discovery to Cockcroft and Walton. And the reason is that these days that is usually, though not always, what people are referring to when they use the term, and so it seems sensible, particularly when dealing with laymen, to accept the colloquial reference. But we are physicists, and we need to get the facts straight. Smithson is right when he says that I was there when Cockcroft and Walton artificially disintegrated lithium. But I also remember newspaper reports two months earlier, claiming that

Chadwick had split the atom, when he had in fact discovered the neutron. They said he'd split the atom because he was performing artificial disintegrations too, quite a lot of them. And long before the famous Cockcroft and Walton experiment, even I was disintegrating atoms.'

Smithson looked awestruck. Walter smiled. A bit of hero-worship didn't go amiss in the learning process every now and then.

'Well,' said Aitken. 'Church committees. Dinner parties with pacifists. You seem to have taken your duties rather to heart.'

George sniffed in annoyance. If that wasn't what he was supposed to be doing, what was? How was he meant to know, when no one had told him? He clung to his triumphant mood through Aitken's scornful patronage, then replied.

'The really interesting thing,' he said, 'is that Nunn May was supposed to be at the dinner too. And he didn't show.'

For a moment George thought he could detect a flicker of interest on his employer's face, followed by something almost like frustration. Both expressions were quickly expunged.

'Didn't show, you say? Must have been detained at work.'

'That was what the Dunnachies thought. She was quite upset.' He suddenly felt a stab of guilt. Reporting on Dunnachie was something he could do with the work part of his brain, an organ he was usually reasonably successful at keeping separate from his conscience. But the mention of Dunnachie's wife confounded all that.

'Spoiled the dinner, no doubt. What did you eat?'

George could not see how this could possibly be relevant. 'Tomato soup followed by Lancashire hotpot.'

'Very nice too. Must have saved up her coupons.'

'We brought ours.'

'Neighbourly of you. Well, next time you'd better let me know before you embark on any such mission. You aren't the only person I have working on this. It is necessary to coordinate.'

'I'm sorry,' said George, crestfallen.

'Did you find out anything of interest?'

'Well, actually,' said George, getting into his stride, 'he was most vehement about pacifism.' Despite initial appearances, Dunnachie had ended up behaving like a particularly contemptuous science teacher after all. Phoebe had remonstrated with George about the foolishness of that comment about the tablecloth all the way home. It had rankled with him ever since, and it was not often he had the opportunity to wreak revenge on his persecutors. 'In fact he was quite offensive about the British Empire. He described us as having made war all round the world.'

Aitken puffed scornfully through his nostrils. George felt encouraged and continued.

'What's more, it was his opinion that we do not currently have peace.'

'Don't currently have peace? What the devil did he mean?'

'It was Russia that brought us on to it. My—' He stopped. He'd been about to say, 'My wife's brother'. No, no. He was not going to mention Leonard.

The muscles in Aitken's face tautened a little. 'Russia?'

'Yes. We were talking about the fact that they were allies. Dunnachie talked about war machines. He listed the countries. Russia, America, Britain, France. That they were somehow ranged against one another once more.'

'Did he mention Russia favourably or otherwise?'

'Neutrally, really. He spoke of all countries equally. Even Germany. He mentioned that we once went to war with them against France as allies.'

'Yes,' said Aitken. 'I've heard that sort of thing before.

Holier than thou. All men equal under God. Precisely the sort of attitude with which to justify treachery.'

George had never before heard Aitken utter the affirmative. It was enough to give him the courage to ask the question he'd wanted answered from the start. 'Mr Aitken,' he said, 'do you really think that Dunnachie is a traitor?'

'Oh, most certainly. You can get him to admit to it any day of the week. It's all down in writing. He stood in opposition to his own country in its darkest hour.'

'You mean the conscientious objection. But do you think he's done anything illegal?'

'My dear boy, he doesn't have to have done. You weren't under the impression you were employed by the police force, were you?'

Aitken's words came out so quickly they felt like a slap across the face. George recoiled.

'No,' he said. 'Sorry, sir.'

Aitken continued to sit still and regard him. George knew there was something else he had wanted to say but was struggling to remember it. Oh yes, that was it.

'The strange thing is,' he said, 'Dunnachie's made no contact with the pacifists ever since I started following him. He was supposed to preach a sermon about Peace right at the beginning, but he didn't turn up. It's like Nunn May all over again. And yet he seems so keen on it. I can't work it out.'

Aitken's body appeared to be incorporating itself into the chair. George picked his fingernails.

'And your job is?' said Aitken.

George jumped. 'To work it out,' he mumbled.

'That's right. Go to it.'

On the day the atom was split, in April 1932, though once again they did not know it, Alan and Walter were in the laboratory, debating hard about Peace.

The expedition to China had been prevented by the government even as a small band gathered at Harwich. Walter felt as though he'd failed an exam. He'd done all he could – writing letters to newspapers, handing out leaflets, helping to liaise with the ship and its crew – and it had all come to nothing.

Alan did not miss the opportunity to rub his nose in it. 'I told you so,' he said.

'What did you tell me? You told me they'd all die and the sacrifice would be in vain. You didn't tell me they'd never even be allowed to set sail.'

'It was futile. That's the point. Weapons are more powerful than words. This is the victory the strong have over the weak. It's wrong, and it's nasty, but it's unavoidably true, and you might as well face up to it.'

Alan was getting extremely sure of himself these days and Walter was not sure he liked it. He had a way of deftly destroying anything that hinted at being a solution to the world's problems, without ever bothering to propose an answer of his own. He flirted with communism, but refused to commit to it, too ready with criticism even of the ideology closest to his heart to be prepared to defend it. Sometimes Walter thought it rather a cowardly way of going about things. But the arguments were too enjoyable to be resisted. He attempted to assemble a riposte, and then stopped, because Chadwick was advancing across the laboratory towards them.

'Good evening, gentlemen,' he said. 'Working late again, I see. Don't let Rutherford catch you.'

Rutherford had a rule that all Cavendish men should down tools at six, in order to 'take advantage of all the other opportunities which Cambridge has to offer'. Chadwick in particular was scrupulous in its avoidance.

But though his pace of work had barely slackened since his great discovery, he was terribly mellow at the moment.

'Seeing rather a lot of you lately, Nunn May,' he said with an amused raise of the eyebrow. 'You'll be spending quite enough time here next year. Time enough to get sick of the sight of the place. Isn't that right, Dunnachie?'

'You don't mind, do you, sir?' said Alan anxiously. 'You said I could ask Dunnachie to show me round his work.'

'That was four months ago. Dunnachie, don't tell me you're still doing the same experiment as in December.'

Walter blushed. The truth was, he was.

'It's going much better now,' he said. 'Since we got the plasticine. And Cockcroft's kindly agreed to switch off his particle accelerator while I'm working with the source. It was a bit of a difficulty before. That's the problem with having a source with such a short half-life. Whenever the accelerator sparks over, all my equipment gets knocked out, and by the time I've fixed it, the radium's decayed.'

'That was *very* kind of Cockcroft,' said Chadwick.

Walter didn't think it was that especially kind. Cockcroft and Walton's equipment had grown and grown, and the voltage had reached higher and higher intensities, until it threatened to take over, or indeed explode, the entire laboratory. They'd moved it to a room close to Walter's table, and this relocation had caused Walter great stress. And despite the revolutionary impact of the plasticine on his own work, it was proving hard to get hold of any. Cockcroft and Walton had spent the last two months applying eight pounds of the stuff to the cracks and joins in the accelerator. That was nearly half the manufacturers' output to date.

Still, it was clear that they were under a certain amount of pressure. A few weeks ago, when Walter had gone into Cockcroft and Walton's room to ask them to switch the machinery off, Rutherford had stormed in. It was a rainy day and the director had been dripping wet. He'd pulled his coat off and thrown it onto a hook. The room had filled with a blinding flash. Walter had been knocked sideways by the impact. Rutherford had stood there with his moustache sticking out straight and his hair standing on end. He'd bellowed with pain and Ernest Walton had dived for the switch.

'Good God, what are you men trying to do to me?' he'd shouted.

Walter had cowered, trying to dissociate himself.

Rutherford had pulled himself together, snorted extensively, and sat himself down, trying to calm himself in communion with his pipe. But he always smoked very dry tobacco, and as soon as it ignited, it had gone off like a volcano in the charged atmosphere of the room, with a great cloud of smoke, flames and ash. As the flames and smoke subsided he'd glared up at them through his singed eyebrows.

'Get me Cockcroft,' he'd roared.

Walter had scampered from the room to fetch the machine's owner. Cockcroft had been advising a colleague on an engineering problem. He'd treated his summons with nonchalance. 'Suppose I'd better go and see what bee the old Crocodile's got caught in his bonnet,' he'd said.

'Cockcroft,' Rutherford had boomed, cutting a dangerously comic figure and looking for all the world like a scientist in a second-rate horror film, 'what the devil are you doing with this monstrous contraption?'

'We've managed to get the protons accelerated to a pretty good speed now. We're observing their properties.'

'Properties? What sort of properties?'

'How far they will go in air. How they behave in a magnetic field. What colour the glow is. That sort of thing.'

'COLOUR?' The professor had been almost apopletic. 'You're employing the most expensive and infernally DAN-GEROUS equipment this laboratory has ever had the misfortune to house, and you're using it to find out what COLOUR a proton is?'

'There are important implications—'

'Implications my sainted aunt. I tell you, man, you'd better stop messing around and wasting your time. For pity's sake get on and do what I told you to do months ago and put those protons to good use.'

Walter had not been party to what good use Rutherford was talking about, but even Cockcroft had looked chastened and promised to follow his orders. Since that day, he and Walton had spent their lives on ladders looking for leaks in the plasticine and rubbing it with grease to make everything airtight.

'Oh, talking of Cockcroft and Walton,' said Chadwick now with a sphinx-like smile, 'have you heard what they did this morning?'

The two students shook their heads.

Chadwick fumbled in his pocket. 'CTR told me about it. He was so excited he couldn't talk. Had to write it down for me. Here you go. This is what they've done.'

He handed Walter a scruffy, crumpled scrap of paper. Walter smoothed it out. He took one look and looked up at Chadwick in astonishment.

'What is it?' shouted Alan in excitement, trying to grab the paper.

Walter showed it to him.

'And the piece of paper read—'

Walter scrawled the equation on the blackboard.

$Li + H \rightarrow 2He.$

He spun round to face the students. 'A lithium atom was bombarded with an accelerated proton and split down the middle to form two helium nuclei. That was the good use Rutherford had been talking about. I wish I had the photographs to show you. Perhaps I will bring them in some time. They were stunning. The one showing the disintegration of lithium was a little difficult to make out, as it was distorted by a square white smudge on the lens. Still, the straight paths of the two diverging nuclei were clear enough. But the boron photograph looked to me much as one would envisage a nova exploding. Three straight clear lines shooting out from a white cloud of what looked like dust but which was actually water vapour, with a dark, empty circle at its heart.'

Lectures did not often go like this, but when they did, he remembered why he liked to teach. The audience was following his every breath.

'It was the most extraordinarily important experiment. The press were told that it was important, and so they said again that it was the splitting of the atom. Only this time we did not bother to correct them. We supposed that now that one atom had been split directly into two, they might as well have their way. And we wanted Cockcroft and Walton to have the credit for what they'd done. Because we knew even then that their experiment would pave the way for much of the scientific progress in nuclear physics that came afterwards.'

A hand shot up.

'Ridley?'

'You mean that led on to fission?'

'NO!' roared Walter. 'Good grief, man, have you been listening to a word I've said? I said scientific progress, not technological! Do you think that the scientists who were working during the war were exploring the properties of the atom? They took what we already had and worked out how they could use it to further their countries' own ends! There's barely been a single scientific advance since 1939!'

He caught his breath. It had always been a strict rule to keep his science and his politics separate. He had never broken it before.

'I'm talking about the development of nuclear accelerators. I'm talking about the machine Cockcroft had in that room of his. That was technology, but it was technology designed to further the advance of science. Accelerators had absolutely nothing to do with fission. But it has been possible to explore so much with those accelerated particles since then.'

Ridley's face had contracted with hostility. He was not going to let it go. 'Then what *did* lead on to fission?'

Walter was silent.

'Sir?'

Smithson's hand was in the air once more.

'Sir, it was the discovery of the neutron, wasn't it?'

The silence crackled. The roof began to bear down on him. When he spoke Walter could barely hear his own voice.

'Yes, Smithson,' he said. 'You are right. It was.'

11

On Sunday morning the tug of science could no longer pull Walter into the office, as it had done the previous weekend. He sat at the breakfast table long after Grace had cleared the plates away, until he had read the newspaper from cover to cover. Then he stared at the wall, unable to think of anything to do.

'Walter,' said Grace, 'if you are going to honour us with your presence, then you might at least condescend to *talk*.'

He stared at her. There was nothing to say.

'Look,' said Grace, 'I have an idea and I'd be grateful if you could give it your consideration. It's been a difficult winter and we've all been cooped up indoors for far too long. A bit of fresh air and exercise will do us all good. Let's go and fly kites in the park.'

'Kites?' Patrick sprang to his feet from the floor, where he was constructing a scale model of the Science Museum with spent matchboxes he'd been saving for more than a year.

Walter looked at the window. 'It looks rather cold,' he said.

'And windy. Perfect kite-flying weather.'

'I'll go and get the kites!' cried Patrick, and ran off upstairs, confident that his mother would sort out his reluctant father.

'Come *on*, Walter. Stop moping. Let's just go.'

They went.

She was right, of course. The fresh air did make him feel a

little better. Even the slight ache in his muscles as he propelled himself and Bridget up the hill was a sign that his blood still flowed.

'Daddy,' said Bridget.

'Yes, Topsy?'

'When's Uncle Jim coming back to stay?'

Grace spun round, dropping Patrick's hand.

'Bridget,' she said sharply, 'you don't remember Uncle Jim.'

Bridget was perched on Walter's shoulders in the blustery air. 'Yes I do,' she said from her elevated position. 'He used to play planes with us.'

'She does remember,' confirmed Patrick.

'We saw some planes yesterday,' said Bridget. 'It's *ages* since we've seen some planes. I like playing planes. When's Uncle Jim coming back?'

Grace reached up and retrieved her from Walter's shoulders. 'Bridget, we're playing kites today, not planes. Patrick, do you want to sort the kite out?'

'But we're not at the top of the hill yet.'

'We soon will be,' said Grace, and took off, running ahead of husband and children. Bridget whooped and followed her. Patrick held back for a moment and was then seized by the competitive imperative of beating his sister.

Walter watched them, skittering helter skelter up the hill, and felt a terrible stab of love. Jim had adored Grace and the children. It had been so miraculous that the boy Walter had abandoned in Australia should have come to Wales fully grown and have so utterly bewitched his ready-made family. Jim's leave in Bangor had been difficult at times but overall it had been a very happy time. It wasn't so long ago. Today it almost seemed possible to recapture it, to feel for Grace as he'd felt for her then.

He walked slowly up to the scrubby summit. By the time

he got there, Grace was already holding the kite while Patrick walked backwards, frowning.

'Ready?' shouted Grace.

'Steady, go!'

Grace tossed the kite aloft. It bobbed and faltered above her head, then Patrick gave it a tug, it caught the wind, and soared straight upwards. Bridget danced beneath it. Grace walked back to Walter. The mention of Jim had made them both a little more tender towards one another.

'Well,' she said, 'I don't know what that was all about. Probably the fact that they saw planes yesterday. Or perhaps even the kite. Jim used to fly kites with them.'

'I'm so glad she remembers him.'

'I'd be surprised if she really does. She was barely two. It's probably Patrick. You know the thing he's got about planes. But—' she rubbed Walter's back '—on the other hand, she was so completely besotted by him. Perhaps he's a bit of a character in their stories to one another. You know? And she remembers him that way.'

Walter looked down at her, his heart still hurting. 'Do you remember all those postcards I used to send to Jim, when he was a boy?'

Grace's face lit up. 'Of course I do! He told me when he came to Wales that he'd got half his education by means of your postcards.' The laughter in her voice was a tonic. 'His commanding officer was most put out about it, apparently. That Jim was just a sergeant and had so much more general knowledge. Of course you were always very determined to be informative. Do you remember – there was a rather hilarious card you wrote when we went on holiday to Cologne that time, when we were still students. We'd just visited the cathedral, which, I think, was one of the largest in Europe, and you copied out the whole entry for it from Arthur Mee's *Children's Encyclopaedia*. And Arthur Mee was terribly rude about it. Said it was typical of the Germans to imitate a French style and get the measurements wrong. But we thought it was wonderful.'

Walter looked down at the grass. Her memories were so blithe and spirited. He was sure that was the way things had been at the time. But the darkness in his soul was a rage and a disease. Even up here, there was nothing he could do to keep it out.

'*Walter*. Don't go again.'

But it was too late. He was already gone.

The holiday in Germany was the greatest miracle that had ever happened to him. Greater than the Travelling Scholarship, greater than meeting Ernest Rutherford, greater even than the discovery of the neutron. It should not have happened. But it did.

His first year in Cambridge had spun on with such excitement that he had been forced to let his reveries of Grace Padgett recede. He had not wanted them to go – they made him feel happy and sad in a combination that was more beguiling than anything else he knew. But in the end he had to admit that his constant reimagining of her was wearing away any reality she had possessed. He allowed what remained of her aura to glow around Peace, and other than that, slowly let her go.

At the beginning of the long vacation, he took what valiance he hoped he had left and travelled up to London to express his regret to Henry Brinton that the Harwich mission had failed, and to ask how he could be of service now. One or the other of them mixed up the dates – afterwards they never quite determined which – and Brinton was not there. So Walter was left adrift in London, with science all over for the year and Peace stolen from him, as hopeless and homeless as he'd been in his first days in England. There were two options.

One was to take the next train back to a Cambridge devoid of all his friends, and the other was to make the most of his time in London. He did not feel very capable of the latter, but could not bear the defeat of the former. So he undertook a sightseeing tour, alone and in the coldest murk of summer he could ever have thought imaginable.

Waterloo Bridge was a grey crossing across heaving waters, opening onto a choppy vista which could only have been construed beautiful by a heart equal to Wordsworth's. Westminster Abbey was a morgue, crammed to the rafters with the graves of dead soldiers. No spire or trellis could uplift him, not with those corpses beneath the stones. Who was he to say they had got it all wrong when they had lived their short lives with more glory and conviction than he was capable of? In the vast space of this fusty old monument it was hard to believe that he knew better than them. Still, relentless and ever more of a curse to himself, he trudged out of the church, stomped up Whitehall avoiding Nelson's eye, and turned right into the Strand. Hopelessness was upon him now, and nothing could divert him even for a second. Law courts older than any building in Australia passed him without a glance. He hated himself for feeling miserable, and in hating himself felt miserable all the more. There was no point now, except to mooch back to Cambridge where for another week at least there was a bed to call his own, somewhere to crouch with his books and hide from his sorrows and throw his socks around.

The voice stole up on him, so that the end of the sentence drifted into his mind, and, with the shock of recognition, coiled back again to the beginning, so that he heard it all in replay.

'Well, I don't care whether Uncle was whispering or shouting,' said the voice, rising out of the empty street air, the hubbub of strangers suddenly condensed into a clear, cool line of speech, 'but I certainly didn't hear him.' It was a signature of humanity. He knew her.

Above him, St Paul's. Its massive shoulders sprawled into the city, and its filigreed dome rose above them. It claimed earth and sky.

'I heard *every word*,' said a petulant middle-aged voice.

'You only believe you did because they call it the Whispering Gallery. I think its magic wore out centuries ago.'

He did not dare look. While he did not look he would still believe it was her. Even the possibility of such a deliverance—

'*Mr Dunnachie!*' she shrieked.

Now there was no choice but to look. There he was, standing in no particular direction on the pavement. He attempted a saunter. Then he petered to a halt.

'Hello,' he said, keeping his eyes on the hair.

'I should *think* hello.'

She'd called him Mr Dunnachie. She used to call him Walter or even Walt, just as they did at home. It was all gone. Nothing could be worse than this.

'Do you know this gentleman, Grace?' asked the male part of the couple that was with her.

'Mr Dunnachie. My uncle Arthur. My aunt Rose. Mr and Mrs Johnson to you, Mr Dunnachie. I met Mr Dunnachie on the ship, Aunty. He is studying at Cambridge.'

They all stared at him expectantly.

'I am most pleased to meet you,' said Walter.

'Well,' said Uncle Arthur, 'what brings you to London?'

Stupidity. Hope. Grace. 'I am on a sightseeing tour,' he said.

'Which sights have you seen?'

'Westminster Abbey.'

'We are just on our way there. Did you enjoy it?'

'It was wonderful!' he gushed. 'I – I would appreciate the opportunity to show which bits I liked the most—'

Grace laughed. He had expected her scorn. But it was not a scornful laugh. She was laughing the way she had on the ship.

'A guided tour would indeed be most pleasant,' she said. 'If, of course, that is acceptable to the assembled company.'

'I was going to *write* to you and tell you that I was going to be visiting Aunty,' she hissed behind an arch. 'I was going to *suggest* that we meet up. But you never replied to the letter I sent you at Christmas. So I thought you wouldn't want to come.'

'I was too afraid,' he said simply.

'Afraid of what?'

She was absolutely real. All his common sense had been wrong, and his imaginings had been right. At the sight of her face, little and charming beneath his, he smelt the zest of the ocean. 'That you didn't want me to write to you. That you'd replied to me just to be polite.'

She frowned fiercely. 'What utter nonsense.'

'Yes,' said Walter.

'So I didn't tell you I was coming. And yet you came anyway. Walter, there must be some science to it. Why should we both have been in the same place at the same time?'

A hundred thousand molecules, a million particles, all zipping around in the void, minding their own business, until the collision took place. 'There is no reason why we should not have been,' was the best he could come up with. No reaction meant anything other than its consequences. This, like any other, would be utterly trivial unless it led to a significant and permanent change. Yet her eyes were burning into him as if she were quite convinced that the change had taken place already.

They stared at one another for a moment, eyebrows

crinkling, then Walter decided to take the initiative. 'We should rejoin your relatives. They will think—'

The pair of them scuttled out, bound by what might be thought. The sightseeing tour proceeded without any incident other than the to and fro of conversation, weaving itself around what was expected by aunt and uncle. But this time there was no landing card to lose, and at the end of the afternoon they succeeded in exchanging contact details properly. Walter did not intend to let her go again.

'The thing about writing to you, my dear pen pal,' Grace wrote, 'is that I think of you *almost* as being someone from home, because I met you the day after I left. But the difference is that I can write to you about what I am up to and it is only a few days before I receive a reply. I am sure you find the same thing, but I find it terribly distracting to receive letters from Mother commenting on things I did months ago which I can now hardly remember.'

He did find the same thing. But her letters were more than that to him. They gave him a glimpse of a life beyond the bright, crisp air of Cambridge science – a cosmopolitan world of parties on the Champs Élysées, nights at the opera, and people speaking a dozen different European languages.

'It's not in the least glamorous here,' protested Grace's letters in response to his hesitant comments about how much more exciting her life was than his. 'We don't go around discovering new particles or anything like that. Mostly I just go to lectures and have tea with Vera.'

But for all her objections, the letters brought Walter the seductive scent of something softer, subtler, more shadowy, than the life he was coming to know. Paris, in his head, was irretrievably associated with the allure of the female.

Germany was her suggestion, thrown out casually. 'The

high summer will be occupied by a Grand Tour of England, Scotland and Wales,' she wrote. 'I am most fortunate to be hanging on to the coat tails of this expedition. Vera's parents, having already been so kind as to take me out to dinner, have decided in their wisdom that I am a suitable companion for their daughter. But it seems I am not to be satiated by three countries; I must do more. Because after that I am going to Scandinavia with Margaret and Jean; and have taken it into my head to part from them before the end of the trip and take the ferry across the Öresund and make my way to Germany. After all, it's about time I made use of all those expensive German lessons. If you happen to be free at the beginning of August, company would be most acceptable.'

He'd had to read it three times to make sure he had understood it right. And then, when he was certain, he was thrown into an almighty panic. He'd dreamed all summer of seeing her again, but now that it was a real possibility, he just could not imgine it. To spend a week with such a woman – someone who had spent a year being educated in Paris, and who was prepared to tour the whole of Northern Europe in such an independent and confident manner – was he really capable of it? Would he be able to think of anything to say?

'Yes!' he replied to her, and then 'No!' and finally, 'Oh, Grace, you will think me so disorganised and inefficient, and really I would like to come more than anything in the world, and if I possibly can I definitely will, but there are a number of things I have to fit in here, and I just can't quite work it out now, which means I suppose that I will be too late to make the decision, because soon you will be on your Grand Tour, and there will be no time to worry about my plans.'

'Dear disorganised Walter,' said Grace's reply, 'you do not

in the least have to make your decision now. I am quite aware that you lead a very busy life and that it would be most foolish of me to worry about your plans. So I shall not. I will be going to Germany, with you or no, and plan to arrive in Nürnberg on or around 4 August. Hopefully there will be an opportunity to provide you with more details of my train nearer the time, and if I should happen to find you waiting for me at the station, then I will be filled with joy, and if not, I promise not to be too inconsolable in my disappointment.'

Such a challenge proved in the end impossible to resist. In August Walter packed his bags and took the boat train to Dover, the ferry to Ostend and the train to Nürnberg. He had never spent a journey in such cosmopolitan company; he met a fellow Australian, a Siamese physicist, a Belgian, a German girl who was returning home after three years in London, an English woman who was returning to Hungary with her Romanian husband, and a Czechoslovakian who spoke the languages of everyone there with the exception of the Siamese. This last gentleman was recovering from a misadventure in Brussels, having lost one of the two pedigree dogs he was taking back to Prague. By the time Walter stood waiting for Grace on the platform at Nürnberg, he felt he'd had a crash course in world culture.

He saw her unload her own luggage from the train, looking smaller, quieter and more restrained than he remembered her. Walter hesitated for a moment, then started to walk towards her, slowly at first, then breaking into a run. She turned.

'Walter!'

Her face cracked into a huge beaming smile. She dropped her bag and jumped up and down. 'Walter! Oh, I'm so glad! I'd decided you weren't coming!'

'Why not? Why wouldn't I come?'

'Because it was best if I decided you weren't, silly. Better to have a nice surprise than a bad one. Oh, this is going to be so jolly! Have you found somewhere to stay?'

It was indeed quite wildly, ecstatically jolly. Nürnberg, Heidelberg, Frankfurt, Cologne— They wandered through the cobbled towns, climbed hills and looked out across the Rhine Valley, and went walking in the Black Forest. Amongst all the old buildings, and for all the mutterings about hyperinflation, a truly modern nation shone through. Grace had a job to drag Walter away from the various mechanical wonderlands he found.

In one extortionately expensive tearoom he retreated to the lavatory and did not emerge for a good five minutes. 'What's wrong?' asked Grace. 'Are you ill?'

He confessed that he had thrown good money after bad by spending thirty pfennig in washing his hands. 'It was done by an automatic machine,' he gabbled. 'I wish you could have seen it. The money was placed in the slot, a button pressed and then things started to work. Both hands were placed just below the machine, then water came out for two seconds, then liquid soap for one and a half seconds, water for six seconds, hot air to dry the hands for fifty seconds, and cream for one second. There was an interval of a few seconds between each of these processes and a dial indicating when each was to start and finish.'

'And that cost thirty pfennig?'

'It cost ten. But I had to do it three times. I wanted to remember the timings properly.'

After that they dispensed with the tearoom part of the adventure and fed themselves from an Automat. The Automat was a café where all the food was displayed in glass compartments, each equipped with a metal slot. When the correct money was put in the slot the compartment magically opened and the meal was delivered. The food was a little stale and not terribly wholesome, but Walter was so entranced that he could not be persuaded to eat anywhere else. When they could find the Automat, that was. They got lost in town after town after town.

'Where are we now?' was Grace's constant refrain.

'Well, I think – is that the Rathaus? Or it could be the castle.'

Grace's laughter pealed against the walls of the ancient lanes. 'You know, in all the time I travelled with Vera and Margaret and Jean, we never once got lost.'

'Well, they had proper guide books, didn't they?'

'Oh, I'm most *frightfully* sorry. It was you who saw fit to bring the *Children's Encyclopaedia*.'

'And if I hadn't brought that, we'd have nothing.'

'Here, let's ask this chap.'

And they tried out their German on another unsuspecting local.

'*Wie kommen wir am besten zum Cathedral?*' demanded Grace, rolling her Rs and distorting her vowels in what sounded to Walter like the most outrageous fashion. But it must have convinced the German, because he proceeded to rattle off a procession of long, complex and, to Walter, utterly incomprehensible instructions. Grace smiled and nodded enthusiastically. '*Ach, ja,*' she said at intervals, and '*Vielen Dank, mein Herr.*'

'What did he say?' demanded Walter when he had taken his leave.

'Haven't the foggiest. But I got the general impression that we need to take *die Straßenbahn.*'

So they caught the tram in what they considered to be the general direction of the cathedral.

'What's that?' Grace pointed.

'I think that's the Exhibition Building,' said Walter, his nose in the *Encyclopaedia*.

'There seems to be some sort of event going on. Shall we take a look?'

'I thought we were going to the cathedral.'

'We can go to the cathedral after we've been to the Exhibition Building. Come on.' She grabbed his sleeve and pulled him off the tram.

Whatever it was that was going on was terribly popular. They pushed their way through the crowds and were suddenly inside. Walter turned and saw that Grace was close to being swept away by the tide of people. 'Grace!' he shouted and tried to push backwards. On the stage a row of men sat on a podium, shuffling papers as if preparing speeches. Above them were draped a series of enormous flags, emblazoned with a spiky, twisted black symbol they had seen only in newspapers.

Grace and Walter looked at each other. She said something he could not hear above the noise of the crowd. 'Pardon?' he shouted, and she said it again, louder.

'It's a political rally, isn't it? We don't want to listen to it, do we?'

He did not. As a hush fell unevenly across the hall they started to push their way back out. Behind them one of the speeches had begun. Speech was not really the right word, for the man's voice was like a percussion instrument, banging out the sentences in a kind of monotonal music. The crowd made their own noise in time with his words, the bodies flowing forward with the rise of his voice, and back when it dropped. Grace and Walter fled. They did not look back.

'Oh, thank goodness,' said Grace as they escaped into fresh air. 'Politics are terribly rowdy. Your peace meetings aren't like that, are they?'

'Goodness, no. They're – well, peaceful.'

They grinned at one another and set off in search of the cathedral.

*   *   *

'Thank you for a lovely holiday,' said Grace.

'I don't want you to go back to Australia,' said Walter inconsolably.

They were standing outside Charing Cross station, waiting for Grace's bus. Nelson looked loftily down upon them from his column, as if all their cares were nought in comparison with the grand sweep of history to which he, like all the dead, was witness.

The bus would take her to Worthing, for her time as a student in Paris was over, and she was to spend her last months in Europe living with relatives and teaching in a local school.

'Well,' said Grace, 'I have to. I have a job in Perth to go back to, remember? It's not that I want to go. I don't want to go back at all. I've made so many friends here. Not least *you*.'

Walter blushed and eked out a smile.

'And I really think it suits me better over here. The culture. There's so much more to it. And the climate.'

'The *climate?*' said Walter disbelievingly.

'Oh, I hate the heat. I know it sounds strange, having been brought up in Perth. Probably Mother's influence. She always has to have something to complain about, and the heat is fairly reliable.'

'Then why not stay? There are always jobs for teachers.'

'I have to *go*,' said Grace. Her chin was tilted upwards in stubbornness, and her eyes were inscrutable. Walter thought she had never looked so lovely.

The bus pulled in. Walter detested it. They heaved her luggage aboard, squeezing between the other passengers and treading on one another's toes. When she was safely seated, Walter stood in the aisle, gazing at her and getting in everyone's way.

'Walter,' said Grace, 'it's probably best if you don't end up in Worthing. You haven't got a ticket, for a start.'

He frowned, feeling the most intense unhappiness. 'Will I see you again?'

'There's always half-term. I could come and see you in Cambridge. I've never been to Cambridge. Would that be acceptable?'

'Oh, yes!'

Suddenly she smiled and Walter felt the warmth of it wash over him.

'And now you really must get off the bus.'

'Thank you! Thank you! Goodbye!'

'*Au revoir*,' said Grace, and Walter stumbled backwards down the aisle.

Walter was waiting to take his turn with the bat. He and Alan were sprawled on the grass at the perimeter of the cricket pitch, the insects buzzing around them in the last frenzy of August.

'Alan,' he said, 'I've got a visitor coming to stay in October.'

'October? That's rather a long time to be planning in advance.'

'It's – the person I went to Germany with.'

'Graham?'

The time had come to make his confession. 'Erm – the name wasn't Graham. It was Grace.'

'*Grace?*'

They stared at the batsmen. The bowler ran up to his crease and the ball looped in a tall arc towards the wicket. There was a flurry of bat and ball, and the fielders dived. Walter began to get to his feet. Then the ball trickled out from the feet of the competitors, and Walter sat down again, rearranging his pads.

'She's going back to Australia soon,' he said mournfully. 'I think I'm going to have to ask her to marry me. I don't suppose she'll accept.'

Alan looked nonplussed. A moment ago, he had not even heard of this woman, and now Walter was proposing her as a candidate to become his wife.

She came to Cambridge. He showed her around the town, after a fashion.

'Look, look!' whispered Walter, pointing. 'Is that him?'

'No, of course it isn't. He's wearing the wrong clothes.'

'He's in England. In his book he wore English clothes when he was in England.'

'Yes, but he doesn't now, does he? You've seen his photographs in the papers. He wears that sort of nappy arrangement.'

'A dhoti.'

'I know what it's called. I still think it looks like a nappy.'

Walter had planned the itinerary for Grace's visit to Cambridge down to the last second. But it had all had to be scrapped, because at the last minute he'd received intelligence from his Indian colleague, Chaudhri, that Gandhi was in town to give a speech to the Indian students at the Unitarian Church. And so here they were, scouring Cambridge in the hope of a sighting.

'When's the service?' asked Grace.

'Not till four. But I think he must be in town already. The place is crawling with his followers.'

'How do you know that they're followers? They could just be normal students, like your friend Chaudhri.'

'They aren't. They don't have gowns. And – oh golly! Look at that woman over there!'

'Which woman?'

'The English woman in a sari. That's Miss Slade.'

'Miss Slade?'

'Gandhi's English disciple. She's quite famous.'

'How funny it is that the Indians are all in English dress, and the English woman is got up like an Indian.'

'Chaudhri came into the laboratory once in his Indian dress.'

'*Really?* In a dhoti?'

'Oh, no. Most Indians don't wear dhotis. That's just for—' He stopped, because he didn't actually know who it was for. 'But he looked pretty odd all the same. He wore a pair of very light brown trousers which fitted tightly on his legs below the knees, like riding breeches, and no stockings so that his ankles were exposed, and a long coat with buttons reaching right up to his neck.'

'How very exotic.'

'Well, yes. But that was nothing to what happened when he took off the coat.'

'What did he have underneath?'

'It looked like an ordinary silk shirt, but instead of having it tucked inside his trousers like anyone else, it hung quite loose, so that it looked as if he was in the middle of getting dressed. He was getting about the lab like this, when he came across one of the women, who was so embarrassed that she fled the building.'

Grace giggled. 'I wouldn't have run away. I would have been interested.'

'The strange thing is, Gandhi had just the same problem when he came to England and had to wear English clothes. He thought they were terribly indecent. Because the shirts were so short, you see, and they revealed the waistline. Which only goes to show that all the things we think are normal for us are just – well—'

'Arbitrary?'

'*Yes,*' said Walter, very pleased with her for finding the right word. 'And it shows that we should always strive very hard to see things from the other person's point of view, especially if they come from another culture. Which all ties in with what Gandhi has to teach us about Peace.'

'I wish we could go to the service. It seems a bit narrow-minded to restrict it to the Indians. If what you say is true. He should treat us all the same.'

'I suppose it has to be restricted in some way.'

They failed to track him down on the street and resorted to waiting outside the church.

'Can *that* be him?'

A luxurious saloon car drew up in front of them. Walter and Grace hurried backwards to let its passengers out. Sure enough, a small weedy man with bald head, spectacles and cotton robes stepped onto the pavement.

'Golly, one couldn't possibly mistake him,' whispered Walter.

'Don't you think the car and his array are rather incongruous?'

'Shhh!'

The tiny man walked past them and disappeared into the church.

'We were so close!' said Walter in awe.

'Mmm,' said Grace.

They wandered away.

'It's a bit of an anticlimax really, isn't it?'

Walter looked at her in fear. 'Are you bored? Are you not having a good time?'

'Oh, Walter, of course I'm not bored. I'm having a *lovely* time. And I'm very glad to have seen Gandhi. But it was a shame not to hear him speak, after all you've told me about him.'

'I'm sorry.'

'It's not your fault! And I don't really mind. It was just tantalising, that's all.'

'I've booked a punt for five,' said Walter shyly. 'If you want to go, that is.'

'A punt! How very Cambridge. That would be wonderful. Are you any good?'

Walter did fancy himself as a bit of a dab hand with a punt. But when it came to trying to steer a boat with Grace in it, everything seemed to go wrong. The punt zigzagged down the river. She laughed at him mercilessly.

'It's that blasted rowing boat,' expostulated Walter. 'Keeps getting in the way.'

'No it's not!' shouted the rower. 'It's you!'

'You tell him,' said Grace to the rower. 'He gets completely out of control.'

Walter jammed his pole into the river bed, trapping the punt against the bank, sat down, and sulked.

'Do you want me to have a go?' Grace teased him.

'No!' He sat for a bit longer. The end of the boat drifted towards the middle of the river. 'I'm having a rest.'

'You have a rest, then. You deserve it.'

He stared at the flowing water, feeling as much out of control as she'd said he was. The time was slipping away from him. Soon she would be gone for ever.

'It's all going wrong,' he said.

Grace's face creased with an affectionate smile. 'What's going wrong, muggins? I think everything's lovely.'

'We didn't hear Gandhi speak. I didn't go to China. I've run out of polonium and I haven't finished my experiment. And – and—'

'That seems quite enough to be going on with. And what?'

'And you're going back to *Australia*.'

Grace said nothing. She was serene and collected, her hair bright in the sunlight.

'I've left so much over there. I don't want – the only thing I really care about here – to go there too—'

She was serene and collected no more. Her eyes were suddenly frail.

'Grace,' said Walter in a sudden rush, 'will you marry me?'

'Yes,' said Grace almost before he had finished the sentence.

They stared at one another.

'Oh, goodness,' said Walter.

'My darling—'

She was beautiful. She was clever. She was unfathomably lovely. She had called him darling. And she had just agreed to marry him.

'Oh, Grace,' he said, 'I shouldn't have done it like that.'

'Walter,' she said, 'don't you see? I don't *care*—'

'Oh, Grace.' He stood up. The punt wobbled. She stood up and it wobbled some more. He caught her waist and her smell washed over him. The softness of her dress and skin were against him. He kissed her.

There was a cheer beside them. They stumbled apart, laughing and blushing. The punt tipped and Walter sat down, pulling her with him. She buried her face in his shoulder. He looked over her head to see a group of nine men in rowing clothes jogging along the towpath, the tiny cox in the lead. One of them waved. Walter smiled.

'I'm just a student,' he whispered to her, joy bubbling over in him. 'I have nothing to offer you.'

'You have everything I want.'

'I won't be able to marry you for years. Not until I've got a job. I don't even know where I'm going to be.'

'You certainly won't be able to marry me for years. I'm going back to Australia, remember?'

He drew apart from her. 'Going back to Australia?'

'My love, I can't change it now. The passage is booked and everything. They're expecting me back at the school.'

'But for how long?'

'Two years was the original contract. But that's all right, because that's how long you'll be doing your Ph.D.'

Two years. With her skin against his, it was more unbearable than ever.

'Of course it's not all right,' she admitted. 'It's not all right at all. But – nobody ever said it would be *easy*—'

'I love you,' he said helplessly, as if that would make a difference.

'Oh, Walter,' she said, and now her eyes were closer to his than any living thing had ever been. When he kissed her a whole world seemed to open up before him. Just letting her go to speak again felt like the most enormous loss.

'I suppose if things are as wonderful as this it doesn't really matter, does it?'

'It doesn't matter at all. Because Walter – you have realised this, haven't you? – we are talking about the rest of our lives.'

He hadn't, really. He shivered in the sunlight and then pushed the chill away. 'I'm sorry I don't know more about the rest of my life.'

'Nobody ever knows. I know enough, now.'

'Oh, Grace, you are so lovely.'

'I'm not lovely. No one would ever accuse me of being lovely. I'm just in love.'

It did not seem possible that anyone could ever deserve to be as happy as this. 'Do you remember that poem?' he said.

'What poem?'

'The one you showed me on the boat.'

'Sir Walter.' She snuggled. 'My knight in shining armour. We're going to explore the world together.'

'Why, yes!' It was the most fabulous thought. Anything seemed possible. 'He came to a nasty end, of course.'

She took his hands and squeezed them so hard they hurt, and stared at him with blazing eyes. 'We won't, my love,' she said fiercely. 'I'll make sure of it. We won't.'

Patrick was packing up his kite.

'Do you think it's going to rain?' said Grace loudly, to no one in particular.

The clouds were racing fast across the sky. Still running away from him, after all these years. 'I think it'll probably hold off until we get home,' said Walter weakly. He did not want to go home. He wanted to stay out here, in the cool fresh air.

Bridget was pelting towards him, a small cannonball zig-zagging across the muddy grass. He picked her up and twirled her round him.

'Aeroplanes!' shouted Bridget breathlessly when he'd returned her to the ground. 'Again!'

'Not again. Daddy's tired. Hup!' He scooped her up and put her back on his shoulders.

He looked across at Grace, who was striding across the grass, her face screwed up in concentration. What was she thinking about? Him, probably. For a moment he wanted to say out loud the thought he'd had about Jim and Cologne, the memory which had swept him away from her just when they were about to achieve closeness.

But it wasn't going to help.

Jim had sent Walter a postcard after a trip to Cologne too. It was shortly after he'd left Wales, to embark on active duty, and he'd sent it the day after the first thousand-bomber raid. As the planes circled above the firestorm, Jim had remembered the postcard he'd received as a child, and had thought to look back for the spires of one of the largest cathedrals in Europe. But amidst the flames and smoke which rose up from the wreckage, not a trace of the ancient city could be seen.

12

'Good morning, Professor Poltine.'

Edward Horatio Poltine sat at his desk, fidgeting in ill temper.

'Is this going to take long, Mr Henderson?' he said. His voice was a nasal whine.

Henderson felt very foolish. He was doing his best to act on Aitken's command to 'go to it' but he had still been given no further indications of what he was supposed to do. How could he investigate a pacifist who had no involvement in peace? The only option was to go to the place where Dunnachie actually did spend his time. But it was hard to see what he could possibly discover here. He sat very straight in his chair and tried to emulate Aitken. It was a challenge without the accompanying flesh. 'I'm sure we can cover the various details reasonably speedily,' he said in as unconcerned a tone as he could muster.

'Because I have all sorts of things to be attending to. There are people out to get me.' He twitched.

Henderson's eyebrows rose. This was the last place he'd expected to encounter paranoia.

'The Board of Governors. They're trying to force me out. So as you can imagine, this is all rather inconvenient.'

'But necessary, I'm afraid.'

'So you said on the telephone. So, come on, what are you going to ask me?'

'I wanted to check a few facts about Dr Walter Dunnachie.'

'*Dunnachie?*'

'That's right.'

'The man's completely harmless. What on earth do you want to know about Dunnachie?'

What did he want to know? This was the most difficult thing, thought Henderson, about trying to do this job properly. Poltine almost certainly knew things that were valuable to Henderson, but didn't know what they were, and if only Henderson heard them he'd know what they were, but he didn't know yet, and so it was impossible to know what to ask.

'Is he a good scientist?' he hazarded.

'Was once. The best of his Cambridge crop. Job market was overflowing with talented Ph.D.s in 1934. Refugees, you name it, and hardly any academic jobs. So I could pick and choose. But still it was a coup to get him.'

'Was once, you say? Not any more?'

'Might be again, I suppose. But I doubt it. Past it, you see. He's thirty-seven.'

'And that's past it for a physicist?'

'Not necessarily. If you're on a roll at that age you can generally keep going for another ten years. But most people's greatest achievements take place in their early thirties. After that it's mainly a matter of directing your protégés. If you haven't made it by then, then you tend not to have any protégés, and the best option's administration. And you can't get into those jobs without a distinguished research record. I know. I've been there. It's been hard, you know, very hard, they don't understand. And Dunnachie doesn't have my – *grit*.'

The man peered at him through small weasel eyes.

'So Dunnachie hasn't made it?'

'He's just a lecturer,' said Poltine, as if that explained everything.

Henderson remembered a comment of Mrs Dunnachie's. 'And he won't be promoted?'

'Not unless he gets his finger out and publishes some decent research. Messed around with some god-forsaken theoretical chemistry throughout the war, and goodness knows what good that's supposed to do a physics department. I have the reputation of my school to consider, you know. We're flagging. They think it's my fault. But what was I supposed to do, out in Bangor, with nothing but a bunch of invalids and conchies—'

Henderson's chest tightened. He willed himself not to cough. 'He was a conscientious objector. Is that why he hasn't made it?'

'What do I care?' snapped Poltine.

Henderson stared at him.

'What do I care if he's a conchie or a communist or a *bloody* blackshirt? I recruited the best scientists and they let me down, and now the Board of Governors is blaming it on me.'

He sat with his hands folded on the table and glared at Henderson over his half-moon spectacles.

'I suppose it's the pacifism you're interested in?'

Henderson wanted to say something profound. But he couldn't think of anything. 'Yes,' he said.

'Why didn't you say so, for goodness' sake? Honestly, you civil servants are all the same. Had exactly the same problem during the war. Types like yourself sniffing around after equipment. They never said what they were after, but they may as well have saved us all the trouble and just come out with it, because they always got it in the end. Well, if it's that, then perhaps I can help you. I've had a complaint.'

Henderson perked up. 'Really?'

'Load of nonsense, if you ask me. Navy chap, liked fighting, wants to carry on with it, and has decided to pick on Dunnachie. Neither here nor there. Not planning to follow it up. Wouldn't look good, under the circumstances. But if you want to have a word with him—'

Henderson nodded, trying to keep his enthusiasm under control.

'Might kill two birds with one stone. That'll shut the blighter up, if he thinks I've spoken to someone from the – what did you call it again?'

'The Bureau.'

'Yes, that would do very nicely. A bureau will appeal to him. But I must have an assurance from you.'

'What?'

'That not a word of this goes to the Board of Governors. Not from him, and not from you.'

'You can be assured of my absolute discretion,' said Henderson, feeling a burst of confidence. 'That's my job.'

'Well, sir,' said Ridley, 'I must say I'm very glad this is being taken seriously.'

Sir. Henderson swelled with pride. Ridley's bearing was military in the extreme, and he spoke as if he were addressing a senior officer.

'Not that I want to get Dr Dunnachie into trouble. But you can't be too careful, as I'm sure you know. I certainly do.'

'What seems to be the trouble?' said Henderson, and then realised that he sounded like the family doctor.

'Well,' said Ridley, 'he's a nice enough chap, I'm sure. But he's a crackpot.'

'In what way?'

'He's very hostile to me, for a start. And all the other veterans. Can't abide us. Apparently he was a conscientious objector.'

'He was.'

'Yes, well, and that speaks for itself, doesn't it? The government was always very decent about them, too much so if you ask me. Give them an inch and they take a mile. Most of the ones I came across were shirkers, plain and simple. But with Dunnachie I think there's more to it than that.'

'What makes you think that?'

'It's his attitude to fission.'

Oh God. Henderson's hope subsided. If the man's complaint was about his school work, it was hardly going to be of any use to him. And he really was not qualified to interview scientists. 'Fission?'

'Yes,' said Ridley kindly. 'Do you know what fission is?'

'Well—' It was not pleasant admitting ignorance, but this man gave the impression that he'd enjoy it if Henderson did, so he capitulated. 'No.'

'It's what happens to trigger an atomic bomb.'

About three seconds later George remembered to close his mouth.

'I'm sorry,' he heard the student say, 'did I say something that disturbed you?'

Science. Physics.

It was so obvious. 'You're so *stupid* sometimes, George,' he could hear Phoebe saying. 'Why don't you see what's in front of your nose? It's because you don't want to see, can't you even see that? You'll never make a success of anything unless you start looking around you.'

She was right that he did not want to see. The bomb. A weapon created by scientists. He remembered the terror he had felt on seeing those first newspaper reports. All the other bombs – even the doodlebugs, even the V2 rockets – had been possible to understand. They'd got bigger and more devastating as the war went on, but he knew about explosions. Logs rolling from the hearth and scorching the carpet, stink bombs, bonfire night, sparklers – the Blitz had consisted of the direct descendants of things he'd seen around him all his life. But the thing they'd dropped in Japan –

stripping bodies of their skins even when buildings were left intact, working by rules which only a few people in the world could comprehend – it was too horrible even to begin to contemplate. So after that day he had not thought about it. And he had assumed somehow that everyone else had done the same. But now it was clear that the bomb had not sprung into existence on its own. There were people who had made it. And those people would logically work in places like this.

Having failed to get a response, Ridley continued anyway. 'Fission's why I'm doing this degree, if the truth be known. They offered me a chance to get an education, and I thought, well, if they're paying for it, then I might as well take them up on it. And then I had to decide what to study. And as I was an engineer on the ship, some sort of science seemed the right thing to do, and then the news came from Hiroshima, and it ended the war. And I thought, that's the future. That's what I'll do.'

But I'm investigating a pacifist, thought George helplessly. What about the Peace Army, all those plans for standing unarmed between two opposing armies? How could such a thing possibly be reconciled with this? And then, if *that*'s what this is about, why have they put *me* on to it? The enormity of the situation yawned beneath him like a pit.

'And it has to be said,' Ridley pontificated, 'it's a waste of time so far.'

'Oh,' said George, and then, realising that more inquisitiveness was expected of an inquisitor, managed to phrase a question. 'Why's that?'

'I'm sure protons and electrons and neutrons are all very well, but they're no good to man nor beast. I want to protect this nation against its enemies. I was in the Battle of the Atlantic, you know. I remember what it was like when we were hanging on by a thread, about to go under. My friends died to save this country and I want to make sure that no one gets the upper hand over us again. Dunnachie's responsible for giving my generation the tools we need to do that. And he won't give them to us. He just won't teach it.'

'Erm – what?'

'He was there, you know! He was there when they split the atom. But whenever anyone asks him about it, he just fudges the issue and talks about the difference between science and technology, and says that it's science that's important, and fission has nothing to do with science. I tell you, if fission has nothing to do with science, then I'm a March hare.'

Ridley's very wide eyes and prominent ears did momentarily give him a hare-like aspect. 'Mr Ridley,' said George, gasping a little, 'you must make an allowance for the fact that I do not have a scientific background. I would appreciate it if we could go over a couple of things again, to make sure that I have them clear.'

'Oh, sorry,' said Ridley. 'What exactly do you need me to explain?'

What indeed? George flailed for a bit, and then started to pull things out of the mess in his brain. 'Fission. You say that fission is something you learn in physics. Is that right?'

'Yes. It's what happens when a uranium atom captures a neutron and splits, and it lets off some more neutrons, and they get captured by more uranium atoms, then there's a chain reaction.'

No, no, he could not deal with any of that at all. Every time the man started using words like *uranium* and *neutron* George's chest began to constrict, as it used to in science classes at school. He tried to calm himself by taking deep breaths. 'And you say that it's something to do with building an atomic bomb.'

'Exactly.'

'Do you mean that Dr Dunnachie was involved in building the atomic bomb?'

'Oh, golly, I don't think so, sir. That all happened in America. And anyway, he's a conchie. I told you that.'

Well, yes, exactly. 'But you said he was involved in something. I can't remember exactly what you said now. You said he was there, or something.'

'Splitting the atom?' suggested Ridley.

'That was it. Is that something to do with fission? Or is it to do with the bomb?'

'Well—' Ridley's air of confidence dissipated as his forehead creased. For a moment George thought he could see the cogs of the man's brain turning, unevenly and painfully, and he felt a little better. 'I think you might find the science a little complicated, sir.'

Henderson straightened his back. 'I'd be grateful if you'd spare me the science, Mr Ridley. I just need you to tell me whether it's to do with the atomic bomb. And if so, in what way Dr Dunnachie is involved.'

'Well—' Ridley was still floundering. Then he pulled himself together. 'You see, sir, that's the problem. He won't tell us. He won't tell us how they're related. Whenever I ask about fission, he gets extremely angry and changes the subject.'

'And why do you think that is?'

'Because he's a crackpot,' said Ridley triumphantly, proving his point.

'Right. But what you still haven't told me is what this splitting the atom business has to do with it.'

'He was there,' said Ridley simply.

I am getting nowhere, thought George. An image of himself sitting in the British Library reading a tome on atomic physics presented itself to his brain. He expelled the thought very quickly. It was much easier to let other people do the reading and then get them to explain the important bits. He looked at Ridley's muscular face and wondered whether he should try again.

'How are your grades?' he asked.

Ridley's face turned bright red. Then his eyes flashed with anger. 'Very poor, sir, very poor. I told you, he's biased. This is important to me, you know. I've signed away three years of my life. I'm just trying to do my best for my country, and he's trying to stop me. Doing everything in his power to stop me, in fact. And he shouldn't have that power.'

'I see.' Bias or no bias, it appeared that Ridley was not exactly a star student. And the chances were also that he didn't know anything more about Dunnachie than he had already told. Still, if only George could subdue the panic he felt when presented with the science, this had been a successful interview. He'd learnt a great deal. The thing now was to go back to Poltine, if he could bear it.

'Are you going to get them to get rid of him, sir?'

Henderson was touched by his trust. 'I'm afraid that this is only one part of a much wider investigation,' he said.

Ridley looked impressed. 'Well, if there's anything I can do to help. Anything at all.'

'Thank you for your diligence. There is a favour you must do for me now. You mustn't speak to anyone of this interview. Professor Poltine knows I'm speaking to you, of course, but he's not aware of the wider implications. And we must keep it absolutely quiet.'

'Oh, completely, sir. You can rely on me.'

The man looked as though he was a hair's breadth away from a salute. Henderson swelled with pride once more.

'Good afternoon, Miss Alderton,' said Henderson to Professor Poltine's secretary.

He knew he was not very skilled in this spying business. But if there was one means of getting things done which was at his disposal, it was being polite to the little people. He was, he considered ruefully, a little person himself, and he knew how they thought. Secretaries appreciated it if one remembered their names.

'Oh, good afternoon – Mr Henderson, isn't it?'

Miss Alderton had very full breasts. The stomach beneath them was a little on the plump side, and she had made an attempt to hide both the credit and debit sides of the equation, but the disguise was not entirely effective, and merely added to the impression of spilling out of herself. He gave her a calm smile.

'That's right,' he said. 'How clever of you to remember.'

She blushed with pleasure and the skin above the top of her blouse coloured very slightly. 'Well, it's my job, you know, to remember who the professor's associates are, and ensure that everything runs smoothly. What can I do for you, Mr Henderson?'

'Well, I'm aware that the professor is terribly busy at the moment. But I wonder if you could do me a great favour and arrange another appointment with him as soon as possible. It's a rather urgent matter, you see. The professor knows all about it.'

'I'll do whatever I can,' said Miss Alderton. 'But I'm afraid he's over at the Senate House in committee meetings for most of today. I could try to get a message to him, I suppose—'

'I can wait until tomorrow,' said Henderson, smiling.

'I'm afraid tomorrow is rather difficult too. Oh dear, I am sorry. The following day looks a bit better, though. Would that be all right?'

'That would be fine.'

'I think the morning would be best – though I'd suggest coming earlier rather than later. There's always the chance he'll have got caught up in something if you leave it too late.'

'That's very sound advice. You've been most helpful, Miss Alderton. I'm extremely grateful.'

'Oh, it's nothing, Mr Henderson, absolutely nothing.'

George felt a spring in his step as he walked out of the door. She was not a pretty girl, but there was something rather voluptuous about her, for all her attempts to be prim. The sort of woman whose dread of spinsterhood was an all-consuming passion. He imagined that if he touched her she might swoon right away. The thought made him hot with pleasure. She was his for the taking, if he wanted her. Of course, she was out of bounds for professional reasons, but still—

Or was she? Might there not be very good professional reasons for continuing the flirtation? As he walked down the brown-painted corridors of the institution, he allowed his mind and body to be swept away on a tide of images, of flesh, tangled hair, moist smells, female adoration, and himself as the most potent sort of spy—

'Mr Henderson.'

The voice was female and abrupt. George stopped dead and saw two hostile blue eyes glaring up at him through schoolmistress's spectacles. The effect on his anatomy was sobering and immediate.

'Why are you following my husband?' demanded Mrs Dunnachie.

I am not, George had stuttered.

Oh yes you most certainly are, Mrs Dunnachie had replied. And now I'd like us to proceed to a place with a little more privacy, so that you can start telling me *exactly* what you are trying to achieve by insinuating yourself into our lives.

So, obedience itself, he had taken her to the obvious place, which was the coffee house on the Euston Road. They had received their cups of coffee and he was now in the midst of a coughing fit, while Mrs Dunnachie sat opposite him with a look of patient fury on her face, waiting for him to get it over and done with.

I am not doing it on *purpose*, George protested in his head, because her expression stated that he most certainly was. The mucus was catching between chest and throat, and his diaphragm had begun to convulse uncontrollably. He had not had an attack as bad as this for a very long time.

'Stop it!' shouted Mrs Dunnachie suddenly, as if to a hysterical child.

George stopped.

'For goodness' sake,' she said irritably.

The water was streaming down his cheeks. He had by now exhausted both his napkin and hers, and stood up briefly to grab a third from a neighbouring table.

'Take deep breaths,' said Mrs Dunnachie.

He obliged.

'Now. As soon as you have got yourself under some sort of control, I would like you to explain what you think you're up to.' And then, as his chest began to tighten again – 'No!'

'Mrs Dunnachie,' stammered George, 'I am in the most dreadful position you can imagine.' He really was. It was no exaggeration. This was so much worse than what had happened outside the British Museum. The whole mission was completely sabotaged. Mrs Dunnachie would tell her husband, and Dunnachie would tell Nunn May, and – well, he was really in no position to understand what would happen after that, but there was every possibility that Nunn May would tell the Russians. The table and the ground beneath him began to shudder, and George jumped, expecting at any moment a blinding white light and a mushroom cloud rising above the streets of London. He stared at the floor in horror.

'Mr Henderson,' said Mrs Dunnachie, 'it's the tube.'

Oh yes. So it was.

'You are clearly in an extremely overwrought state,' she said, 'so I will keep my questions simple, in the hope that you will have some success in answering them. Are you conducting – these activities – on your own behalf, for some private motivation, or is this something you do to earn a living?'

'I do it to earn a living,' said George miserably. He knew that he was not supposed to have said that. Some plausible excuse for being in University College ought to have been made at the start, and then he should have got out, gone straight to Aitken, told him everything, and left the next steps up to his employer. But none of these things had happened. He was lost and bereft, and the only person available to guide him was her.

'Who pays you?'

'The government.'

'The *government*?' Now she was actually shaking with anger. 'Well, I suppose you did tell me that you worked for the civil service. I have clearly been quite unfeasibly stupid. I suppose it was rather a stroke of luck for you when I invited you round for dinner.'

'Yes,' agreed George.

'So. Do tell me. What exactly does the government want to know about Walter that he would not tell them himself if they had the courtesy to ask him?'

I don't know, he pleaded in his head. And then, confronted by her frankness, a wild thought occurred to him. Perhaps, if he had the courtesy to ask her, she would tell him herself.

He was still contemplating this thought in surprise when she spoke again.

'I suppose it's the pacifism, isn't it?'

'That certainly seems to be part of it, yes,' he confirmed.

'Well, I can give you my absolute assurance that Walter hasn't lifted a finger for Peace since the end of the war. He's been given every opportunity and he's rejected all of them.'

'I – I had come to that conclusion myself.'

'In that case, why on earth are you following him? There are hundreds of people who are still active in the Peace Movement who might better occupy your time. Or does the government have people tailing each one of them as well? It sounds like the most extravagant waste of our taxes, if you ask me.'

'I—' He might as well say it. Things could not exactly get any worse. 'I think it's because of the science.'

'The science.' She frowned in concentration. 'They aren't very easy bedfellows these days, are they? Science and Peace, I mean.'

He supposed not. The rumble of another tube train vibrated beneath his feet.

'But that still doesn't make sense to me, Mr Henderson. I mean, I can see how the sort of science which Walter does might be very interesting to the government indeed. But he was a *conscientious objector*. He has been excluded from every field which was associated with military developments during the war – in fact he excluded himself. So we're back in the same position as we were with the Peace. He's the worst-informed nuclear physicist you're likely to come across. Specifically because he *is* a pacifist. So why not follow one of the others? Any of the others?'

'Mrs Dunnachie,' said George, 'what do you mean by the others?'

'The ones who were actually involved, of course! The ones who built the bomb! Chadwick, Cockcroft, Oliphant – that lot!'

'But I thought all that happened in America,' said George weakly.

'Mr Henderson, are you putting on an act? Or do you really know as little as you appear to? Because if you are a spy, I fear that doesn't make you a very good one.'

'I'm not a very good one,' admitted George.

A rather odd smile flickered on Mrs Dunnachie's lips. 'I do hope you're telling me the truth.'

'I am!' He'd told nothing but the truth since they'd entered the café. In a way, it was the most tremendous relief.

'You lied that you worked night shifts. You lied about wanting to join the Methodist church. What else have you lied about?'

He thought about it. 'I don't live in Watford.'

'Really? Your wife was most convincing on that point. Does she know that you're a spy?'

'Well—' Did she? 'Sort of. Not exactly.'

'That sounds like a rather odd way to conduct a marriage.'

Was it? Surely couples all over the world had secrets from one another. Something occurred to him. 'Mrs Dunnachie,' he said, 'do you mind if I ask *you* a question?'

'You can most certainly ask it. I don't guarantee to give you an answer.'

'What were *you* doing in University College?'

'Following my husband,' she snapped back, too quickly for him to even wait for the response.

'Oh,' said George. Then, 'Why?'

'I'm not going to answer that one. You are, you must understand, a difficult person in whom to place one's trust.' She took a deep inward breath, eyeing him over the rims of her glasses. 'Nevertheless, I can see that there are ways in which we might be able to help one another. Particularly if you are, as you claim to be, a very *bad* spy.'

'Oh, I am, I assure you,' said George breathlessly.

She laughed. 'I believe you,' she said. 'Shall I tell you why? It's because I caught you so easily, when I wasn't even trying. You said that my catching you puts you in a very difficult position. How difficult?'

'I don't know. I don't know what they will do to me.'

'What if you don't tell them? What if this little conversation never happened?'

He stared at her. 'Well, naturally that would make things very much easier.' Then his heart fell. 'But they would find out. And then it would be much worse than if I'd told them.'

'How will they find out? Do you think they can see us now? Do they have spies spying on their spies? That sounds like a rather inefficient use of manpower in the current economic situation.'

'But you'll tell your husband,' he explained. 'And that will cause things to happen – I don't know what, but I'm sure it will – and then they'll know.'

'What if I don't tell my husband? What if he doesn't know about this either?'

That sounds like a rather odd way to conduct a marriage, thought George, but then hope caught hold of him and he buried his surprise. 'Would you not?' he asked eagerly.

'I might not. I haven't thought this through properly yet, but I think I might be about to propose a deal to you. Give me a moment.' She rested her forehead on the palm of her hand and stared at the tablecloth in deep thought. George left her to it and resolutely did no thinking of his own.

'Mr Henderson. This is the point. I have absolute faith in Walter. I have been married to him for more than a decade and I know him to have more integrity than anyone I have ever met. He has sometimes taken issue with the course of action taken by the British government, but he has always been absolutely open in saying so. And he always would be. So in many ways I have nothing to fear from you. I know, you see, that there is no way that he has done anything which is immoral or underhand. So whilst your investigations may turn up facts of which the government is not currently aware – even of which *I* am not aware – I very much doubt that either he or I have anything to fear from the truth.'

She paused, waiting for a response from him.

'I see,' said George.

'There is, of course, another possibility.' Her eyes narrowed. 'I have a certain respect for the British establishment. In general, I believe that it is not corrupt. But I have also known it to do things in the past which are not *entirely* honourable. I would say that the fact that you are following my husband is a further example. And it has to be said that I don't know very much about these things. I am out of my depth. It could be a great deal worse than I think. You see, there is the possibility that what you, or your masters, are after is not the truth at all.'

Such thoughts had never crossed George's mind. He thought of Aitken's jaundiced eyeballs and implacable stare and shivered.

'If that is the case, then my husband may be in real danger. My first instinct, naturally, is to tell him so. But I am not sure that is the best course of action in the circumstances. As you say, if I tell him, then things will happen, and your masters will know about it. Even if I try to ensure that things *don't* happen as a result of my telling him, you will most likely tell them yourself, and they will react. We may even find ourselves allocated a more professional operative than yourself, which I certainly don't want. I think my best chance is to assist you.'

'Assist me?'

'Assist you. I shall answer your questions, whenever I can. I shall help you become a better spy, and guide you towards the truth, because, as I have said, I have nothing to fear from the truth. In return, you will assist me. I want to know everything you're doing, everything you find out, everything your boss says to you, everything you are told to do. You see, even if my worst fears are confirmed, and something corrupt is going on, then my best chance is to know about it.'

'I don't think anything corrupt is going on,' said George. 'I think they just want to know.'

'I agree. In which case, it is in everyone's interests to arrive at the truth as swiftly as possible. So. If you will give me your word that you will not tell your employers of what has passed between us, then I give you my word that I will not tell Walter. I will keep my word absolutely unless you break yours. Do we have a deal, Mr Henderson?'

'Oh, yes!'

She stuck out her hand. They shook. George felt faintly ridiculous.

'Now, I can't spend very much more time here, as the children will be back from school. We will meet again, in less conspicuous circumstances. At the church. You're going to have to increase your involvement. I'll put you on the pastoral committee. It involves visiting the old and sick. You don't mind that, do you?'

He did not have much choice. 'That's fine.'

'You know,' said Mrs Dunnachie, 'I really don't think this can be a terribly serious matter. Or they would have appointed someone with a little more *experience*. I know that we have a labour shortage, but still.'

Her smile was long-suffering and affectionate, as if she were dealing with a recalcitrant but redeemable pupil. George felt humiliated, but also oddly hopeful. He had the feeling that she was taking over the mission, and that she was going to run it rather better than Aitken had. Certainly she promised to be a little more thoughtful in her treatment of *him*.

'Oh yes,' she said, 'before we go, there is one thing I'd like to establish. I realise that you don't know much about pacifism, and you don't know much about science. But you must, surely, have some idea of why you are following Walter. What prompted it? What made them send you?'

George thought about it. It took him a while to remember. 'Oh – I know. It was because he received a visit from Dr Nunn May.'

She was halfway through standing up when he said the last words. She shot upright. 'Alan?'

'I believe that's his first name. Why? What do you know about him? Is he—'

But all traces of openness had vanished from her face. 'We shall speak further. At the church. I'll telephone you. Goodbye, Mr Henderson.'

And she was gone.

13

Knock-kneed, coughing like hags, we cursed through sludge . . .
Flashed all the sabres bare, flashed as they turned in air . . .
The blood comes gargling from the froth-corrupted lungs . . .
Only the monstrous anger of the guns, only the stuttering
rifles' rapid rattle . . . Into the mouth of Hell rode the six
hundred.

The first speech Walter ever made was preceded by a
nightmare. He'd stayed up writing it until well after two in
the morning, fretting over his phrases, devouring old poems
for inspiration, until he could no longer keep his eyes open,
and he was forced to crawl between the sheets of his bed,
leaving the sheets of paper spread around his desk. He set
the alarm for six o'clock and was sucked instantly into
slumber.

And the chamber into which he sank was a battlefield
strewn with corpses from every conflict since the Norman
Conquest. The mud sucked, the arrows swarmed, the cannons
roared, the armour flashed, the horses screamed, the chlorine
gas drifted across the trenches, the smoke suffocated, the
aeroplanes swooped, the tanks rolled—

He gasped for breath, flailing his arms, trying to drag
himself into consciousness.

The arms of the dead reached out for him, their mouths
writhing in the shape of the words he'd written.

Walter struck out for his bedside table and clung to the
wood.

The wood melted away in fire, the bed collapsed beneath

him, and the shells tore through the ancient walls of Trinity College.

'I am awake!' he tried to shout.

But he was asleep.

The next blast threw him out of bed. He lay on the wooden boards for a moment with his eyes open, watching the curtains sway in the breeze from the window, and then crawled away from the bed as fast as he could. Walter reached the desk with his limbs still moving but his eyes shutting again, the shells exploding at his feet. He grabbed the chair and dragged himself onto it, fumbling for the light switch. The flash threw him backwards. Then he picked up his pen and carried on writing his speech.

'You look rather odd,' said Reverend Barnes in the morning.

'I had a bad night,' said Walter.

'It is a bit nerve-racking, public speaking, isn't it? Rather like doing an exam.'

Like an exam? Walter always woke for exams clear-eyed and with a sense of excitement. Today he felt like the walking dead.

The venue for his speech was a soapbox on the corner of Petty Cury. 'I've cleared it with the police and the proctors,' said the Reverend cheerfully, 'so they shouldn't bother us, unless we manage to incite a riot or something untoward like that.'

Walter was relieved to hear it. When the gaggle of speakers arrived at the site, armed with their soapbox, he saw Alan waiting for him, leaning nonchalantly against a wall with his arms crossed.

'*Alan*,' said Walter, 'I told you *not* to come.'

'Couldn't resist it. Sorry.'

'Well, you mustn't heckle.'

'Oh, I wouldn't dream of it.'

Walter eyed him doubtfully. Reverend Barnes smiled. 'It's good to start off with an audience,' he said. 'Encourages other people to stop. Good of you to come along, Mr—?'

'Nunn May.'

Hmph. Walter stood as far away from Alan as he could while the first speaker took to the box. He couldn't help seeing what a ridiculous figure the man cut, talking to thin air while the shoppers hurried past, with only Alan looking thoughtfully up at him. The panic rose in him. What if he couldn't do it? There was nothing to suggest that he could. Perhaps once he got on that box he would be back in his dream once more, unable to speak or move.

'And,' concluded the speaker, 'until the world is free of war, we cannot consider ourselves truly free.'

'Bravo!' shouted Reverend Barnes.

Alan clapped loudly.

The speaker shuffled off his perch. Barnes prodded Walter in the back. Walter felt the butt of a rifle. He jumped, and scrambled onto the box.

'Hello,' he said to nobody.

Alan tilted his head in an encouraging manner. Walter twitched, and tried to imagine Grace standing there instead. He had fretted at great length about this speech in his last letter to her in Australia, but of course she would not even have received it yet, let alone have had time to send a reply. If she were here, he was sure he would have known what to do. He wished he could have talked it through with her, instead of having to compose it on his own. In the week before she left, he had booked a hotel in Worthing near where her aunt lived, and they'd spent five dreamy days wandering along the cliffs, talking and talking, and quite often not needing to talk at all. During that short space of time he'd felt he'd got to know her better than any other human being in the world. She'd asked the right questions, and he'd always known the answers, even if he'd never thought of them until she asked. But she was twelve thousand miles away, and he had to do it for himself.

He summoned every ounce of courage he possessed. 'We owe it to the *dead*,' he shouted.

The last word bounced against the yellow walls of the shops on the other side of the street. A woman pushing a pram looked up at him in annoyance.

'To strive for *peace*.'

The guns rattled in his head. He pushed his voice above them. 'The dead are wiser than we are,' he said. 'But they cannot come back and tell us what they know. We owe it to them not to follow them to their fate. They died for us. If we do not hear them they died in vain.'

And he began to hear a music in his own words. The memory of the man beneath the banners in the Exhibition Building in Cologne surfaced, and he suppressed it with the thought of Grace, taking his hand as they fled from the hall. He followed the rhythm of his own speech, rising, falling, and the clattering guns faded and ceased, until all that was left was Walter's words, aspiring, reaching out for minds.

He paused and looked down. To his surprise there was a small crowd. Amongst them, beside Alan, was a familiar face. It was Henry Brinton.

Walter stared in surprise. Alan began to clap.

'I haven't finished!' shouted Walter before anyone else could join him in applause. 'There is *no* rest for those who strive for Peace. There is no finer calling. I do not disparage those who died for their cause. I simply call for their children to fight for a grander cause still – that it should never happen again.'

The man who was next up to speak gave Walter's sleeve a tug. Walter looked round in annoyance. He still hadn't finished. But Barnes gave a little nod to indicate that his task was complete. 'Thank you,' said Walter breathlessly, and slid down to the street.

The small audience applauded.

Walter did not hear any of his successor's speech. His head was still soaring. When it was over, Henry Brinton came over and shook his hand. 'Well, Mr Dunnachie,' he said, his face sparking with pleasure, 'you certainly seem to have learnt a thing or two about this public speaking lark.'

'It was my first one,' said Walter proudly.

'Your *first*? But that's absolutely terrific. My goodness, that's terribly promising.'

'I read your book,' said Walter.

'Did you? Thank you *so* much. Not many people did, I'm afraid. Did you enjoy it?'

'I thought it was wonderful.'

'Did—' Mr Brinton glanced at Alan, who was walking slowly towards them. 'Did your friend read it?'

'No, I'm afraid not. Alan's rather contrary. Aren't you, Alan?'

'I didn't need to read it,' said Alan. 'I've had it quoted to me verbatim. But Walter tells me it's very good.' He managed to convey his scepticism with the lightest turn of a vowel.

'Of course events have moved on now. Overtaken me rather.'

'You virtually *predicted* those events,' said Walter. 'It's all the more reason to believe everything else you had to say.'

For the thing which Brinton had said was least likely to happen had happened. The threat, once again, was Germany.

Since Hitler's edict disallowing Jews from working in the civil service, more than one quarter of Germany's physicists had lost their jobs and all hope of getting one in their native country. They had been forced to flood into other places, and those other places were overwhelmed. Rutherford had been one of the first to set up a fund for the refugees, and when they wrote to him asking for places at the Cavendish, he said yes as often as he felt he reasonably could. But when they arrived, despite the frantic fund-raising efforts, there was no money for them to live on, no space in the laboratory, and no equipment for them to use. As always, it was Chadwick who was left with the task of accommodating them.

'I find it difficult to believe that such a thing could have happened,' Chadwick huffed as he and Walter moved all the tables in an attempt to squeeze yet another one in. 'The Germans I know are such *civilised* people.'

This was one of the things which Walter admired most about Chadwick. His attitude to Germany was quite different from that of his contemporaries. Walter had once made some comment about how terrible it must have been to have been interned during the war.

'It was no great hardship,' Chadwick had responded tersely. 'Frustrating. Bad for the digestion. But no more. My friends were dying in the trenches at the time. On both sides.'

Now Germany was expelling its own scientists. Walter tried to follow his supervisor's example and moved the tables as willingly as he could. But he knew that the arrival of the Germans was not good news. He was looking for a job himself, and in the depth of the depression there were hardly any advertised. And now experienced and needy candidates were presenting themselves in their thousands.

Walter found one single job to apply for and duly appeared at an interview in Manchester. He caught his final train of the day back from London to Cambridge in a very low mood, because he had met the other candidates – all English – and they all appeared to be formidably well qualified. When the man joined him in the carriage at King's Cross and asked if the seat opposite him was taken, he recognised the accent immediately.

'No, it's free,' said Walter, speaking as clearly as he could. 'Do take a seat. I hope you don't mind me asking. Are you German?'

The man's forehead creased in pain as he nodded. Walter noticed that his only luggage was a small rectangular parcel. He saw the distinctive edges poking against the brown paper and recognised that it contained nothing but books.

'Are you going to Cambridge to work?' he asked.

'Yes,' said the German. 'I have an appointment with Lord Rutherford.'

Hope flickered across his face as he spoke the magic words. Walter felt like a very poor sort of human being.

'I am a research student at the Cavendish Laboratory,' he said. 'We will be colleagues. I'm sorry. I've been rude. I'm Walter Dunnachie.'

'Otto Klemperer,' said the German.

They shook hands.

'We will be colleagues only if I am very lucky,' said Herr Klemperer. His English was impressive. 'I was a Privat Dozent in Germany, I had many responsibilities. It does not seem that there are such things possible in England now. My wife, you understand, and small childs. Small children. They are in Germany. I cannot be here if they cannot be here also.'

'Oh,' said Walter helplessly. He thought of the children he and Grace had assumed they would have and realised that it might just be an impossible dream.

'Tell me,' said Herr Klemperer suddenly, with an air of desperation, 'I had heard that it is necessary to live in a college at Cambridge, and that it is – requiring a lot of money. Is this true?'

'There are cheaper ways,' said Walter, who was no stranger to penny-pinching. 'But it is better to be in a college if you can.' He remembered the loneliness of his own arrival, and how comforting it had been that Trinity College had prepared everything for him. 'Do you not have a job, then?'

'I have an introduction.' He pulled an envelope from his pocket and held it in front of Walter, his fingers keeping firm hold of it. 'It is from Herr Professor Geiger. Ernest Rutherford has told that he will speak with me. But that is all I have.'

'They will find a place for you,' said Walter with sudden passion. 'They are good men. Whether there is room or not, they will find a place.'

'A place? What do you mean by place?'

'A table. Somewhere to work. Something to do.'

'Something for food for small children?'

Walter had no idea how much it cost to feed small children. If this man had nothing, it seemed quite unlikely that enough money would be found even to match his own meagre scholarship funding. And he could not quite imagine how it might be possible to divide that amongst four or five bodies. 'I don't know,' he said.

When they got off the train neither of them knew where Herr Klemperer ought to go.

'Do you have any money at all?' asked Walter. It was an indecent question, but necessary. 'Enough for a guest house, I mean? Just for tonight?'

'Yes. But it is expensive. I would like to talk to the university tonight if it is possible.'

Walter did not know what to do. Then he remembered Chadwick's nocturnal habits. 'Look,' said Walter, 'let's try the laboratory. There's bound to be someone around.'

'Thank you,' said Klemperer quietly. Walter saw the hardship of being forced to accept hospitality from strangers. 'You are very kind.'

I am not very kind, thought Walter, because I do not want you to be here. If this man had nothing but an introduction from Geiger, then he was not one of those for whom tables had already been prepared. He would be yet another. Walter's Ph.D. would soon be completed, and after that the only way of staying in Cambridge while he looked for a job would be by getting work around the Physics Department. Why should Rutherford and Chadwick bother to keep him while men like Klemperer needed food for their small children?

They stood in the twilight at the Cavendish doors and Walter pushed his big key into the lock while Klemperer stood back and examined the inscription in the stone. Walter remembered the day he'd stood there for the first time himself, in the brightness of morning, and shivered. He wanted so much to stay. Time was running through his fingers and the world outside seemed a darker place than it had been the day he'd entered. The lock turned. He pushed at the heavy wood and the door creaked open. They sidled in and stood in the gloom of the unlit entrance hall.

'There,' said Walter, 'you're in the Cavendish Laboratory.'

Klemperer did not look as impressed as Walter felt he ought. 'Where are the scientists?'

'This way.'

Walter had tripped through these empty, night-time corridors dozens of times before, dashing back to do more work after grabbing some food. Chadwick was there more often than not. Once the assistant director had left the laboratory in a hurry, announcing that his wife was holding a dinner party but that he would be back as soon as the cheese course was dispensed with. Sure enough, a couple of hours later Chadwick had returned. He had not reported the reaction of his wife.

The lights were still on in the main laboratory. As they entered, Walter could hear the sound of movement from Chadwick's office. 'Dr Chadwick!' he called softly.

There was no reply. 'Don't worry,' whispered Walter. 'I think he's in there. If he's working he won't hear us until he's finished what he's doing.'

Sure enough, when they hovered at the office door, Chadwick was there, bent over his equipment. 'Dr Chadwick!' said Walter again.

Chadwick jumped and cursed. He looked round. 'Dunnachie! What is it?'

'Dr Chadwick, this is Otto Klemperer. He has come here from Germany.'

Chadwick stared at them. Then he stopped work and emerged from the apparatus. 'From Germany, you say?' A dozen thoughts appeared to pass across his face. Walter could not work out what they were. Then Chadwick proffered his hand. 'Good to meet you, Dr Klemperer.'

Klemperer shifted his little parcel to his left hand. 'Dr Chadwick, it is a great honour.'

'You're one of Geiger's men, aren't you? I have found the Geiger-Klemperer counter to be a very useful advance.'

That Klemperer! Walter had not made the connection.

'It is very kind of you to say so.'

'I used to work with Geiger, you know. Before the war.'

'He speaks very highly of you. He was most excited about the neutron.'

The quietness and respect with which the two men treated one another in such strange circumstances left Walter feeling unnecessary and excluded. The question of what Klemperer was doing in the laboratory at this time of night had not even been raised. Walter felt he should make a contribution.

'Dr Chadwick,' said Walter, 'Dr Klemperer has arrived from Germany this evening. He does not have a job and he has nowhere to stay. We – he – wanted to make some contact with the Physics Department before finding a guest house.'

Chadwick glanced at Walter very briefly and then his gaze reverted to Klemperer. 'No job?'

'I have a letter from Herr Professor Geiger.'

'We don't need a letter, Dr Klemperer. We know who you

are. But I do not have a job waiting for you. This is all most irregular.'

'Many things are irregular these days.'

'You are right.' Chadwick sighed. 'You must stay, of course.' He looked at his watch. 'It's a bit late to be getting a guest house now. I'm sure Aileen can rustle up some bedclothes for you in the spare room if we are very nice to her.'

'I cannot accept—'

'I don't see that you have very much choice. Unless you fancy bedding down here, and that has not been done in the Cavendish since we got rid of the troops in 1919. No, it will be all right for one night. Aileen will make a bit of a fuss, but she will not mind. She knows how much I owe—'

Chadwick and Klemperer contemplated one another, united by their opposite yet oddly symmetrical experiences.

'But we will have to sort out something better for you tomorrow. I suppose if you don't have a job you don't have a college either.'

'I was just speaking to Dr Dunnachie of a possibility of finding other ways of accommodation. I have heard that Fitzwilliam House is cheaper than a college.'

'*Mr* Dunnachie. Fitzwilliam House, you say? No, no. You must join a college. They do things for you. You can go and have a look round tomorrow morning. Now, you must be very tired after your long journey. If you don't mind waiting a few moments while I tidy things up, we'll get on.'

Walter stared in amazement. He had never known Chadwick be so mindful of creature comforts.

'Dunnachie,' said Chadwick, 'have you come back to do some work?'

'No—' It was as if he had played no part in the redemption of Klemperer at all.

'Well then, you may as well get back to your rooms.'

Walter left. The following afternoon he discovered that Klemperer's mission to find a college had been successful. Chadwick had pointed him in the direction of the 'good colleges', St John's, Trinity, and just to give him a chance, Magdalene. When Klemperer visited Trinity he discovered that they were already full up. At St John's he was told that they would let him know in six weeks. Then at Magdalene he had managed to find the Senior Tutor, who had said, 'Ah, you are a refugee. I suppose we ought to have one.' Then he had added, 'I suppose you have no money; we had better give you a hundred pounds.'

It was not enough to support small children, but it was a start. A hundred pounds was half of Walter's annual income.

'Chadwick is an extraordinary man,' whispered Walter to Alan over their apparatus. Alan was an official collaborator now; he was a year into his Ph.D. and working with Walter on the same experiments.

Alan looked inclined to agree. 'It is rather untypical,' he conceded.

'It's not untypical at all! How is it untypical?'

'Shhh!' Chadwick was on the prowl around his room. Then Alan did what he generally did when losing an argument, and changed the subject. 'Have you heard the latest about Einstein?'

'What about him?'

'He's recanted.'

'*Recanted?* What do you mean, recanted? Relativity's proven. He can't recant.'

'Not relativity, you idiot. Pacifism. He's recanted his pacifism.'

Walter felt as though he had received a blow to the stomach. He stood there winded for a moment, and then felt sick. It had always been a point in Walter's favour that the greatest mind of modern times was on his side. 'He can't have,' he breathed.

'He most certainly can. He's a Jew, remember?'

It was the first of many such blows. As life in the laboratory continued in its usual intense and chaotic manner, events outside swirled darker. Walter spent his last official term at Cambridge writing up his thesis and playing cricket for the Cavendish against teams such as the Low Temperature Station, the Ouse Catchment Board and the Observatory. The sun in his eyes and the slow momentum of bat and ball were a welcome distraction from life's more pressing questions. He was lonely. Grace had been gone for a year and a half. He wrote to her every night, and received long letters back, full of words which danced with her personality and brought a whole world to life. Her mother's moods, her trials at school, the concerts she attended with her friends – each of her days seemed to be packed with incident and amusement, and at the end of each instalment she assured him that it was all nothing in comparison with him. He immersed himself in their correspondence, afraid it was taking him away from the world around him, but too captivated by joy and pain to stop himself.

And he was frightened. It seemed there was no prospect of getting her back. Grace's contract was drawing to an end, but there was no point in her coming all the way to England while he did not even know if he could support himself here. Since the Manchester rejection there had been no jobs for which he could even apply. He completed the thesis and had it taken to the binders, and when he received it back, looking for all the world like a real book, he realised that it was over and this was all he had to show for it.

There was a viva to stay on for in December, but nowhere to go while he waited, and nothing to do. For the first few days afterwards he could think of nothing better than to hang around the empty laboratory, deep in the long vac, and take as long as he could about tidying things up.

Rutherford found him there one morning.

'Dunnachie!' he said in surprise. 'I thought you'd finished.'

'I have,' said Walter miserably.

'Then what are you doing here?'

Walter said nothing.

'Have you got a job yet?'

He shook his head.

'Oh dear,' said Rutherford sadly. 'Difficult times, difficult times. I suppose you will be going back to Sydney, then.'

'It's worse there,' said Walter. 'There are no jobs in Australia either.'

'Do you want to go back?'

Walter tried to sort out his thoughts on the subject. The thought of seeing Grace again was almost unbearably tempting. Sometimes when he wrote to her he longed to say that he would spend his last pennies on a ticket home the next day. But as she had once said, the two years apart was of little account in comparison with a lifetime together. He knew also that she had no particular desire to spend her life in Australia. It was too small for her. If he went back that would be the end of his academic career. He would have to be a teacher or something, and they would settle down to be an ordinary Australian couple. Neither of them had been ordinary since the day they had met. He felt he ought to be able to do better for her than that.

'I want to be an academic,' he wailed.

'You know many of the chaps are taking jobs in television,' said Rutherford gently.

'I know.'

Rutherford gazed at him in compassion. 'You want it very much, don't you? It does seem terribly unfair. You are a fine physicist. In normal circumstances there would be no question of your not getting a job. I am sure if you are so determined you will get something in the end.'

Walter was on the verge of tears. The compliment was a prize greater than any he could ever have hoped for. But it was useless. His determination was worth nothing if he could not feed himself while he kept trying.

'I tell you what,' said Rutherford. 'I'll have a bit of a scratch around amongst the Commonwealth funds. I'd have used them already for the Germans if I could, you understand, but there are a few bequests which are restricted. And – have you done any demonstrating?'

'A little.'

'Well, we can always do with another demonstrator.'

Walter knew that the last thing that Cambridge needed was another demonstrator. The place was awash with them. Not a lecture passed without a demonstration of the experiment involved. But he was not going to argue.

'And – hang on. Chadwick's been complaining terrifically about his supervision workload. What's the name of that chap you've been working with? Nunn May?'

'Yes—'

'Well, as soon as you've got your doctorate you can take him off Chadwick's hands. There! You see! There's always a solution! That way you'll have another academic year in which to find a job. And if you don't manage it by then, well, at least you'll have had a chance to think about what else you want to do.'

Walter was not sure what Alan was going to think about this, but he was bursting with gratitude. As Rutherford folded his arms in satisfaction and strode off across the laboratory, he remembered the affinity between Chadwick and Klemperer, and thanked his lucky stars that Rutherford was a New Zealander.

Another year. Walter felt he owed it to Rutherford to prove that it was enough. He worked as hard as he could. But in his spare time he felt moved to grapple with the seriousness of the world that was forming around him. These days the question of different countries and how they got on together was not just a matter of favours and kindnesses between men who recognised their own troubles in others. The situation was becoming very grave indeed. Walter might not be in a position to support a wife, but he could at least try to be worthy of her. He threw himself headlong into the quest for Peace.

His experiment with speech-making had been successful enough to demand a repeat, and soon the soapbox was replaced by real stages in halls. To begin with it was the Reverend Barnes who coordinated the events, but soon Walter started to play a part in organising them himself, and as his experience grew, the demands to speak came in from further afield.

'Nottingham,' wrote Henry Brinton from London. Then, 'Sheffield'. Leeds. Coventry. Swindon. Walter scraped together his pennies to afford the rail fares and was always greeted on platforms by the bright, industrious figure of Brinton.

The dreams the night before a speech had become a regular fixture. 'You're looking well,' Brinton always assured him. 'I feel *dreadful*,' was Walter's invariable response. But the worse the dreams, the better the speech, and the greater the peace which descended upon him afterwards.

'You're a lunatic, do you know that?' Alan assured him as he set off from the Cavendish one evening to catch a sleeper to Glasgow.

'One day the world will know that it is we who are sane,' said Walter pompously. He had come to use his sparring matches with Alan as practice for the real thing. But as time went on even Alan's ebullient opposition began to become more sober. The world outside was growing too dark for jokes.

'Oh, Grace,' Walter wrote as the time apart stretched on to eternity, 'I'm tired of political intrigues. When I think of you and of our future together I am sometimes quite scared. Do not listen to me too much about this, I am just being cowardly, and wonder occasionally if I will ever be fit to make a life for us. I know I should not say any of this but somehow I cannot help it. I feel that I can say anything to you and you will understand, and so of course I say it. Please think kindly of me. You know there is nothing more important to me in the world than that we will be together again and I will do everything I can to make it happen.'

He made it happen. In the end he got a job in London, and Grace set out on a ship from Perth to marry him. Three years began to whittle down to months, then weeks. The last frantic days were a blur of arrangements, of trying to obtain a special marriage licence, of telegrams between Cambridge and the cargo ship on which Grace was travelling, attempting to ascertain whether it would dock in Southampton or Liverpool, then another day's delay caused by bad weather. When he had lost her the first time he had found it difficult to believe she existed. Now they had spent years sharing every last emotion they felt. It seemed extraordinary that the mind he'd come to know and love so well was being conveyed towards him in a real human body. He did not know what would happen to him when she arrived. It seemed impossible that his constitution would be capable of withstanding such happiness.

And then, under grey north-western clouds, she was there above him, the girl on the deck of a ship, vivid in a trim little yellow frock, waving and laughing and crying as she ran down the boarding plank and threw herself into his arms. He cried a little himself but he did not explode, as he had feared. Nothing was strange at all. She was in his arms and it was where she ought to be. He had a job, a country to live in, and love. And for no other reason than that happiness had finally claimed him, for the first time in his life he felt as if he deserved all of it.

14

Walter got his history back out of the drawer. He read what he had written, and when he had finished, felt almost ready to write again. He realised that the reason he'd stopped was not just his emotions about the neutron. It was also that after that there was no more to say about his time in Cambridge, and he still felt as much of a tug against leaving it as he had at the time.

Yet the years in London before the war had been happier, in their way. He and Grace had married in March 1935, in a funny little ceremony with witnesses taken from her ship's crew and no guests, because they did not think it would be fair to invite anyone else when their parents could not be with them. They honeymooned in a flat in Bermondsey, borrowed from a friend of Walter's for the week, and had spent most of it looking for a home of their own. Then, when they had found a place, they set up home with two hundred pounds to last them to the end of the year. Nothing could have been more perfect. Grace had spent part of her last year in Perth topping up her domestic accomplishments, and with the profusion of crocheted table mats, crowded window boxes and water-colour paintings which soon populated their tiny flat on Gordon Street, the place became a little heaven. Walter popped home each day for lunch, and between them they unravelled the infinite mysteries of professional academic life. The workload of a junior lecturer was huge and the politics of London University unfathomable, but neither of them minded. This was it, at last. This was the beginning of the rest of their lives.

The period was uneventful scientifically in comparison with what had gone before, but looking back, it was a time of the most intense emotions. Love, of course, but also fear. For all his speechifying, they knew that Walter's exertions for Peace were not working. That only prompted him to try harder. Brinton, while he never took the platform himself, was a great inspiration. The worse things got, the more excitable Brinton became.

'We must *fight*!' Brinton hectored Walter, jumping up and down on his tiny feet.

'Fight?' Walter queried.

'Struggle! Oppose! Oh, goodness, the devil has all the vocabulary, doesn't he? Persevere. That will do. Walter, we must persevere with all our might!'

Walter persevered. Grace attended every meeting she could, her clear attentive eyes a well of calm amongst the masses.

'If it happens, and I haven't done absolutely everything I could have done, I will never forgive myself,' he told her after one particularly fractious rally.

'I know, my darling,' Grace had said, curled up in his arms. They kissed. There was something about the sense of impending doom which heightened their appetite for life even more.

Yes, he thought, it was very heaven in that time to be young.

October 1937. A thunderstorm, the rain bouncing off policemen's helmets in surprised arcs, the sky looming and flashing, and Alan rushing in through the front door, splashing Walter and Grace with his umbrella and his clothes. He had come up to London from his home in Bristol for a conference, and would be staying with them for the weekend.

'Alan, *darling*,' protested Grace, 'you're getting me wet.'

'Walter, Grace, I have terrible news,' said Alan melodramatically, throwing the umbrella to the floor. A thunderclap exploded behind him, emphasising his point. Walter shut the door.

'Oh no, not another political disaster,' groaned Grace. 'I don't think I can deal with another of those.'

'Not a political disaster. A scientific disaster. I bumped into Cockcroft at the conference. He told me.'

'A *scientific* disaster?' Walter had never come across such a thing.

'Rutherford is dead.'

It was indeed a disaster. They all sat down in shocked silence.

'He can't be dead,' said Walter in the end. 'I saw him the last time I went to Cambridge. It was only two months ago. He was just the same as ever. I tell you, he had a lot more energy than me. Or anyone else.'

'How old was he?' asked Grace quietly.

'Sixty-six.'

'Then *how*?' Walter was inconsolable. 'He never had a day of ill health in his life. And he wasn't the type to fall over with a heart attack. I tell you, he just wasn't.'

'No, he didn't fall over with a heart attack. He fell out of a tree.'

They were silent again, but somewhere just above them bobbed the image of the bulky, robust Rutherford, perched upon a branch.

It was Grace who gave way to the giggles first. Just very briefly. 'Oh, boys, I'm so sorry. I don't mean any disrespect. It's a terrible tragedy. It's just that—' And a tear slid down her cheek.

But now the tension was broken and Alan and Walter gave way too. They sat there and laughed and cried.

'What the devil was he doing up a tree in the first place, anyway?' demanded Walter.

'Cutting back the branches,' sobbed Alan, holding his stomach. 'He was trying to improve the view of the river.'

'Why didn't he get someone else to do it, like anyone else? Good God, that's just typical of Rutherford.'

'How's Lady Rutherford bearing up, do you know?' said Grace.

'She was with him at the end. Apparently his last words were that he wanted to leave a hundred pounds to his old college in New Zealand. She's as well as might be expected, I think. After all, they did have a very happy life together.'

Walter grabbed Grace's hand and held it hard.

'Do you remember—' said Alan, and the memories came rushing forth. Rutherford standing over experiments and making them go wrong, ruining his suit with photographic developer and being reprimanded by his wife, calling Chadwick at three in the morning to give him the benefit of whatever intuition he had 'felt in his water' that night.

'I wonder how Chadwick's taken it,' said Alan. 'They worked together for so long—'

'But not any more,' Walter reminded him. Chadwick had taken up a professorship at Liverpool University soon after Walter had left Cambridge. 'The last time I went back it wasn't the same as the old days. Everyone was gone. There was only Rutherford left.'

And now Rutherford was gone too. 'It's the end of an era,' said Alan dolefully. 'We shall not see his like again.'

But still, despite their solemnity, they managed to rouse themselves to go out to the cinema as planned and watch a rather diverting comedy, and as the three of them wandered home, skipping arm in arm along the rain-splattered streets, they agreed that Rutherford would never stand for it if they stayed too sad for too long.

'We must remember him,' said Walter, on the verge of tears again. 'And we must remember what he taught us. That's the main thing.'

12. FISSION

Fission was first performed in 1938 by Hahn and Strassman, but they could make no sense of it, as it defied all current understanding of nuclear processes. It appeared that a free neutron had split a uranium atom into two much lighter particles, and there was no accounting for how this could have happened.

'How could barium be formed from uranium?' wrote Otto Frisch, a young Austrian working for Niels Bohr in Copenhagen, and one of the first to see the experimental results. Uranium was the heaviest naturally occurring element, and even in Cockcroft and Walton's revolutionary experiments, no larger fragments than protons or helium nuclei had ever been chipped away from nuclei. 'The thought that a large number of them should be chipped off at once could be dismissed: not enough energy was available to do that. Nor was it possible that the uranium nucleus could have been cleaved right across. Indeed a nucleus was not like a brittle solid that could be cleaved or broken; Bohr had stressed that a nucleus was more like a liquid drop.'

It took Frisch himself, along with his aunt, Lise Meitner, to work out what had happened. Meitner was Jewish and living in exile in Stockholm. The pair sat on a log in a Swedish pine forest that Christmas, and drew pictures of what might have happened. Their calculations were based on the surface tension which bound Bohr's liquid drop. Suddenly it made sense that this phenomenon was occurring when a neutron was captured by the heaviest of all elements. Any atom much larger than that of uranium would contain too much energy for the surface tension to keep it stable.

The addition of the neutron had, in effect, made the nucleus go 'wobbly', making it oscillate and elongate, until its shape formed two bulbs connected by a bar. The electric force between the two bulbs pushed them apart, until the waist gave way and formed two smaller nuclei. Then these two new atoms spun apart with great energy. Meitner calculated the energy produced to be two hundred million electron volts.

Not only that, but the process had released two or more free neutrons, which were free to fission further uranium nuclei. Leo Szilard's prediction of an atomic chain reaction was no longer science fiction.

The two scientists were astonished by their own conclusions and meant to keep it quiet until they could publish a paper establishing priority over the idea. But Frisch confided in his tutor, Niels Bohr, and Bohr agreed to check their calculations. Another scientist, who assisted him in the work, was so excited that he told a colleague all about it. A chain reaction was sparked and the news spread all round the world.

By the end of January 1939, a brilliant young scientist named Robert Oppenheimer had drawn a diagram on the blackboard in his office at the California Institute of Technology. It was, according to one of his students, 'a very bad, an execrable drawing – of a bomb.'

Patrick was born towards the end of 1938. Walter touched the new creature. It screwed up its eyes. Walter grappled with the intensity of an emotion which he could not name because he had never felt it before.

'Are we wrong?' Grace said one quaking night soon after she had fallen pregnant again. 'Are we selfish to have children at a time like this?'

'We can't give up on *life*,' Walter had insisted in his wretchedness. 'I am sure that hope is a duty.'

His time with Grace and Patrick had become very precious. Every spare moment was spent up at the Peace Pledge Union with Brinton, planning campaign after campaign. 'Hope is a duty,' he told audiences who had fear in their eyes. 'We must not give up hope. No rational person in any country wants war. We must trust our enemies and our friends to see sense. Peace is possible. Peace is the *only* thing that is possible.'

But the audiences were drifting away. The duty Walter prescribed for them was beyond them. And now the nightmares which had always preceded each speech started again immediately afterwards, in anticipation of the next one.

In August 1939 Chamberlain issued an ultimatum to Hitler. 'Should we still go to Aberdeen?' was the chorus resounding through the corridors of London University at the time. The annual meeting of the British Association for the Advancement of Science was to be held there at the beginning of September and many academics decided that it was fruitless to go. Walter sided with life once more and took his son and pregnant wife up to Scotland on the train. By the time they got there many of the delegates had pulled out and it became clear that the conference would not take place. Walter and Grace listened to Chamberlain's announcement on the wireless in the dining room of an austere and airless hotel. When it was over, the sirens began to wail in the streets of Aberdeen to announce the outbreak of war. The woman at the next table left to throw up in the lavatory. A young man with a feeble moustache accosted them as they hurried Patrick up to their room. 'We're all going to die!' he proclaimed.

'Don't be ridiculous,' said Grace, pulling her son away from him.

'No, no, you don't realise,' he said, his voice rising, 'it's true, we're all going to die.'

They hurried up the stairs. Walter had made the same prediction of the next war from too many conference platforms for either of them to be able to counter his hysteria.

The done thing was to call one's employer and find out what was going on at home. As a result of the millions of such calls made that day, the phones were beset with queues and the lines were jammed. When Walter finally got through to Poltine he was told to proceed directly to Bangor.

'Where?'

'Bangor. Godforsaken hole in North Wales. I daresay there'll be trains, even in this mayhem. Anyway, if it takes you a week, get a train. I've got an address for you somewhere. Evacuation plans, you know. Pages and pages of 'em. Some poor blighter has been entrusted with the task of putting you up until you get more permanent accommodation. I'll find it in a minute.'

'But we can't go to Wales. All our stuff is in London.'

'Good God, man, don't you know there's a war on?'

It was the first time Walter heard that phrase for real. The receiver slipped in the sweat of his palm.

'We're expecting air raids at any time now. Think yourself lucky, Dunnachie. I tell you, this town is insufferable. I'm having the most intolerable difficulty with my arrangements—'

'That's fine,' Walter said, knowing that to extend his protest would be to hear every detail of Poltine's difficulties. 'We'll get the train.'

Half the country was abroad that night. The passengers piled deep at station platforms at midnight. They shuffled around in uneasy silence in the darkness, stumbling over the heaps of luggage. Each of the connections was delayed. The carriages were cluttered with gas masks and blackout fabric. Grace was uncomfortable but stoic. Patrick slept as much as a baby could be expected to, but by the time they had travelled the last interminable stretch along the North Wales coast from Chester in the morning light, he was, like the rest of them, beyond sleep.

They passed Snowdonia. Walter gazed up at the mountains.

'They're beautiful, aren't they?' said Grace. 'Vera and I came here on our Grand Tour. I wanted to be able to show them to you at the time. I never thought—'

There were a thousand things they had never thought. It was of no help now.

13. THE WEAPON AGAINST WHICH THERE IS NO DEFENCE

It was suggested to Professor James Chadwick by his friends that a family holiday in Sweden in the late summer of 1939 might be inadvisable. Chadwick told them in no uncertain terms that Britain and Germany would never go to war again.

As a result, in September he managed to find himself in Europe at the outbreak of war for the second time in his life.

It took him more than a month to get back, but this time he made it, complete with wife and children. When he got back to Liverpool he found a letter from the government's scientific agency, the DSIR, asking him for his opinion on Hitler's hints of 'a new weapon against which there is no defence'. The DSIR was concerned, the letter said, that this was a reference to some kind of uranium bomb.

Chadwick was infuriated by the fact that a war was going on at all, and responded vigorously. He made the point that neutrons occur quite naturally on earth as the by-product of cosmic radiation from the sun and other stars. The fact that the Belgian Congo, the earth's richest supply of uranium, had not ignited long ago suggested that there were good reasons why it had not. And Chadwick was pretty sure he knew what these reasons were.

The first was that a very large quantity of pure uranium was likely to be necessary for a chain reaction to take place, making it very difficult to transport in the form of a bomb. The second was that, even in pure uranium, most of the atoms which captured neutrons did not actually split, making the chain reaction itself unlikely even in a very large mass. Niels Bohr had recently put forward a convincing theory that the reason for this was that fission took place only in a very rare isotope, uranium 235, which constituted less than one per cent of natural uranium, and there was no known process for separating the isotopes. And the third objection was simply the question of how to prepare a uranium bomb which would not blow up immediately, hoisting its inventor by his own petard.

Still, the leading German nuclear physicists – Hahn, Geiger, Bothe, Heisenberg – were all men Chadwick knew and respected. He knew that if Hitler took it seriously he had a team as strong as any in the world with which to pursue it.

So he promised the DSIR that he would look into it. By the end of the year his attitude had changed. He wrote a letter suggesting that there was a possibility that it could be done.

The letter was seized by the Committee of the Imperial Defence. On reading Chadwick's letter, the chairman declared the chance of fission having a military application to be 'quite 100,000 to 1, but if the issue were successful it might be of such great importance that the 100,000 to 1 chance should not be ignored'.

15

On the Saturday before Christmas 1939, Walter cycled up into the foothills of Snowdonia to buy a tree from a village smallholder recommended to him by the professor who lived next door. He managed to make the transaction despite the fact that the farmer spoke no English and Walter had no Welsh. The farmer strapped the pine tree to Walter's back and he proceeded triumphantly back down towards the town.

He was not sure whether the tree was allowed – the number of things restricted to war use was growing day by day – but all their Christmas decorations were back in the house in Gordon Street, and there were none in the shops, so it was all he'd been able to think of to create a little festivity around the house. Walter scooted along the lanes, the cold air whistling through the branches of his tree. He'd always loved Christmas, and having been without their own families for so many years, he and Grace were all the more determined to celebrate it properly now.

The war was gathering slow momentum in Europe. But in Bangor Walter was robbed of opportunities to promote Peace, and with only a handful of students and very little equipment for research, his workload was a fragment of what it had been in London. So he had the chance to spend more time with Grace and Patrick. They'd found themselves a house of their own, and the new baby was due in late January. And though he felt guilty for being so insular, his wife and children were the only people who had any use for him now.

As he entered Bangor the children in the streets laughed

and pointed at the strange man with a Christmas tree on his back. Walter frowned and continued regardless. When he reached the front door the tree almost unbalanced him as he attempted to dismount, and he was just starting to fiddle with the rope when the professor ran out of the neighbouring front door.

'Dr Dunnachie!'

'Good afternoon, Professor.'

'Your wife! She's—'

Walter dropped the bike.

'It's all fine—' said the professor breathlessly. 'My maid's taken her to the nursing home – your son's with her – with Blodwen, I mean—'

'I must go to the nursing home!' Walter jumped back on the bike and began to pedal back down the hill.

'Dr Dunnachie!'

Walter looked back over his shoulder and found his face immersed in branches. He skidded to a halt and the professor ran down to him and helped rip the tree from his back.

'Thank you,' said Walter, covered in pine needles, then he was gone.

It was, they agreed later when they got to know her better, absolutely typical of Bridget to arrive with such dramatic timing. Walter and Patrick collected mother and baby from the nursing home on Christmas Eve, and Patrick examined his sister with scientific fascination, giving her a good poke in a spirit of Rutherfordian experimentation.

'Oy!' scolded Grace, and cradled the baby protectively.

'She's very small,' said Patrick critically.

Walter beamed at them, glowing with pride, and took them home. On Christmas Day, he made his best attempt to cook the joint of gammon. He decorated the tree with paper chains cut from the pages of old academic journals, and the mantelpiece was enlivened with cards from home and abroad.

Walter slipped a farthing into the Christmas pudding Grace had made back in October to the accompaniment of his old recording of 'Hark the Herald' on the gramophone.

'Merry Christmas, darling,' he whispered to Grace, ready to burst with happiness, and she treated him to the biggest smile he had ever seen.

By New Year's Eve Grace felt ready to repay their professorial next-door neighbour for all his kindness during her pregnancy. Walter tried to persuade her that she and the baby were surely still too tired, but she wouldn't have it. They got all their best tins out of the larder, and Grace instructed Walter in their correct preparation. The professor turned up on cue and greeted each dish with a suggestion for shops where they might be able to find something better.

'It is most charming to see such a lovely family together in these times,' said the professor.

Grace and Walter blushed with pleasure.

'Such a shame it can't last,' he added.

Grace's back shot upright. 'What do you mean, it can't last?'

'Haven't you heard?' said the professor with the sad pleasure of one imparting bad news. 'It was announced today that conscription has begun. All men between the ages of twenty-one and twenty-eight are to be called up.'

Walter was about to point out that he was thirty, but he did not get in fast enough.

'But Walter's a pacifist!'

'Oh yes. You mentioned. But you'll drop all that when you're conscripted, of course.'

Grace glared at Walter expectantly.

'No I won't,' said Walter. 'I will apply for conscientious objector status. And if I do not get it, I shall still refuse to fight.'

'Really?' The professor raised an arch eyebrow. 'Horses for

courses, I suppose. I daresay for some the comforts outweigh the ignominy. Understandable, in the face of such domestic bliss.' He smiled benignly at both of them in turn.

The insult hit home and then bounced off again. They will try to make me feel guilty, he thought, for the happiness they all say they're fighting for. Up to a point they would probably succeed. But that was no reason not to value the things in life which were most important.

'The ignominy I can bear,' said Walter quietly. 'The comfort may be harder.'

The professor frowned for a moment, then Grace rushed in again. 'Will you be fighting, Professor?' she demanded of the grey-haired man. 'Do you expect to be begrudged your own comfort?'

The old man glared at her over his spectacles. 'If you expect to rescue your husband with that kind of comparison, my dear, you will be sorely disappointed.'

She flounced from the room, and Walter was left to engage their guest with talk of mountaineering.

'I thought he was such a gentleman!' raged Grace when he was gone. 'An educated man like him! There's no excuse for it.'

'Many educated men have been in favour of war,' Walter said. 'It's no distinguishing factor at all. Harry Moseley was regarded as the brightest physicist of Chadwick's generation. He was killed at Gallipoli.'

A few days later, they received a letter from Alan in Bristol. Despite being twenty-eight himself, he reassured them that Moseley's fate was not for him. 'The scientists have found a use for me,' he crowed. 'At last physics and politics can join in action. Do reconsider your position, Walter, there's a good fellow. You won't have to kill anyone at all. But if you stay where you are, you're going to have a terribly dull time.'

He showed Grace the letter with reluctance. If even Alan

could not see the fallacy of such a distinction, they really were alone. And behind it all, reality was pushing through, making those smudged paper chains look tawdry. The government had taken the twenty-eight-year-olds, and it would not be long before they came back for the next lot. The only important decision of Walter's war would soon be upon him.

14. CRITICAL MASS

In the early months of 1940 a committee consisting entirely of ex-Cavendish men was tasked with the job of overseeing the uranium investigations. Chadwick pursued a number of lines of enquiry in Liverpool and liaised with all the other centres, including Bristol, Cambridge, London and Birmingham. In April 1940 two refugees based in Birmingham handed the Maud Committee a paper containing the first blueprint for an atomic bomb.

The refugees in question were Otto Frisch, who had escaped from Copenhagen just days before the outbreak of war, and Rudolf Peierls, an earlier immigrant who had lived in England ever since joining Chadwick at the Cavendish in 1933. As foreign nationals, both were barred from working on the serious things connected with the war, such as radar, and whilst they were allowed to work in a general sense on the uranium question, they were not party to the progress of the various teams assigned to answer it. But they struck up a friendship immediately on Frisch's arrival in Birmingham, and one day over coffee Frisch suddenly said, 'What would happen if someone gave you a quantity of pure 235 isotope uranium?'

The Maud Committee had been flummoxed by the difficulty of obtaining such a substance and was mainly concerning itself with trying to find a way of achieving a chain reaction in untreated uranium. The scientists did so in the knowledge that even if they managed to crack that problem, the other obstacle – the sheer immovable volume of uranium which was likely to be required – was looming at them from the other side.

No one had got as far as working out what kind of weapon could be created using the pure isotope. Peierls and Frisch, unfettered by official instructions, decided to take the successful separation process as a given, and to work out the size and behaviour of a weapon containing pure uranium 235. Within weeks they had written their memorandum.

'The attached detailed report concerns the possibility of constructing a "super-bomb" which utilises the energy stored in atomic nuclei as a source of energy,' it began. 'The energy liberated in the explosion of such a super-bomb is about the same as that produced by the explosion of one thousand tons of dynamite. This energy is liberated in a small volume, in which it will, for an instant, produce a temperature comparable to that in the interior of the sun. The blast from such an explosion would destroy life in a wide area. The size of this area is difficult to estimate, but it will probably cover the centre of a big city.'

The memorandum then went on to calculate the radius of a critical mass of the substance.

'One might think of about one kilogram as a suitable size for the bomb,' they said. One kilogram. So it could be transported by aeroplane after all. 'If one works on the assumption that Germany is, or will be, in the possession of this weapon, it must be realised that no shelters are available that would be effective and that could be used on a large scale. The most effective reply would be a counter-threat with a similar bomb. Therefore it seems to us important to start production as soon and as rapidly as possible, even if it is not intended to use the bomb as a means of attack. It would obviously be too late to start production when such

a bomb is known to be in the hands of Germany, and the matter seems, therefore, very urgent.'

The judge seemed half asleep. His gaze wandered all round the room as he spoke, never once alighting on Walter.

'And what,' he said in a voice sing-song with the traces of Welsh, 'would you do if a German soldier burst into your house with a rifle, held you at gunpoint, and threatened to rape your wife and kill your children?'

Wales was in the heady midst of the loveliest spring for years, a warmth as rich and gentle as love itself. The garden at their home in Bangor had burst into unexpected beauty. The wanton extravagance of the creaking, over-laden boughs and the soft wet blades of grass that reached up to meet them was shocking in comparison with the shrinking ration books, the disappearance of the railings from the edges of streets and parks as they were plundered to make armaments, and the occasional rattle of planes overhead.

Hitler's weather, it was called. Belgium, Holland and Luxembourg were flattened under a Blitzkrieg – a ghastly storm of mechanised battles, bombed oil tanks at Hamburg shooting flames ten thousand feet high, and towns, art, literature, all steamrollered flat in the rush to the coast. Amiens, Arras, Abbeville – the poppy-strewn burial fields of a generation which would have still been young enough to bear arms, taken by invading hordes once more. Germans up to the Channel ports, and the news growing steadily more grave and obscure as the whole Maginot line collapsed and the Nazis pushed through from Sedan to Boulogne in four days. The Belgian King ordered his country to capitulate, and the road to Dunkirk lay open. The British Expeditionary Force was lost to death or retreat.

'Which,' continued the judge, his voice as languorous as

the sunshine, 'in days like these, appears to be an increasingly likely eventuality.'

The court consisted of three officials, chaired by the judge, a couple of clerks, and Walter. There was a buzzing somewhere in the courtroom – a fly or a bee or a wasp, its insistent, intermittent drone reminiscent of the planes flying out from unknown airfields, their bellies packed with bombs like a bee with pollen.

That old question, thought Walter. He felt immeasurably weary, as if he had been tried a hundred times before. And so he had, on conference platforms and in meetings all round the country, and now that it was happening for real it felt like a dream.

'I would place myself between my family and the aggressor,' he said, hearing his own voice like a gramophone recording being played on a turntable which was revolving very slightly too slowly and whose surface was marginally warped, so that there was a rhythmical, repetitive lurch downwards and back, shoom, shoom, in time with the buzzing of the fly. 'I would do everything in my power to defend them, to the death if necessary, except—'

'Except for the use of force. Do you really believe that?'

Oh, nobody believed in these question and answer sessions any more. In the last war, when this whole rigmarole had been worked out, each party thought that those court battles were a fight for civilisation itself. Walter's own generation of pacifists had no such delusions, and neither did the judges. Strange, that the number of conscientious objectors in this war had already risen to three times, five times the number in the last, and still nobody really cared. There were dark hints that they might be members of a Fifth Column, and slurs on their patriotism, but it did not matter. The authorities seemed proud of their tolerance. Perhaps it helped them believe they were superior to the enemy, defining themselves against its

CLARE GEORGE

dictatorship. We may kill thousands in foreign countries, the rationale seemed to be, but here at home we still know how to conduct ourselves like civilised human beings.

The judge who tried Walter had a reputation for being particularly strict. He did not seem very strict. He just seemed bored. And yet though it all washed over every other person in the room, still Walter's skin was clammy with sweat. In the last war these questions had been asked and answered in the spirit of pure rhetoric, and this time it was a matter of icy, vicious fact. The question did not belong in a courtroom, it was a matter for his own home. What would he do? How could he bear— And he wanted to be at home, for now the only good news was of tens of thousands of hungry, tired, half-clad soldiers getting back across the Channel, in any kind of boat that would take them, bombed all the time. No one knew how long they had before German planes came, or before the troop ships followed. It could not be expected that a force which had trampled all Europe would stop at Britain. Even the BBC was trying to prepare the country for what was to come. Bangor – locked to the coast by mountains – might be one of the last places to go, but if resistance proved to be as useless here as it had everywhere else, it would go.

One of the officials rustled through his notes. 'In 1932,' he said, 'you joined the Peace Army.'

'Yes.'

'You wrote a letter of support for the departure of an unarmed party due to set out for China with the intention of standing between the Chinese and Japanese armies and preventing hostilities from breaking out.'

The judge suppressed a snort of laughter.

'Yes, I did.'

'Why?'

'Because—' Oh, that infernal gramophone sound. 'Because it was quite clear to me even then that if the nations of the world did not find new ways of sorting out their differences then we were doomed to walk a path to destruction.'

'But you did not go,' drawled the judge. 'Why not?'

'It was stopped. The government put a stop to it.'

'And when the National Socialists came to power in Germany, did you or your—' he paused '—comrades – consider employing the same tactics against Hitler?'

'It had by that time become apparent that war could not be stopped while the choice of waging it rested in the hands of governments who believed in armed support for national power.' How odd, how devastatingly futile, to be translating his own speeches from the present to the past tense. The whole world seemed to be slipping into the past tense, hour by hour. 'We chose to try to bring pressure on those governments, by enlisting the huge but largely latent support of the peace-loving people they governed.'

And then, the only possible conclusion:

'We failed.'

There was a silence.

'Do you have any brothers?' demanded the judge.

'One.'

'Older? Younger?'

'Younger.'

'And has he joined the armed forces?'

At the beginning of the war Walter had written to his parents telling them what they must have known already in their hearts: that he would be a conscientious objector. The letter from his mother in reply was breathless with relief, and she had persuaded his father to put pen to paper as she always required him to do at moments of significance. His father had strung some sentences together saying that he was glad Walter had followed his heart and his conscience, and that he knew that Jim would do the same, though it might not lead to the same course of action.

'No,' replied Walter. 'There is no conscription there. Yet. You will have noticed that I am Australian by origin.'

The judge raised his nose and eyebrows. 'I had taken you for a Cockney,' he said in tones of amused disdain. The official to his left smirked.

Oh, really. They'd known about the Peace Army. It could hardly have been possible for them to miss the country of his birth.

'So,' continued the judge, 'you presumably have friends or associates in this country who are active in the fight for freedom.'

There was no point arguing over terminology. Yes, he did. The drift into khaki was gentle and almost intangible, the whole country slowly turning mud-green. It was generally the first indication that a decision had been made which would transform a man's life irrevocably. It wasn't just the soldiers, either. Daily he received news of his scientific colleagues, diverted from teaching and research into some branch of the war machine.

'Yes,' he said.

'And how do you regard their activities?'

Some of Walter's old friends from the Peace days had been amongst those who, confronted with the force of imperial fascism, had thrown their lot in with the government and had decided against conscientious objection or had even joined up. The choice had faced every one of them. As enemies rose in massed ranks on the other side of the Channel, many of the leaders of the Peace Movement laid down their white poppies and declared that they could see no way of escape without force. Such a state should never have been reached, they said, but Peace, on this occasion, had failed.

'It hasn't been easy for anyone,' said Walter.

'Very good of you. You respect their right to defend you.'

He said nothing.

'But you will not defend them.'

He opened his mouth. Only sophistries presented themselves.

'Not if it means using force,' he said in the end.

'Well, thank you for your time, Dr Dunnachie,' said the judge. 'You may go now.'

Walter was never in much doubt about the verdict. Mainly all the authorities needed to see was that his conscience was not something he had invented for the occasion. Consistency was all, and Walter had a fine record of questionable activities dating back an entire decade.

He arrived home to find all the street signs gone or tampered with. 'A lorry blazed through today,' Grace told him, 'and uprooted them all and stuck them up in other places. Why the Germans would want to go to Llanrwst or Pwllheli I can't imagine. I would have thought the Welsh language was quite enough to confuse any Nazi. I've had an idea. When they come we will speak nothing but Welsh.'

'But I only know about six words.'

'You will have to learn.'

Walter smiled despite himself, but shook his head. 'It's way beyond me. You can speak Welsh. I'll have to be a deaf mute.'

But now that his trial was over it seemed there was no more he could do or say. He felt somehow that a deaf mute was a fair description of what he had already become.

15. DUNKIRK

As the Nazis stormed across Europe, Frederic Joliot, the man who almost discovered the neutron, remained with his wife at the Curie Institute in Paris and rejected all the pleas of the various British delegations sent to encourage him to leave. Joliot was a patriot to the core, and he chose to stay behind and become the leader of the National Front, the largest French resistance movement of the war.

But Joliot was as aware as any other scientist of the atomic threat. More so, because he had in his possession a store of a material which was needed to assist the manufacture of plutonium from uranium, one of the possible routes for building a nuclear bomb. The material was an isotope of hydrogen called deuterium, containing a neutron in addition to the sole proton in the hydrogen nucleus, and was more commonly known as heavy water. It was extremely rare, constituting only 0.0156 per cent of natural hydrogen, and it was imperative that it should be out of the reach of the Nazis. So Joliot sent it to Bordeaux in the care of one of his researchers, Halban, with instructions that it should be spirited away to England if at all possible.

The Paris representative of the British scientific establishment, the Earl of Suffolk, had spent the previous months holding court at the Hotel Ritz, surrounded by champagne and beautiful women. When things started to look grim, the Earl decided to do his bit, and got together as many French scientists and engineers as he could find. They decamped to Bordeaux, carrying a large cache of industrial diamonds which the Earl had obtained at pistol point in Antwerp.

The Earl commandeered a vessel, and kept it waiting by plying the crew with drink until Halban had got aboard with his twenty-six cans of heavy water. The journey was terrifying, but there was so much champagne that few of the passengers were much aware of it. The boat docked safely at Falmouth and the heavy water was unloaded.

The diamonds remained in England. But the threat of invasion was intensifying, and the heavy water was regarded as being too dangerous to stay. It was spirited away to Canada, and in due course Halban followed it.

Meanwhile, the German planes followed the boats across

the Channel, and began the assault on military targets which would become known as the Battle of Britain. It was designed to remove the obstacles to invasion, and the bravery and skill of 'the few' prevented this nightmare from ever taking place. But the battle was never formally won; when the Germans realised that the loss of their planes in these targeted raids was too great, they simply abandoned hope of an immediate invasion by sea, and took the war to the cities of Britain by air instead. After months of the Blitz, Britain began to respond. The bombing offensive on both sides of the Channel brought civilians into the front line of battle for the first time.

Walter sat on Bangor station, waiting for his little brother. He pulled his scarf more tightly around his neck. Above him was a full harvest moon, the bomber's friend, lighting up the fields and houses far more surely than the lamps extinguished by the blackout ever had. A thin cloud was drifting across it, silver and violet, lit from behind by light reflected from the sun on the other side of the earth. He sat very still and thought he could hear the uneven thud, thud of bombs falling. Liverpool, perhaps. On a night as still as this the sound could travel fifty miles across the Irish Sea.

'When I've finished my training in Canada I'll be getting on a ship to England,' Jim's letter had said when it had arrived three months before, back in the summer of 1941. 'My CO says I'll get leave when I get there, so Mum said I should stay with you if that is all right with you.'

He was twenty-five years old.

In the ten years they had been apart, the enthusiasm of the replies Walter'd received to his bombardment of letters had waned. The boy grew up, and presumably had experiences of his own which he did not feel able to relate to someone who had become a stranger. Walter's own correspondence had slowed and then stopped. In the end the brothers had communicated mainly via their mother. Then the news had come that Jim had joined up. As he sat on the platform Walter realised that he did not even know what a Royal Australian Air Force uniform looked like. He had a go at reading his book by the light of a torch but quickly gave up, and just sat there, blinking into the moonlight.

He heard the train before he saw it. The noise separated into a rhythm, and he watched the row of lights wind round the corner of the track. As it pulled into the platform, he could see into the brightness of the carriages, where the people had started to stand up and collect their bags and trunks. It was a blur of khaki. Even the civilians seemed to have modified their clothing to merge into the yellow and brown. He glimpsed a woman standing on a seat, pulling at the rack, and a child with his face pressed against the glass. The windows opened and the warmth fogged out of the carriages into the crisp night air. The engine wheezed and hissed and then chugged into silence, the sound replaced by the opening of doors, the clunking of luggage and the buzz of conversation.

He walked slowly down the platform, keeping well away from the edge. The passengers were all struggling with their own trunks, with no porters to help them. As he walked, he stared intently into the face of each uniformed man he saw. A dozen times he thought he'd caught a likeness, and was never sure when they turned away again that he had not missed his brother. He squinted through the dappled light, his heart pounding.

'Walter.'

He tripped over the edge of a trunk. An arm caught him, steadied him, and set him upright. He looked up at his benefactor, fearful, and his little brother's eyes looked back out of a firm, unfamiliar face.

'Jim!'

They embraced awkwardly across the trunk. A spasm of joy

surged through Walter, and he found himself laughing. 'Jim! Jim!' And then, not able to help himself, 'You've grown.'

Jim was by several inches the taller of the two of them. He grinned. 'Well, yeah,' he said. 'That's what happens to little boys.'

Hippens. Walter did not remember accents ever having been so strong. He frowned for a moment, peering at this strong, square man, and then gave him an almighty thump on the back. 'It's going to be a struggle with the luggage, you know,' said Walter. 'No taxis. And there's quite a hill.'

'It's all right, I'm in training.' They each took one end of the trunk and strolled towards the exit. Jim looked at him curiously. 'You talk like a Pom.'

'The Poms don't think so.'

'Bleeding Poms,' said Jim.

They laughed, and their eyes met. Likenesses confuse, but the real thing was unmistakable. It did not matter that every atom in his face had been replaced. Identity lay like a fingerprint around his eyes and mouth. For a second ten years disappeared.

And then returned. At twenty-five, the tiniest lines creased Jim's skin where he smiled or frowned. He had gone from being a child to being almost a contemporary, the same age as many of Walter's colleagues and friends. When Walter left Australia, no one had known that he would not be back in a few years. Did Jim mind? Or had he just accepted it, slowly, letting him slip out of his life as the years rolled by?

'How are Mum and Dad?'

'Last letter I got was a month or so ago. Keeping well, from what I could make out.'

Walter hadn't meant that. Of course, for Jim, the past few months away from home would have been an eternity. He had entered a new world as enveloping as the Cavendish had been for him. But what he'd meant was, how were they *then*, how were they when you were there. And this question was unconveyable. Walter realised that even if he managed to phrase it, there would be no sensible answer. *Jim, how have your parents been, these last ten years?*

'Mum's made up about me coming here,' said Jim.

'So are we,' said Walter. His words sounded very poor in comparison to what he actually felt. Grace had been preparing for the visit as if it were Christmas, saving up her coupons, planning the meals and lining up entertainment. Walter had been very glad of her excitement. It had distracted him from his own turbulent joy and fear.

And now Jim was really here.

'Walter,' said Grace, 'you mustn't think so hard.'

'What do you mean?'

'If you keep thinking so hard about every little thing that happens in the war then I think it will kill you.'

Walter frowned. 'I have to say, Grace, I must be one of the people in Europe at the moment who is in the least danger of dying.'

'You know exactly what I mean. There is so much unpleasantness out there. Sometimes we have to cushion ourselves from it if we want to go on living. We have to be a little *stupid* about things. I am pretty well cushioned myself, and I can spare a little stupidity for you. But it doesn't seem to be enough. You mustn't mind so much. It isn't your fault. We'll have enough of our own troubles to deal with before this mess is over. You cannot grieve for every death.'

But he had to. He'd tried to stop it happening and he'd failed. The travails of all the years looked as pointless and pathetic as his very first flirtation with the Peace Army, when he'd declined the invitation to Harwich. He expected her to share at least a little of his self-scorn and could not understand her turning things on their head in this way. 'You aren't stupid,' he said. 'You care too.'

'I don't, Walter, really I don't. I don't care in the least that Jim is a bomber, and I don't care an ounce for the children he will kill.'

'Grace!'

'I mean it, Walter. I may have as well-developed a moral sense as the next woman, and I'll stand up and condemn those raids as soon as you will. But not in front of Jim. Because he's your brother, and he's the most complete dear, and you love him to distraction. In my mind, I don't want German children to die. But in my heart, my cares stretch only so far.'

'I have never—'

'Condemned him? Oh, Walter, you know as well as I do that you have.'

The game looked so harmless. He'd been upstairs when it had started, searching out boots and warm clothes for his walk in the mountains with Jim. When he got down to the dining room he found a scene of perfect, suspended silence, and stood by the door to watch.

On the table was a house of cards. Jim sat in front of it with Bridget on his knee, clasping each of her hands over two red balloons. Opposite them, Patrick stood still, holding a paper plane above his head.

'All right,' said Jim softly. 'We're ready to go.'

And as Patrick's back and arm arched upwards in expectation, Walter suddenly saw what it was all supposed to represent.

'Now, Bridget,' said Jim. 'This house is our house. The barrage balloons are here to protect it from that nasty Australian bomber. We've got to stop him from knocking our house down. And we don't want to knock it down either. Do we?'

Bridget shook her head.

'Patrick, you know what you've got to do, don't you?'

'KNOCK IT DOWN!' He began to swoop, holding his plane above his head.

'Not yet, not yet, you haven't had the word from Bomber Command yet. Be very quiet and still.'

Walter opened his mouth.

'Go!' cried Jim.

Patrick began to dance. He ducked and dived with his plane but each time he was fobbed off by Jim, who deftly punched him away with the balloons.

Bridget squeaked with excitement. Jim dropped one of the balloons, and, still beating Patrick off, put another plane into Bridget's hand and guided it into the air. Patrick was becoming frantic.

'The German fighter planes have spotted the bomber!' cried Jim. 'Whoah, the fighter swoops in, shhhh! Shhhh! Zhzm! Can the bomber fight it off? Fore-Gunner Dunnachie is tight in his position. The fighter comes in from the rear—'

He was standing up now, balancing Bridget on the table. Patrick gathered himself for a final assault on the target. He threw himself at the house, and finally managed to hit it. Bridget screamed and dropped her plane on the cascading cards.

'DIRECT HIT!' shouted Jim. 'Hitler's headquarters are destroyed! Australia has won the war!'

Patrick ran round and round the room, shouting and holding his plane aloft. Jim picked Bridget up properly, and she clung to him, giggling.

'Stop!' shouted Walter, throwing the clothes to the floor. 'For pity's sake, Jim, stop!'

Jim turned, his eyes wide with amazement. Then his face tightened. The two brothers faced one another in fury. Walter stormed from the room.

*　　*　　*

'And the thing is,' said Grace, 'really, it isn't even Jim that I care about. It's you.'

He'd expected that in talking to her he would get from her what he always had. Her support had always been the one thing in the world that he could count on absolutely. Certainly she was harsh with him sometimes. 'Well, if you want to fret, you can fret,' she said when he was being difficult, 'but don't expect me to help you with it.' But now, when he needed more than anything to be told that he was right, she was taking Jim's side. He did not know how to counter such an attack. His only resort was the one he'd always had, with other people, in extremis.

'I'm so sorry, Grace—'

'No, no, that's exactly what I mean. *It isn't your fault.* In theory there is absolutely no reason why you shouldn't condemn Jim. The pair of you disagree fundamentally. The only reason why you mustn't is that it hurts you too much.'

'The children,' he said. 'It was the children. He said it was Bridget's house, and then it got bombed. It'll lead to nightmares.'

'No it won't. It's perfectly commonplace. You played war games when you were a child too. You probably played them with Jim. Did that lead to nightmares?'

His eyes began to sting. He stared obdurately at the table.

'Oh, Walter,' she said, suddenly seeing what she'd sparked off, 'I didn't mean that. You didn't start it. And you didn't finish it either. It wouldn't have been any different if you hadn't left Australia, you know. You couldn't have influenced him any differently. It's the man he is. You can't blame yourself. Not for that, and not for any of the rest of it.'

'Grace, it's wrong to absolve oneself of all blame for anything. That's the way wars start.'

'You can't be perfect! Don't you see? You can't expect it of yourself! It's too much.'

She used to say that he was perfect. He'd known she was wrong, even then.

'Do you really think it made much difference to him that you left?' demanded Grace. 'Do you really think he cared?'

'*Yes.*'

She looked at him, and her eyes conceded to his vehemence. 'He won't be here for very long,' she said. 'You've got to let yourself enjoy him.'

'I wish I could stop him from going.'

Her eyes lit with triumph. 'Aha! Deep down, my love, that's just selfishness. And selfishness is what you need just now, if only a little of it. Just let's not let all of the other things get in the way.'

Her certainty was a rock and he could bash himself against it no longer. He felt his muscles begin to relax in exhaustion, because he wanted to rest against it instead, as he always had done in the past. But in those days she had always seemed one step ahead of where his own heart was leading. It was he who came up with the ideas, but it was Grace, with the imperturbable logic of her questions, who built a safe structure on which to found them. Now she was undermining them.

'Be selfish, Walter,' Grace implored him. 'For me.'

Why had she ever encouraged him to be a pacifist, if she wanted him to be selfish? She had always been more important to him than Peace. But until now he'd never had to make the distinction. With a shiver, he had an inkling that her fiery belief in him had been a sort of selfishness of her own, all along. They might have talked about sacrifices before the war, but they'd never had to make any, not really. Now that it came to it, she did not want to see him hurt, even if being hurt was right. For her, love was the only true guide.

And suddenly he knew that love was not necessarily on the side of peace.

*   *   *

He relented far enough to renew the invitation to climb Snowdon. But Walter could not rid himself of his anger. He took Jim up the Horseshoe, the hardest path, and beat a pace so fast it humbled a man who was younger and stronger but who was also less used to walking up hills. Jim bounded breathlessly behind him, wriggling like a labrador trying to win back his master's affection, and every now and again summoning breath enough to attempt conversation. Walter dispatched each foray with icy courtesy and increased his speed until Jim gave up on talk.

But in the end the spiky rocks gave way to sky and even Walter could climb no further. Jim threw himself down on an outcrop, spread-eagled in the autumn sun.

'Wow,' he said to the blue air, 'it's beaut, ain't it?'

'Yes,' said Walter primly, and leant on his stick.

'Look at the mountains. Don't they just look great.'

Walter looked. The tops of the hills were skimmed by clouds. And suddenly he wanted to shake his brother. He loved Snowdonia because it was the opposite of everything that was hurting the world. Durability, beauty. The serenity of nature. And yet all of that was false. The mountains were an absence, not a presence; the crags and escarpments were sculptures carved by water and air. They had been slipping away for a hundred thousand years. Their creation had depended on forces that would just as surely destroy them. Even mountains die.

'Those clouds,' said Jim. 'Just itty bits of things, floating about up there. You always had a thing about clouds.'

Walter spun to face him. His memories did not include any vouchsafing of those particular dreams.

'Have you ever seen clouds from above?' said Jim dreamily.

'No,' said Walter. 'I have never been in an aeroplane.'

'It's incredible, I'll tell you that. First time I saw it, I wanted to write straight to you.'

And though he fought it, Walter sensed his frostiness beginning to melt, and felt a pain as hard and prickly as that of a frozen limb coming back to life.

'It was like cotton wool,' said Jim. 'But not like that. Like the coat of a little lamb. But not like that either. It was softer, and lighter, and, I dunno, *surer*, than those things, or anything else. There wasn't anything I could liken it to, because I'd never been up there before, and I'd never seen anything like that. It went out, up to the edges of the earth, and round it. I wanted to jump out of the plane and bounce.'

Jim's eyes were as clear as the sky. Walter looked at them, and saw a mind which had seen things he'd never experienced. Flying was, he realised, for Jim, just as physics was for him. Another world, as real as this one, but bigger, more mysterious, and more unknown.

'Jim,' he said, because he could not help himself, 'have you thought of what will happen when your bombs hit the ground?'

Jim did not move. His outstretched pose looked inappropriately vulnerable. 'Yes,' he said.

'Really? Have you really thought of what will happen?'

'No,' said Jim, in the same tone of voice.

'Then you *should* think about it.'

Jim shot upright. 'I've never said a word about what you've done. And I don't agree with that either.'

'You didn't need to say a word. I know what you think.'

Jim sat on the rock. Then he drew his long legs up to his chest, and hugged his knees. 'Walt,' he said, 'you were the best man I ever knew. But you left.'

He'd been right all along. He'd always known he was right about that.

'I was jealous of you, when you went. I knew I'd never be

as clever, or as good, and I thought I'd never be able to go myself. You left us all behind.'

'Jealous?' Of all the emotions he'd construed for his brother, it had never occurred to him that he might have dreams of the big wide world too.

'I never thought I'd be able to come, and now here I am. But it's not like I thought it would be. I thought this place would be too good for me. But I'm scared for it. Nothing as bad as this has ever happened here before. I've come to defend it. I never thought it would need my help.'

'Oh—' Walter had acknowledged the reality of heroism a hundred times before. It had been a formality of every Peace speech, something to be got over with. But he'd never witnessed it before, not in someone he loved. This boy had forced himself to be prepared to give up his life to save something he believed in.

'And what I can't understand,' said Jim, his voice still as young and helpless, 'is how, after everything that's gone on, you can stand by, and not help.'

'I—' And now he felt as Grace did. He did not want to explain it to Jim. That things were deeper, and nastier, and uglier than he thought. That good intentions could spiral into bad acts, which would never be undone.

'Jim,' he said, 'I don't ever want to kill anyone. I don't want ever to do what they have done to others. I've made my choice and I can't unmake it. I can – understand – how you see things. You see things differently. You—' He wanted to say that Jim might be right. It was how their father would have seen it. Their father had sent them on their different paths with his blessing. But Walter could not do it. He could not summon up the selfishness – or the selflessness, he could no longer see which it was – to lie. 'I'm sorry,' he said finally. 'I can see how much you've given up. For us. I am grateful. I do—' He took a lesson from Grace. 'I do care.'

'Thank you,' said Jim quietly.

'Are you afraid?'

'Yes.' He traced a finger along the contours of the rock. 'But I'm like a dog with two tails too. I've not done very much with my life, you know, not compared with you.'

The old note of hero-worship was still there.

'Now I get to do my stuff too. And I've been trained. They're the best men I ever met, you know, Walter. You see, we're the first wave of wartime recruits. No one's ever had training like this before. The Jerries won't know what's hit 'em.'

No, thought Walter, they probably would not, because they would be dead. He tried to suppress the images of the people he'd met in Germany, dying in the remains of the buildings he'd visited. It was not – could not be – Jim's fault. He was as innocent as they were. Or far more so, by now. Walter forced the words out. 'I'm very proud of you,' he said.

Jim blushed.

'I don't want you to go,' he added.

'I didn't want you to go either. But you had to. Now I have to go.'

'I know.'

And Walter knew that no sacrifice he could make for Peace could compare to this.

It was a bad Christmas and things did not get any brighter in the new year. The Japanese had bombed Pearl Harbor, and the US was in the war. By the time New Year came there were more countries at war than ever before in the world's history. In the bitterness of the coldest English winter ever recorded they read the news. Hong Kong gone; Sarawak going. Penang gone, and war surging into Malaysia; Rangoon and Singapore bombed. Manila burning, and the outnumbered Americans fighting a hopeless battle in the

Philippines. By the end of January New Guinea was invaded, Malaya evacuated, and all forces defending Singapore itself. Mid-February and Singapore was gone, its inhabitants duped by British censorship into staying until it was too late; and the papers plainly prophesied that soon little of the Empire would be left. Would Burma go? Would India? Would – Australia?

And then the Japanese bombed Darwin, and their troops were four hundred miles from the Australian coast.

'Perth,' hissed Grace, stooped over the newspaper. 'They're bombing Perth.'

Newcastle had suffered its first attack a week before. The Japanese were preparing for invasion. A force invading a nation with Australia's geography was hardly going to meet the sort of resistance that the Germans had feared at Dover.

'How could they do it? How could they be – so callously cruel?'

The spring sunshine streamed through the windows, but Grace's anger outblazed it.

'I can't begin,' said Walter.

Her mind was still with his. If anyone so much as came close to criticising his stance, they generally found their comments sliced apart by a concise blade of sarcasm. But he knew now that her anger, though pacifist in stance, was not motivated by thoughts of Peace.

'Listen,' said Grace. 'This is Vera Brittain. "In the South African war it took the British two and a half years to conquer the Boers, but the Japanese have conquered an Empire in two and a half months." Two and a half months, Walter! Because Churchill had to fight in Europe, and leave the whole thing as good as undefended! The Americans are asking openly what we did with the armaments they sent, and are accusing us of sending Dominion, not British, soldiers to die. Oh—' Her rage rendered her temporarily speechless. Then she recovered.

'When I think of Jim, fighting for Churchill over Europe, while his own home is defenceless – I tell you, Walter, if Jim has to fight, I wish he hadn't joined up so early. He's an Aussie through and through. If he'd stayed a bit longer, he'd be fighting the Japanese right now, and if I were him, that's where I'd want to be.'

Jim was posted to an air base in East Anglia. With the brightest and the best, he looked down into the firestorm of Cologne, and then a few days later destroyed Essen. Then he was whisked from Europe and dispatched to Egypt, to assist Montgomery in the scramble for Africa.

The battle lines were scratched like severed veins across the maps Walter scrutinised for hours in his study. Grace stopped buying newspapers and so Walter went out and bought them for himself.

'Stop it!' she shrieked at him as he unfolded the pages across his buttered toast.

He gazed up at her, uncomprehending. 'I have to know where he is,' he said. Once Jim had learnt his geography by following the tracks Walter made across the globe. Now it was Walter's turn to do the same. His knowledge of obscure North African towns increased apace. So did his parrot-like comprehension of the grim statistics of war.

'Walter,' pleaded Grace, 'do you think somehow that if you know the precise probability of him being killed, it will save him?'

No. It was not like that at all. The life expectancy of an Allied bomber was short and getting shorter. Walter knew perfectly well how unlikely it was that the figures would allow his brother to slip through their net. But it was the only solidarity he could offer. To know.

Then it turned out he knew nothing at all.

*   *   *

Jim died.

'I wonder if we should wear black,' said Grace, her eyes flickering with distraction, digging out a small pair of leather gloves, which was all she could find. 'I feel we should wear black, at least for a day. But it's very difficult, with there being no funeral to go to.'

Walter stared at her, woozy with the expectedness of it, with the crippling lack of shock. A young man at the height of his youth and vigour, whose spirit had burst out of his every pore, had been reduced to nothing in seconds, and it was not even a surprise. The telegram had arrived, and its coming had been so formulaic that they had been unable to speak for fear of using other people's words.

'I suppose it is always like this,' Walter had said eventually, and as soon as he said it, a pit opened beneath him. Please not this death. Not Jim. If it had been expected, it ought not to have happened. And if it had happened, it ought to belong to Jim, not be buried along with his life under this mound of official stoicism. The telegram was stiff with the pride of the Empire. They had claimed his soul along with his body. The paper shivered in Walter's hands. Surely he did not know, thought Walter. Surely he did not know that it would be like *this*.

'I should contact Mum and Dad,' said Walter. So he did. He sent a telegram. It was as meaningless as the one he had received from the government. He followed it up with an air letter, and filled it up with enquiries about things that would be long gone by the time it was received. Things such as whether there would be a memorial service – how could the church possibly find time for them all? – what they would do about flowers, if there were any, and whether they knew if Jim had had a girl. He needed to know what was going on at home, how Jim was remembered. Walter saw the look in his father's eyes when he'd explained to him the gap that was left for ever by the death of a child. The shape of that hole was all that remained of Jim. And Walter did not even have that.

It was an ignominious end. Jim's plane had set out on a raid of Tobruk, but the bomb-release mechanism failed. They returned to base with the rest of the squadron, and the landing gear was damaged by flak on the way back. When the plane landed at base, the bombs hit the ground and exploded.

Grief felt at first like anger. Jim was hoist by his own petard. Those bombs had been built to kill, and they had achieved their mission with the imprecision for which they were famed. Walter wanted to write letters, make speeches from podiums, shout about the injustice and stupidity of it all to the roar of a surging crowd. But there was no point. He had done all that, years ago, when it was not Jim, when it was mere humanity which had been at stake. But humanity had not listened, and now it was dying in its millions, and its agony drowned out any care the world might have had for the singular death of Walter's brother.

'What about Mum and Dad?' Walter blurted out in fury. 'He should not have given his life. It wasn't his to give.'

'Yes it was,' said Grace. 'I'm afraid it was. No child owes a parent their life. Not in the end.'

Their own children had been sent next door until Walter was fit to do the duty his father had performed for him: to explain the meaning of death. He dreaded their eyes. Their comprehension would hurt beyond imagining – the first wound to his babies' immortality, the first shudder towards all their graves. And their incomprehension would hurt Walter even more. They would forget Jim. There would be no more kite-flying, no cards on their birthdays, no news of him from Grandma, no cousins far overseas, no future. Uncle Jim would stand for them as the first sentinel of the kingdom of the dead. And in the end, for Walter he would do that too. Don't *go*, screamed Walter to his brother's living soul, feeling the corrosive tide of memory start to wash over the formless hole already. The small moments they'd shared as children in their mother's kitchen, on the verandah, out on the beach, were shared no longer. They lay trapped, dying, in his own mind. Now all there was of Jim was a name and serial number on a grave in Africa, in a town where none of them had ever been.

And when the fires died down, and the tatters of grief hung about him, and the anger sank in his blood like ash, he was left with the emotion that had been there at the first. Was it a defence against grief, or did it lie at the heart of grief? He did not know. He saw only a harbour, and his mother and father smiling through their tears, and the blue eyes of a fifteen-year-old boy, blazing with accusation, refusing to bid him farewell. Jim had known back then what it meant to go away. Walter had not understood it until now.

His guilt confronted him at every turn. The guilt of having left him alone; of having buried Peace to give him his blessing; of having allowed him to go out to fight; of having failed to save him.

But most of all it was for having sat warm and safe at home while Jim lay bleeding in the flames of the wreckage until he died of his wounds.

It was the guilt of having survived.

16

'Well, Mr Henderson,' said Mrs Dunnachie, as they settled themselves into the small room she'd obtained for them at the back of the chapel, 'shall we have tea to accompany our conversation again?'

'I'm fine, thank you.'

'That's good. Because I'm fine too. Now, I've made a list of things I want to ask you about. Have you?'

'Pardon?'

'Have you written a list?'

'No—'

'I suggest next time you do. And for your other interviews as well. It's so much more effective a use of time.'

Good heavens. No wonder people told her she behaved like a teacher. Still, he thought, it wasn't altogether a bad idea. Next time he would bring a list, if only out of sheer fear.

'Well,' she continued, 'as I am the only one with a list, we may as well start with my questions. Do you agree?'

George agreed.

'Tell me everything you know about my husband.'

That was reasonably easy. He did not know very much, so he might as well start with the basics. 'He is Australian. He emigrated here in – the early 1930s, I think. To take up a place at Cambridge University and study physics. He joined the Peace Movement shortly after his arrival and had some sort of involvement with the Peace Army in 1932.' George stopped, feeling rather pleased with himself for remembering the date. 'After he left Cambridge he took up the position as physics lecturer at University College London which he still holds. At some point he married. I don't know which year, I'm afraid. He has two children, Patrick, aged seven, and Bridget, aged six.'

'You know that because of *me*,' pointed out Mrs Dunnachie.

'Erm, yes.' George hurried on. 'During the war he was evacuated with the university to Bangor. He was registered as a conscientious objector and remained in Wales until 1944.' There must be more. 'A few weeks ago he was visited by an old associate from Cambridge, Dr Alan Nunn May.' He waited for her to react, but this time she did not. Then he realised that there was something he knew which she probably did not. 'His employer at the university is a Professor Poltine. Poltine is very busy at the moment because he feels that the Board of Governors is trying to oust him—'

'Poltine is a paranoid psychotic,' said Mrs Dunnachie briskly. 'The medical fellows have diagnosed him from afar and there's absolutely no doubt.'

'Yes, yes,' said George, 'but you see he's also very twitchy about your husband. You see, Dr Dunnachie is currently under investigation by the university.'

'Under investigation by the university? Whatever do you mean? Who's investigating him?'

George thought about it and realised that the only person Poltine had commissioned to do any investigating was himself. 'Well, perhaps that's putting it a bit strongly. But there's been a complaint. From a student.'

'Only one? He's doing rather well, then. Most lecturers have three or four under way at any one time. Demanding creatures, students.' She paused expectantly. 'Do carry on,' she said.

But George had nothing more to say. 'That's it,' he said.

'That's *it*?'

'Yes.'

'How long have you been following my husband?'

'Three weeks.'

'Well, that brings me very nicely on to my next question. What the devil have you been doing all that time?'

George blushed speechlessly, feeling as though he'd failed an exam.

'I mean, let's count it off. You went to the Methodist church and made contact with me. You attended one of our services, to which my husband failed to turn up. You came round to our house for dinner, at which my husband was rather bad-tempered about pacifism. You've clearly spoken to Poltine—'

'And to the student who complained,' broke in George.

'Was that a fruitful meeting?'

'Well, yes, it was rather. You see, the complaint he made was about your husband's pacifism.'

'Presumably you must have already *known* that he was a pacifist. What new information did he give you?'

'He spoke about fission,' said George. 'And about the atomic bomb.'

'Yes, but as we have already established, my husband is a pacifist and had nothing to do with the development of the atomic bomb. Was the student under the impression that he had?'

'He said your husband was there – for splitting the atom!' spat out George desperately.

'Aha. Splitting the atom. Do you know what splitting the atom is?'

'No—'

'Well, we can come on to that later if you want to, but I really don't think it will be necessary. Can you assure me that what you have just told me is the sum total of everything you have gleaned?'

'I think so. About your husband, anyway.' He considered mentioning his reading session in the British Library, but knew that it would receive the same response as everything else.

'In that case, could you now let me in on your plan for your future enquiries?'

Plan? No one had ever asked him to have a plan. 'I have another appointment with Poltine first thing tomorrow morning.'

'You're going to see Poltine. Pray, Mr Henderson, what exactly do you think Poltine can tell you?'

'Erm—' It was a good point. 'Well, I was getting a bit confused with all the science. I was hoping Poltine could tell me about Dr Dunnachie's involvement.'

'I can tell you as much about that as you like. Probably far more willingly, and certainly with a lot less spitting. From my point of view I'd really rather you didn't persist in raising needless suspicions in my husband's irrationally suspicious employer. Would you do me a favour and cancel the appointment?'

George thought wistfully of Poltine's admiring, pliable secretary as he began to nod in submission, and then suddenly remembered the other thing he'd wanted to find out from Poltine.

'I was also going to ask him about Nunn May,' he said.

Her expression was opaque. 'Poltine doesn't know Alan,' she said.

He rushed in, realising he'd hit her weak spot. 'He's bound to know *of* him, though. They're both physicists at London University. I was going to ask him what Nunn May's connection with your husband was. But I suppose I can find that out from you now too, can't I?'

She was silent for a moment. 'I can most certainly tell you of their connection,' she said in a low voice. 'I have a feeling, however, that I am likely to find out more from you than I can tell you about Alan himself. I have not seen him for three years. As you know, he failed to turn up at our dinner party.' She pulled herself together. 'Anyway, you will cancel the appointment with Poltine. Won't you?'

'Yes,' said George.

'Now, I have another question. It is about your own employer. For the sake of the convenience of our conversation, I would like to be able to refer to him by his name. What is it?'

George considered the options, and shook his head.

'We'll call him Mr Jones, then. Is Mr Jones satisfied with your progress so far, do you think?'

'Not really. At least I don't think so. But you see he's never really told me what he wants me to do, and rarely ever comments on what I've done, so it's very hard to tell.'

'He must have told you to do something.'

George pushed back into his memory. 'He said to find out where he lived, what he did, who he spoke to, and what he said. Especially that.'

'You're right. It's not a very specific brief, is it? I suppose you have already fulfilled it, up to a point.'

George sat up in surprise. 'Yes,' he said. 'I suppose I have.'

'But the thing you and I need to discover is why he asked you to do all this following, and what he expects it to achieve. Don't we?'

In George's opinion all he needed to do was keep his head down and his nose clean. But keeping Mrs Dunnachie happy was now essential to achieving this aim, and so he supposed it came to the same thing. 'Yes,' he said.

'And to stand some hope of doing that,' she continued, 'we are going to have to pool our knowledge. Which means that you are going to have to start asking me some questions. Because, you see, my best guide to what this is all about is what you want to know.'

They stared at one another.

'Go on,' said Mrs Dunnachie. 'Ask away.'

George thought of a question. He knew it was a good one. 'Tell me everything you know about Alan Nunn May,' he said triumphantly.

When Walter had left Grace that morning she'd seemed to have recovered her animation. He could not imagine why. Things had not improved between them at all. But still, there it was, the air of preoccupation, the sense of bustle, and above all, a greater patience with his own silence. As he'd kissed her farewell and she'd smiled gaily but absent-mindedly, he'd felt a sudden stab of suspicion. What was she up to? What wasn't she telling him?

But it was hardly an accusation he was in any position to make. He'd been staying later and later at work, sinking deeper into the old griefs, which somehow seemed all the fresher for seeing them in the harsh context of the present.

He hadn't cried when Jim died and he hadn't cried for him since. Good God, Jim had died like a man, and the least Walter could do was respond to his death with the same fortitude.

He almost laughed at himself when he heard himself thinking such sentiments. The guilty tendency to come over all stiff-upper-lip when confronted with a military death was ironic, to say the least. But he knew he must not laugh, because then he would be back where he was the day Grace laughed at Rutherford in the tree, sobbing like a baby, and he was afraid that if he started to cry for Jim he would never stop.

There was no point in going down that route, not now, because he knew exactly where it led and it was not the way out. Instead he must persist with the mission he'd invoked Rutherford's ghost to help him with – to understand. Because we must remember what Rutherford taught us, thought Walter. Whatever we've done, we must at least do that.

So he picked up his pen and descended once more into the morass.

16. TUBE ALLOYS

The Frisch-Peierls Memorandum was read by the Maud Committee and they set up a project code-named 'Tube Alloys'. It was to be led by James Chadwick. In 1941 Frisch was transferred to Liverpool to work with him there.

Shortly after the new member of staff arrived, the bombing of Liverpool started in earnest. At night Chadwick listened to the cacophony of sirens, anti-aircraft fire and the whistling of bombs, and the fear he felt was of a different order to that of his fellow citizens. Each time a bomb fell he half-expected it to bring the Armageddon portrayed in Frisch's note. He persuaded the Chief Constable to give him a permit to test the bomb craters, and stole out in the early mornings with a Geiger counter. Chadwick brushed past the shocked and weeping homeless, brandished his permit in the faces of bemused air raid wardens and firemen, and crouched in the rubble, waiting for the lethal 'click, click, click' on the dial. If ever he were to get a positive result, he knew that simply by standing there he was as good as dead. Even if they had not dropped a uranium bomb that night – and the fact that he was still alive attested to the fact that they had not – he could see no reason why the Germans might not use bombs to disseminate large quantities of radioactive material. His tests were negative. But just because they were negative one morning, he saw that as no reason to believe they would be again the next, and out he went into the smoky light once more.

In these circumstances, the progress of Tube Alloys felt

*agonisingly slow, but in fact it was incredibly fast. In August
Peierls came up with the idea for an ingenious separation
method. Four months later a German refugee in Oxford
had produced a report called 'Estimate of the size of an
actual separation plant'. Meanwhile Chadwick's Liverpool
colleagues were making inroads into obtaining experimental
data on which to base the finer points of the construction of
the bomb. In Montreal, Halban was making good progress in
setting up facilities in bomb-free Canada, assisted by a young
physicist seconded from Bristol, Alan Nunn May. Chadwick
coordinated the whole thing, directing the research, collating
the results and communicating with the Maud Committee.*

*In the spring of 1941 Chadwick realised that a nuclear
bomb was not only possible, it was inevitable.*

*He did not get another undisturbed night's sleep for the rest
of the war.*

'I cannot tell you everything I know about Alan Nunn May,'
said Mrs Dunnachie quietly, 'because what I know does not
amount to facts and figures. He is a human being and a friend.
And a soul will not fit into a jar, Mr Henderson.'

Her turn of phrase should have confused him as much
as Aitken's more peculiar sayings. But the softness of her
voice told George exactly what she meant. He wanted to
say that it didn't matter, that she didn't have to tell him
anything she didn't want to. But they were not in that position. Neither of them had the freedom to withhold evidence.

'What I can tell you, however,' she said, 'is the thing you are
probably most curious about. And I may as well come straight
out with it, because it's common knowledge anyway, and I
have a feeling that you would take rather a long time getting
around to it.'

She did not come straight out with it. He waited.

'Dr Nunn May was an employee of the Manhattan Project,' she said eventually.

He knew that this statement was supposed to have a dramatic effect on him. But he could not help that it did not. 'What is the Manhattan Project?' he asked.

George thought the eyes would pop out of her head. She jumped out of her chair in outrage, and then threw herself back onto it. 'The bomb, you fool! Robert Oppenheimer, Niels Bohr, Leo Szilard! I'm talking about the goddamn, bloody, evil, murdering atomic bomb!'

'Oh,' said George. 'That.'

17. THE MANHATTAN PROJECT

By the end of 1941 the British already had a clear idea of how an atomic bomb could be constructed. They also knew that it would be a tall order to actually build it. The continual bombing of all the major industrial centres made a difficult task almost insuperable. The Maud Committee had been lobbying the US government for support since the summer of 1940. There were occasionally some words of encouragement, but there was very little action.

Then, on 7 December 1941, the Japanese bombed Pearl Harbor, and the US entered the war. From then on, the United States put the full weight of its resources behind the race to build the bomb. The British 'Tube Alloys' project continued, and for more than a year Churchill was determined to maintain its independence, but the Americans quickly overtook it, despite its head start. By the end of 1943 the British decided to throw in their lot with the Americans. Chadwick, Frisch, Peierls – all were sucked up into the Manhattan Project. Even the laboratory at Montreal was handed over and came under the general command of the project's new leader, Robert Oppenheimer.

And on that vast continent, still untouched by bombs, the undertaking which had so far been pursued on sheets of paper and in test tubes began to sprawl into reality.

There was ice on the inside of Alan's window. He sat on his bed with the sheets wrapped around him and could feel the cold blast at his shoulder. It was distracting him from the business of staying alive.

I could boil the kettle and steam it off, he thought. He stared at the kettle. It was perhaps two yards away. The deep torpor in the muscles of his legs forbade any movement towards it.

He watched the second hand of the clock clunk its way around the minutes. Twenty-six minutes past three and eleven, twelve, thirteen seconds.

It was Sunday. During the weeks he could escape the skin of this flat and inhabit the blessed dry sticks of the faculty routine. Each moment was accounted for, bleached clean and colourless by the dull expectations of the faces of strangers. At the end of the day his nightmares lay in wait to strangle him, but in the darkness he could struggle, and scream silent screams, and know at least in his dreams of death he was alive.

But the weekends had become a torture so dreaded that sometimes he felt he was on the verge of hallucination amidst the slow, relentless, formless daylight. By Sunday afternoon he had already borne thirty hours of the weekend and there were still six more to go.

A pile of letters lay on the doormat. He had not opened any of them for weeks. Once or twice he had picked one or the other of them up, and examined the envelopes, but they failed to make any contact with him. The problem was the first line of the address. Dr A. Nunn May, they read.

'Who is that?' he asked.

He received no reply. The letters dropped from his fingers and fell back onto the mat.

17

From the beginning of the war, the restricted circumstances did not stop Alan and Walter from communicating with one another. They were both living in relative isolation – Walter, in his self-imposed exile from the mainstream of science, and Alan, in the ghetto of censorship. The two men needed one another to talk to, if only by letter, even if Alan was not allowed to write about science, and Walter was, but had nothing to write.

So they gossiped about the conditions in their respective laboratories, and railed at length about the impotence of the ideologies in which they'd believed so passionately before the war.

'Each day I am more relieved that I never joined the Communist Party,' wrote Alan in the summer of 1941, when the Nazis invaded the Soviet Union, 'and am more sure that I made the right decision to part company with them when Stalin made his terrible pact with Hitler. It does not surprise me at all that it has backfired on him now. The two of them are behaving like the tribal warlords of a millennium ago, except that these days they have tanks and aeroplanes and bombs at their disposal and can inflict their rivalries on the whole of mankind. My own egalitarian principles have, of course, never changed. But I have the feeling that those of Josef Stalin waned a long time ago.'

There was, as always, a barb at the end of the letter: 'Of course *you* must have had some sympathy with Stalin's decision in 1939 not to oppose the Nazis. His policies were exactly the sort of "pragmatic pacifism" that your crowd always used to espouse when you were trying to make yourselves plausible to governments. Well, I hope you have seen what happens when you stand aside for a fascist imperialist regime. I personally think that the Soviet Union is a society worth defending. Even Britain's relative freedom must be defended against Hitler. And that is why I am defending it with all my might. Though it must be said that my might does not always feel very powerful when I am fiddling around with my vacuum flasks and my equations, and I long to go out and give Hitler a jolly good drubbing with all the rest. But on other days I feel that this is the most fulfilling time I've ever had in science. Do you remember how we used to say how frustrating it was that science was so remote from our beliefs? Well, now it is not. Oh, Walter, I find it so absurd that this is the case and you don't even know it! I wish I could tell you everything because I know that if you knew, you would join us. You would have no choice.'

The beauty, however, of an epistolary debate was that they did not have to rise to one another's taunts as they would have done in person. They could ignore the other's ranting and plough on with the point they themselves wanted to make.

'Pacifism still is and always will be an absolute for me,' wrote Walter in his reply. 'The death throes of the millions roar about my ears and prove it more vividly than my words ever could. Yet still mankind is deaf. Even you, Alan, are deaf. And now there is no point in my shouting. The bombs and screams drown me out. If the death of a best friend will not prove to a man that killing is evil, what will? Sometimes I think that the old maxim was true, and that while human nature is human nature we shall always have war. But this I must not believe. Because when I believe that, all hope is gone.'

Yet Walter could not help but admit the futility of his

position. The subject of physics had been taken over by the military machine of which Alan was now part. All experiments of a purely academic nature had ceased due to lack of equipment and materials, and those which continued were top secret. There did not seem to be a single avenue he could pursue without in some way contributing to the war effort.

'I must say I'm getting very depressed about it,' he wrote shortly after Jim's departure to East Anglia. 'Everything I was doing before the war is impossible here. I feel as though I have been left behind. There are so few students here that even the teaching isn't keeping me busy. So I'm occupying myself in some research into theoretical chemistry, which at least doesn't need any laboratory apparatus. The problem is that the work is highly mathematical. Almost all of Bangor's calculating machines have been commandeered for war work, and all I have is an ancient contraption which perpetually jams. The results register is on a hinge, and each time I multiply by a factor of ten, I have to lift the hinge, move it manually one space and then lower it again to engage with the mechanism. The research requires precise and complex calculations to many decimal points, so I have to do this dozens of times for every sum. Each time it seizes up I have to stop, mess around with the cogs and the grease, and start all over again. I tell you, Alan, sometimes I fear for my sanity.'

Walter was in the middle of a calculation one day when the woman from the Ministry came to visit.

'Dr Dunnachie?'

She was dressed in a neat twinset and was carrying a clipboard.

He lost count. 'Yes,' said Walter.

'Oh, good afternoon, Dr Dunnachie. I'm Mrs Sharpe. Can you spare a few minutes?'

'Of course. Take a seat.' It was not, he realised, likely to be good news. Women with clipboards did not bear good tidings. 'How can I help you?'

'Well, I think you can help me, actually. I'm from the Ministry.' The blustery good cheer with which she said these words made Walter absolutely certain that she had been apprised of his status as a conscientious objector. Overwhelm 'em with jolliness, that was the official policy. 'I have it down here – I'm not sure whether it's correct, the records haven't been very well kept – that you are in possession of a calculating machine.'

'In a manner of speaking.' He pointed at the contraption which was sitting on the table directly between them.

'Oh!' Mrs Sharpe gave a brief laugh. 'Forgive my ignorance. I was unaware of what it looked like. I assumed that was some sort of typewriter.'

'It's extremely old. It was all they could leave me.'

'Ah. Well, as you know, there's some very important work going on.'

Oh no.

'Incredibly important. I can't give you the details – I don't know much myself – but I can assure you that it's absolutely essential for the defence of the nation.'

'And you want this machine too.'

'That's the long and the short of it, yes.'

He shut his eyes for a moment. Be calm, he told himself. It is not the end of the world.

'Well,' he said, 'it's not my machine. So I daresay it's not for me to say how it is used.'

'I'm afraid not, no.'

'When do you need it?'

'This afternoon, really.'

'Oh.'

She brought in some under-age lackeys and they removed the machine. When they were gone, Walter stared at his equations for a while and then laid his head on the desk where the machine had been.

'Even that old junk heap is of more use to the nation than me,' he complained in his next letter to Alan.

'I think even the junk heap knew that,' Alan wrote back.

And despite himself and all his misery, Walter laughed.

'Dear Walter,' wrote Alan in September 1942. 'I have some exciting news. As always, I can't actually tell you what it is. Suffice to say that I am setting off to Canada very shortly. I think I am allowed to tell you that. Perhaps I am not, but if it is supposed to be a secret, they have got so worked up about the other points of my necessary silence that they have forgotten to tell me about that. Well, anyway, I will continue to tell you the things they haven't told me not to tell you. Essentially I am to stop fiddling around with equations and become the scientific equivalent of the operatives in the bomb factories over whom you affect so much moralistic sorrow. Yes, you are right, to put a screw into the casing of a radio control in a bomber plane is to kill. And hurrah to that, say I, for we are at war, and killing is necessary to defeat the evil with which we are confronted.

'It is also rather exciting to be going to Canada. I have not been abroad since my trip to Moscow in 1936, and I have never lived in a foreign country. I begin to understand the fear and excitement you must have felt on leaving Australia. Well, wish me bon voyage, my very dear Walter, and may we meet again, soon, and in happier times.'

It took Walter two weeks to find it in himself to answer the letter. 'Alan,' he wrote, 'your letter has hit me rather hard. We have been separated by war for three years now, and there was no near prospect of that changing. But in Bristol I always felt that you were quite close by. You are the only one of the old crowd – Chadwick, Cockcroft, and all the rest – with whom

I have managed to maintain contact. I cannot bear to think of you going abroad. You see, the news has come at a particularly difficult time. My brother Jim died three weeks ago. He was the victim of one of the bombs you spoke of. The bomb in question was in his own plane. I had better not write any more. I will say something I will regret. But I thought that you should have some note from me before you go, to explain my silence. I will write a better letter when I can. Walter'

18. NIELS BOHR

Niels Bohr, along with Albert Einstein and Ernest Ruther-ford, is one of the greatest physicists of the age. As a young man, working under Rutherford in Manchester, he was the first to apply quantum theory to atomic structure. He then took up a professorship at Copenhagen, in his native Denmark, and soon built it into a world centre for physics. In the 1920s he developed the standard model of quantum theory, which has become known as the Copenhagen Interpretation.

He expressed the characteristic feature of quantum physics in his principle of complementarity, which stated that it was impossible to separate the behaviour of atoms from their interaction with the instruments that measured that behaviour. The implication of this was that evidence from experiments conducted in different conditions could not be united in a single picture – instead they must be regarded as being 'complementary'.

Bohr also developed the 'liquid drop' model of the atomic nucleus, which was to prove so important to Frisch and Meitner's interpretation of fission. When war broke out soon after that momentous discovery, his colleagues all round the world encouraged him to flee to the United States. He was half Jewish, and the small, flat nation of Denmark could offer no resistance to Nazi invasion. But like Joliot, Bohr was determined to stay. He planned to remain in Copenhagen as long as the war lasted, to protect the freedom of Danish institutions and the scientists who worked in them.

Denmark was invaded in 1940, and the government agreed to cooperate fully and continue to govern the country itself, on condition that the Nazis guaranteed the security of the Danish Jews. But Hitler lost patience with the semi-independent state, and in August 1943 Copenhagen was occupied once more. One of the reasons for the takeover was that Hitler was infuriated by the Danish Jews' protected status. And so by the end of August the Jews of Copenhagen started to disappear.

Bohr continued to stay and helped arrange the escape of those of his colleagues who were in danger of arrest. Then he received word that his own arrest had been authorised in Berlin. He and his wife had to get away the same day. They hid in a gardener's shed in a friend's garden by the beach. When night fell they crossed the beach and were picked up by a motorboat, which ran them out to a fishing boat. The boat dodged minefields and Nazi patrols and crossed the Öresund to Sweden. In Stockholm he helped persuade the Swedish King to receive the Danish Jews cordially, but there was a danger that Bohr himself would be assassinated by one of the many German agents swarming in the town. The British sent a small plane to fetch him. His enormous head was too large for the helmet he was given, so he did not wear it; unfortunately it contained the earphones necessary for communication with the pilot, and so he did not hear the instructions to put his oxygen mask on. The pilot noticed he had fainted only when he did not receive a response to a question, and as soon as they were over Norway he had to descend and fly low over the North Sea. Fortunately Bohr survived and by the time they landed in Scotland he was conscious.

The British 'Tube Alloys' scientists were in the process

of packing their bags to join the Manhattan Project. They quickly adopted Bohr as their figurehead to give the mission influence and prestige. Since Rutherford's death, Bohr had emerged as the father figure of the world of physics; and Bohr, a more measured and thoughtful man than Rutherford, was well equipped for the role. He also had very strong ideas about what part an atomic bomb might play in the future of the world, and once he got to the United States, it was Bohr's vision which sustained the hundreds of scientists working on the project.

It was another railway-station reunion and Walter found himself full to the brim with the previous one. So many things were similar. Like Jim, Alan had been gone for many years, and like him, he'd travelled all the way from Canada to be on this untidy little platform in Bangor. Both men were his on temporary lease from the war. And like Jim, Alan would soon return to the fray.

But many things were different too. Alan was still a civilian, and his jacket seemed to be the same one Walter had last seen him wear, in London. There was no danger of him flying in aeroplanes over hostile Europe, the target of every flak ship and fighter plane in range, attempting to kill people. The terrible, disabling worry he'd felt for Jim was absent. And so was the guilt. Their last parting had been jolly and down-to-earth. Nobody had been abandoned. No one had been betrayed.

Alan looked tired. 'Too many journeys in too few days,' he excused himself.

'I'm sorry I can't arrange some sort of transport—'

'Oh, I'm not on my last legs yet. Has Grace baked a cake?'

'Do you know,' said Walter, 'she has.'

'Jolly good. Your wife may have her faults, but she can always be relied upon to bake a cake. I've been looking forward to it all the way from Birmingham.'

'Alan, I'm so glad you could spare the time to come to see us. It means a great deal. We have a constant flow of visitors, of course, but none—'

'No scientists.'

'No.'

'I think a lot of them are too wrapped up in their own moral dilemmas to be able to accommodate conversations with a pacifist right now.'

Walter detected a change in Alan's tone since his last barnstorming lectures on the topic of pacifism. He looked at his friend curiously. 'How about you? Can you accommodate conversations with a pacifist?'

'Oh, you're not a pacifist to me. You're Walter. I never took you seriously anyway.'

Walter laughed. 'Alan, I've missed you.'

'You too. You don't know how much. Walter, I just want to say – I'm so sorry about your brother's death.'

'Thank you,' said Walter. He had learnt that it was the only sensible response.

'My stupid comments about bomb factories—'

'It doesn't matter. You were excited. What you said had nothing to do with Jim. It was just bad timing. If we took too much notice of bad timing in this war we wouldn't be able to say anything at all.'

'Well, we can't say anything anyway, can we?' pointed out Alan.

'You can't. I can say whatever I like, as long as I do my first aid sessions at the hospital. That's the way they've chosen to deal with it this time. Here I am, in total opposition to the government of my own country, and they've managed to hide the fact by stamping a label on me, which says "Conscientious Objector", letting me get on with it, and by ignoring me ever since.'

'Yes. It must be rather emasculating.'

'Sometimes I think I'll go mad with boredom. Which is *why*—' Alan was labouring rather with his suitcase. They had drawn almost to a halt halfway up the hill. Walter grabbed it from his hands and stormed ahead '—it's so wonderful to see you. Come on. Grace'll need to get that cake out of the oven soon.'

'Well,' said Grace, 'it's not quite what I've been able to offer you in the past. I suppose you have eggs in Canada. And fruit.'

'What is it?'

'Carrot cake. At least it turns out moister than that horrible eggless sponge. I've gone a bit overboard with the icing in compensation. I hope it isn't too sweet.'

'Grace,' said Alan, 'I'm sure it will be a triumph over adversity.'

'Tell me about the food in Canada,' she said, leaning forward hungrily.

'Oh, we have caviar for breakfast. And quails' eggs for lunch. And the most wonderful venison you ever did taste—'

'No, truly. I'm starved of information.'

'Well, they tell me some things are a bit shorter than they used to be. Can't imagine why. It's probably psychological. But actually they eat like kings out there. I should think it was the same back in Australia. The food seems to be much bigger. All that open space. Big, big steaks. Loaves of bread the size of a picnic hamper.'

'It wasn't at all like that in Australia. You see, we always thought we should be eating whatever they did in England.'

'Oh. Anyway, the Canadians all grow very big because of it. I find them quite frightening. Enormous hulks of humanity. Not very bright, though. Except for the scientists, but then they're much weedier.'

'Ted Nicolls wasn't weedy,' interjected Walter.

'Walter,' said Grace, 'he's pulling our legs. As always. Were you *ever* serious, Alan?'

'At Cambridge Alan had the reputation of being an exceptionally serious young man,' said Walter. 'It's only with us that he plays the fool.'

'I still have that reputation now,' said Alan. 'Being deprived of your company makes me rather morose, I'm afraid.' For a moment he looked a little sad. Then he took a huge bite from his slice of cake. His face brightened, then looked bemused.

'Carrots,' he said. 'An interesting idea.'

'Oh, come on. You must have had carrot cake before.'

'Never. My mother had aspirations to gentility. I think she would have thought carrots were beneath us in a pudding.'

'Well, she'd have to revise her opinions now.'

'How's your father?' enquired Walter. Alan had come from visiting him in Birmingham.

'Dying, I think. I doubt he'll last out the war.'

'I'm sorry.'

'He isn't. I think he's had enough. First they take away his livelihood, then just when things are getting back on an even keel, they bomb him, kill his wife, take his only son away to Canada, and finally inflict him with a crippling illness with a highfalutin Latin name. I think he intends to die just to spite them.'

'Poor man. He's had a hard life.'

'The thing about Father is that he takes it all entirely personally. I mean, the depression was never a matter of wider economic forces or class conspiracies. It was all done to get at him. Likewise he is convinced that Hitler has a personal agenda to cause him maximum inconvenience. I suppose it makes the struggle livelier. But to listen to him, you'd think that the destruction of the bus shelter down the road was a greater bereavement than Mother's death.'

'I didn't know your mother died in the bombings,' said Grace.

'She didn't. She had a heart attack. But it was Hitler's fault, you see, because she lost so much sleep over the bombings, and it was entirely deliberate on his part, and it was also the fault of the Ministry of Food, because they specifically took all her favourite things out of the shops, and it was the fault of the local council, who didn't repair the steps up to the street from the main road, and it was also *her* fault, because she chose the day before his birthday to die, just to make things awkward. Sorry. I don't mean to make him out to be awful. He's a good man really. And as you say, he's had a hard life, and that's been his way of dealing with it. Sometimes I've wished that my own outlook could be as simple. That I could always find someone to blame.'

'Well,' said Walter, 'you did, in a way. Didn't you? The class system was always to blame. For pretty much everything.'

Grace sprang to attention with delight. She loved Alan and Walter's good-humoured ideological sparring, and particularly enjoyed weighing in on Walter's side.

'Now come on,' said Alan, stiffening. 'That's rather simplistic, as you know.'

'All right,' said Walter, because it had occurred to him that Alan's father's illness was not a particularly good pretext for an argument. 'It is quite simplistic. You're right.'

'That's because communist theory is simplistic,' said Grace.

'I'm not a communist,' said Alan.

'Not a communist?'

'I haven't been a communist since about 1935.'

'Alan,' said Grace, 'I first met you in 1935. And you've been spouting communist theory at me ever since then.'

'That's because you provoked me.' He chewed. 'And I still think that most of what Marx had to say was right. But I've never much liked absolute positions, and I like them less since Hitler. Anyway, you two can't talk. Pacifism is nothing if not simplistic.'

'There's nothing more complex in the world.'

'Oh yes? Your position is based on the conviction that there is nothing, and I repeat nothing, which is a greater evil than war. That is your only justification for avoiding it at all cost. And that's hardly an opinion which is based on an unbiased evaluation of the external evidence available. It's not an opinion at all. It's a faith. And there is nothing simpler than faith.'

'Nonsense,' said Grace, but the resort to such a cursory dismissal was a sign that he had been effective, for the time being at least.

'Come on,' pleaded Walter. 'This is supposed to be a holiday, especially for Alan. Let's not argue.'

'Hmph,' said Grace. 'That's just because you don't like to mix arguments with food. You'll only take Alan to the top of a mountain and argue with him there, without me.'

And both men suppressed a smirk, because they knew she was right.

19. DETERRENCE

In 1943, when Niels Bohr arrived in the United States, the Manhattan Project faced a crisis of conscience.

The further the project progressed, the bigger it became. Bohr had always predicted this. He had long cast scorn on the possibility of the bomb on the grounds that 'you would have to turn the whole country into a factory'. When he arrived in America, and Oppenheimer proudly showed him the fledgling nuclear pile at Oak Ridge to prove him wrong, Bohr surveyed the enormous industrial installation and said, 'But you are turning the whole country into a factory'. Millions of dollars had been spent already; hundreds of scientists employed; mountains of mineral resources deployed.

The British, arriving bomb-fraught and malnourished from their homes in the cities of England, stared around them in disbelief. If proof had been needed that the decision to decamp was the right one, it was this. There was no way under the sun that this could have been done at home.

And it was then that they realised that if it could not be done in Britain, the chance of a bomb being built in Germany was almost non-existent.

Ever since the first thousand-bomber raid in 1942, 'Bomber' Harris's assault on the population of Germany had escalated. Night after night, cities were razed to the ground. Even if military installations this size had survived the onslaught, there was no way they could have escaped the notice of the spy planes. The naval blockade which was starving half the peoples of Europe prevented any materials from being brought in. And now the tide had turned against the Germans. The Battle of the Atlantic was over; the Allies had invaded Italy; Mussolini had fallen. The Nazi Empire was on the defensive. It was unthinkable that they could spare resources on this scale.

The crisis of conscience for the Manhattan Project scientists was this: if they were no longer building a deterrent against a German atomic bomb, what on earth were they doing?

Walter and Alan talked and talked. They talked until their voices were hoarse, repeating all the arguments they'd rehearsed in their letters, varying them, and then repeating them again. They charged mountains, stormed beaches, assaulted escarpments. And always the negotiations broke down upon a single point: that of what Alan could not tell.

'Don't you realise,' shouted Walter above the crashing of the waves, as they raced one another across the rock pools stretching out to sea, 'I don't *want* to know! It's completely irrelevant to me. You are serving your own government in the defence of your country and you believe it to be right. That is all I need to know. If my brother taught me one thing, it was that.'

'But what we're doing now is finding a *pacifist* agenda!' cried Alan, as Walter attempted to steer their rowing boat away from the bank of the river. 'There is nobody who would understand it better than you. We need you, Walter! You can abdicate the right and the responsibility to bear arms, but you can't abdicate the right and responsibility to know.'

'It is not me who has given up the right to know,' bawled Walter above the wind on the summit of Snowdon, in the exact same spot where he and Jim had come to the understanding which they would take to their graves. 'It has been taken away from me by a military government. This is what war is, Alan. Secrets are as potent a weapon as bombs and I will not be party to them.'

'You must have some inkling,' murmured Alan as they sprawled, exhausted, on the sofas in the living room, nursing their cups of tea long after Grace had given up on them and gone to bed. 'You must have some idea in your head of what I'm talking about. It's perfectly obvious if you think it through. I think you do know really and just won't admit it.'

You were wrong, Alan, thought Walter, staring at the words he'd written about what had happened during the war, and at the piles of books from which he'd scraped every last morsel of knowledge. I don't know how I managed it, but I had no inkling at all back then. Honest to God. I did not know.

18

'Now,' said Grace, 'it is time for you to tell me what *you* know about Alan Nunn May.'

George told her. He watched her turn very pale. 'I'm sorry,' he said when he'd finished.

'The Russians? But I don't understand it. I mean, he had some vague communist sympathies when he was a very young man. But he never stuck to them very well, and he never joined the Party. You see, Alan's opinions were always rather chaotic. He was never a man of conviction, like Walter. It was the argument he was interested in, not the truth.'

'He visited Moscow in 1936,' pointed out George.

'Oh, but that was just a sort of – ideological tourism. He visited Germany as well. So did we. And anyway, as soon as Stalin made the pact with Hitler, Alan discovered where his sympathies lay. He wanted to fight the Nazis, and if the Soviets wouldn't do it, then he'd join the British.' She faltered. 'You have to realise how complicated all of this is. People's opinions are never black and white. They change.'

'Perhaps Nunn May's opinions changed again,' suggested George.

'But not—' For a moment George thought she was going to cry. Then she sniffed hard. 'You say he never kept the appointment.'

'That's right.'

'Definitely?'

'Definitely. I followed him for four months. Ait— Mr Jones said he was supposed to make contact in October last year.'

'Then perhaps it's all nonsense.'

'Perhaps.'

'But you say they're going to arrest him. Do you really think they will?'

'George thought about it. There was no doubt in his mind. 'They will.'

'But what *for*?'

'I don't know. But you said – that he was involved in—'

'The Manhattan Project. Yes. I suppose it's obvious what they *think*. But do they have any evidence? Is it just because he happened to work for his government during the war, and because he happened to say a few things that were a bit left wing about ten years ago? Is that a good enough excuse to go trailing around after him for *four months*, and then start persecuting his friend, who never had anything to do with the whole bloody mess at all?' She sniffed again.

'I don't know,' said George.

'And if they have got proof, why don't they just arrest him and be done with it?'

'I think—' George thought very hard, and realised that he might have an answer to that question. 'Well, you see, the reason why I was following Nunn May in the first place wasn't to find out anything in particular about him. Jones always said he already knew all he needed to. Or he wouldn't have put me on to it. That's what he said. I was just a – dogsbody. All I was supposed to be doing was letting Jones know when he kept his appointment at the British Museum. And then the plan was to pull him and his contact in together.'

'But he didn't keep the appointment.'

'No. But it wasn't just that he didn't keep that appointment. He didn't keep any appointments at all. Until the day he went to see your husband.'

'You mean that Walter is the *only* person he has seen since he came back from Montreal?'

'Yes. And so—' Why had he never bothered to think about it like this before? 'I suppose what Jones really wants to know now is why Nunn May went to see your husband, and what he said to him when he was there.'

Grace was very quiet. Then she said, 'You know, what I want to do most is go to Alan and tell him he is going to be arrested.'

'Mrs Dunnachie, you can't.'

'*Grace.*'

'Grace. He will be arrested anyway, whether you tell him or not. You mustn't go to him. Don't you see? That's what they're waiting for.'

What am I saying? thought George. Why was he giving Dunnachie's wife advice on how to protect her husband? He was supposed to be on the other side. Of course, there were good reasons for trying to stop her from tipping off Nunn May. But still—

'Can't you ask your husband what happened?' he suggested.

'I did at the time. He wouldn't tell me. All he said was—' She took a sharp intake of breath. 'That Alan hadn't liked the secrecy. And something about the Canadian Mounties.'

'The Canadian Mounties?'

'Behaving like secret policemen, apparently. Oh God—'

'Grace,' said George, feeling momentarily as though he were her equal, 'I think we have to assume that Nunn May did whatever they think he did. The question isn't that. The question is what he told your husband.'

'I can't believe Alan would do anything that would put Walter in danger. Even – even if he has betrayed his country, I can't believe that he would ever betray his *friend*.'

'But,' said George, 'as far as the authorities are concerned, your husband is a traitor anyway.' He could hear Aitken's voice saying the words. *You can get him to admit to it any day of the week . . . He stood in opposition to his own country in its darkest hour.*

Her eyes blazed with anger. 'So am I. If Walter is a traitor, I am one too.'

20. OPENNESS

The essence of Bohr's vision was that the prospect of an arms race after the war was a very frightening one, and that it would threaten the very existence of the world. But he believed that the problem contained its own solution, a solution not just to atomic rivalry but to the conundrum which had vexed every peace-lover since the close of the First World War. How do you make war an anachronism? How can man's capacity for killing be curbed?

'We are in a completely new situation that cannot be resolved by war,' said Bohr.

He felt that the atomic bomb was not really a weapon at all. It was 'a far deeper interference with the natural course of events than anything ever before attempted,' he wrote; it would 'completely change all future conditions of warfare'. The anarchic, self-interested negotiations between independent national entities which had characterised the political organisation of the world for a millennium or more would no longer be possible. The last resort of such negotiations had been war, but in an atomic future, war would no longer be a negotiation but the end of the world.

'It appeared to me,' Bohr wrote after the end of the war, 'that the very necessity of a concerted effort to forestall such ominous threats to civilisation would offer quite unique opportunities to bridge international divergences.'

And Bohr believed that there was only one way to turn those opportunities into reality. 'The prevention of a competition prepared in secrecy will demand concessions regarding exchange of information and openness. The very fact that knowledge is itself the basis of civilisation points directly to openness as the way to overcome the present crisis.'

Niels Bohr took a plane to see Churchill in London as the lead-up to D-Day intensified. Churchill was confounded and outraged by what he heard. The idea of telling the Russians about the bomb went against all his most secretive inclinations. Some of his scientific advisers tried to explain to him that this was not the sort of secret that could be kept, and that Stalin would end up with the bomb either way.

But Churchill knew that British power was starting to slip away. The bomb, and Britain's knowledge of it, gave him one of the few safeguards of Britain's place in a post-war world.

The scientists at Los Alamos, Oak Ridge and Montreal knew Bohr's views and knew also that he had the ear of leaders of state. They trusted him to guide the Allies into responsible custodianship of the terrible technology they were building.

They did not know that those leaders had ignored everything he'd said.

Grace was asleep. Walter lifted the bedcovers very carefully and crept downstairs to the dining room.

All the old letters were stored in the bureau they'd brought with them to Watford from the flat in Gordon Street after the war. Few from Walter's early years in England had survived, because he'd received so many that he'd been forced to conduct mournful letter-burning sessions every six months or so. But all of the letters Alan had sent after his return to Canada were still there.

He laid them out on the dining room table, steeled his courage, and read. They were like words from beyond the grave, the last missive from a dead friendship.

'Walter,' Alan had written in 1944, 'things have become rather odd here. Halban has fallen ill and so Cockcroft has been dragged out from Cambridge to lead the laboratory. I thought I would be glad to see him, but he brings the whiff of the Cavendish with him, and I cannot reconcile the memory of Rutherford with what is happening now. Cockcroft has not changed one jot, which makes it stranger still. Chadwick has now become the leader of the British contingent here and he has been elevated to some sort of diplomatic role, rushing about between Washington and the various laboratories. Can you imagine Chadwick as a diplomat? I cannot, even though I have seen it. He no longer seems to be interested in the science at all. All he cares about is whether we British are thought of with approval by Oppenheimer and General Groves, who is the American soldier running the project. Their approval, according to Chadwick, requires that we say nothing at all about our opinions of what we are doing, even to each other. Shut up and do your sums is the general attitude. Oh, I know exactly what you will say to all this. That I have chosen to become part of a military machine, and I should expect it to be run with the dictatorial callousness of an army. Oddly enough, in effect, that is what Chadwick and Cockcroft say too.'

Walter had not enjoyed reading these letters even at the time. Alan was a friend, and his fallibility was acceptable, up to a point, but Chadwick and Cockcroft were amongst the best men he had ever known. He remembered their dedication to science, their academic courage, their quietness and their fairness. Those memories were remote enough as it was, divided as he was from the people who had made them. He did not want them destroyed entirely.

'Good news from Europe!' rejoiced a later letter. 'Paris in the hands of the Allies at last! Now that we have it back, the awful years we have lived through seem all the more surreal. Halban is beside himself with joy. Unlike me, he is a real exile, who watched his homeland fall to the Nazis, and left it only to save it. He keeps a copy of Churchill's "We shall fight on the beaches" speech taped to the wall by his desk, with the final words underlined – you know the ones, about the new world stepping forth to the rescue of the old. Halban says that Churchill was right and that the war will be won from here. Anyway he is back in the laboratory after his illness, though working under Cockcroft now, which he has taken very well. He is desperate to go back to visit his family and meet up with Joliot. Cockcroft gave him permission to take leave only yesterday. I shall miss him while he is away. He is the only person here I have been able to get any sense out of lately.'

In the next letter the mood of celebration was gone. 'All hell has broken loose. Cockcroft wrote to Chadwick informing him of Halban's plan to go back to Paris. It was just a formality – Washington has to be told of every move we make – but Chadwick has not taken it that way. He sent a telegram straight back saying that Halban must be stopped from departing. By that time Halban was already on the ship to England. Now Chadwick has come to Montreal, screaming at Cockcroft, interrogating all the other Frenchmen, and making our lives a misery. The Canadian Mounties are crawling all over the place looking for treachery. I cannot understand it. Cockcroft, who is racked with guilt, says that it is because Halban is French, and now that the French Provisional Government has been formed, he owes his allegiance to a foreign power. The fear seems to be that he will tell Joliot about what we have been up to here. But Walter, in the name of heaven, we have been fighting to *liberate* France, and at last we are succeeding. How dare they treat the French as if they were our enemies? Both Joliot and Halban have contributed immeasurably to our work. In fact without them there would be no laboratory here in Montreal at all.'

The letter ranted on for several more pages. It ended with a plea for advice.

'Walter, there is no one else for me to ask. Chadwick and Cockcroft are the kind of men I would have gone to in the past if I had been placed in some sort of scientific dilemma, but now they are part of the problem, not the solution. I think I wrote to you in a previous letter about Bohr's ideas on the openness of science and technology being applied to military matters. Well, they are just not following them. And I believe strongly that something must be done about it. But I don't know what to do. I always thought I knew what you were going through as a pacifist, but now that I am in the same position I realise that I did not understand at all. My God, it is a cold feeling to stand against what everyone else believes is right. What should I do? What *is* there for me to do?'

How did I reply? thought Walter desperately. He remembered having felt a rush of pleasure at Alan's acknowledgement of his own trials. It had made him feel as he had all those years ago when Alan had shown sympathy for his being an Australian in England. And he had also felt rather smug at being asked for advice. For once Alan did not have all the answers. For once he was deferring to Walter's wisdom.

What on earth had he written? Walter knew that he had replied at great length and with very little substance. Of course he'd had no idea what dilemma Alan was actually facing, so he was forced to stick to generalities. But what generalities?

Walter opened his eyes. The light of the bulb above him was suddenly harsh and unnatural and he longed for the softness of the natural world. He went into the kitchen, unlocked the back door, and stepped into the silence of the garden.

He stared up at the stars. What a small, small planet this

is, he thought, feeling very frightened. Small, vulnerable and dangerous. The chains of cause and effect were threaded through its every atom, and were so multifarious and complex that a single picture of them could never be seen. The questions he had been asking himself the past few weeks were all causal. How was this caused? Why did that lead to this? And what will happen next? It occurred to him as a scientist that even the questions about what had gone before were not answerable. If even the past could not be understood, what hope was there of planning for the future?

He heard a sound from inside and stood stock still. Another. He began walking and then ran. At the doorway to the dining room, he stopped.

Grace was standing over the table in her towelling dressing gown, her hair sticking in all directions and her eyes screwed up against the light.

'What are you doing?' he demanded before he'd had time to think.

'I might ask the same question of you,' said Grace.

They stood divided by three yards of furniture and air. 'Are you reading my letters?'

'They are *our* letters. Do I need to remind you that we are married?'

She clearly thought he needed to be reminded. And the sense of intrusion and guilty secrecy was overpowering. Something in Walter broke, and an emotion which he had been barricading up for months flooded through him. It was resentment. He did not know how much longer he could go on being cooped up in the same small space as someone who did not in the least understand the contents of his brain.

The fear he'd always lived with was that he would not be allowed to keep her. The awful vision of a life without Grace had hovered at the edge of his brain ever since he'd won her, impossible to contemplate but there nevertheless, and it had made their life together all the sweeter. What, after all, would he be without her? Now he began to realise that he was beginning to find out. And that it was not she who was slipping from his grasp, but he from hers.

Of course there had always been parts of him to which she had no access. Neither of them had minded. Science was to her as music was to him, something mysterious and slightly alien whose ownership was surrendered utterly to the other person. But there had always been plenty of other things they could share. Now those other parts of Walter were withering away, and the bits which persisted were no business of hers.

She was right that he ought to have nothing to hide. But he had never been very good at explaining himself, not without her help. When they were young she had interpreted his moods and he had been guided by her reasoning. 'You're doing x,' she had said, 'because of y.' Her emotional algebra was way beyond his own. But it no longer worked. This time there was real, scientific algebra involved and she was not equal to it. Yet she still went on as if every problem in the world could be solved. And it could not.

'What are you going to do about Alan?' she said.

He had no idea what he was going to do about Alan. For a second he toyed with the idea of telling her everything, and giving her the chance to puzzle it through. And then he realised that she should not have been able to ask him that question. She was not supposed to know that the problem of Alan required anything to be done.

'What do you mean, what am I going to do about Alan?' he demanded.

She folded her arms and shook her head. 'You really aren't going to tell me what went on between you, are you?'

Her posture was exactly as it might be if she found the biscuits gone from the cupboard and was demanding a confession from one of the children. Her consistency on such occasions meant that Patrick and Bridget knew that if they owned up before she was forced to name the crime, their punishment would be more lenient. They generally confessed, because they knew they'd been caught already.

But this was not a theft, nor a betrayal. There was nothing in those letters that could implicate him any further than his months of silence already had. She was the one who had been caught, and yet he was being treated like a child.

Walter could bear it no longer. The letters lay on the table in front of her. He made a dive for them and gathered them up into his arms.

'Don't *shove* me!'

He could not bring himself to apologise. Or even speak.

'Walter, what are you trying to do to me? Do you expect me to live in this atmosphere? You've barely *seen* the children for weeks. Can't you see that I'm going out of my mind with worry?'

Still he was silent. He watched her rage intensify.

'Go back to Alan if that's what you really want!' she shouted. 'Have it out with him and damn the consequences if you think it will cure you of whatever disease you have. It is clearly absolutely no concern of mine.'

She turned and left the room. A half-second after the echo, Walter turned towards the door she had slammed behind her.

What did she know?

19

Walter read Alan's last letter in the bathroom, beyond Grace's prying gaze.

'Walter,' it concluded, 'if only you knew how your letter has sustained me. I am so terribly alone here. Your advice has been the only guide I have had in an impossible situation. I have returned to it again and again. You know that however much we have argued about our beliefs, in my heart and in my actions I have always supported you. It is my most fervent wish that you will never need to hear what it is that I have done, but if you ever do, then I can only trust that you will stand by me as I have stood by you.'

Trust. When he'd first received that letter, he'd been as frustrated as ever by its opacity, but the war was drawing to an end, and they and their friendship had survived. Soon Alan would come home, he'd thought, and they'd be able to have a good talk about it all without all this nonsense.

It had never happened. Even at the time, Alan must have known that it would not. One does not mention trust until it is on its way out.

Walter and Grace returned to London at the end of 1944 along with the rest of the university, when the risk of bombing was thought to have subsided. In fact they arrived just in time for the examinations to be interrupted by the V2 rockets. Walter heard the boom and felt the shake of the floor beneath his feet when one of them exploded half a mile away, as he began a lecture addressed to an almost empty theatre. In those first days back in the city, the corridors and common rooms were still half deserted. If he chanced across any of his fellow staff, they would inevitably shake hands in enthusiastic reunion, and insist on meeting for coffee. Sometimes they even managed to find themselves some students to teach.

For more than six months after that, what passed for peace stumbled its agonising path across Europe, and as the months went on, the news grew worse and worse as the soldiers turned over the rubble they'd created and found the things they'd destroyed. Priceless masterpieces, their canvases scorched beyond repair. Ancient places of worship, Cologne Cathedral amongst them, which had stood for a thousand years and were now reduced to little more than dust. Smoke stacks, treasure hoards, strange medical-looking implements whose use could only be guessed at. And the bodies. Fifty million souls had perished in this war. Our war, the newspapers said proprietorially.

It was natural enough, on returning to his old haunts, for Walter to return to his old habits too. And his most time-consuming habit had always been Peace. He walked down the hill from Tufnell Park tube station to the Peace Pledge Union and demanded to know what was going on.

The fight seemed to have gone out of Brinton. 'There isn't very much demand for speeches these days, Walter,' he said. 'Nobody wants to know about Peace. They're too busy preparing themselves for the *peace*.'

'You can't call what's going on peace,' Walter expostulated. 'Henry, you of all people must not do that. It isn't called peace. It's called victory. One man's victory is another man's defeat, and in defeat are sown the seeds of future war.'

'We can call it what we like but I'm afraid that's the way it is. Be patient, Walter. Wait a while. The future will come, and when it does, the world will see that we have a place in building it.'

Walter marched home and wrote a long letter to *The Times* about the distinction between victory and peace. It was not published. He wrote another attacking the complacency of success and pointing out that if this war had risen from the ashes of the last with twice its might, then the world would be lucky to survive the next. It was ignored.

'Damn them all, Grace!' he shouted. 'Anyone would think they *wanted* to die.'

She laughed at his vehemence and said, 'You're preaching to the converted, my love. If the war ends, Alan will come home, won't he?'

'What does that have to do with it?'

'Well, with any luck you can shout at him instead of me.'

21. DESTROYER OF WORLDS

On 16 July 1945, more than five years after the Frisch–Peierls Memorandum sparked the British into action, a group of physicists was driven to a desolate spot in the New Mexico desert, two hundred miles south of the Manhattan Project's base at Los Alamos. The place was known in Spanish as Jornada del Muerto, the Dead Man's Trail. A steel tower, one hundred feet tall, was tethered to the desert rock with concrete reaching twenty feet deep. The temperature was well over one hundred degrees and storms were on the way. The scientists continued to execute their plans anyway.

One physicist speculated as to whether their experiment would ignite the atmosphere, and, if it did, whether it would merely destroy New Mexico or destroy the world. The project's military commander, General Groves, called the governor of New Mexico to prepare him for the possibility that he might have to declare martial law.

The timing device was started at minus twenty minutes, just before 5.10 a.m. The busloads of observers arrived from Los

Alamos, James Chadwick amongst them. They were twenty miles from the site of the experiment. Instructions were given to lie down on the ground, turn their faces away from the blast, and bury their heads in the sand. No one complied. They wanted to look the beast in the eye.

The scientists pressed welders' glass to their faces, shielding the sides with their hands. Isaac Rabi said afterwards that it was the brightest light they had ever seen or that anyone had ever seen. The intense pinpoint mushroomed to a great ball. The hills and desert were bathed in radiance, as if the sun had been turned on by a switch. It blasted; it pounced; it bored its way right through them. It was a vision which was seen with more than the eye. The ball burned through orange to red and was surrounded by purple luminosity. About one hundred seconds after the appearance of the pinpoint of light, the skies cracked and the earth shook, the echoes thrown back by the hills.

When the blast was over Oppenheimer led the party out of the shelter. He stood and quoted a line from the Hindu scripture, the Bhagavadgita: *'Now I am become Death, the destroyer of worlds.'*

'The war is over,' they reported to base.

Four hours later, the ship carrying Little Boy set out from San Francisco into the Pacific.

The *Enola Gay* travelled to Hiroshima in the early morning of 6 August 1945 with two escort planes and no maps. The planes travelled at a height of thirty-one thousand feet. There were no clouds. They came in over the island of Shikoku and crossed the Inland Sea. Hiroshima lay on the far shore, a crow's-foot delta surrounded by hills. At the centre of the city was the target. It was a T-shaped bridge spanning the Ota River. The moment arrived. The bomb was released. It weighed four tons and dropped through still, shimmering air.

Beneath, the sun shone gently on gardens and three hundred thousand civilians began their working day.

22. LITTLE BOY

The bomb looked like a tall black rubbish bin with fins. Inside was a long tube, which effectively contained both a gun and its target. At the base of the bomb was a bullet consisting of cylinders of pure uranium-235 mounted on a steel slug. The target lay at the far end of the tube and had a uranium-235 post centred in the hole. The separate masses of bullet and target were substantial, but they were below the critical mass first estimated by Frisch and Peierls. Together, they exceeded that mass. All that was needed for the bomb to explode was for the uranium bullet to hit its target with enough momentum to hold the critical mass together. The bullet was fired by a conventional explosive detonated by radio signal when the bomb was halfway to the ground; it made contact; and the shock of the impact triggered a tiny initiator stored just beneath the target rings. The initiator was a neutron source, almost identical to that created by James Chadwick in 1932. It fired alpha particles into beryllium and released neutrons into the now-critical mass of uranium; and above the city of Hiroshima, the chain reaction commenced.

A flash extinguished the sun, a blast ripped the earth, and as the *Enola Gay* looped upwards and away, as fast as its fuel could carry it, the death of a city began.

The ball of fire swelled, cooling into visibility. Then the ball began to rise, supported by a neck of smoke. The stem narrowed and twisted, and the ball spread outwards into the sky, its red core surrounded by a bubbling mass of purple-grey cloud. In the shadow of the mushroom, the city beneath boiled like a vat of burning black oil. The flames shot up, and the mass of dust and smoke flowed outwards like lava up into the foothills, fires starting up around the edges of the bowl, until it was impossible to see anything for smoke.

Birds ignited in the air. On the ground, those humans within half a mile of the fireball had their internal organs boiled away whilst their bodies were seared to small bundles of smoking char. Within that radius, no life remained to experience the chemical and physical reactions that ensued. After the blast, there was silence.

Beyond the centre, there were still bodies to feel, but no eyes to see. Eyelids and noses and ears melted away, leaving only white teeth to stick out and beg for water in the last moments before death. Further still, vision returned after the flash, and the eyes of the people who had survived the blast looked down at their bodies and saw that their clothes were gone, and their skin peeling away, falling in strips from wet flesh. The buildings collapsed and the men, women and children stumbled out into the streets, staring at one another, seeing bowels and brains erupting from bodies, watching the fires ignite spontaneously around them, breathing the ashen air, not screaming or crying but simply stumbling in any direction which might herald safety. In the midst of all the wreckage, the Communications Hospital remained upright, a dull beacon in the mire, and the rows of naked, hairless people trudged in ant-like lines across miles of scorched earth towards its protective walls. By morning they lay in piles on the roads. Those who reached the hospital crammed into every room, lying in the toilets, the doctors tending patients whilst their own burns bled, until the hospital itself caught fire.

The screaming began. The river bloated with the floating corpses of those who had gone there to drink or to cast their burning flesh into the waves. The streets were empty except for the dead, and the buildings gone. As the day turned to night and then day again, the bodies stacked up and began to decompose. They were gathered into piles, oil poured over them, and were burned once more. Some jerked back to life, found themselves in flames, and ran from the pyres. Those who did not die seemed for a time to improve. But then they became sick once more. They bled, they lost their hair, they vomited, and the life seeped slowly out of them.

By the end of 1945, half the population of Hiroshima was dead.

The day after the blast, the news arrived in London.

The city was no stranger to death. Each member of the populace had lost someone they loved, had grieved, and gone on. A communal personality had been stitched together in adversity, and its face was stoical, tenacious, and unshockable.

But for a moment that morning, London stood still in horror. The holes in the roads gaped. The tatters hanging from the sides of widowed buildings shivered. The sun flickered and dimmed.

'The first atomic bomb has been dropped on Japan,' the newspaper announced. 'It has two thousand times the blast power of the RAF's ten-tonner, which was previously the most powerful bomb in use. Thus British and American scientists have achieved what the Germans were unable to do and have won "the greatest scientific gamble in history". The announcement was made yesterday by President Truman, who said, "We are now prepared to obliterate more rapidly and completely every productive enterprise the Japanese have above ground in any city. If they do not now accept our terms they may accept a rain of ruin from the air the like of which has never been seen on this earth."'

A way had been found to impose peace upon the whole world. In its moment of victory, London flinched.

'The authorities are still unable to obtain a definite check on the extent of the casualties. Medical relief agencies from neighbouring districts could not distinguish – much less identify – the dead from the injured. The impact of the bomb was so terrific that practically all living things – human and animal – were literally seared to death by the tremendous heat and pressure set up by the blast. All the dead and injured were burned beyond recognition. Those outdoors were burned to death, while those indoors were killed by the indescribable pressure and heat.'

And though it had been proved scientifically half a century before, London knew for real that morning that a rock is made from the same materials as a human heart.

A word is the echo of a thought. A bomb is the echo of an intention. A death is the echo of a moment in which the balance between positive and negative totters and falls.

And in Walter Dunnachie's head the echoes swelled and reverberated, beating back and forth from one side of his skull to the other. Niels Bohr's genial smile and bloodhound jowls, humbly declining Lady Rutherford's offer of pudding that Saturday evening at Newnham Cottage. Cockcroft, offering to switch off his particle accelerator while Walter completed his experiments. Chadwick, pursued through the laboratory by journalists, rebuffing them, while Walter tried to liberate some of those elusive neutrons using his own malfunctioning apparatus.

And Alan. Alan as an undergraduate, hurrying after Walter, almost running in the attempt to keep up. Alan as a doctoral student, making arch comments about world affairs. Alan as a university lecturer, laughing and crying over Rutherford's untimely demise. Alan as a military scientist, pleading with Walter to believe in something he did not even know.

'*I did not know*,' screamed Walter.

But though his lips formed the words, he was a man in a dream of death, and no sound emerged.

After Hiroshima the invitations to give speeches began to flood in. 'Your special position as a physicist and a pacifist,' was the way Brinton put it. Everyone wanted to know his opinion. They wanted him to stand on conference platforms and explain to them what it meant for a man to learn that his best friends had taken vacuum flasks and spectroscopes and killed one hundred and fifty thousand human souls.

At first the blood in his brain was too red and clotted for him even to realise that he was not going to accept the invitations. They remained hidden under newspapers, shoved in between the pages of Grace's cookery books, interleaved with the pages of Patrick's maths homework. Then he started to burn them. Grace took to snatching them away before he could get to them and filing them for herself. He did not mind that. All he cared about was that he should not have to look at them.

'Walter, how can I help you?' Grace pleaded.

Still that insistence on attending to *his* needs. What was he, in comparison with this? At night the equations pounded in his brain. One neutron, fired into the core of the uranium atom. Two more stray neutrons, heading out towards their defenceless targets. Eight. Sixteen. Thirty-two. Sixty-four. One hundred and twenty-eight. At 3 a.m. one night he got all the way to five hundred trillion in only fifty moves. It took him about three minutes, but a neutron could do it in a fraction of a second. The bomb dropped on Hiroshima – the second ever built, a prototype, at most – was nothing to what might be possible.

He'd thought sometimes in the war that his brain was being addled by the sheer numbers of the dead. But even when Jim had taken off in his bomber plane to raid Cologne, one plane and one bomb had hit one house and one family. It had been simple at the outset and had become complex at the end, the human end, when Jim had flown as one man in a mighty dance of death, with a thousand plane crews and a thousand individual targets. With the atomic bomb it was simple at the end. One plane, one bomb, one hundred and fifty thousand deaths. It was the process leading up to that moment which was complex, and Walter had been tangled up in it ever since the day he had walked through those Cavendish gates, his heart singing with the injunction to delight in the works of the Lord. Webster's cloud chamber, now up in his office as a souvenir, had been right in the thick of it. The only way to have kept his pacifism pure would have been to turn around that autumn morning and go straight back to Australia.

He could not have known it then. But he should have known earlier. There had been speculation at the madder fringes of science back in 1939, after the discovery of fission. It had gone nowhere, or so Walter had persuaded himself. Everything had gone quiet and all he'd known was that real science had shut down in the headlong impatience to build bombs and defences against bombs. Was it innocence which had prevented him from believing that it was possible, or wilful stupidity?

'*Don't* help me,' Walter hissed at Grace.

Brinton came round to talk to him about it. Walter knew from the way he talked that it was at the behest of Grace.

'Walter,' he said, 'I know you must be suffering very much, knowing that your friends were involved in this thing—'

'My suffering is irrelevant,' said Walter.

'It *isn't* irrelevant, Walter. Now is the time when people want to learn about Peace and how we can build it. You must be going through a very difficult time, but the dilemmas you face are something we can all learn from. Your reflections—'

'I have no reflections,' said Walter.

'But Walter – Walter, you don't have to talk about the bomb, you know. There are plenty of other questions to address.'

'Really?' Walter grabbed the pamphlet Brinton was clutching. 'This is your next meeting agenda, I presume. Item one: "The Absolute Weapon: Atomic Power and World Order". Item two: "Manifesto for the Atomic Age". Item three: "One World or None: The Full Meaning of the Atomic Bomb". What other questions would those be, Henry?'

'There *are* other things.' Brinton's mind was as agile as ever. 'The administration of the United Nations. The relationship with the Soviet Union. The question of Palestine.'

'Don't you think it would be a little dishonest of me to talk about the Jews and the Russians when the Jews and the Russians are standing up before me and talking about nuclear physics?'

Brinton's ebullience was starting to dent. 'Walter, you used to tell me that speaking to the public about Peace was the best cure for bad dreams. You said that the only way to confront the bad dreams was to replace them with good ones.'

Castles in the air. The clouds floating out to sea, changing their shape as they drifted beyond his grasp. A cloud in a bottle, the water vapour condensing around a single alpha particle, captured at last. And now a cloud in a new shape, created by man.

'Dreams, Henry?' said Walter. 'Dreams are dangerous things. You are right that I have had good dreams in my time. My dreams for Peace were crushed by war. My dreams for science led to death. I have had enough of dreaming now.'

Brinton left. Walter knew that he had treated him badly. But he was glad that he was gone.

20

'So, Henderson,' said Aitken, 'I am to be treated to another little update.'

George was cold with fear. He felt like a double agent. Perhaps he was. Grace had given him exhaustive instructions on how to handle the meeting. A piece of paper had been pushed across the table towards him, and a pen. 'Write it all down,' she'd told him. 'Then memorise it. Then burn it.'

Her voice had been steady but her eyes were stark and scared.

'Tell him all the details of Walter's friendship with Alan. Explain how they met and what they did together at college. You should let him know that they stayed in touch throughout the war, and that Alan came to visit us in 1943. The reason why you were able to get these details out of me is that you asked me why Alan didn't turn up to our dinner, and I immediately entered upon a conversation about how untypical of Alan it was, and I related a history of his friendship with Walter. You then asked me what had changed between them, and I said that I thought the difference was that they might have quarrelled when Alan went to see Walter in London. I admitted to not knowing what passed between them on that occasion, but my conjecture was that they talked about the atomic bomb. Alan wanted Walter's blessing and Walter would not give it.'

George had begun to worry whether he had actually gained anything from all this talking with Grace. 'But is that true? Is that really what you think?'

'Yes,' Grace had said.

'Might they not have talked about – something else?'

'If they did would I know about it?'

No, he'd admitted, she would not. But sitting before Aitken now, he wondered whether it was wise to follow her instructions so implicitly. Yet he could not see what else he could do. He could not go halfway.

Aitken listened without interjection, as unmovable as ever. The account petered to a close.

'What an extraordinarily chatty woman,' said Aitken.

George tensed with fear. Then he forced himself to relax. 'Yes,' he said. 'It rather suggests that whatever Dunnachie has done, his wife has no suspicions of him.' That too was true. As far as George knew.

'You say that Mrs Dunnachie thinks that her husband and Nunn May quarrelled about the bomb. Can I take it that she is under the impression that Dunnachie is steadfast in his opposition?'

'Yes.'

'And Dunnachie and Nunn May corresponded throughout the war.'

'Yes.'

'Very good. Do you have any plans for further liaisons?'

'Yes. You see, I'm on the pastoral committee.'

'What does that involve?'

'Visiting the old and sick,' said George lamely.

A very mild look of amusement twitched Aitken's eyebrows. 'Really. Have you done any of this visiting yet?'

'Erm – no.' Grace had been too preoccupied to force him into it.

'And when is your next appointment with Mrs Dunnachie?'

'Tomorrow morning.'

'At the church?'

George nodded.

'What time?'

Why what time? Aitken had never been very bothered about such details in the past. George's discomfort increased. 'Half past ten.'

'Thank you, Henderson. Your work has been adequate.'

Somehow the unprecedented burst of praise scared George even more.

'How did it go?' Grace asked George as soon as she had shut the door behind them. She looked as though she would pounce upon him and drag the information from his throat if he did not surrender it instantly.

'I think it went all right,' said George, not feeling very confident at all.

'Why? Why do you think it went all right?'

'He was pleased with the information I gave him.'

'Is that all right? Or is that a bad thing? Why is that all right?'

George shook his head. It was beginning to occur to him that her attempt to control Aitken might not have been a very wise thing to undertake.

The details released by the US government lay before Walter, alongside the summary in his own handwriting. The bomb was not such a difficult thing to build after all. The only barriers were the expense, and the industrial enormity of separating the necessary volumes of uranium-235. Of course the travails involved in discovering that this was the case had been immense, and would have taken decades in a time of peace. But now that the work was complete, its most important effect had been to show the world that it could be done. There was little to stop any nation with the necessary resources from following in America's footsteps. Except, of course, sanity. And given that the two nations which had already exploded the bomb were those which Walter had always regarded as being the most trustworthy on earth, there was little hope of that.

The telephone rang. Walter jumped, then stilled himself and picked it up. It was Grace. She was breathing in short, shallow gasps.

'We've been burgled,' she said.

'Burgled?' For a moment Armageddon faded into the background. 'Grace, are you all right? What's been taken?'

She was crying. 'They've taken the letters,' she said.

'The letters? What letters?'

'Every letter Alan ever sent you. They've gone.'

He stood up.

'Walter—'

But Walter was already out of the office. The receiver dangled by its cord from the edge of the desk.

George had been summoned. He crept into Aitken's office.

'Ah, Henderson,' said Aitken. 'The great detective. Do take a seat.'

George sat down, clutching the sides of the chair in dread. Whatever he had achieved, he did not want to have done it. It was better to be stupid and incompetent than actually make things happen.

'It turns that you were right about Nunn May's correspondence with Dunnachie. This—' it was placed in front of George '—is the last in the series. I think you will find it illuminating.'

George looked fearfully at the page and awaited revelation.

Several sentences had been underlined. 'I am so terribly alone here'; 'I cannot tell even you what choice lies before me, and so I am forced to make my decision alone'; 'Your advice has been the only guide I have had in an impossible situation.'

The letter did not seem to say very much at all. He looked up in relief.

But Aitken's bearing had changed. The atmosphere of disgrace was deeper than for any of George's previous misdemeanours. 'Tell me,' said Aitken, 'how long exactly have you been investigating Dr Dunnachie?'

'Three weeks, sir.'

'And can you explain to me exactly why this letter was not in my hands three weeks ago?'

The excuses leapt into George's head. *Because I didn't know it existed. Because I didn't know you wanted it. Because you never told me what to do. Because you have never told me anything at all.*

'I—' he began. He fell silent.

'Do you have any comprehension of how much pressure I have been under from the Americans to get this thing sewn up these past three weeks? Do you realise the number of men I have employed investigating Nunn May's case?'

There was only one possible answer. 'No,' he said. He summoned up the courage to ask a question of his own. 'Mr Aitken,' he said, 'what is it in that letter that is so dreadful?'

'*Look* at it, man.'

George looked again.

'Why do you suppose Nunn May has kept his liberty all this time?' stormed Aitken. 'We've always known his guilt. But he's not the only traitor in our midst. The security of this nation is under as great a threat now as it has been during any of the past six years. An external threat can be countered and defeated. This time the enemy is within. But of course the Americans don't care in the slightest about British security as long as it doesn't affect them. It was only with the greatest difficulty that they were persuaded to give us time to find Nunn May's accomplices before arresting him.'

'Accomplices?'

'Spy networks, *Mr* Henderson.'

'But I – I didn't know I was looking for a spy network.'

'You weren't, for pity's sake. Do you think I'd employ *you* on such a mission? Dunnachie has never had any communist connections other than Nunn May. I needed an eye kept on him, that's all. It was the others who were looking for the real villains.'

'Others?' George had never been aware of any others. But he supposed they must exist. He looked back down at the letter and searched it for a clue to the source of Aitken's disgust.

And then he saw it.

There was one particular word which had been under-scored so deeply that the paper was almost pierced.

Alone.

George looked up in surprise.

There had never been any accomplices to find.

And suddenly, for the first time in his professional life, George Henderson knew exactly what was going to happen next.

For Alan, it was one of those moments which will live too strongly in the memory to ever be experienced in the present. He walked from the lecture theatre into the courtyard. The air was concise and deliberate. There were students to either side of him, existing on a separate plane, as they always did.

The men in dark blue uniforms and erect hats did not have to stop him. They did not need to say the words. His head recited them alongside the metallic voices.

'Will be taken down in evidence—'

'Thank you,' he found himself saying to them, uselessly, and accompanied them to the Yard.

*   *   *

Like every other person in the courtyard, Walter stopped and stared.

Alan's shoulders were stooped and he shuffled like an old man. His clothes were creased and grubby, his tie askew, and his chin displayed uneven stubble. He looked straight ahead of him, and did not acknowledge the existence of anything in his path, as though the view before him was an empty canvas. As he and his companions drew close to Walter, Walter stepped forward and opened his mouth. Alan's gaze washed over Walter, along with everything else. There was not the slightest flicker of recognition.

Walter tried to reach out as he passed, but he was repelled by a strange smell coming from Alan's clothes. It was an odour of neglect more normally associated with academics of far more advanced years.

The stench of loneliness.

21

Alan sat with the police officers for about an hour. It was a very unnatural form of existence. He did not speak to them, and they did not speak to one another. He knew well enough what they were all waiting for. Eventually the very fat man arrived.

'Dr Nunn May,' said Aitken. 'Most pleasant to make your acquaintance again. Are you in the mood for a confession this time?'

'Yes,' said Alan.

'I am most relieved to hear it. Shall we get on with it?'

'I want to be sure I have it right. If you don't mind, I'd appreciate it if you could spare me some paper and a pen so that I can write it down first.'

The policemen looked at Aitken expectantly.

'That will be no problem,' said Aitken.

The policemen twitched with surprise.

'Go get the paper and pen,' Aitken commanded them, and they jumped.

When they had all left him alone in the room, Alan stared at the blank sheet before him. The moment of decision was upon him.

He had two options. One was to write something extremely brief and efficient, which conveyed the basic information and no more. The other was to embark upon the quest on which he'd always hoped Walter would accompany him, and start telling a story designed to shock the world.

*   *   *

Walter locked himself in his office for as long as he could, but he had to go home in the end. Although the police had already been round and written their report, Grace had left everything as she'd found it. She wanted Walter to see what had happened.

It was a neat job. The burglars had clearly gone to the bureau straightaway, having identified it as the most likely place, and had placed each of the drawers on the floor. A few piles of paperwork lay on the carpet, but most of it remained where it had been found.

'Have they taken anything other than the letters?'

'Nothing. I've checked everything.'

'And they've taken every single letter Alan wrote?'

'Yes. What—' Grace looked very frightened. 'What will they have found out, Walter?'

He sat down. Then he looked at her. She had not expressed any surprise at all from the moment he had got home. It was no longer possible to pretend that she had no knowledge of what had happened. 'What do you mean, they?'

The guilt on her face was unmistakable. She smothered it and spoke. 'The government.'

The worst possible suspicions were racing through his mind. 'What do you know, Grace?'

'I know that Alan was arrested this morning.'

'*How?* Was it on the news? Did someone from King's call you?' He was desperate to find an excuse for the sinister extent of her knowledge.

'No.' She took the chair next to him and sat down. 'Walter, you must listen to me properly when I tell you this.'

'Tell me what?'

'George Henderson told me.'

Walter's mind was a blank. 'Who's George Henderson?'

'The man who came to dinner. With his wife. The man from the Methodist church.'

Someone from the church? For a moment all Walter could see were the fires of hell.

'Except that the stuff he told me about the church was all a lie,' said Grace. 'I believed him but it was a lie. He made it up to find out more about us.' She paused, and even in her palpable fear Walter could sense her making the most of the drama of the moment. 'George Henderson is a government spy.'

Walter's brain tumbled over and over. A spy? In all his torment it had never occurred to him that anyone might want to spy on *him*. He tried to dredge the memory of the dinner party from the recesses of his mind. There had been a man. With a wife, as Grace had said. Rather a ridiculous man, as he remembered it. There had been some cursory talk about Peace and Walter had been forced to retire to the kitchen and stuff a teacloth in his mouth.

'He came here to spy on me?'

'I didn't know he was a spy. There was no reason for me to suspect—'

But the protestation of innocence brought his suspicion flooding back. 'You know now. When did you find out? How long have you known?'

'Three days.'

In a fury, he grabbed her by the wrists. 'Why didn't you tell me?'

And with that motion, the Grace he knew vanished, and a wildcat replaced her. '*Let me go!*' she shrieked, her face screwed up, her arms attempting vainly to flail, her body flying away from him. He was too strong for her. She opened her palms and tried to push him away. 'Let me go or I won't tell you a thing!'

He did not want to give her her freedom. She was too frightening an entity to be allowed independence. Grace struggled to her feet, knocking the chair aside with her foot, trying to drag herself loose. Walter dug his feet into the carpet and stayed exactly where he was. Then, suddenly, he looked down at his hands. Her thin wrists were red and white where his fingers dug in. He looked up again and saw her face creased with pain, holding in a scream.

The use of force.

He dropped her wrists. She fell backwards and toppled over the chair. He heard her gasp as she hit the floor. At that moment remorse overwhelmed him and he rushed over to her, crouching beside her, cradling her in his arms.

'Get *away* from me!' She clambered to her feet and ran to the other side of the table.

There was a click at the hallway door. They both turned to it in alarm. A small figure was looping its way under its own upstretched arm, holding the handle whilst pushing the door open.

'Bridget!'

Bridget looked from one to the other and then back again. Her lip was wobbling. Then, with an expression that was pure Grace, she pursed her mouth and jutted out her chin.

'I'm thirsty,' she said. 'I want some water.'

Walter did not know what to do with himself. Grace ran to her daughter. 'Bridget, you naughty girl—' But her voice contained none of the sharpness with which she would normally have responded to such a plea. She bundled Bridget into the kitchen.

Walter quickly righted the chair and stared at it in horror. He could hear their voices from the room next door. 'I can't sleep,' said Bridget. 'I want a story. We haven't had a story for ages. I want to know what happens to Peter Pan.'

He grows up, snapped Walter's thoughts, and then his bitterness evaporated in the swirl of softness that was the echo of Bridget's demure voice.

'Bridget, I offered to read you *Peter Pan*,' said Grace, 'and you wouldn't have it.' The sound of a cupboard being opened, and a running tap.

'I want Daddy to read it.'

It was a put-up job, he realised, as the depths of guilt were plumbed within him. It wasn't that mother and daughter would ever have planned such a thing. No, they were both too guileless and instinctive for that. But they were opportunists. They knew he was listening to every word, and they had their hopes, in their different ways, for what it would do to him.

Walter forced himself to walk into the kitchen. Grace was bending down to place the glass in Bridget's hand. Together, their shapes formed a circle in the dim light. Two faces turned to regard him expectantly.

'Bridget, I'll read you *Peter Pan* tomorrow, I promise.'

A child's trust might survive any number of late nights in the past, but it will not stretch twenty-four hours into the future. 'Not tomorrow. Tonight.'

Walter glanced at Grace. Which course of action would be acceptable to her rather strict notions of child-rearing? Would it really be a good idea to disturb the children's routine to start reading stories in the middle of the night? He made his decision. 'No, Bridget. We'd wake Patrick up. I give you my word that we'll read *Peter Pan* tomorrow. Come here. Give Daddy a kiss.'

Walter dropped to his haunches. Bridget stepped forth easily from her mother's protection and planted a soft posy of lips on his mouth. He gave her a hug and did not want to let her go. Then he realised that the very vehemence of the action might alarm her, and he loosened his grasp. 'Good night, darling,' he whispered. 'Sleep tight.'

'Make sure the bugs don't bite!'

He laughed, close to tears. 'If they do—'

'Get a shoe—'

'And bash their little heads in two!'

The last phrase was chanted together. Grace was leaning against the sink, her body both limp and taut. 'Nighty night, Mummy,' said Bridget, marching back to her. She was making a meal of it, revelling in the attention. There were the beginnings of a smile at the edges of Grace's mouth, and the beginnings of a sob in her eyes, and her muscles resisted both, as if they might rip her face in two. 'Come on, nutkin,' she muttered, swept Bridget off her feet, and carried her back to the bedroom with the glass of water.

Walter walked into the dining room and waited in dread for his wife to return.

Alan sat in his cell with his head in his hands.

He had destroyed Walter's last letter along with the rest of his possessions before the long journey back from Canada. But he knew it by heart. It had been the only scrap of companionship or support he'd had in his moment of decision.

'Openness is essential to our dealings as scientists and as human beings,' Walter had written. 'Narrow ideas of nationality and ideology are as nothing in comparison with what we can accomplish when we talk to one another. You know as well as I do that the gravest problems our friendship has faced in this war have not been caused by our differences but by the fact that we cannot talk frankly. It is the same between nations. So talk, Alan, I implore you, talk. Talk as loudly and repeatedly as is necessary to make people hear you, even if talking brings punishment upon you. It will be worth it, because at least you will have acted according to your own conscience.'

No doubt Walter had been thinking of the sort of talking to which he was himself accustomed. But there had been no conference platforms or letter pages available to Alan. No newspaper, government agency or scientific authority would have touched what he had to say. Even Walter had forbidden him from telling him a word of it.

So he had told the only people who were prepared to listen.

It should never have been me, thought Alan in infinite weariness. He had always been the one who could see the failings in every absolute position, the one who believed in compromise and in flawed justice. Yet somehow here he was, exiled to the fringes of human existence by an act so extreme it must have come from some sort of faith. He did not regret what he had done – the glow of warmth as he had handed over the little jar and freed himself from the dirty secrets inside – but the small steps which had led him there had not been choices of his own. There had only been room for one big choice in his life, and it had been at that moment. Now he felt disconnected from it, as if he'd handed over his heart too, and it had decayed to nothing, along with the isotope in the glass.

He took up his pen and wrote.

'Grace—'

'Don't bother apologising. Not yet, at least. We've got a long night ahead of us before we get to apologising.'

'How did you know—' The unshared knowledge felt like the deepest possible insult to his soul. He felt an almost physical revulsion at the idea that a man named George Henderson might have been party to Grace's confidences. 'How did you know that Henderson was a spy?'

'I caught him hanging around UCL. There was only one possible connection between hanging around the church and hanging around the college, and that was you.'

'But—' Three days ago? Grace had not visited him three days ago. 'What were *you* doing at UCL?'

'Checking you were there.'

Walter stared at her.

'Walter, I didn't know what to think. You've been living in a world that doesn't include me. You might have been doing anything and I wouldn't have known. I – just wanted the peace of mind of knowing that you were where you were supposed to be.'

The enormity of it hit him. '*You* were spying on me too.'

'What else could I have done? You and the children are my whole life. I knew you were in trouble and you wouldn't tell me anything about it. If you were in trouble I wanted to help. I wanted to be part of it. I had to be. What choice did I have?'

Walter heard the sound of Alan's voice, railing at the keeping of secrets. He pushed it away. 'Did you— What happened when you caught Henderson?'

'I confronted him. I got him to tell me everything he knew. You see, he isn't a very good spy. At least—' Her firmness cracked a little. She stopped.

'What did he know?'

'Virtually nothing. Only what anyone might have known about you, except that he also knew that Alan had visited you, because before he was following you he was following Alan.'

This, at least, Walter should have known – that Alan would have been followed, that to be associated with him was to be cast under suspicion. 'What did he want to know about me?'

'I think the general idea was – that there might be a possibility – that you might be involved.'

Of course. He had been a suspect character from the start. Presumably the authorities thought pacifism at least as menacing as actual treachery. During the war, the British had treated all the prominent advocates of Peace as potential German infiltrators, while the Germans had placed the same names on a list of people they intended to arrest as soon as the invasion was complete.

'*Were* you involved?' blurted out Grace.

He was aghast. 'Grace! Surely you trust me that far!'

'I do, but on the other hand, how can I? You didn't tell me. I knew about Alan for three days. You knew for three weeks. What happened, Walter? What passed between you that day? What's written in those letters that worries you so much?'

He thought. Were the letters harmless, or not? Was he safe? Something occurred to him. 'What I don't understand is how they came to take so long. If they've been following me ever since Alan came to see me, then why wait till now to take the letters?'

'I think—' and Grace had clearly already been doing some thinking on this point '—that perhaps they couldn't be bothered. I don't think they took you very seriously as a risk. It was only worth their while when – Walter, I think it was my fault.'

'Your fault?'

'It was all so difficult to work out. And I was so worried. I can't believe some of the things I've done these last few days, but on the other hand it was all so strange and frightening that it really did seem to be for the best. But perhaps— You see, Walter, I *did* trust you. You wouldn't talk to me, but I still trusted you. And so I thought it wouldn't matter if I told Henderson the truth. I thought the truth would protect you. So I told him that you and Alan had kept in touch during the war—'

Walter shuddered. 'Grace, how on earth would *that* protect me?'

'And then the burglary happened when they knew I would be out of the house, because I was at the church with Henderson—' And now, at last, she began to cry, nursing her red-blotched wrists. Grace was not a weeper. The sobs were held hard back and burst out angrily. He made a motion towards her and then thought better of it. 'What have I done, Walter? Have I hurt him, or you? He was arrested straightaway after they took the letters. They must have got something they wanted. What was it? What did he say to you?'

Now she had told him the worst, he no longer feared her. Her tears reminded him of Bridget's fury whenever she scuffed her knees on the pavement.

He spoke to her gently, almost as if she too were a child. 'You wanted to find out, didn't you? You wanted Henderson to find out for you.'

She nodded and sobbed. 'Because I had to. Otherwise it would all happen without me, and there would be nothing I could do. I thought it would be safer. Walter, I love you. I have to be able to help you. It's what I'm all about.'

The betrayal no longer mattered. She was as fallible as he was, and she'd done what she'd done trying to protect him. No one else in the world would do that for him now. And he wanted to protect her too. He wanted to kiss her better. Perhaps there was still a chance he could.

'I knew Alan went to the Russians,' Walter confessed. 'He told me.'

'DON'T SAY IT!' he shouted, facing Alan across his office, defending his last scraps of innocence as if they were not already gone.

Alan gazed at Walter in disbelief. Then he drew himself upright. 'The Russians approached me,' he repeated in a very soft whisper. 'They offered me the chance to be true to what Bohr had taught me. What *you* had taught me. I took that chance, and handed over a report telling them everything I knew. On the day of the Nagasaki bomb, I gave them a sample of uranium-235.'

Walter was crouched with his head in his hands. He realised he had his fingers over his ears. He took them away. It was too late to shield himself now. 'The Russians—'

He looked up. There was a strange innocence in Alan's eyes.

He looked as hopeful and expectant as he had the day he'd first accosted Walter outside the Cavendish. He was, Walter realised, waiting to be congratulated.

'The Russians know about the bomb—' he choked.

'They would have worked it out in the end anyway,' explained Alan. 'But you see it was clear enough by then what would happen if it turned into a competition prepared in secrecy. If you do it in secret, you end up using it. Don't you? That's what happened to us. So the Russians had to know as soon as possible. They had to have exactly the same knowledge as the Americans. We have to treat this in just the same way that we treated scientific knowledge before the war. *Everyone* must know. If everyone knows, no one can use it.'

'But Alan – oh, you fool, you fool, you fool—'

'Fool?'

The sweat was cold on Walter's chest and forehead. Alan had given Hiroshima's blueprint to Josef Stalin. The gaping eye sockets and the melting flesh of his nightmares returned to him as vividly as any dream. From the moment he'd seen the awful photograph of that cloud, he'd known it would loom over every city in the world for the rest of his life. But he had never thought it would drift towards London so fast. 'You fool,' he whispered. 'The bomb is not scientific knowledge. It is a bomb.'

Alan's face crumpled in frustration and disappointment. 'Walter, you said I should talk. You said it was the only thing to do. And you were right.'

'*No!*' How dare he suggest that it was his fault? 'You can't ask my advice about things you won't tell me and then pretend that my answers have anything to do with what I believe.'

'If you remember, I didn't tell you because you wouldn't let me.'

Because— 'Alan, you should not have gone to the Russians. You must know that they will kill people.'

'Who else could I have told?'

'You shouldn't have told anyone.'

'Walter, you can't *think* this thing out of existence. It's there. It's been there ever since Chadwick discovered the neutron. Or since Rutherford disintegrated the atom. Before that even. Since the human race evolved a brain big enough to work it out. Oh God, Walter, neutrons and uranium have been around a lot longer than mankind. It's *always* been there. Not telling anyone isn't going to stop it from existing.'

Walter racked his brains. 'You could at least have gone to the pacifists. There were plenty of them in America.'

'I did go to a pacifist. In Wales. He didn't want to know.'

They both said nothing.

'All right,' said Alan, 'if it was wrong, what would you have done?'

'I would never have done that. You have given yet another country the means to kill more human beings than has been possible in the history of the world.'

'Walter, you can't keep telling me what you *wouldn't* have done. That's what you always used to accuse *me* of. You said that it was cowardly always to criticise other people's solutions and never come up with any of my own. Well, now I've done something about what I believe. You say I was wrong. Why can't you tell me what's right?'

They stared at one another. Alan's delivery of this perfect little irony was so typical of him. Walter felt as though they might at any moment find themselves tripping through one of the hot-headed debates of the past. But all of it was gone.

'Alan,' he said, 'it's pointless asking me what I would have done. I am a pacifist. I would not have been there.'

'Yes,' said Alan. 'That always did make rather a good excuse, didn't it?'

'It carried on like that for ages,' said Walter. 'I told him it was a tragedy and that whatever good or bad he'd done for the world, he'd ruined his life. He said he didn't care. But he did care. He was frightened. And I was frightened too. He wanted me to help him out of the scrape he'd got himself into. And I couldn't. Or wouldn't.'

'How did it end?' asked Grace.

'I threw him out. I shut the door.'

They sat in silence. Grace stretched a hand across the table and clasped it around Walter's. She seemed to accept his shame, share it, even. He raised his head.

For the first time in six months, he looked her in the eye.

'I suppose it is a formality of sorts,' said Aitken. 'But it is rather expected that you speak your confession. So I would be grateful if you could read it out to me. In the presence of these—' He dismissed the policemen with a wave. 'Witnesses.'

Alan took a deep breath. He had imagined this moment so many times, and had never foreseen how deep the trap they'd set for him would be. Every word he spoke would be filtered through the establishment which Aitken represented. Then, when his statements made their tangled way out of the police cell, through the courtroom and into the press, who was there to hear him? Openness was fruitless. He did not stand a chance.

He read his confession. It was a simple statement of the facts, containing no accusations, no philosophy, and no science. It did not last very long. 'The whole affair was extremely painful to me,' he concluded, 'and I only embarked on it because I felt this was a contribution I could make to the safety of mankind. I certainly did not do it for gain.'

'Really?' said Aitken.

'That is my statement. I am not going to say any more.'

'Describe the man who approached you.'

'No.'

'This could go on for a very long time, you know.'

'I have—' He took a deep breath. 'A lot of time before me.'

22

'Good morning, Henderson,' said Aitken. His eyes were raw with tiredness, the skin below them sagging over his yellow cheeks.

'Good morning, sir.'

The silence stretched.

'I would say that I presume that you have read this morning's papers,' said Aitken eventually, 'except that I seem to recollect that you are not much of a newspaper-reading man.'

'I've seen them.'

Nunn May's arrest had been hailed as a triumph of Anglo–American cooperation. The reports stated that George's employers had possessed cast-iron evidence of his guilt since last September, a month after the bomb, when a cipher clerk named Gouzenko had defected from the Soviet Embassy in Ottawa with a stash of incriminating documents stuffed up his shirt.

'This afternoon I have an audience with the American ambassador,' said Aitken, wincing as he pronounced the word 'American'. 'He expects me to inform him what treasures these past six months have bought us. I will be forced to explain that we have nothing.'

George tried to imagine Aitken being ordered around by a Yank. It was an impossible picture. In such a circumstance he would surely frustrate him using every ounce of Britishness at his disposal.

'I'm sorry, sir,' said George.

'There is,' said Aitken, 'no use crying over spilt milk.' His tone suggested that if milk were really spilt he would require George to get down on his hands and knees and lick it up. 'The Nunn May affair is over and with any luck we'll manage to brush it under the carpet.'

'Brush it under the carpet? But how?'

'Nunn May has no constituency, no audience, no one who understands why he has done what he has done. The overriding objective now is to ensure that it stays that way. We have enough enemies without creating more. Lone warriors are of no particular interest to us, and should most definitely not be of interest to the nation.'

'You want—' George found himself closer to Aitken's thought processes than was comfortable. 'To silence him.'

'Precisely. We are, at any rate, fortunate in that Nunn May appears to have lost the appetite for a fight. He will be made an example of, but not too shining an example. We can expect his cooperation in this and if we do not receive it, we will enforce it.'

'But what about Dunnachie?' said George.

'What do you mean, what about Dunnachie?'

'He – he knows why Nunn May did what he did.'

'Yes.' Aitken subsided a little. He looked tired. Ill, even. 'He is an extremely dangerous individual.'

'What will you do?'

'There is little we can do for the time being. He has the annoying habit of remaining on the right side of the law. But I will put my best men on to it. If he makes any attempt to cause damage, he will know about it. It is imperative that we succeed in our battle against the destructive forces which threaten us. You, of course, must sever all connections with him. I don't want you blundering in there and queering our pitch.'

Relief surged through George. The dread of bumping into

Grace again was as bad as anything he feared from Aitken. Perhaps now, at last, he had performed badly enough to be sent back to the files. 'No, sir,' he said hopefully.

'I have a new duty for you,' said Aitken. His mouth opened into a parody of a smile. The sight of his teeth was unfamiliar and terrifying.

'I—'

'Chap named Cunningham. Lives in Dagenham.'

'*Dagenham?*'

'Find out what he does. Where he goes. Who he talks to. I've got an address. You can start tonight.'

The jaws of the trap descended. George sat, shackled. He could still glimpse daylight through the gaps. He opened his mouth again.

'Yes, sir,' he said.

Walter dreamed of a boy's blue eyes on a harbour, glimpsed through the coloured streamers which connected the ship's passengers to the hordes of people on the shore. The boat pulled away and the streamers began to break, flying loose and waving in their thousands across a widening gap which would never close.

'No!' Walter shouted in his dream, and there was a clambering, the streamers somehow robust enough to support his weight, and Jim holding their ends. 'It's all right! I'm coming back!'

Then the ship's horn became the shrill of the alarm clock, and the streamers broke, and Walter plummeted once more into the present.

He opened his eyes. 'Oh God,' he said.

Grace stirred, rolled over, and lifted her head. Her face hovered over his. 'Walter, you're crying.' She dabbed at his tears with her fingers. 'You were crying in your dreams—'

It was a sea of tears, gaping between ship and shore. He had barely skimmed the surface. Outside somewhere the tanks were rolling, the test tubes were being prepared, and Stalin had the bomb. And still it was his own griefs which hurt the most.

'Alan woke in prison this morning,' he said.

She gazed despairingly into his eyes, too far away to help, and then rolled onto her back. They both lay there, and the light crept in through the curtains and exposed the cracks in the ceiling.

'What are you going to do?' asked Grace.

'I don't know. Go to work, I suppose.'

It wasn't what she meant, but she let it pass. 'Do you have to? Are there lectures?'

'Not until this afternoon. But I've got a meeting.' He let out a sigh at the thought of it. Walter had agreed to the meeting before discovering what it was about, and then when he'd found out, had reacted by burying his head in the sand.

Grace did not miss the sigh. 'What sort of meeting?'

'Poltine wants me to tell the Board of Governors that I'm going to do some research.'

'Oh,' said Grace. She groped for enlightenment through her ignorance. 'Don't you want to?'

'I don't see how I can,' said Walter.

'Why not?'

'You wouldn't understand. It's too technical. It would bore you.'

She scowled. 'Don't underestimate me. Anyway, isn't that where it all went wrong? People thinking that science didn't have anything to do with them, and the scentists thinking that it would be all right not to tell anyone what they were doing?'

'I suppose so.' After so many confessions, this one could not be so very much worse. 'All right. It's about fusion.'

'Fusion.' The linguist in Grace was hard at work. 'Fusion, fuse. Is that joining two atoms together?'

'Yes. It's the energy source of the stars. It's what keeps the sun burning.'

'Oh!'

Fusion was wonderful. He could see reflected in her eyes how wonderful it was. 'The thing is,' he said, 'the sun is quite a powerful thing.'

'Yes.' And he saw the dread recreated in her, simple and pure, as if she were a very intelligent child.

'The energy given off is many times that produced by fission,' he said.

'Yes.' And now the burden of asking to know was becoming too much, even for her. 'Walter—'

'We are finding out how to create the conditions at the centre of the sun on earth.'

'Can't we ever *learn*?'

'But we have to learn, Grace. Don't we? We can't draw a moratorium on knowledge. I can still see that we ought to be able to restrain ourselves from building things to hurt people, but I just can't see how the human race can possibly ever resist the temptation to *know*.'

'No.' For once even she did not have a solution handy. 'Oh, Walter—'

'It's all very well not going to this meeting. Or going anyway and fudging it. But I'm a physicist. I have to do something, or leave altogether. And nothing in science is entirely safe.'

'I suppose—' He could hear her thoughts. That nothing in life was safe either, and that the consequences of one's actions could never be known in advance. But she did not say it. Perhaps she had learnt by now to spare him her platitudes.

'I don't know what to do,' he confessed. 'I could leave well alone, as I always have—'

'You never did!'

'Yes, I did. I thought that if I didn't get involved I would at least be in the right. But it isn't possible not to be involved.'

'That's just Alan talking,' said Grace fiercely. 'You did get involved. You stood firm when the whole world thought you were a crackpot or a coward. There wasn't a moment when you even flinched. When people made those horrible remarks – I was so embarrassed and ashamed. But you – you just asked them to talk, and let them try to explain, and they ran out of steam. You never cared about yourself. You were so gentle, even when provoked. I was so proud of you.'

He started in surprise, and basked for a moment in her opinion of him, letting himself believe it. Perhaps if he believed it, it would be true.

'The things that could happen are so terrible,' he said eventually. 'How could I ever make a difference?'

The children were beginning to stir in the next room. Grace pulled herself together. 'I'd better go and get breakfast,' she said.

He watched her pottering around the room, finding her clothes, reaching for her hairbrush. Her make-up was spread around the dressing table, interspersed with the photographs they had no space for in the sitting room. There was a snap of Alan and Walter in their cricket whites at Cambridge, Alan with his arm loosely around Walter, laughing. Walter's parents on their wedding day, his mother seated and looking incredibly sweet, his father standing with his hand on her shoulder, looking as though he wanted to sink through the floor. Jim, in his RAAF uniform, posing like a matinee idol.

'Don't go,' he said as she began to open the door.

She rushed over to him, knelt by the bed, and put her arms around him. 'I'm so sorry there isn't anything I can do,' she whispered.

'You can. You're still here.'

But she had to leave him anyway, because if she did not

make breakfast the children would be late for school. Their voices clattered along with the cutlery downstairs, and the merriness of the sound jarred against his unhappiness. And now he longed to be part of it, to be the husband and father he'd always thought he'd be. He was tired of being unhappy, tired of the boredom and frustration and fruitlessness, tired of keeping quiet. I want to *live*, he thought. It was just that lately he seemed to have lost the knack.

With an effort, he thought of the meeting ahead of him. Poltine's motives for putting him there were as self-serving as ever – to convince the Board of Governors that the department was capable of doing things of which the government would approve, and thereby save his own beleaguered job. When it came to fusion, Walter was the most qualified academic to hand. He was also a scientist with a reasonably distinguished track record who had contributed no research since the war. And so he supposed that Poltine was right that it was about time he got going.

But the problem with fusion, tantalising though it was, was that however purely he might stick to science in his own research, in the country as a whole it was being led not by university professors, but by government ministers and army generals, and the results were not published.

So publish, then, Walter told himself. Talk, as he'd urged Alan to talk. The only other option was to withdraw from the fray, as he had during the war, and let all the discoveries and the decisions be made without him.

He looked up at the dressing table and stared at the paper faces of the past. One way and another, he had left them all. Alan was alone in a prison cell. Walter's parents were as childless now as they had been on the afternoon of that photograph. Jim was dead. Yet here they all still were, pulling him backwards, pinning him to opinions he'd never held and decisions he'd never thought he'd made.

But, he thought, confronting Jim's cocky gaze – I am *alive*. If all of this is to mean anything at all, one of us has to survive it, and it looks as if it has to be me.

He stiffened with fear. The thought was so callous and disloyal, so scornful of the past. It meant leaving the dead behind. But he knew it was the only way forward. In a single movement, he threw back the covers and got out of bed.

Grace found him in the dining room, rifling through the drawers of the violated bureau.

'What are you looking for?' she said tentatively.

'That stuff you put away. Brinton's stuff.'

'Henry's pamphlets?' She jolted with hope. 'Oh, Walter, are you going back?'

'I might.'

She edged him away from the bureau, closed the drawer he'd been looking through, and opened another. 'There you are.'

He looked down at the leaflets. 'There's something I've written which I think I could use, if I can think how to finish it.'

'What is it?'

'It was meant to be a lecture for the Modern Physics course. But it just went on and on.'

He'd known as he'd written it that no student would ever consent to listen to it. It was long and ragged, and lay in his office drawer with no ending, exactly as he'd left it when he'd tormented himself over the horrors hidden in Alan's last letter, and had taken his revenge on his friend and himself by writing a description of the bomb.

'I can't imagine addressing a Peace meeting about science,' said Walter, 'any more than I could talk to scientists about Peace. And I suppose I'll have to do both.' He saw Chadwick's face in the audience, his eyebrows flickering in outrage, readying himself to respond. In the past Walter's targets had all been faceless. He had never had to address a criticism to someone he admired, or face their wrath. But whether he was right or wrong, he felt he owed it to them to tell them what he thought as much as he owed it to himself. The killing must be stopped. In many ways it was the same story as it had always been. The only difference was that he was now in a better position to understand it. And that, perhaps, was the hardest thing of all.

'Science and morality are going to have to talk to one another,' he said. 'That's all I know.'

'Are you going to Poltine's meeting?'

'Yes.' He looked at her. 'No one will listen, you know. Not the people who matter.'

'They never did. That's no reason—'

'For not trying. I know.' He lowered his head. 'There's more trouble ahead, Grace. I could lose my job. Anything could happen.'

'You always were trouble. I never minded the *trouble*.'

'No.' His throat tightened with the nausea of dread. 'I did, though.'

'I know. You're very brave—'

He shook his head. Brave he was not. 'There's no choice. Not if I'm going to go on living.'

They stood tight in one another's arms in front of the bureau, Walter's face buried in her cardigan, while the toast burned.

He left the house and looked upwards. The clouds were scudding across the sky, his companions once more. A gaggle of workmen were setting up their equipment on the roadside, preparing to make a start on repairing the holes in the road. The city was broken, but it was doing its best to mend.

Then he saw the man in the brown overcoat. He was standing on the opposite pavement behind a car. Walter stopped at the edge of the road and stared. The man shuffled, as though he hoped to wriggle himself into invisibility.

He wavered for a moment, confounded by the oddness of the situation. Then he stepped forth, crossing the road towards his adversary.

'Good morning,' he said to the man. 'I haven't seen you around these parts before.'

The stranger could no longer look away.

Walter stuck out his hand. 'I'm Walter Dunnachie. I live just across the road. Are you a new resident?'

The man allowed his hand to be shaken and mumbled something incoherent.

'Well, I must get on,' said Walter. 'Perhaps we'll bump into one another again some time.'

And as he turned and left, feeling the echoes of the man's shock in the air behind him and waiting for the footsteps to follow, a thought occurred to him. That man would be forced to travel to wherever Walter took him. He would have to sit at Peace rallies and report the proceedings religiously back to his masters.

The blood rose within him, his appetite scenting the fight ahead. His step quickened.

They'd have to bloody listen to him now.

Acknowledgements

My grandfather, Dr W. E. (Eric) Duncanson, was an Australian who won a scholarship to study at the Cavendish Laboratory and travelled to England in the autumn of 1930. Whilst at Cambridge, he conceived a passionate interest in the Peace Movement, and was a conscientious objector during the war. After receiving his doctorate, he married my grandmother, Olive Webster, a fellow Australian whom he had met on the ship over when she was on her way to take up a place at the Sorbonne.

These and many other facts and incidents have been taken from the lives of my grandparents. But this is not in any sense a biography. It is a novel, and far more than the names have been changed. Walter Dunnachie is not Eric Duncanson. Most significantly, Eric was not at all close to Alan Nunn May and did not keep in touch with him after leaving Cambridge, until Nunn May appeared mysteriously in his office one day shortly before his arrest, before disappearing again. As a result, the clash of loyalties which is portrayed in this book never took place. But even if it had, I believe my grandfather would have acted differently. Eric was a far sunnier man than Walter, with a deep faith in God that sustained him through the worst of times. In part, in creating Walter, I imagined how I would have behaved myself.

My debt to my grandparents goes beyond the wonderful story of their lives. I hope that my retelling of their tale does not disrupt the real memories of those who knew them, which are better than anything described in this book.

My grandparents' diaries, letters and memoirs were typed up by my aunt, Patricia Gravatt, and edited by my uncle, Peter Duncanson, who made sense of a hundred fragmentary mentions. Both they and my mother, Kay George, Olive and Eric's third child, went to some lengths to help me with my research. Without them this book could not possibly have been written.

As a non-scientist I am very fortunate that my father, Clive George, is by training a nuclear physicist too. He explained to me what happened scientifically in this story, and corrected my bungling attempts to retell it. The final decisions, and any mistakes, are mine.

The published sources which I have plundered most extensively are Richard Rhodes's *The Making of the Atomic Bomb* (Touchstone, New York, 1986) and Andrew Brown's *The Neutron and the Bomb: A Biography of James Chadwick* (Oxford University Press, Oxford, 1997). These books are essential reading for anyone interested in finding out more about the real events described in this novel. Both Andrew Brown and Richard Rhodes kindly read the manuscript and corrected some factual errors. Their wise advice has been incorporated to the best of my ability. My other major source was *Cambridge Physics in the Thirties* edited by John Hendry (Adam Hilger Ltd, Bristol, 1984).

Extensive passages from *The Peace Army* by Henry Brinton, FRAS (Williams & Norgate, London, 1932), are printed with permission of A & C Black Publishers. An extract from *Rutherford, being the life and letters of the Rt. Hon. Lord Rutherford* by A.S. Eve (1939), is printed with permission of Cambridge University Press.

Whilst both Henry Brinton and Otto Klemperer were real people, both appear in fictional form in this book. Klemperer was a nephew of the famous conductor, who travelled as a refugee to the Cavendish Laboratory and became a good friend of my grandfather's. I have combined the story of his arrival in Cambridge with that of Maurice Goldhaber, another talented refugee, whose story can be read in *Cambridge Physics in the Thirties*.

Caroline Egginton translated long sections of my grandmother's diaries from the French. Emma Maxwell and Mark Adamson read and commented on the manuscript while it was in various states of disarray, and Edward Paleit has been my first port of call in all matters, from literary advice to helping me fix the printer.